A RIVAL CREATION

At thirty-nine Liberty Turner's manuscripts were no longer being published. As relentless rejections pulverised her every effort she faced up to the whimsical truth that while she was absolutely bursting with creativity, the talent just wasn't there. She began to observe her friends and neighbours in the village of Tollymead (not quite the perfect rural idyll that everyone liked to imagine) and their 'creations'. Evelyn Brooke and her fight against pollution, the vicar rebelling against his middle-class parishioners, even Nancy Sanderson the magistrate, rejecting her long-accustomed role. Then Oscar Brooke moved into the village and suddenly Liberty's creative urge was flowing again...

A RIVAL CREATION

Marika Cobbold

Chivers Press
Bath, Avon, England

Thorndike Press
Thorndike, Maine USA

This Large Print edition is published by Chivers Press, England, and by Thorndike Press, USA.

Published in 1996 in the U.K. by arrangement with Transworld Publishers Ltd.

Published in 1996 in the U.S. by arrangement with A.M. Heath & Company, Ltd.

U.K. Hardcover ISBN 0–7451–3954–X (Chivers Large Print)
U.K. Softcover ISBN 0–7451–3955–8 (Camden Large Print)
U.S. Softcover ISBN 0–7862–0615–2 (General Series Edition)

The text of this Large Print edition is unabridged.
Other aspects of the book may vary from the original edition.

Set in 16 pt. New Times Roman.

Printed in Great Britain on acid-free paper.

British Library Cataloguing in Publication Data available

Library of Congress Catalog Card Number: 95–62141.

To Jeremy and Harriet,
with love

ACKNOWLEDGEMENTS

My warmest thanks to Diane Pearson, my editor, and everyone at Transworld, to Sarah Molloy, my agent, and to my husband, Richard Cobbold, for all their help and support in the course of writing and editing this novel.

Many thanks too, to Martin Roberts and his staff for their advice on herbicides.

CHAPTER ONE

Liberty wondered if she was alone in imagining herself far prettier as a corpse than she would ever be alive. She stood on the podium at the back of the village hall, admiring the image of her dead self, draped across the trestle table which was long enough to take at least four bodies laid end to end.

'So beautiful,' they would sigh as they arrived at the hall and saw her there, dead. 'So young.' There were few things for which one was considered young at thirty-nine, but dying had to be one of them.

'I think I can hear a car.' Nancy Sanderson, secretary of the Tollymead Women's League, popped her head out from behind the curtain that separated the small kitchen from the podium. 'You all set?'

Brought back to the present, Liberty nodded, picking up the bunch of A4 papers that lay on the table in front of her.

'It really was good of you to help us out like this at the last minute.' The whole of Nancy appeared. 'But I knew of your little classes, so when that wretched woman let us down again, I said to myself, "Liberty Turner is the girl you want."'

The door of the hall squeaked, hesitated, then opened altogether, letting the first of the ladies through to find their seats.

At eight o'clock the hall was as full as it would get with most of the thirty or so members of the League in place. Nancy welcomed them all and went on to say how the evening's speaker needed no introduction. She spoke on the subject for a good ten minutes before finally calling on Liberty.

Liberty cleared her throat, then flinched as the sound was amplified with startling efficiency by the small microphone in front of her. Feeling she had not achieved an impressive start, she smiled apologetically.

'I know you all came here tonight expecting to hear a talk on how to paint your walls to achieve an effect not unlike marble but, as you've just heard, Belinda Harrison, your speaker, had to cancel at the last minute. As I know very little about decorating, I will speak to you on an entirely different subject, deeply unfashionable but dear to my heart…' Liberty put her hand out for the glass of water thoughtfully provided by Nancy and, looking out over her sparse audience, took a deep gulp before continuing, 'Tonight I will speak to you of The Failure.

'The yearning in man to do more than just survive is the making of both the greatness and the tragedy of being human. From that yearning stems every painting, every piece of music, every great garden and every book.

'Now I expect most of you are familiar with

2

the idea of the struggling artist who battles through neglect, even ridicule, poverty and illness, to win recognition in his or her chosen field. Less talked of is another kind of artist, one who shares the same burning desire to create and to breathe spirit into the stuff of life, the same need to describe and interpret the world around them, even the same foibles and neuroses. So where lies the difference, you might ask. The answer is simple: talent. When God created The Failure, He popped in all the right traits but that single vital one. Was this a deliberate act, or simply an oversight? Who knows?' Liberty paused and blinked nervously out across the hall, stretching out her hand for another drink of the water. One woman, her stout legs planted firmly apart, her modesty covered by a voluminous grey poplin coat, glanced at her watch.

*   *   *

Liberty had been surprised herself when she accepted Nancy Sanderson's late invitation to speak to the Tollymead Women's League. The call had come at a bad time.

'You're obsessed!' Tom had shouted as she sat weeping over the letter from her agent. 'You know that, obsessed!'

' "I am sorry to have to return yet another of your manuscripts, but as we have already discussed on so many occasions, the market for

3

your kind of books has all but disappeared. I do feel now that we have done all that we can for you and that with the country in an ever deepening recession..." What's that Tom?' Liberty looked up from the letter.

'I'm off, leaving for good!' he yelled. 'I've had enough living with a woman...'

'Week-ending,' she muttered. It seemed important somehow to get the facts right.

'... who is only half there, if at all. Who spends the nights not in bed with me but locked away with a bloody computer. I'll put up with playing second fiddle to your son, but not to a damn word processor. I've had enough. I want a woman who puts me before her hobby.'

The word hobby made her flinch. She looked up at his handsome face that was all red and angry and at the eyes, brown like the skin of a conker and round with outrage. 'It's finished, I'm not a writer any more,' she said finally. 'I've quit trying. From now on, I'll come to bed early every night and there'll be no more ink stains on my nightie.'

Tom looked hard at her for a moment. 'Well it's too late,' he said finally.

Liberty's gaze sidled off in the direction of the letter, and with a deep sigh she said, 'I suppose you're right to go,' her voice emerging much quieter than she had meant.

'Look at you. Even now you care more about getting the boot from your agent than you do about me going.' Most of the noise had

4

gone from Tom's voice now, leaving it twanging with grievances. 'You are obsessed you know, neurotic too, and most probably a manic depressive.'

Liberty had buried her face in the crook of her arm, but now she looked up at him with a small smile. 'Just because you've stopped loving me you'll grasp at any little fault.'

Tom had given her a look that was a close cousin to hatred, and she had hidden her face again, feeling the puckered skin of her scarred cheek against her hand. When she looked up he was gone.

She had decided a long time ago that two errant fathers were quite enough in any child's life, so it was only when Johnny, her son, was practically grown-up that she had allowed herself to become close to Tom. And now, with Johnny away and her work rejected, Tom too was gone. Her face had ached with all the crying, and her cheeks were so sodden that she half expected the skin to peel away like the label from a jam jar. It was then that the phone had rung. She only answered in case it was Johnny and, steadying her voice, padding it with false cheer, she picked up the receiver and said hello.

'Mrs Turner?' The woman at the other end had said. 'Nancy Sanderson here. We haven't actually met ... quite terrible really, after all these years living in the same village. I do know of you, though, so anyway we, that is the

Tollymead Women's League, are having our monthly meeting...' Liberty moved the phone half an inch away from her ear; her head ached and Nancy Sanderson had a voice like a hammer beating a tin tray.

'... You can say anything you like on any subject; we're very catholic in our tastes. I'm sure you have some jolly interesting stories from your glory days. So many people seem to be keen on writing; anything you say will be fascinating, I'm sure. Mind you, they don't seem to read as much as they used to. Maybe it's because they're all busy writing.'

'Of course I'll do it.' Liberty had said when all she wanted, like Miss Otis in the Cole Porter song, was to give her regrets due to a sudden death: in Liberty's case, her own. But she never could say no. Cowardice, her father called it, not kindness, cowardice.

So she had sat down in the kitchen alcove where her computer stood, drawn back to the blank screen like a child to an abusive parent, trying to think of something to say to Nancy Sanderson's ladies. She sat there until it grew dark outside and then, as she got up to switch the light on, Tom returned and gave her a subject. 'I forgot my violin,' he said. Then, leaning against the doorway he looked at her not unkindly. 'You know Liberty,' he said, 'you really are the definitive failure.'

*   *   *

6

Liberty was coming to the end of her talk. 'But ladies...' then she noticed Neville Pyke at the back of the hall so she added, 'and gentlemen, my intention tonight has not been to depress,' this bit was spoken with deep insincerity. 'There are thousands of us out there failing; getting the sack from the organization to which we gave forty years of our lives. Seeing our business taken into receivership, being divorced by the husband to whom we dedicated our youth, having our golden-haired little cherubs mug old ladies, sitting on a small hard chair still playing second violin after twenty years in the symphony orchestra, being offered yet another part as the heroine's overweight friend in a BBC sit-com. It's hard, wanting so much and finding out that, quite frankly, you haven't got what it takes to get it. But as I said, it's no cause for despair. Failure is good, failure is necessary. Just think, without it, how could there be success?'

The applause lasted just long enough for Nancy to take Liberty's place at the microphone. 'Mrs Turner will be glad to answer questions,' Nancy said.

Liberty drank some more water. There was silence. People looked around at each other, expectantly at first, then disapproving; surely someone could think of something, anything, to ask, they seemed to say. Liberty was easily embarrassed; a sign of conceit her father said, and she thought how she need not have put herself through this humiliation, minor though it was. She could just have gone right ahead and killed herself as she had planned, instead of agreeing to do the talk first. Mealy-mouthed to the end, she thought bitterly. No wonder she was a no-good artist, a no-artist, in fact. A real artist was strong and true, straight and good, not weasely and measly and frightened of things that did not even go bump in the night.

'Surely,' Nancy said invitingly, 'someone has a question raised by tonight's ... stimulating talk.'

It was the same when Liberty was eight and at a birthday party, one of those to which the whole class was invited whether the birthday girl wanted it or not. (No darling, you do have to ask Liberty. It would be very unkind to leave her out and besides, we know her father.) Liberty could see it before her still. She could hear the birthday girl's mother's voice with its barely masked irritation, 'Now who will be Liberty's partner? ... I'm sure someone will ... no?'

Neville Pyke, who was a member of Liberty's writing class, stood up, and relief rose like a pleasing scent from the audience.

'I have to admit,' Neville said, 'that I took Mrs Pyke's place here tonight, expecting to hear about how to achieve a marbled effect on any surface by the simple use of paint, but after my initial disappointment I must say I enjoyed the talk very much. You see when I was a lad

8

I . . .' From her place at the podium Liberty saw Neville turn pink as his voice trembled. '. . . dreamed of playing cricket for my native Essex. I was quite good too but, like Mrs Turner here, not quite good enough.' Neville smiled up at the lighted podium. 'But I found great satisfaction in my life with the railways, and I would like to say to Mrs Turner that I'm sure she too will find some other, equally satisfying occupation.' Neville sat down to a fair amount of mumbled approval.

A woman with a face like a cockatoo stood up. 'Your story makes me think of Shirley Temple, Shirley Temple Black as she is now of course. She became an ambassador. But she was very, very famous wasn't she? Anyway, when did you realize your career as a writer was over and what have you decided to do instead?'

'I think it was yesterday,' Liberty answered, thinking with some pleasure that to embarrass someone you only need to tell them the truth. 'Yes, yesterday, when I had my fifth rejected manuscript in eight years returned with a letter saying I should think of taking up some other profession. Call me hasty if you will but I decided it was time to bow out.'

Before sitting down, the woman added that Liberty's typing skills would come in handy, and Liberty asked if Shirley Temple typed.

The next question was again from Neville. 'I meant to ask you in class, do you write under a

9

pseudonym? I've been searching for your work in our local library. They suggested you might be writing under a pseudonym.'

'No,' Liberty said with a deep sigh. 'No, I didn't use a pseudonym.' As if I would, she thought, after all the trouble I went through to get a decent name.

*   *   *

'The children at school say my name is silly.' Six years old, fair-haired and plump, Liberty Bell had turned accusing eyes at her father. 'And they say their mummies think I've got a silly name too.'

Hamish Bell couldn't help but look amused, but there was no corresponding flicker in his daughter's anxious face. 'Why did you call me a silly name?'

'It's not silly, it's interesting. People always make fun of what's unusual. It shouldn't bother you.'

'Mormor and Morfar don't like it either.'

'Your grandparents are Swedish; a lot of things probably sound strange to them.'

The child thought of tea with her grandparents. They had given her a watch for her birthday, so she knew that tea was always at four o'clock. Milky tea and ginger nuts, always at four o'clock. The thought caused a brief smile to cross the child's solemn features before she turned again to her father. 'They

10

wouldn't think Anne sounds silly. Anne is a nice name,' she said nodding emphatically, ensnaring her father's neck in her podgy arms. 'A really nice name.'

Hamish had freed himself with an irritated flinch. 'It might or might not be a nice name, but your name is Liberty.' And he had stood up and walked from the room.

Liberty had gone into her bedroom in their flat at the top of the school's senior boarding house. Sitting down, straight-backed, on the green shag-pile rug that looked just like a lovely patch of grass, she was a very pretty girl called Anne on a picnic with her mother and father. Anne looked at her watch. It was exactly four o'clock, so she knew tea would be served right then. As she ate her ginger nuts another very nice girl appeared and asked, 'What's your name?'

'Anne,' Liberty-Anne would say in a proud sort of voice.

'That's a nice name,' the other girl would say.

* * *

In the village hall a woman, much younger than the rest, put her hand up.

'Yes?' Nancy said in the voice of a teacher to a promising pupil.

Liberty looked at the lovely young woman who sat at the back of the room, as out of place

11

as Colette at a Tupperware party. 'What did it feel like, producing a book?' the woman asked. She lowered her voice. 'I imagine it's rather like the birth of a child.'

Liberty was taken aback. The birth of a book, the birth of a child, it was such an obvious comparison that she had never paid it any attention. Was it like Johnny being born? And if it was, did that matter? Did it make either event more, or less, important? 'I regained my figure quicker after the books.' Liberty felt annoyed at herself as soon as she had said it; a serious question, however commonplace, merited a serious answer. She tried again. 'Both events were marvellous and both are in the past, my creative part in them, over.'

'I don't think you should call yourself a failure, though,' the girl said. 'Everyone is good at something.' There was a general muttering of approval.

Wouldn't they just like to believe that, Liberty thought. She looked across at the young woman. 'I don't know that I agree with you. There is a tendency in modern society to abolish anything uncomfortable. We used to have a heaven and a hell; if you believed in one you had to believe in the other. Nowadays ... it's all right to tell a child that Granny has gone to heaven. But even if Granny was a well known axe murderer and paedophile, try getting away with saying that, in your view,

12

odds are that Granny has, in fact, gone straight in the opposite direction. Opposite is the word here. I think it's wrong to tell people that they can have just one side of the coin. It's too easy and life, as we all know, is not easy. Failure just isn't fashionable; it goes against all modern ethics and ideas of what is right and above all fair. Failure is not politically correct unless of course it's the failure of a politician—but failure is there, all about us.'

Nancy hastened up from her seat. 'And on that truly fascinating note,' she concluded, 'I invite you all to join Mrs Turner and me for a glass of sherry.'

Liberty stepped down from the podium. Smiles like nervous tics were all around, as the ladies of the Tollymead League sipped their sherries and tried to think of something to say. A few of them had known Liberty as a child, when she lived with her schoolmaster father at the nearby prep school, Tollymead Manor. But now it seemed that she confused them by being someone they felt they ought to know but didn't. Most of the ladies, though, were barely familiar faces to Liberty, glimpsed in church or at some drinks party. Tollymead was like that: you drove through it on your way to somewhere else, even when you lived there. In fact, Liberty often thought it was just the sort of place where you could lie dead in your house for days without anyone noticing, particularly if your milk was stacking up by the back door rather than the front.

The beautiful young woman who had asked one of the questions earlier made her way through the group of ladies to the empty circle round Liberty, hips swinging. Liberty admired her calf-length, tight-fitting, black skirt and the pale face with its full lips painted in pillar-box red. She had to be interesting, Liberty thought, to look so wonderfully out of place.

'I'm Victoria Brooke,' the woman said in her slow, thick voice that made the words drop from her lips like honey from a spoon. 'I really enjoyed your talk. If you are still taking that writing class, I'd love to come some time. They say those who can, do, and those who can't, teach, so I'm sure your classes are very good.'

Liberty's eyes widened. Did this lovely girl intend to insult with an elegance matched only by the cut of her clothes, or had she happened on the skill by luck? But she said, 'Victoria Brooke, of course; you're married to Evelyn's nephew. Evelyn and I are next-door neighbours.'

Just then the door to the hall opened for a tall man of about forty who brought with him a blast of chill air, like the wicked fairy at the christening.

'Oscar!' Victoria hurried towards him. The man bent down and kissed her cheek. Liberty looked round for someone else to talk to, but Victoria returned. 'This is Oscar,' she said, and Liberty smiled and shook hands, annoying

14

herself by pushing her hair over her cheek to hide the scar. She hadn't done that earlier, with only women and Neville looking at her.

She looked up again, and her smile grew warmer. 'Your aunt told me you had moved down here.'

Oscar was just about to answer when Neville Pyke joined them, aiming words even as he crossed the room. 'Mr Brooke, pleased to meet you. Very pleased to meet you indeed. I hear you're our new editor. You'll be glad to know that I've read *The Tribune* ever since I moved here and I think it compares very favourably with other local papers. I see myself as rather an expert on local papers you see, reading them wherever I find myself, and I have found myself in some strange places I don't mind telling you.'

Oscar had put a polite and interested look on his face, and it remained in place as Neville carried on. His eyes are wandering though, Liberty thought. He's probably thinking about taking his beautiful wife home to bed.

'But I had hoped that since our new editor...' Neville went on.

'I saw your book on the Colombian drugs trade,' Liberty interrupted before apologizing to Neville. 'It must be quite a change, coming down here?' As she asked, Liberty found she was not really interested in Oscar's answer, she just wanted to go home; home where razors and aspirins, brandy and ropes waited for her like a loving family. Then it occurred to her that at almost forty she still did not know how to tie a noose. Her cousin Bertil had promised to teach her one summer on the Swedish island when they were nine, but he had never got around to it.

She realized that Oscar was speaking to her but, feeling she was coming from so far away she could not possibly hear, she excused herself and said goodbye. She could feel his surprised gaze on her back as she struggled to open the heavy outside doors. Those doors, inserted into the rickety walls of the village hall, always made her think of the story of the three little pigs, where one little pig's house, made of straw, was blown clean away, leaving just the sturdy door standing with the little pig hiding stupidly behind it.

She walked out into the autumn night and through the low-flying smoke from a dying bonfire in the vicarage garden. She got into the car and drove slowly through the village, across the bridge over the river that divided Tollymead in two, and down River Lane towards her cottage.

Coming home used to seem like a reward to Liberty. It was the first place she had actually owned: pebbledash with a bow-window that looked all wrong, like pink ribbon on a bulldog. The narrow hall boasted a multicoloured stained-glass window more suitable to a suburban semi. Liberty liked that too; it

16

had made the move away from London easier. It amused her to think of all these town dwellers striving to make their homes into Marie Antoinette's idea of a country cottage, and there was the builder of Liberty's house, working away all those years ago, making his home a little piece of suburbia in the middle of the Hampshire countryside. She had christened the house Laburnum Terrace and placed a large aspidistra in a blue-and-white china pot on a stand in the hall. She was fond of the plant. It had survived alternate bouts of neglect and lavish care, to welcome her for five years now, but that evening even the sight of its blowzy abundance did not bring her comfort.

She wandered aimlessly round the house, finally settling in the kitchen. She filled the kettle and put it on the Aga hot plate. She might be a failed writer, but she was becoming a nice little literary cliché herself: suicidal and Aga-owning. At least the Aga was unfashionably beige. She actually loved the thing: the way it had no buttons or controls and could not be set to cook your dinner half-an-hour before you returned home in the evening; the way it did not pretend to be a charcoal grill or a pizza oven. It just stood there, gently warming your home, a one-cooker stand against state-of-the-art technology, a solid hunk of metal protest. Liberty poured the water into the teapot and brought it to the table. Just as she was thinking she was too tired even to bother to die, the telephone rang. Hoping that this time it really would be Johnny, she leapt up to answer.

'Would she,' the operator asked, 'accept the charge for a call from Sweden?' She would, of course she would.

'Johnny darling, how lovely!'

Johnny just wanted to say hello. He was spending the first months of his gap-year in Sweden, working as assistant gamekeeper in a forest on the shores of a wide lake. He was an undemonstrative boy, but he liked to keep tabs on his mother, to make sure she was all right and not lonely without him.

'I thought maybe you could come over here before I leave for Adelaide. I'll miss Christmas at home.'

He misses Christmas at home, Liberty thought. How can I kill myself when my son misses Christmas at home?

* * *

She had become pregnant with Johnny in her second year at St Andrews, by a guest lecturer from the Outer Hebrides. Callum McLaughlan was a doctor of literature who had taken a year off from his teaching post in London to write a novel. He was also married, but Liberty had not thought to ask about that. She had listened to his lecture in the half-empty hall and looked at his lower arms that were covered in reddish-

18

blond hair like the limbs of a golden fly. She had thought his lecture brilliant, marred only by the shuffling and whispering of some of the other students who, it seemed, failed to see what beauty of thought and body was offered to them by Callum McLaughlan. When the talk was over she had stayed behind, and later they had walked together to the restored old gypsy caravan in which he had travelled down. Had she had a mother, Liberty felt later, that mother might well have warned her daughter about men who travelled to work in purple-and-yellow caravans; but as she stepped through the fringed velvet curtain that night, Liberty thought only that if her life ended then, she would at least have known love.

The next morning Callum had hung his head as he explained that he was married, with a small child, and that his wife was not strong like Liberty, but a soft vine that needed him to lean on or she would not survive. He left, and Liberty had found herself empty of all feelings other than a mild curiosity as to the softness of vines.

It had not been easy to explain the pregnancy to her father. 'We had so much in common,' she had tried. Hamish's eyes could be mild and yielding but that evening they had been like blue mirror lenses returning her worries, taking nothing.

'There was literature...' Liberty said, 'and him being Scottish and me half...'

19

'In Scotland, such men are not difficult to find. Will you be sleeping with all of them?'

*   *   *

What a thing for a father to say. Even now, nineteen years later, Liberty blushed at the memory as she spoke on the phone to Callum's and her son.

'Love you,' she said as she always did, as they rang off. And that love, she thought as she put the phone down with a sigh, was about the only sure thing in God's strange creation.

By now the tea was cold, so she tipped it into the stained sink and poured herself some dark Jamaican rum. She always kept a bottle to make the drink her grandfather used to make when she was small and had a cold: one tablespoon of dark rum, one tablespoon of demerara sugar and top it up with hot milk. Tonight she skipped the sugar and the milk, making up the difference with some more rum. She downed it and made herself another drink.

'How could you do it, God?' she muttered into her glass, as if He was lurking below the surface of the thick, dark spirit, 'How could you let it happen? Were you sitting there, creating? "Artistic temperament and sensitivity: one teaspoon of each. Dedication: two heaped tablespoons. Passion for expressing herself in writing: three cupfuls. Talent ... Whoops, there's someone at the

20

gate. Oh you're getting it St Peter, thanks old chap. Now where was I? Finished I think. Down the hatch." Was that the kind of day it had been?'

She leant her head in her arms, mumbling, 'God, Peter, Patrick...'

CHAPTER TWO

Liberty had not been back long in London when she met Patrick Turner, a young architect, in the Friends' Room at the Royal Academy. She had returned with Johnny from five years living in her grandparents' wooden house on a small island off Sweden's west coast. She rented a basement flat in Fulham and continued her work as a translator of children's books. In her spare time she took Johnny for long walks in the park or round the museums, and at night she thought a lot of the past and of the future, and dreamed of a modest kind of glamour. Back in Sweden when Johnny had been a baby, she had pushed him in his pram along the streets of Gothenburg, and she had seen the students, no younger than her, sitting alone or in groups at the small tables in the cafés along the Avenue. She loved her son, but she had felt that sitting like that at a white wrought iron table, drinking cups of coffee and studying—hours and hours of studying—would be paradise. She would wear a red scarf, she decided on those long tramps along the slushy winter streets, and the books would pile up high as she turned the pages dense with text, and scribbled notes in the pages of her loose-leaf binder.

When she moved back to England, her father paid for her to become a Friend of the Academy so that she could go in free with Johnny to all the exhibitions. She discovered they had a room, a nice, airy, café of a room where she could work on her translations with her books heaped on the table in front of her.

One day she looked up to find a man standing by her table, smiling. He was older, about thirty-five, dark-haired and crinkly-eyed, and he was wearing a red scarf thrown carelessly round his neck. He introduced himself, saying his name was Patrick Turner. Turner: such an easy, sensible name, and so apt, considering they were in a gallery. Liberty had raised her eyes to the ceiling, thinking that this was surely a sign.

She had spent her life dreading every new meeting: the embarrassment at each new introduction. Speaking her name was like having to admit that the tipsy old thing in a black leather mini skirt and fishnet stockings really was your mother. When the moment came she would sometimes mumble, 'Libt Bl,' in a muddly quiet voice, hoping they would not bother to say, 'Sorry, what was that?' At other

22

times she shouted out as if to silence any comment, 'LIBERTY BELL,' defying them to laugh. Still, it would be wrong, Liberty felt, to say she married Patrick just to have his name. People married each other for many reasons; her grandfather, for one, swore he married Liberty's grandmother because she had a body like Mae West and the lightest touch with pastry of any woman on this earth. It was what happened afterwards that mattered, and for a long time Liberty and Patrick were happy. At that first meeting Patrick told her she looked like a cherub with a dirty secret. Liberty had not been sure quite what he meant, but it had made her laugh and she had packed away her books and walked round the exhibition of Italian architectural drawings with him.

Patrick, who had spent three years in the States, said Johnny was a really neat little guy and it was obvious that Johnny thought Patrick was pretty neat too. After two months, Patrick proposed. Liberty asked if he could see Johnny as his son, because she could never have another child. Patrick had thought for a moment, his dark head bent, his chin resting in the palm of his hand. Then he had looked up with a smile and told her that yes, he could. He wanted her and he wanted Johnny, and to get them both was enough for any man.

They got married, and at the wedding Patrick's mother had cried at the thought of her lost grandchildren. At the time everyone thought they were tears of happiness.

'What other tears are there at weddings?' Hamish had said to his daughter, who had become quite alarmed at the crying that seemed to go on far longer than was necessary when seeing a son married. Liberty and Johnny moved from the dark little flat, where the loo had to be cajoled into flushing and where the kitchen cupboards were the colour of a sick orange, to Patrick's house on Putney Hill. Liberty stopped going to the Friends' Room at the Academy; instead she worked at a round mahogany table in the sitting-room bay with the long, narrow garden outside.

'What's mine is yours,' Patrick said, and Liberty cared for each of his things as if she had chosen them herself. She polished the mahogany table with beeswax until it shone like a child's newly washed hair, and Patrick thanked her and called Johnny and her, 'my little family'.

Four years later, when he told Liberty he was leaving her for the love of a fertile woman, there were tears in his eyes. Could she, would she understand that having Johnny had only made him long for a child of his own all the more?

Now she had got what she wanted, Patrick's mother had been very kind to Liberty. She persuaded her son to let them stay on in the house until they found somewhere else. Patrick, she said, could move in with her.

Hamish found her the cottage in Tollymead. It was derelict, but she had the money for a down payment from her pay as a translator. 'Johnny can be a day boy at Tollymead Manor,' Hamish had said. 'Staff get reduced fees.' So that was settled and, as it happened, Johnny and Liberty moved out of the house on Putney Hill on the day that Patrick's son was born.

As a child, Liberty had scribbled stories full of death and love in endless notebooks, and she had started no less than three newspapers, written and produced by her entirely, and bought by her family and a few friends who even at such a young age were not immune to the charms of seeing their names in print. She knew with quiet certainty that one day she would write books; she was just waiting for the right moment. That moment came when Patrick left her steeped in her grief and frustration, and with more time on her hands now there were only Johnny's shirts to iron (her own things were almost entirely drip-dry) and no dinner parties or client lunches to arrange. The book she wrote was about an architect who lived alone in a villa in the Umbrian hills and got drunk one day after designing a particularly beautiful house. He got into his gleaming car and he drove down the steep, winding road, right into a young woman and her small son. The man got out of the car and looked at the woman and child, who lay in a twisted embrace on the dust track, then he got back in again and drove off, leaving them to die. But the child survived, although no-one knew who had killed his mother, no-one that is until an English tourist, another young woman, staying in the small hotel owned by the dead woman's aunt, decided to find out. It was a book with a mystery, some love and even a few good jokes, and she wrote it in the early hours of the morning, between four and seven, when Johnny was still asleep and the phone did not ring. As this was when there was still plenty of money around, a publisher bought it.

Liberty had begun to feel her own life was like one of those American films where the woman loses the man but finds herself, and she was happy. For three years and three more books she was happy, and so was Johnny. Then came the day when her new manuscript was turned down. Her publishers were giving their big annual party that Thursday, and Liberty had organized a baby-sitter for Johnny and bought a black velvet jacket for herself. On Wednesday morning Alistair, her editor, called to say he wanted to tell her straight away, what with the party the next day and everything, that it was with great regret they had decided to let her go. He had talked a lot about shrinking markets and changing fashions and, sounding genuinely distressed, he had said goodbye. Liberty had cancelled the baby-sitter and taken

26

the jacket back to the shop. The assistant wanted to give her a credit note but Liberty had said could she please have the money back; she needed it now.

All that was eight years ago; eight years, two lovers and five rejected manuscripts. God, Peter, Patrick ... she fell asleep at the kitchen table, her head in her arms.

*   *   *

She woke at five the next morning, with a stiff neck and a dry mouth, surprised and not at all pleased to find herself still alive. Getting up from the table she reasoned with herself, 'You drank some rum and then you fell asleep, so what did you expect, spontaneous combustion?' She eased herself up from the hard kitchen chair and, grabbing her sweater, scuffed across the tiled floor, trailing the sweater by its sleeve as if it were an old teddy. She stopped for a moment by the cork board on the wall next to the Aga and looked hard at the pictures of Johnny, blond and smiling, before plodding upstairs and into bed.

When she woke again it was half past ten, and it took her a few minutes to remember that it was Harvest Sunday and she had paid for a ticket to the Harvest Lunch in the village hall. Two tickets in fact; Tom was meant to have come with her. She slid out of bed and padded into the bathroom, showered and dressed in a

27

brown-and-white flower print frock that was meant to turn her into a fashionable waif, but managed instead to make her look like a washed-out matron. But there was no time to change as she was running late already for the church service at eleven. It was such bad form, she thought, to turn up to the lunch without having been to church first—rather like missing the funeral but being the life and soul of the wake.

*   *   *

At noon she was back in the hall where she had given her talk the night before. Although Tollymead was a large village, the congregation now gathered for the Harvest Lunch was small and today outnumbered, at least twenty to one, by apples. Bramleys, shiny as if polished by a crazed housewife, and dusty-looking Coxes, their colours subdued like neglected ornaments, lined the podium, spilled out of carrier bags, and lay stacked in the deep windowsills. Harvest was a good time for being charitable and getting rid of one's apple glut all in one go. Liberty could almost hear her neighbours all thanking God for arranging things so . . . well, so sensibly.

The table where last night she had imagined herself laid out, had been removed from the podium and joined with another at the centre of the hall to form a large T, so, Liberty thought with a small smile, her corpse would be on the floor now amongst the apples, as if she had drowned in a river of fruit. Maybe it was more affecting that way? Liberty cocked her head a little to one side; less of the mortuary slab about it.

'A plague on their fruit trees.' Ted Brain the vicar was at her side, a lone apple in his small hand. 'I don't know what they think the poor and needy of the district can want with all these apples. Shove them up their gas meters maybe.'

Liberty laughed weakly. It worried her that the vicar did not seem to like his parishioners very much. She was not overly taken with them herself, but that was different. She was an amateur, not like Ted, paid to love and forgive. No, from her vicar she wished for better; she liked to imagine a soft duvet of tolerance and love covering them all and their miserable failings. The other day, when she was giving Ted a lift into Fairfield, she had argued with him.

'You know, middle-class country dwellers have problems too, souls even, if you look hard enough. We need saving just like everyone else.' But she didn't feel she had convinced him. Ted cared only for what he called Real People, and in Tollymead, if there were any, they did not seem to attend church. Whenever she spoke to Ted, Liberty tried to be more Real, but somehow she always had an uneasy feeling that she disappointed him. The drinks party,

29

for example, that she had given to mark her's and Johnny's tenth year in the village, had been all wrong. Ted had arrived with a pleasant enough smile, what he was expecting she still had not worked out, a single parent support group maybe. He had stayed chatting to the Hampshire matrons, schoolmasters and commuters with a look on his face of a reluctant saint washing the feet of a particularly sorry lot of poor and needy. But afterwards he had told her she had fallen straight into her slot in the village, marked by outmoded and class-ridden values. When he had first met her, he said, he had hoped for something different. Liberty had been upset by his words but she kept on trying to please. She always did. It was a habit she felt sure owed much to her appalling start in that direction. Her father had loved her mother, her grandparents had loved her mother. Liberty had killed her. Not deliberately of course, and had she had a chance she would have loved her mother as much as anyone; but as it was, she had killed her. It was knowledge so painful that even now she would step gingerly through her thoughts like a heron picking its way through marshland.

'Here,' she handed Ted the basket dangling from her arm.

'Jam,' he said. 'Excellent.' He peered into the basket. 'And chocolate cake.'

'It's been frozen I'm afraid,' Liberty

muttered.

Ted Brain carried on rummaging through the contents of the basket. 'Instant cappuccino, asparagus, butter ... and what have we got here? Tinned mussels and a string of garlic. A bottle of Chablis too.'

'I've written down a very good recipe for baked mussels in garlic butter. It's sellotaped to the tin, here.' Liberty showed him. 'Mussels are supposed to be very good for you, unless they're bad of course, when ... but this is a very good brand. Garlic protects against colds, not to mention passing vampires,' she smiled, 'and we all know there are lots of them around Hampshire.'

'Great stuff!'

Liberty felt warmed by his approval as he put her basket down on the podium. She had planned her gift a couple of days before, imagining the pleasure of some house-bound old dear getting the basket full of inessentials. You could have life's necessities piled up around you and still feel poor; it was the chocolate cake that made the difference.

'Hello there Liberty. I'm sorry I missed your talk last night, didn't know you were on actually.' Evelyn Brooke peered up at her through round glasses. 'That bore Nancy tells me it was "different".'

Liberty smiled tiredly, but she liked Evelyn. She had known her since she was a child. Evelyn had been old then and she was old now.

It was comforting in an uncertain world that some things remained the same.

'I wasn't feeling terribly well. I was thinking of killing myself, you see ... I suppose I still am. I just don't seem to be getting round to it.' She regretted her words the moment they were spoken. She did that sort of thing quite often. A perfectly innocuous phrase would be making its way to her lips, when it would be unceremoniously elbowed aside by a string of unsuitable words that embarrassed her even as they were uttered.

'People do commit suicide,' she added lamely. 'Look at Hemingway.'

'You, my dear child, are not Hemingway,' Evelyn said.

'Well there you are; another reason for doing away with myself.'

Evelyn's mouth turned down at the corner as she gave Liberty a disapproving look, but before she had a chance to say anything Oscar Brooke came up to her, taking her by the elbow. Nodding hello to Liberty, he hissed to Evelyn, 'When does this thing end?'

'We haven't eaten yet. You two know each other already do you?'

'We met briefly last night,' Oscar said. 'Victoria was at the talk last night. She enjoyed it.'

'Well you're not likely to forget each other, both having such silly names,' Evelyn said.

Liberty had not looked properly at Oscar

last night, and he had been wrapped up against the cold and rain in a large overcoat, with the collar turned up. Now she looked closer at him and found herself thinking that, if she was to die soon, his face was not a bad one to take along as a last image, apart from Johnny's, of course. Oscar did not look much like his aunt, standing as tall and slim as she was short and square. His straight hair was blond, whereas Evelyn's had been black before turning wire-wool grey. He did have the same high-bridged nose though, and Evelyn's deep-set eyes must once have been the same vivid blue. He wore glasses, of course, with round, tortoise-shell frames, but he seemed to Liberty the sort of man who had ended up with the latest fashion in spectacle frames purely by hanging on to the same ones for twenty years.

'If you'll excuse me,' he said, 'I think I saw Victoria calling me.'

Liberty looked after him as he hurried off to his wife, who was standing on her own, her hand raised in a little wave.

'What is it do you think,' she said to Evelyn, 'that makes a man prefer the company of a ravishing twenty-five-year old with a heart-shaped face and magnolia complexion to a thirty-nine-year old with a fat, scarred face and dimply thighs?'

'You're being very silly today Liberty,' Evelyn said. 'Even by your standards.'

Ted Brain announced that lunch was being

33

served.

'Luncheon,' Nancy Sanderson muttered in a long-suffering way just behind Liberty.

Liberty wandered off towards the table. A large, misshapen Bramley was knocked off the podium and rolled unevenly across the floor, like someone running with only one shoe on. It came to a halt right by Liberty's feet and she bent down to pick it up. 'You're a miserable specimen, aren't you, just like me,' she whispered. She put her hand out, but Neville Pyke's square, paint-stained paw got there first.

'Waste not want not,' he said rubbing the dust from the apple with the sleeve of his blue club blazer before placing it on the white paper table-cloth. Taking a step back to survey the scene all the better, he said, 'I don't think one could see a prettier sight anywhere in the land.' He beamed at the table, which stood bedecked with all manner of twigs and berry-laden branches as if the decorating had been left to a rather untidy beaver.

'All across the country folk are sitting down to Harvest Lunch,' he said, 'but I don't think there's a table anywhere to rival this one, not even in Everton.'

He made Liberty feel guilty. Where she saw cheap china and a mess of twigs on a make-do table, he saw beauty. There he was: getting old, quite fat, quite bald, a little stooping, making ends meet on a pension in a village that was

34

nothing like the old-world idyll he had dreamed of finding when at long last he retired to his country cottage. There he stood, seeing the best in everything. Either that, Liberty smiled suddenly, or he had very bad taste.

'It's lovely,' she said, 'really lovely.' She didn't mind lying. It was like when a friend had bought a new dress and showed it to you, all pleased and proud: a smile, a little twirl; a 'What do you think?' You didn't say, 'Bloody awful,' whatever you thought.

Nancy Sanderson and her helpers busied around the table carrying plates of food, their church hats perched like insults on the back of their heads. 'Sit over there Liberty,' Nancy said over her shoulder. 'Next to me.'

Ted Brain's place was at the top of the table, marked by a particularly large apple speared through its middle by a lit candle. Liberty sat next to Evelyn a few places further down, and soon Nancy joined them, plonking down on the empty chair between Liberty and Ned Simpson. She did not mention the talk, but with a tactlessness that Liberty could not help but admire, asked about the scar on Liberty's right cheek. 'I wanted to ask you last night. It's very bad isn't it?' She peered closer. 'A nasty wound. Doesn't look as if it's healed properly, you know.'

Liberty said nothing, hoping she could ward the inquisitive Nancy off with a persistent smile. As her smile stiffened out in the cold, she

35

found herself wondering if that was the secret of Mona Lisa's smile: she was fed up with Leonardo asking her all those really intimate questions about her love life.

The conversation round the table was growing quieter as people's interest seemed sucked towards her and Nancy.

'I said, I hear it was a dog.' Nancy went on. 'Now why was there nothing about it in *The Tribune*? I thought dog attacks were all the rage these days. I've had several cases before me on the Bench lately. You could sue, you know.'

Liberty felt a moment's pride at being so fashionably maimed, but she said, 'It was only a very small attack.'

Neville spoke from further down the table. 'I can't say I'm surprised nothing was written. I said to Mrs Pyke only yesterday that our little village seems rather neglected in our local paper. I often find myself searching in vain for a mention in the Village Diary, but it's always Everton this and Everton that.' He made an artful pause. 'Maybe now we've got the new editor in our midst we will see a change for the better.'

'Being new here,' Evelyn said, 'maybe my nephew thinks Everton is a football club. That would certainly justify the interest in their jam-making and beauty pageants.'

Oscar opened his mouth to speak, but Nancy got in first. 'Don't be silly Evelyn. Anyway, the pronunciation is completely

36

different. Ev'ton. E.v'.t.o.n.' Her cyclamen lips stretched and pursed as she enunciated.

'The Village Diary is very little to do with the staff or the editor,' Oscar said. 'It's more of a community notice-board made up of entries from the residents of the different villages themselves. Apart from asking my staff to make up entries,' Oscar smiled patiently at Neville, 'there really isn't much I can do to raise the profile of the village. I know I've only been living here for a few weeks, but Tollymead doesn't seem to exactly throb with activities. Today being an exception of course. Now something like this Harvest Lunch...'

'Luncheon,' Nancy muttered.

'... is just the item for the Diary if anyone would care to write in. Of course, if something happens that is of more general concern—'

'Like the attack on Mrs Turner here,' Nancy interjected.

'—then of course it gets taken up elsewhere in the paper by our staff. There's no discrimination intended,' Oscar said to Neville, 'I assure you.'

'And none taken, none taken I'm sure.' Neville nodded his bald head vigorously. 'But we have the makings of a very fine community here, very fine indeed if we'd all just try a bit harder. What better tribute to God's creation than the close and caring community of a traditional English village?'

Liberty joined in the murmured approval;

37

Neville was right. Had she herself not come running back to Tollymead when life got tough, her head full of images of village life that would have Miss Read suing for copyright? They all seemed to want a fully formed, up-and-running village community as a pretty back-drop to their busy lives but, like the corkscrew at a picnic, everyone counted on somebody else to provide it. Everyone, that was, but Neville and Nancy Sanderson and a handful of others, who valiantly flogged the dead donkey, organizing the Christmas Bazaar and the Summer Fête, the Women's League and the odd fund-raising event; all about as integral to the day-to-day life of the village as a monocle to a child's eye. There soon would come a time, Liberty thought, when busy commuters would have to hire the services of professional villagers. 'Of course we're very lucky, what with the mother's help and the gardener, not to mention the simply marvellous little man who looks after the Village Spirit. He takes care of everything: those annoying visits to church between Christmas and Easter, slide shows in the village hall, the cake stall at the fête, although he does charge extra for bell-ringing. And his wife's rather a treasure too; regular as clockwork at the WI meetings, never fails to twitch the net curtains first thing in the morning and last at night. She even offered to do the gossip at the Post Office counter, but I said, "Mrs B," I said,

"I'll take care of that, you're doing enough as it is, and I wouldn't want to take advantage." Where did we get them from? Oh this splendid little firm in Cobham.'

'Anyway Liberty,' Nancy's voice roped her thoughts back in line. 'Do tell us what happened.'

'It's not really very interesting,' Liberty tried. 'My hand's fine and the wound's healing nicely.'

'I hope you reported the dog's owner to the police.'

'No, no I didn't.'

'Why ever not?'

Liberty was beginning to get upset. The more she wanted not to carry on with the subject, the more interest she seemed to generate.

'Because it was my father's dog,' she admitted at last. That did nothing to quell the curiosity of the others.

'Oh the poor man,' Nancy said briskly. 'He must be feeling simply awful.'

*   *   *

'This is my fault.' Hamish's voice, heavy with a thousand burdens, had floated towards her as she bent double on the orange plastic chair in the surgery waiting-room, clutching her bleeding cheek with her hand that was also bleeding and wrapped in a soiled tea towel. It

39

was a voice Hamish liked to use quite often, but this time she had been in too much pain to bother with the comforting denial of facts that he expected from her. Instead she had wondered tiredly, was this enough? Had the wounds, caused by her father's ill-disciplined and grossly indulged dog, coupled with the goddamned awful name he'd given her and that she had carried like a stigmata, at last atoned?

No, of course not. Not when measured against the loss of a wife. She had sighed and turned away from her father's face and his relieved smile that waited in the corners of his mouth, like a prima donna in the wings, poised to rush out and receive her applause.

*   *   *

'Poor man,' Nancy said to Piglet in an encouraging sort of voice. Liberty jumped as she was dragged back to the Harvest Lunch via yet another detour of her mind. Maybe it was not so surprising after all that she had failed as a writer, when her stream of consciousness revolved around Winnie the Pooh.

'Oh. Right.' Liberty opened her eyes wide in an attempt to look alert.

There was silence at her end of the table. She felt as uncomfortable as when she was nagged to tell one of her two jokes; the more she protested that it was not really all that funny,

40

the more everyone became convinced they wanted to hear it. Now the whole hall seemed quieter and heads were turned expectantly towards her.

Liberty sighed. Nancy was making her feel unco-operative and childish.

'All right, but it's only a little dog bite. Not at all your headline-grabbing kind.'

'When did you say it happened?' Nancy asked.

'That really wet Wednesday some weeks ago. It was pouring down. I was walking across to my father's house at the school, to show him some snaps Johnny had sent. Johnny is my son.' A note of proprietory joy sneaked into her voice, and she paused to allow herself to dwell for a moment on the open-featured, fair-haired love of her life.

'How is dear Johnny?' Evelyn asked.

'Very well thanks,' Liberty smiled at her. 'Sweden is proving a huge success. He's living in a cabin in this real Troll forest: miles and miles of fir trees. And he's off to Australia next month, for the next stage of the great gap-year adventure.'

'I thought he was going to Edinburgh.'

'No, that's afterwards. This is—'

'Liberty, you were saying it was raining.' Nancy called them to order.

Liberty began to get annoyed. They wanted to hear a story. OK, fine; they were going to get one. Her head a little to one side, she looked thoughtfully at Nancy before continuing. 'I thought my father must have been watching "Good-bye Mr Chips" or "Dead Poets' Society" again, because his sitting-room was filled with boys: sweet, small boys smelling of sweat and wet socks. Hamish was standing by the open fire, declaiming—Owen I think—and he was wearing a garland of tobacco flowers in his hair.'

'Nicotiana,' Neville informed the table in general.

'Hamish was standing by the open fire, declaiming, a garland of nicotiana in his hair,' Liberty repeated patiently.

'In all my years as a naturalist,' Evelyn said, 'I've always found English perfectly satisfactory for my needs.'

There was a stubborn streak in Liberty. They had bullied her into starting this story, now they would have to listen until she'd finished. 'Be that as it may,' she said, 'but there I was, shaking the rain from my umbrella before leaving it in a corner of the room. Moments later one of the boys, a rather fat one, got up and began to scramble across the outstretched legs of the others. He tripped and fell, landing on top of Cissy, my father's beagle. I dived forward, hand outstretched, to help the boy up. Arrgh! Cissy, startled by having a fat boy land on top of her when she was fast asleep, sprang up, the whites of her eyes showing. Crunch! Her teeth clamped onto

42

my cheek and then my finger as I put up my hand to protect myself. Whack! My father hit Cissy across the back with my umbrella and Yelp! she let go.' Liberty looked round the table and smiled sweetly. 'I sank to the floor and, holding out my bleeding hand to my father, I quoted: "Thou rascal beagle hold thy bloody hand." Then I fainted, for once fitting my father's idea of the perfect woman: educated but feminine.'

There was quite a long silence after that.

Someone spoke at last. 'Mrs Turner used to be a writer.' The middle-aged woman, whom Liberty did not know, volunteered the information like an apology on Liberty's behalf. Liberty gave her a pained glance.

'It's beadle not beagle,' Evelyn said. '"Thou rascal beadle—"'

'You're absolutely right,' Liberty agreed. 'But Cissy is a beagle.'

'Beagles don't bite,' Neville said.

Oscar Brooke seemed to have cheered up. 'I rather think we should have had that story in *The Tribune*,' he said, smiling across the table at Liberty.

'Well now you've had your little bit of fun,' Nancy's smile, on the other hand, was as tight as if it had shrunk in the wash. 'I can see you're not going to tell us what happened. Of course that's your prerogative.' She turned round in her chair. 'And look, what have we here? Pat's special Harvest Pud, how lovely!'

43

As the apple crumble and vanilla ice-cream were passed round, Liberty turned round with a grin and whispered to Evelyn, 'Every child knows that if you want to be believed, the last thing you should do is tell the truth.'

'Mrs Sanderson,' Victoria spoke across the table in that sweet, thick voice that fused the words together like toffee.

Nancy turned round, her face softening. 'Do call me Nancy.'

'I've experienced the most wonderful sense of community in some of the most deprived inner city areas,' Ted said suddenly on Liberty's right.

'Nancy then,' Victoria smiled. 'Jenny Haville-Jones told me you have the yummiest recipe for crab-apple jelly and I wondered if I could pop over and copy it down. I've been searching for a really good one for absolutely ages, haven't I, darling?' She turned her smile on Oscar who nodded, but without much enthusiasm.

Ted Brain pushed his chair back and cleared his throat. 'So another Harvest Festival draws to a close. I'm grateful to all of you who made it to today's festivities and of course especially those of you,' he nodded towards Nancy and Pat, 'who have worked so hard preparing this meal, and decorating the hall to make this such a pleasant occasion.' The vicar paused for a moment, looking down at his hands. 'Still, I must say that I find myself disappointed to

44

note that the circle of friends assembled here today is not much different to that which I would find at any village drinks party. The church and our festivals must not come across like an exclusive club. Somehow we must find ways of reaching out to our neighbours and drawing them into our circle.' Ted folded his napkin lengthwise, then across, as mouths were opened; but nothing came forth but offended silence.

Some minutes later, when Liberty began the two mile walk back home, a car pulled up alongside her, and Evelyn, seated in the front passenger seat next to her nephew, wound down her window and offered her a lift.

'You went off in a hurry. We're going back to my place. Come and join us for some decent coffee.'

Liberty said she needed the walk but she might drop in later. As the car drove off again, Evelyn popped her head out of the window once more. 'Suicide is so frightfully middle class,' she hissed. 'Don't do it.' Off they went, with the gorgeous Victoria giving a little wave from the back. She is like a young queen, so beautiful and young and adored, Liberty thought as she walked on in the misty autumn afternoon that was so silent and solid in its gloom, it was as if the world was wrapped in a grey blanket. She stopped on the bridge and, leaning over the railings, she gazed down into the shallow water that looked as if it had just

45

rinsed over a pair of muddy boots.

'Suicide is so frightfully middle class,' she heard Evelyn's words.

'But I am middle class,' she moaned as she stood on tip-toe, leaning over the railing.

Oh what was the point? You would have to be unconscious first to drown in that trickle. She wondered if the recent drought and accompanying low water levels had had a corresponding effect on the suicide statistics. There could be yet another gripe at the water privatisation in it. 'It's diabolical! Since the water was taken away from the people and put into the hands of the bosses you can't even get enough for a decent suicide.' Giving the river a last glance, she began the last half mile of the walk back home.

The house needed airing, and on the kitchen table the bottle of sleeping pills waited like a long-suffering housewife with the dinner in the oven. 'Hang on,' Liberty said. 'I've got Friday's episode of *Home and Away* to watch first.' She made herself a cup of tea and sat down in front of the video. She was half-way through the episode when the door bell went. Sighing, she pressed the pause button and got up to answer. It was Oscar.

'Evelyn sent me,' he said. 'She was most insistent you come over and, as you probably know, she never gives up.' He smiled at her. 'She has absolutely no concept of what is known as personal space, either. When she

46

stayed in my flat in London she was quite capable of coming into the bathroom whilst you were bathing, or even on the loo, if she wanted to speak to you.'

'Didn't you have a lock?' Liberty stood back to let Oscar in.

'No,' he said. 'An old Australian tradition.'

'You're not Australian are you?' Liberty said, her voice gaining a little colour. 'My son is about to go to Australia.'

'No, no I'm not.' Oscar smiled again. Liberty opened her mouth to speak but Oscar added quickly, 'You look a little tired, if I may say so. Are you all right?' He looked at her through his round glasses, his blue eyes remote but kindly.

Spectacles on Oscar Brooke, Liberty thought, were rather like hairpins holding up the locks of a gorgeous brunette; you found yourself imagining taking them off. 'Oh I'm fine,' she said. 'I've just had a couple of bad days.'

What stupid things one says: 'Oh it's nothing, I've just lost my job,' or, 'I'm very well thank you, riddled with cancer but otherwise on top of the world.' Ridiculous. But she put her coat on obediently and followed Oscar the few yards along the lane to Evelyn's place.

Glebe House was an Elizabethan farmhouse which had managed through the centuries to remain so. 'Narrowly avoided having a Georgian front slapped on it on at least two

47

occasions,' Evelyn said. She was also fond of complaining, 'If I have to hear the words Desirable Property once more from some spotty-faced yappy or whatever they are called, I will sue for verbal battery.'

Evelyn had inherited the house from her parents, and she had made few changes in her childhood home. Once, when Liberty was admiring the blue embroidered curtains in the sitting-room, Evelyn had thanked her for the compliment. 'They are pretty aren't they. I believe Mother hung them in 1939. I remember her saying if there was going to be a war, at least she could have some good curtains to look at. Though I don't know that they were of much comfort to her when poor Herbert got injured.'

'Of course, you're Herbert's son,' Liberty said now to Oscar as they arrived at Evelyn's front door. Thinking of her own mother she asked, 'Did you ever meet him?'

'No.' Oscar held the door open for her, then followed her inside. 'No I didn't. He died in May 1948, two months before I was born. His ship was torpedoed during the Battle of the Atlantic. It took him five years to die.'

Liberty sighed. 'How sad.' She paused for a moment before adding, 'But at least it wasn't you who killed him. You must be thankful for that.'

At this Oscar looked surprised, but before he had time to answer Evelyn called out to them,

48

'Hot or cold milk in your coffee?'

Liberty wandered through to the kitchen across the worn, pale green carpet. 'Hot, please.'

Evelyn stood, surrounded by gadgets, in the large kitchen with its dark oak beams and old blue painted wooden cupboards. Liberty always wondered why, in this house where new possessions were so scarce, the kitchen looked like an electricity show-room: microwaves and processors, juice machines, ice-cream and yoghurt makers, electric whisks and mincers, even an electric wok.

Heating milk on a ceramic hob, Evelyn said, 'So you didn't kill yourself. Good.' The milk boiled over, frying itself brown on the red-hot hob. 'Blast! I hate cooking.'

'So why do you spend all that money on kitchen gadgets?' Liberty grabbed a cloth and began wiping the spills.

Evelyn piled cups and saucers, made of china so fine you could see your fingers outlined through it, onto the tray. 'I told you,' she said, 'I hate cooking. Now you go on in, I'll be with you in a minute.'

In the sitting-room, water-colours by talented amateurs mingled with oil-paintings of surprising boldness and quality, books spilt from the bookcase onto the carpet, where they were stacked in dusty heaps, and the many little tables positioned round the room were barely visible beneath seed trays and potted

49

plants. Evelyn was a well-respected expert on natural pest control. This room and the converted garage were her offices, the garden running down to the river was her laboratory; an acre and a half of theories put into practice.

Victoria joined Liberty by the french windows. 'I think being busy with her garden keeps Evelyn young, you know,' she said with the air of one conveying new and startling information.

'Yes, absolutely,' Liberty agreed.

'I think any interest like that helps keep the years at bay,' Victoria added.

'True, true,' Liberty nodded, but Victoria's huge dark eyes fixed on her made her feel that something more was expected of her. 'The devil soon finds work for idle hands,' she tried.

'It's so peaceful in the country,' Victoria said. Again they both stared out across the garden.

If you stepped out from the french windows you could walk dry-footed on the York stone terrace until the lawns took over, running down to the riverbank. Even now, the evergreens planted along the walls broke up the grey dusk: Daphne Odorata, Sarcococca with its scented white winter flowers, Lavender lanata, box, lemon verbena. Liberty knew them all, and in the summer their scents mingled with those of the roses and floated inside on the warm breeze. Yes, it did seem peaceful and it certainly was beautiful, but amongst the trees and shrubs and the grass that was green and tall even now, things were going on that would make downtown LA seem cosy. In Evelyn's garden every bug, it seemed, was someone else's meal.

Behind them there was a clinking of cups as Evelyn slammed the tray down on the low table in front of the sofa.

'Ah coffee,' Liberty said, gesticulating vaguely in Evelyn's direction.

'I had another offensive letter from that so-called farmer down the road,' Evelyn said as they all settled down. 'Have you met him, Oscar? Tim Haville-Jones.' She splashed some warm milk into a cup of coffee and handed it to Liberty. 'The sort of man who feels the addition of a second surname is an achievement.'

'They have got the most gorgeous family, though,' Victoria said, turning her long eyes on Evelyn. 'His wife and I had a little bump in our cars on that really narrow bit of road by the bridge. No-one was hurt or anything, but we had a really nice chat.'

'In my days it was visiting cards,' Evelyn muttered, pouring herself some coffee.

Victoria ignored her. 'The twins are adorable. I don't know where Jenny gets their clothes, but they were wearing the sweetest little outfits, and their shoes were like little tiny riding boots with—'

Oscar didn't wait for Victoria to finish.

51

'What's the problem?'

'Oak,' Evelyn said making her mouth into a disapproving line. Like one of those you draw in the sand, Liberty thought, and you cross at your peril.

'Oak?' Oscar found a space on the table for his cup and saucer between the tray of cuttings and the black notebooks.

'The oak in the field, silly.' Evelyn pointed towards the field beyond the river.

'Oh that oak,' Liberty said. 'I thought I heard something about it being cut down.'

'Yes, well that's exactly it.' Evelyn spoke with the sort of stretched-to-snapping-point patience one usually reserves for querulous toddlers. 'And I'm not going to allow him to do it, and that's why he is writing rude letters.'

'I wrote a story about a tree. An old tree that had seen lovers come and go through the ages. I couldn't believe it, but when I sent it into a competition run by our local bookshop, I got a highly commended. It was published in this writers' magazine,' Victoria said in that sweet voice that would have made Liberty listen even if she had not said something so startling.

'You write?'

The magnolia face creased in a smile. 'No, not really. I just feel a story coming on now and then. And then Oscar said, "Why don't you send that one in?" I got this really nice letter back saying that I must carry on, because my writing showed real promise. That's why I

52

thought I'd like to go to your class. Just for fun really. I want to be a full-time home-maker now. I know that's not fashionable, but I've never followed the herd, have I, Oscar?'

'No. No I suppose you haven't.' Oscar uncrossed his long legs and picked up his cup, drinking the hot coffee in big gulps before putting it back, a little too hard, on to the table.

Liberty's cup had rattled to the edge of the saucer. 'Just like that, was it? You thought you'd like to write a story, so you did, and it was accepted for publication?' The words came out of her throat carefully, one by one as if they had explosives strapped to their backs. 'That's simply wonderful.' But inside she raged. It just was not fair. Like giving the pretty doll with the blonde corkscrew curls and the pink smocked dress the teddy bear's growl as well: *de trop*, unnecessary, unfair.

'Maybe you should employ your wife to write in to that wretched Village Diary Neville was carrying on about,' Evelyn suggested.

Oscar stirred in his chair, a sullen expression on his face.

Liberty dropped her jealousy for just long enough to say, 'Yes, why don't you?'

Victoria was leafing through a copy of *The Field* and she said without looking up, 'No, I don't think so, it's not really me. I like making up stories if I'm going to write at all—you know, fiction. Didn't you Liberty, when you wrote?'

53

'Oh yes,' Liberty nodded. 'Absolutely.'

A little later she went back home, having refused an offer from Oscar to walk her back. 'I've got a torch. Honestly, it's only a few yards.'

She paused in her hall, looking at the aspidistra that looked droopy all of a sudden, as if the atmosphere around the house in the last few days had sucked the very life from its stems. Liberty went up close to it, taking one of the fleshy leaves in her hand. 'Don't you die on me,' she said, 'do you hear? Any dying round here comes strictly from me.'

She sat down in the darkened sitting-room, her coat still on, and switched the video back on. The characters from *Home and Away* sprang to life, a small square of colour and some noise to break the silence of the house.

Extract from The Tribune

Tollymead: *The village celebrated Harvest with a gourmet lunch served in the village hall. As usual, this popular annual event brought together people of all ages and occupations in this spread-out but friendly village. Closing the proceedings, the Vicar of Tollymead, the Reverend Ted Brain, said he looked forward to an ever wider circle of villagers joining in future events. Mr Brain, who is well known for his active social concern and support for the less fortunate in our society, was particularly pleased with the many splendid gifts that will be distributed to the elderly and house-bound in the area.*

CHAPTER THREE

Nancy Sanderson had returned from a busy day on the Bench in Winchester. Having made sure that her husband had eaten the lunch she had prepared for him (cottage pie and mushy peas; 'nothing fancy, I'm a simple man'), she settled down in her favourite armchair by the window in the sitting-room, with a cup of tea and a chocolate Hob-nob. With a little sigh of contentment she opened that week's copy of *The Tribune*. Some moments later she called out to her husband,

'Andrew dear, have you read *The Tribune* today?'

From his next-door study, Andrew shouted back, 'No, of course not. I have such a thing as a business to run you know!'

Chastised, Nancy got up and, putting her bony, high-arched feet back into the brown lace-ups, tip-toed into the study.

'Of course dear.' She was using a voice reserved for her husband, a coaxing, softer voice, as though she had been polishing her normal tones with superfine sandpaper before letting them spring from her throat, a voice that would have surprised the young man she had just jailed for driving when over the limit. 'It's just that there's a big Diary entry for Tollymead this week, about the Harvest Festival. I can't think who it would be writing in, but—'

'But what Nancy? I'm trying to work.'

Nancy winced at the impatience in his voice and wished that just for once he'd leave it behind when he spoke to her. 'Oh nothing dear. I'll let you get on.' Having placed a reverential kiss on the top of his balding head, she tip-toed away.

* * *

'Think good thoughts. Keep your mind on what is right and true and beautiful,' Liberty

56

said tiredly to her class, sitting, as they always did on Wednesday afternoons, in one of the three Portakabins lent by Tollymead Manor to the Fairfield Adult Education Department. The cabins stood in a row on the edge of the school car park and were used as back-up classrooms for computer work, CDT and pottery. But not on Wednesdays, Wednesday was a half day.

'If your minds are constantly on petty things,' Liberty went on, 'the irritating barking of next door's dog, your husband's habit of giving one loud belch before he starts shaving in the morning, or how to—'

'You know, Oscar does that.' Victoria had been as good as her word and here she sat, wide-eyed at the front of the class. 'He goes into the bathroom and belches.'

Liberty looked up with a pang of sympathy for Oscar. His wife might just as well have flung open the door to the loo with him in there for them all to see. Neville Pyke, who was working on a *DIY Manual for the Senior Citizen*, cleared his throat, and two young secretaries from the local firm of solicitors tittered. Victoria seemed unperturbed.

'A petty soul, shrunken from lack of exercise, cannot shed light on creation, let alone create something new,' Liberty continued, feeling as if she was reading out the charges in court against herself. 'So don't just work on the techniques, style and syntax and

57

the clever little metaphors, work on your souls, and you'll find that the rest will follow.' Liberty closed her folder. 'That's all for today. See you next week.'

After they had gone, Liberty walked round the room, turning the chairs up on top of the long tables. Victoria, she thought, did not seem very intelligent, but she had cunning and obviously took to truth with as much enthusiasm and discrimination as a Japanese industrialist buying investment art. Liberty had prepared that day's class some weeks earlier, while she still had hope. Now she had no hope, and by next Wednesday Victoria would sit there, looking at her with those big eyes and asking what had gone wrong with *her* soul. She looked at her watch; it was only half past four. She decided to walk the few hundred yards to her friend Penny's house.

Penny had married Donald Mortimer, a resident music master at Tollymead Manor, some ten years earlier and, introduced to each other by Hamish, she and Liberty had become firm friends. Liberty knew no-one in whose presence she felt such calm. Simply sitting down at the Formica table in the large kitchen, with the smell of baking bread hanging in the air, was like half an hour in the lotus position. Penny was a hippy graduate to earthmotherdom, and the combination of dreamy prettiness and militant homemaking was irresistible to Liberty. Penny knew why she was here and where she was going and she gave you tea and home-made cakes on the way. What more could you ask for in a friend?

In the kitchen Penny helped nine-year-old Felicity, the oldest of the four Mortimer children, and her friend to bake tiny cakes for their dolls' tea party. Liberty sat at the kitchen table with her mug of tea, quite content just to be there. She looked at her friend, who wiped up globules of sponge mix from the floor whilst instructing the girls how to grease the frilly paper cake cases. Penny never raised her voice; she never wore jeans, either. Liberty looked down at her own sorry-looking pair. They weren't even scuffed in decent places like the knees, but on the bottom and on the inside of the thighs, because the tops of her legs were so fat they rubbed together. Penny, on the other hand, looked enchanting in frilly apron over a long, doe-skin skirt and one of her husband's shirts. Her husband adored her and called her his Stepford wife. It always made Penny laugh. She had a mind as agile as a marsh frog, leaping across the soggy realities of the day towards her own vision of perfection.

'Have a biscuit, they were made this morning,' she said, handing Liberty a large plate. Edward, her three-year-old son appeared in the door and, without a word, began to undress himself. After a few minutes contemplating his penis, pulling it this way and that until Liberty thought it would snap like a

59

rubber band, he put his trousers back on, placed his pants on his head like a hat, and walked out. 'He's just learnt to undress himself,' Penny beamed after her youngest. 'They grow up so fast.'

'You're telling me,' Liberty said. 'But you're lucky, you have four of them growing up fast. That takes a lot longer.'

'But you could never have stood having four children. I know you would have liked two, but I could never see you with four.'

'I'd love four. In fact,' Liberty said with a vehemence that surprised her, 'I'd have loved four children and a kitchen just like yours and I wouldn't mind Donald thrown in on top so to speak. I've always liked Donald.'

'I know.' Penny helped the two little girls take the baking tray from the oven. 'But you can't have him.'

'She can't have us either,' Felicity said, but she said it nicely, a bit like a shop assistant regretting a popular item being temporarily out of stock.

'I know, I know, you lovely girl,' Liberty grabbed her round the waist, planting a noisy kiss on the child's velvety cheek. She felt happier already, as she leaned back in the Windsor chair with its patchwork cushion in green and red.

'Anyway,' Penny sat down too, wincing as she raised herself again, removing a Stickle Brick from the seat. 'You've got your writing.

60

That's your world, and you know it.'

'Not any more.' Liberty took another biscuit from the large plate. 'Can I at least have one of those?' She pointed to the blue-and-white frilly pinafore apron that Penny wore as sweetly as if she were appearing in a fifties ad for Ovaltine. 'I want to wear it when Johnny comes back. He's always wanted me to be like you. Actually,' Liberty contemplated her friend for a moment, 'it's a truth universally acknowledged that all children want their mothers to be like you.'

'Well they can't have her either. You're being very greedy today, Liberty.' Felicity had a stern look on her small round face as she turned in the doorway.

'Yes I am.' Liberty nodded sadly. 'I always get greedy when I've had a disappointment. I wish someone would get the message that I don't get any nicer when I suffer; on the contrary, I get very mean.'

'You can have one of my cakes. Me and Chloë made them ourselves.' Felicity took the plate of fairy cakes from her friend and held it out to Liberty, who took one. The plate was a heavy blue-and-white pottery one that Liberty had given them years ago. That was another thing about Penny's house. There was not very much of anything, just enough china or glass or furniture, but what was there was loved, and used, and cared for. The kitchen cupboards were the same avocado Formica that had been

61

there since the last-but-one headmaster's wife had the masters' houses refurbished twenty years ago, but Penny had put up shelves, and on each shelf was a frill of red-and-white gingham and hooks to hang cups and mugs. Liberty sat back admiring the ill-matched cups, some with roses, some with animals, one with a painted lighthouse, allowing a feeling of calm to take over. Maybe she should try to adopt. It was not too late, not if they were the sort of children most people did not want. And God knows, there were plenty of those sorts of children around. Johnny would be happy, he had always longed for sisters and brothers. There would be hustle and bustle and shelves in the kitchen just like Penny's ... and then I would shout at them when they made a mess and tell them to be quiet and leave me alone, because I'm not Penny. I am a failure, with a heart so shrunken there's room only for a son and the memories of words spelt out on a screen.

'You don't really miss Tom, do you?' Penny poured them both fresh cups of tea.

Liberty smiled, an apologetic smile, and shrugged her shoulders. 'I miss not having someone around, but no, I don't really miss *him*.'

'I thought as much when you called up and talked for twenty minutes about the letter from your ex-agent and two minutes about your ex-lover.'

'Penny, what will you do when the children leave home?' Liberty asked her.

Penny smiled serenely. 'I've created the perfect place for them to be. They'll come back and they'll bring their children, and the house will be fuller than ever.'

As she left Penny's house and drove towards town, Liberty wondered for the first time if Penny was being quite fair to her family. They might have the perfect childhood, but would they spend the rest of their lives longing for a lost paradise, like the hero schoolboy eagerly turning up at every old boys' reunion, the school song always ready to burst from his lips?

She parked the car at the central car park and checked her face before stepping outside. An infection in the wound on her cheek had festered until the scar tissue had become a raised pink rope along her cheek. That morning at the hospital they had cleaned it up and sealed it with three small plastic strips. It had not looked so bad earlier in the day, but now, hit by the cold air after Penny's warm kitchen, it had turned the colour of hung beef. With a frown of self-disgust, Liberty pulled out a large pair of sunglasses from the glove compartment. Making her way across the lit-up car park she did not see Oscar until she was almost on top of him. 'I'm so sorry,' Liberty said, removing her boot from the black leather of his brogue.

'That's all right. But you'd see better if you weren't wearing those glasses. It's six o'clock, dark and all that.'

Liberty stared at his chest, comfortably wide and clad in a worn tweed jacket and, like a vertigo sufferer staring over the edge of an abyss, she wanted to throw herself against his chest, sob and wail. Going, going, gone, she kept on staring. Think about it, the feeling of release, the final comfort. She blinked and shook herself. 'It's my cheek. I thought I would cover it up.'

'Any particular reason?' Oscar asked lightly.

'It's nearly supper time so I thought it best.'

'I'm sorry, but I don't quite follow.'

Not really concentrating, Liberty explained. 'Well, you know that vet series that was on television some while ago? It was uncanny: the moment you put the first forkful in your mouth, Christopher Timothy would put his arm up a cow's backside.' She smiled apologetically. 'But I don't suppose you ever eat supper in front of the television. I do all the time.' A car passed with its headlights full on, lighting up Oscar's face.

'I promise you,' he said, 'you look nothing like a cow's backside.'

Unable to receive even the mildest compliment gracefully, Liberty changed the subject. 'Are you on your way home?' she asked. 'I had Victoria in my class this afternoon.'

64

'No, no I'm not. I just nipped out of the office for a moment. We've got quite a big story on our hands, well, big for around here anyway. The teenage daughter of a local businessman has gone missing. Her father is Robert Seth. He owns the big Mercedes garage on North Street. The family is obviously extremely worried. It could be a kidnapping.'

'It must be difficult in your position,' Liberty said, 'to know whether to be excited or saddened when things like that happen. I mean, terrible trouble titillates, it sells copies. Wars, nude duchesses—all good for the job. I know when my grandmother lay dying, we all came to say goodbye and, loving her as I did, I still couldn't help thinking that this was an opportunity not to be missed to study death at close hand. I made notes straight afterwards, about the way her breath came so shallowly that it never seemed to touch her lungs at all, and the colour of her skin, grey, really grey with no tinge of relieving pink, and the looks on everyone's faces. Then, after putting my notebook away, I began to cry. Of course I felt guilty for ages.' With a little smile she added, 'It wasn't even as if I ended up creating great art from it.'

'Guilt is a very destructive feeling,' Oscar said. 'Don't indulge in it.' He took a step back. 'I must be off, I'm afraid. Don't drive with those things on, will you?'

'I think I failed to charm,' Liberty said to

herself as she wandered back to the car, depositing the plastic carrier bag on the front passenger seat. 'You're a poor substitute for a lover or a child,' she muttered, placing the glasses on the imagined face of the bag and hooking the sides of the frames through the handles. There were far too many young mothers with families around, loading up the boots of their cars. It was depressing. Only a year ago Johnny had still been home so that she could sigh companionably in the supermarket check-out on a Friday night, 'Teenagers, never stop eating,' as she loaded bag after bag. Tonight she had ended up buying a whole heap of different biscuits because she could not bear to take such a lonely basket through the check-out. As she stood there watching the check-out girl slide first one then another and another packet across the scanner, it occurred to her that it might seem as if she was just a lonely binger. 'My old father,' she muttered to the girl, 'can't have enough of them. If you dunk them for him in coffee, or tea, tea will do just as well, they simply melt in his mouth, right past his dentures.'

'Mushrooms one pound twenty, all right?' The girl chanted.

Liberty had smiled a yes. And back home she smiled again, as she mixed the mushrooms and pasta in a warm bowl. It was lucky she had bought the mushrooms, as Hamish had called up when she got home to say he was

66

coming over.

That evening Hamish was in one of his funky American professor moods. His thick grey hair was cut in a fashionable short back and sides, a lock left to flop across his forehead, and he was wearing a black polo neck under his tweed jacket instead of his normal Viyella shirt. Someone had once asked Hamish if he had ever thought of writing. Hamish had bridled and muttered about lack of time, but Liberty knew he was far too busy reinventing himself, working on suitable sets and plot lines for every new Hamish Bell, to have interest left for any other story. He was a good teacher, an inspired one at times, but his life's work was himself and, like a true artist, his work was never done as he pruned and added, changed a bit here, did an overhaul there.

Hamish declined a second helping of pasta, stretching in his chair and patting his stomach. 'Not bad for an old man eh?' he boasted the way he always did.

'No, very good. Very flat. Norfolk,' she added before she could help herself. She thought of Oscar's remark about guilt being destructive. She was not sure he was right. Would she be half as nice to Hamish if she had not felt bad about taking away his wife?

Hamish leant across the table and peered at his daughter's face. 'It's healing up well,' he said sitting back with a smile. 'You'll hardly be able to see the scar, just as I told you.'

67

He really believes that, Liberty got up to clear the table. And why be surprised? Hamish was, after all, the embodiment of the saying, 'Life's what you make of it.' Son of Pangloss, that was him. Of course the difficulty with having such a man for a father was that he would never help you solve a problem because, quite simply, there never was one; life was so much nicer that way. Now you see it, now you don't. Gone, vanished.

* * *

'Everyone hates me at school,' the twelve-year-old Liberty had wept to Hamish at the end of one school holiday. 'They say I'm weird. They hate my clothes, and when I come to join in a game they just look at each other, like this.' Liberty had heaved her skinny shoulders and rolled her eyes. 'Then they all just walk away.'

'Now I don't believe that is so at all.' Hamish had smiled calmly. 'I think you'll find that you are looked upon as rather a leader by your peers. They admire you precisely because you do not run with the herd.'

Liberty had wanted to say that her dearest ambition was to run with the herd if only she could find a herd that would let her, and that locking someone in an airing cupboard so they missed the school outing to the Theme Park, and cutting up their Sunday tights just after they had been mended, were strange ways of

68

showing admiration. But Hamish wanted his daughter to be popular, so in his mind she was. Now you see it, now you don't.

* * *

'Look,' Liberty said now, pushing her face close to her father's. 'Before you are the beginnings of a puckering scar that will remain until it rots away with the rest of my face, a scar which is pulling at the corner of my eye so that I look like a clown every time I smile.' She sat down and did not look at her father as she poured them both some more wine. 'Can't you see you are taking positive thinking a tad too far. I mean, I was surprised when you didn't argue with the doctor who pronounced Granny dead. Denying that a problem exists won't make it go away. It just goes underground for a while, like a terrorist, sneaking round the innermost corners of your being, leaving little destructive reminders of its existence like parcels of gelignite to detonate just as you think you've won.'

'Very well put Liberty. Very well put,' Hamish nodded wisely and lit his pipe. 'Now let me look at those letters you had back with your manuscript.' Sitting back comfortably he said, 'You know I can't believe they're as bad as you say.'

Hamish stayed until well after midnight. As she washed up, Liberty noticed the outside

69

light coming on at the vicarage. She turned the tap off and hung the tea towel on the Aga rail. Someone is dying, she thought, or in Hamish's world of positive thinking, the vicar is having friends over for a late game of bridge.

*　　　*　　　*

The vicarage was an unlovely fifties' box that acted as a permanent reminder to each new incumbent of his reduced status. It stood some distance away from the church, but not far enough to deny a view of the old vicarage, large, Georgian and mellow. Ted was the first vicar to say he actually preferred the new house. All that he had asked for was some automatic floodlights for the small forecourt, and it was these that came on as the slight black-clad figure moved from behind the large yew tree.

Ted Brain had gone to bed leaving an indifferent Sunday sermon on his desk. Suddenly he felt sympathy for his washed-out mother who, after years of failing to awaken her husband's interest by doing what she did best, cook marvellous meals on a small budget, had sunk into sullen despair, to rise no higher again than some re-heated soup with a dollop of cream on top. He knew just how she must have felt. And that was what his parishioners were getting, a re-heated sermon with a small lump of fresh thought chucked on top. They

70

deserved no better.

When he woke again he did not at first know what had disturbed him. Then he heard the soft knocking on the door and, putting on his dressing-gown, hurried downstairs. He did not open the door straightaway. The old biddies might talk about their peaceful country village until they were blue in the face, but Ted had felt safer in the centre of Liverpool. Here, in the unrelieved darkness of the night, a whole troupe of homicidal maniacs could descend on him and follow up with an all-night rave, and no-one would be any the wiser unless the next day happened to be Sunday and, even then, he thought bitterly, there was no guarantee that he would be missed.

'Who is it?' he called out, opening the door on the chain.

'Please, let me in. I need help. Sanctuary.' The voice outside was a woman's.

'Stand in the light, please,' Ted asked.

The visitor stepped back into the path of the floodlight, and Ted saw a slight young girl, dark-skinned, with long, black hair hanging in a thick plait across one shoulder. There was no-one else with her. His heart pounding, he released the chain and opened the door to let the girl in. She stood in his bare hall, shivering and damp from the dew outside. 'Sanctuary,' she said again. 'I'm seeking asylum.'

Ted raked his thinning hair with his fingers until it rose like a cockscomb from his head.

71

'Where have you come from. Why did you come here?'

'Someone, a friend,' the girl said breathlessly, 'told me about you, that you were active in the movement.'

Ted was about to ask what movement, when he remembered having made enquiries through some radical friends in the church about a group of priests and laymen who ran safe houses for asylum seekers on the run from deportation. Nothing had come of it at the time, but someone must have remembered his interest and passed on his address to this girl.

'Come through to the kitchen,' Ted nudged her before him like a collie with a stray lamb. 'I'll put the kettle on. You tell me everything you can.'

'I had nowhere else to go. I did not know what to do.' Her voice was soft, but the accent puzzling. It was not like anything Ted had heard before.

'Where do you come from?'

'Please, I don't want to talk about it, not now, not yet, but—' she hesitated for a moment as if the story was too painful for her to continue, 'there was a whole group of us hiding in a lorry that had taken us from Holland. Then, while the driver was eating at a café, one of us was spotted and the police were called. I managed to get away.' The girl giggled suddenly, 'You could say that I fell off the back of a lorry.' She gave a little gasp, putting a

72

slender hand to her mouth.

'I'm sorry,' Ted's voice broke with excitement, 'you must be hungry, exhausted too. You stay there and I'll fix something to eat. Eggs and ba ... bac ... eggs on toast all right?'

The girl grinned at him. 'Lovely.'

Ted fried two eggs, sliding them on to the slices of toast that lay ready on the plate. Putting it before the girl he said, 'You did right to come to me. I will not be intimidated by the authorities, whatever the cost to myself. Tomorrow, when you've had a chance to recover, you must tell me the full story, and I will get in touch with the Organization to get some advice about what our next move should be.' Ted let out a sigh of satisfaction as he leant back in the chair. After a moment he had to turn away, blushing from a mixture of pity and anger as the girl emptied her plate with speed and thoroughness, leaving not a crumb on the plate.

'I have to beg your forgiveness,' Ted said, 'for a society that allows a young woman to starve as she runs in fear of the authorities.'

The girl pushed her plate away and eagerly accepted an apple. She sank her white, even teeth into the fruit before looking up again. 'Don't worry about it,' she said. 'But I'm very tired. Is there somewhere I can sleep? The floor will do.'

Ted made up the bed in the spare room, with

the red and navy Habitat bed linen that had been a present from an old girlfriend. He lent the girl a pair of pyjamas and found a new toothbrush at the back of the bathroom cupboard. As he left the girl, he stopped for a moment in the doorway.

'You're safe now, you know. I won't let anything happen to you.' With an encouraging smile he closed the door softly behind him and went back downstairs. He was far too pumped-up to sleep. After pacing the floor for some minutes he poured himself some of the revolting sweet sherry left over from his predecessor and drank it down with a grimace before plonking himself down at the table. His heart was pushing blood around his body at an alarming rate, as if he was suddenly living at twice the normal speed. Taking deep breaths, he looked out of the kitchen window at the village, his village, in darkness. There they all slept, his comfortable parishioners, and here he was, at long last, doing something real, something that actually mattered. All those Sundays preaching to a scattering of people, who thought an hour of their time and a pound for the collection absolved them from responsibilities for the rest of the week, now seemed worth while, leading, as they did, to this night.

'You're safe here,' he mumbled again. 'I'll fight for you.'

Tollymead: *Don't forget, this week is the annual Greenway and Tollymead Brownie Pack's car boot sale, to be held in Greenway church car park. Twenty-five per cent of the proceeds from all sales goes to the children.*

The Tollymead Women's League speaker for their next meeting, on the first Wednesday of the month, is Mr John Trugood, who will speak on the subject of winter colour for your garden. Mr Trugood was Secretary of the South of England Rose Society for many years, and his own garden at Treetops, Haslemere, is open to the public on alternate Sundays throughout the year.

Also this week, Tollymead welcomes a newcomer to the village, Ms Anne Havesham, over here from America for some peace and quiet to work on the script for her latest television show. Proud as we in the village are of our policy of allowing residents to come and go and live and die without interference from anybody, we are sure the newest member of the community will find our village a happy and welcoming one.

Ms Havesham was delighted when neighbour Phyllida Medley welcomed her with a present of a pot of home-made marmalade and half a dozen freshly laid eggs. 'They're from my own bantams,' Phyllida told Ms Havesham, 'so they're guaranteed free of salmonella.' Phyllida added that she knew Americans loved Caesar salad, and with shop eggs that could be a problem.

'I knew the British are meant to be a friendly race,' Ms Havesham told me, 'but even with that in mind, Tollymead obviously takes some beating.'

CHAPTER FOUR

On the Thursday Evelyn woke at seven as usual and, again as usual, the first thing she did on getting out of bed was to open the heavy, rose-patterned curtains and look out across the garden and the Haville-Joneses field beyond. When she was a small child in that same bedroom, she had imagined that the great oak stood guard outside, protecting her from harm, and even now she would nod a brisk good morning. But this morning she lingered, noting, before she walked away, that it was a fine day—cold but fine.

Each spring the huge trunk of the oak was invaded by ivy, and each year, by the time autumn came, unless Evelyn got to it with her

Wilkinson's shears, the ivy grew so that you could hardly see the bark beneath the spreading leaves.

'You want that tree strangled,' she had said coldly to Tim Haville-Jones coming out of church last Christmas Day. 'It's in the way of your machinery, so you want it dead.' It amused Evelyn to remember how shocked everyone had been: to bring up something unpleasant like that on Christmas Day. Surely it could have kept until the twenty-seventh?

This year, a week after Harvest Festival, the tree had received a near fatal injury. The men burning stubble had made a mistake, so they said, when calculating the direction of the wind, so the flames had engulfed the trunk of the tree, charring its bark. The same day a notice had gone up on the parish notice-board and on the entrance to the footpath, warning people to stay away from the area round the tree as it was no longer safe. The tree, the notice continued, would be cut down the following Thursday. Regrettably, with safety foremost in mind, no other action was possible.

When, at nine o'clock, the men came with the tractor and the chain-saw, they found Evelyn chained to the blackened trunk of the tree.

'I'm not moving,' she said, dismissing them with a wave of her thermos flask. 'Why don't you just go on back to your master and tell him there's an ugly old woman chained to the tree,

77

so you can't do your dirty work.'

Grumbling and shaking their heads, they climbed back aboard the tractor and drove off.

Tim Haville-Jones found it difficult to take them seriously. 'You go across and reason with the old bat,' he said to Jenny, his wife. 'I've got a delivery from Sanderson's arriving any minute. And take the girls. I bet behind that bluff exterior she's a real push-over. Old spinsters can't resist children.'

Jenny was not so sure, but she dressed the twins in their blue-and-red striped puffas and green gumboots with frog's faces, and set off across the field.

'Tim's very worried,' she knelt down by Evelyn. She turned to the children. 'Give your Auntie Evelyn a kiss, there's my good girls.' She gave the twins a little push. Reluctantly, they planted a wet kiss each on Evelyn's veined cheeks. Chained up as she was, Evelyn had to content herself with a fearsome glare in their direction, sending them whimpering back to their mother's arms.

'I'm worried too,' Evelyn said. 'That's why I've chained myself to this oak. Normally I don't do this.'

There was a pause. The girls stopped whimpering.

'You'll get cold,' Jenny tried. 'Surely this tree is not worth catching pneumonia for?'

'In my opinion it is.'

Then the telephone rang.

78

'I must be mad,' Jenny said, 'but I thought I heard the phone.'

'"I'm in when I'm out",' Evelyn quoted smugly. Rummaging round the large canvas bag at her side she brought out a mobile phone. 'I think you'll find it's Liberty Turner, my neighbour, calling. I'm sure you've met. I asked her to train her binoculars on me and to call at the first sight of trouble.' Evelyn placed the phone to her ear. Looking sternly at Jenny she said, 'You're trouble.' And she snapped up the aerial. 'Hello, hello, Evelyn here.' There was a pause as she listened to what was said at the other end. The girls stared at her, open-mouthed. Evelyn winked at them, reducing them instantly to floods of tears.

'Yes Liberty dear,' Evelyn said with an evil glance at the children. 'I think you can call my nephew Oscar Brooke, the editor of *The Tribune*. No dear, I don't think there'll be any unpleasantness.' She pushed the aerial down and replaced the phone in her bag.

Jenny grabbed her daughters' hands. 'I'll go and speak to Tim. I'm sure he'll be able to think of something.'

'I'm sure he will,' Evelyn said soothingly. 'Now, if you'll excuse me, I'm going to have some coffee.'

By the time Tim Haville-Jones arrived, the reporter and photographer from *The Tribune* were already there. The photographer, a woman, was snapping Evelyn from every

79

direction. 'Lift your chin a little, that's right, lovely, perfect.'

The reporter, a young man of around twenty, squatted by Evelyn's side. '"Tantamount to murder," did you say?'

'That's right,' Evelyn said with a gleeful look at Tim Haville-Jones. 'Murder.'

Liberty, who had taken the morning off from her translation work to help Evelyn, suddenly felt a little sorry for the farmer and, before she knew it, she had smiled at him. She felt instantly annoyed with herself. Now she was not writing any more, her way of seeing everyone's point of view was becoming nothing but a bad habit. She knelt down by Evelyn's other side and, picking up the mug from the ground, tipped out the remains of the coffee from the cup before pouring in some more that was hot and fresh. 'What about the loo?' she hissed in Evelyn's ear.

'Chamber pot,' Evelyn hissed back, 'under here.' She clanked the chain against the blankets, hitting something hard.

'And how old are you Mrs Brooke?' the reporter asked, respect for whatever age Evelyn would admit to ready to ooze from his voice.

'It's Miss Brooke, and I'm seventy-five.'

'Seventy-five, you don't say.' The reporter nodded at the photographer who moved closer. 'The readers will love that.'

'She sits there like some evil totem, and you

80

lap up every word she says!' Tim Haville-Jones was shouting, his face brick-red. Liberty looked closely at him; if he suddenly began to perspire profusely, it would be a heart attack. 'Don't you understand,' Tim carried on, 'that bloody tree is dangerous. Now do you or do you not want my side of the story?'

The young reporter looked up from his note pad. 'Well let's see, sir. You want to cut down a five hundred-year-old-oak that probably saw Cromwell passing by—'

'And Charles the First,' Evelyn chipped in.

'—and Charles the First, as the lady says, to make it easier for your machinery.'

'I told you, the tree is unsafe!' Tim bellowed.

'I believe it was one of your men that set fire to the tree.'

'Damn it, you turn everything round your way. It was an accident. A regrettable accident but, now it has happened, the responsible thing is to cut the thing down.'

'Well not necessarily,' Evelyn's voice dripped with sweet reason. 'With proper care the tree would heal. I will look after that side of things for free. Just fence it off for now to be on the safe side, and I'll do the rest. For free, as I said.'

'You're saying the tree can definitely be saved?' The reporter looked admiringly at Evelyn, as the photographer took another couple of pictures. Evelyn turned to the camera, her chin a little raised. 'And that you

81

yourself are willing to look after it?'

'That's enough,' Tim Haville-Jones yelled. 'This ridiculous fuss is all because of Oscar bloody Brooke. This is nepotism of the worst kind. I'll call the Press Complaints Commission. We'll see what they have to say about all this.'

'I don't think it can be nepotism,' Liberty interjected mildly, making Tim swing round to glare at her. 'You see, you're accusing a nephew of showing favour to an aunt, not an aunt or uncle to a nephew. It's fascinating really; the word actually dates back to the days when the sons of popes were euphemistically known as nephews, from the Italian *nepote*, a nephew, and—'

'I don't care where the damn word comes from,' Tim Haville-Jones said between clenched teeth, 'but I do care about this waste of my time and money. Now my men will be here in . . .' he glanced at his watch, 'thirty minutes. If you're not gone by then I'll have you all charged with unlawful obstruction.' He narrowed his eyes at the journalists and marched off.

Evelyn and Liberty played 'I Spy' and the reporter made some more notes.

'I spy with my little eye something beginning with T,' Liberty said when it was her turn again. It had taken her almost five minutes to guess Evelyn's 'Newshound'.

Evelyn followed her look. 'Tractor,'

she said.

Two men got off the tractor, and the reporter hurried up to them asking them if they cared for the survival of the planet. 'Have you got kids of your own?'

Evelyn held out a packet of Rich Teas. 'Biscuits?' she offered.

'Mr Haville-Jones told us to start cutting whether you were there or not,' one of the men said, but his voice sounded uncertain as if he was not sure he had heard right. His companion, younger, bow-legged and sturdy, moved towards them with a slow, rolling gait like a cowboy lining up for a shoot-out. 'That's right. Start cutting, whatever.' He lifted the chain-saw with both hands.

Liberty moved closer to Evelyn as the photographer attached her camera to a tripod. 'Evelyn,' Liberty said, 'I think you'd better move.'

'Never!' Evelyn gesticulated, sending biscuits popping from the packet.

The man started the saw and moved the whirring blade closer. 'It don't have any trouble cutting through metal, do it Clive?' the older man said, but he looked nervous.

Clive said nothing, but raised his chin in an upside-down nod.

'You realize this'll be in the next edition of *The Tribune*?' the reporter said, backing away from the blade.

'The smaller the member the bigger the tool,'

Evelyn said in a slow, thoughtful voice as if she was judging the truth of her words.

Clive stopped dead. 'What was that you said?'

'Funny,' Liberty agreed, 'that's what I've heard too.'

Clive glared at Liberty. 'You get away from that tree.'

'Mr Haville-Jones has agreed to pay the damages has he?' Evelyn looked concerned. 'You see, I don't think your insurance will cover you for malicious wounding, and the damages awarded in court could run into millions.'

Liberty nodded and Clive, while not turning off the saw, looked unsure for the first time. 'Is that right Bob?' he asked his companion. Bob shrugged his shoulders. Clive turned back to Evelyn, and suddenly he lunged towards the tree. Then just as suddenly he grinned, turned the saw off and swaggered back to the tractor. He paused on the step and with another grin called out, 'I'll consult with my lawyers, but I wouldn't get too comfortable out here if I was you.'

'Can I quote you on the bit about the smaller the member—?'

Evelyn did not let the reporter finish his question. 'Certainly not,' she said.

'You didn't reckon with the power of the press, did you!' the reporter shouted instead after the departing men. An arm came through the wound-down window, punching the air in a two-fingered salute.

'Liberty,' Evelyn said, 'now those two gentlemen have gone, could you be so kind as to fetch me something to read. Hardy, I think. I don't mind which; I like 'em all.'

When Liberty returned with *The Mayor of Casterbridge*, she found Tim Haville-Jones back too. 'Ah, Mrs Turner, there you are. I was just saying to Evelyn that I don't want any unpleasantness. After all, we are neighbours...'

'This neighbour business, I like it. Now, Mr Jones,' the photographer tried to catch Tim's attention. 'Could you move closer to Miss Brooke, just one more shot; Good Neighbours, we all need them. That's it, lovely.'

'Look here,' Tim leapt away from the tree as if it were still on fire. 'My chaps will be back tomorrow and this time they will not be intimidated. I've arranged for a police escort and I suggest that you, Miss Brooke,' he turned to Evelyn, 'remove yourself from my land well before then.'

As he passed Liberty he said, 'I would see to it that it's sooner rather than later, or she'll die of cold.' Just as Liberty was about to think kindly of him again she noticed the wistful look on his face.

The reporter and photographer left shortly after Tim with a promise that they'd be back the next day. 'If we get our skates on we'll make tomorrow's edition,' the reporter grinned. 'Now, had this happened on a Monday we'd have been sunk.'

Evelyn and Liberty were left on their own in the vast field, the November mist coming down, penetrating their clothes and chilling their bones. 'I have to get back to work,' Liberty said after a while. 'Shall I get you some more blankets first?' She gave Evelyn a worried look. 'Actually I think you should take a break from this now. They won't come back today, and if you froze to death they'd still cut the oak down.'

'I do not intend to freeze to death,' Evelyn said. 'I've taken appropriate precautions.' She had placed herself on a heavy, rubber-backed picnic rug and she was swaddled in blankets already, making her look like some enormous pupa against the tree trunk. 'I would love some more coffee, though, if you've got the time.' She held out the empty thermos. 'I'm all right for sandwiches.'

Liberty took the flask and Evelyn's keys. Walking across the crusty soil, she turned round to look at Evelyn chained so comfortably to her cause. Evelyn was a lucky woman, beginning each day with a purpose beyond its passing.

When Liberty returned, two travel rugs and the refilled flask in her arms, Evelyn asked, in the manner of someone enquiring about a friend's holiday plans, 'Had any more thoughts on the suicide front?'

Liberty shook her head. 'No. What I mean is, I have, and I won't. You're right; I can't leave Johnny, not for a while anyway.' Her green eyes softened. 'He'd miss me. He'd be all dignified and desolate and young and alone, I couldn't do that to him.' She laughed suddenly, 'Anyway, you're not a serious suicide candidate if you put off the moment until after that day's episode of *Home and Away*.' She thought for a moment. 'Or maybe that's precisely what should make you one?' She shrugged her shoulders. 'I don't know.'

'If you're so keen on this writing business, why don't you just carry on? You won't find me giving up my garden.'

Liberty sat down on a corner of Evelyn's rug and helped herself to one of the sandwiches: egg and tomato.

'That's what I would have said too, a while ago. But not any more. There is a fine line to be drawn between perseverance and obtuseness. I've spent close to ten years of my life crying in the wilderness, playing to an empty house, whatever you'd like to call it. Thank God I always made time for Johnny—mostly, anyway—but friends and lovers, other interests, they all took second place to this ... this unrequited passion.' Liberty sighed and shifted on her corner of the rug. 'But a heart can only take so much. I'm dry; exhausted

87

from trying and hoarse from crying. Quite simply, I have no talent. I'm sure there are thousands of people like me, we just don't catch the imagination in the same way as your misunderstood genius. There are no films made about us, no biographies written. I mean, can you see it, the new bestseller? "A Small Life: The Poignant Story of a Poor Sod Who Was Not in the Slightest Bit Misunderstood and Who Suffered No Great Physical Hardship Whatsoever but Was Simply Untalented".' She helped herself to another sandwich, biting into it absent-mindedly.

'If at least I was a painter,' she said, when she had finished chewing, 'I could hang my own pictures, cover my own walls with them until I lived cocooned by my own creations. Then, when I ran out of space, I could give them away as Christmas presents and tombola prizes. There would probably be a hospital or two that could be persuaded to take a few, hang them in intensive care maybe, where everyone is too ill to protest.'

'I had a cousin who painted,' Evelyn said. 'My aunt wouldn't have the pictures anywhere near her, so he hung them in the servants' hall until the housekeeper complained, "It's us or those awful pictures of Master Michael's." The pictures had to go of course.'

Liberty smiled, but it was not a happy smile. Poor Michael, she thought, pulling her red scarf closer round her neck. He and she were soulmates; clowns tumbling off the far side of art. 'I don't suppose there was a happy ending?' she asked. 'He didn't, by any chance, end up selling for thousands in Bond Street galleries?'

Evelyn shook her head. 'No, 'fraid not. One of his sisters, Gabriella, who had absolutely no taste but was a very greedy girl indeed, found them in the attic after he died and hung on to them in the hope that one day they'd become fashionable, but they never did so; in the end, she burnt the lot. It was the biggest bonfire the village had seen; the children were thrilled. So I suppose you could say it was a happy ending of sorts.' Evelyn leant back against the trunk and added dreamily, 'For a brief moment his talent burned brightly, shedding light into the lives of his fellow men.'

Liberty gave her a dirty look. 'Was he very unhappy?'

'No, I don't think he was particularly. You see, we didn't necessarily expect to be happy in those days. The notion that somehow we were put on this earth to be happy was not foremost in our minds, the way it seems with people today.'

'You're right,' Liberty said. 'It's a new thing, this wretched expectation of happiness. Most insidious of all is the message that if you just try hard enough and want something badly enough, you'll get it. Dangerous too; breeds discontent. I reckon you have to be careful with expectations; too little and life is cold and comfortless, too much and you burn up on your way to the sun.' She stretched her legs out in front of her, but tucked them back in as the chill from the damp ground soaked through her thin trousers.

'Look at disaffected youth,' she said. 'I reckon half of them riot because they expect nothing and have no hope, the other because they expect too much and get next to nothing. "Sorry, did we say you could be a pop star and drive a Porsche if only you wanted it badly enough? Just a joke, I meant the guy next door, the one with the talent." I tell you, if Jane Eyre had fallen into the hands of a trained social worker, instead of that unspeakable man at the orphanage, she'd never have got Rochester.'

'Why do you think that?' Evelyn held out the sandwich box to Liberty.

'Because she'd have been all bolshy and angry with her lot instead of a humble little mouse, the way Rochester wanted.'

'The girl had passion though, that's what made her interesting and her life worth while, Rochester or no Rochester.' Evelyn brushed some crumbs of egg from her chest. 'You have to have a passion in life. Now I could tell you things about aphids that would make your hair stand on end and your toes tingle with excitement ... but you have work to do, I know. Another time.'

Liberty stood up. 'You're sure you don't

want me to unlock you?'

'Quite sure, thank you.'

'You can't stay here all night. You'll die of exposure.'

'You're right,' Evelyn said unexpectedly. She brought the mobile phone from her bag and dialled. 'Oscar,' she said after a moment. 'Evelyn here.' Evelyn moved the phone a little further from her ear. 'Now Oscar, it's hardly my fault if your paper decides that my little story is newsworthy. Anyway, I didn't call to chat about that. I want you to bring my calor gas stove across when you come home. It's not much out of your way, only across the field. You've got a key haven't you? Really? I was sure you did. Oh well, not to worry, Liberty will let you in and show you where the stove is.' She clicked the off-button on Oscar and put the phone back in her bag. 'He'll be at my place around six-thirty, could you be there to let him in?'

Liberty nodded. 'I still think you should call it a night and sleep in your own bed.'

'Well I don't, dear. Now if you could bring me the paper tomorrow morning, and some fresh coffee, I'd be most grateful.'

Liberty left Evelyn sitting upright against the tree, her chains spilling out from under the blankets. 'I'll be back before then, with some hot food,' she called as she traipsed back across the field. 'Call me any time. Call me!' her voice sounded through the still air.

CHAPTER FIVE

Liberty had just arrived at Evelyn's when the doorbell rang. 'She's still out there,' Oscar said accusingly as he stepped through the door.

'I'm afraid so. I've just taken her some food. I've got the heater for you.' Liberty pointed to the stove. 'It's terribly heavy.'

'Thanks,' Oscar said, grabbing the stove and turning it on its heel.

'Any news about the missing girl?' Liberty asked, thinking that everybody liked talking about their work; she certainly used to.

'Nothing much.' Oscar let go of the stove. 'The police still don't know if there's been foul play or if she's just a runaway.'

'Teenagers do run away all the time.'

Oscar took off his spectacles, rubbing them against the sleeve of his jacket. Stripped suddenly of the horn-rimmed frames he looked vulnerable, like a knight who'd just removed his armour. 'It's possible,' he said, 'but not likely. There have been no sightings of her. She was doing well at school, lots of friends, good, open relationship with her parents and brothers, apart from some minor boyfriend trouble. There just doesn't seem to be any reason for her to want to run away, especially without a note or phone call or something to her parents.' He put his glasses back on,

92

returning his face to fully-dressed formality, and Liberty, who had been smiling companionably at him, felt him a stranger again.

'Would you like a drink before you lug that thing across?' She took a step towards the front door, expecting him to say no.

'Please, I'd love one.'

'What am I doing offering you drinks in your own aunt's house?' Liberty laughed that ingratiating, overly loud laugh she herself hated so much.

'My mother had a laugh that hit your ear, softly like a puff of white smoke...' she followed Oscar into the kitchen, '...well so I've been told anyway.' She took a double step to catch up with him.

'That sounds delightful,' Oscar picked up the bottle of gin that stood on a pile of dusty detective novels. 'Gin and tonic all right?'

Liberty nodded. 'It didn't get her very far though. She married my father, had me, and died.'

'And from that you've drawn the conclusion that having a laugh like a puff of white smoke leads to an early grave, and have taken steps to avoid that trap. Very sensible.' Oscar passed her the drink, raising his own. 'Good health.'

'I'm supposed to criticize my laugh, you are supposed to disagree. Did your mummy not teach you anything?'

'Of course, you're absolutely right. Anyway,

I like a good laugh, as they say.'

'Victoria's got a lovely voice. Well, she's altogether lovely.'

Instead of looking pleased at the compliment, Oscar drained his glass and placed it on the sink with so much care the effect was more bad tempered than if he'd slammed it down. 'I'd better take that stove across before Evelyn expires from cold.'

Like a dog who'd offended its owner, Liberty padded behind him out into the hall. She stayed in the doorway, watching after him as he dragged the stove across the path, lifting it into Evelyn's wheelbarrow. As he disappeared away from the shaft of light from the open door and into the darkness of the garden, she called out, ''Bye Oscar.'

''Bye,' he called back. His voice sounded soft in the distance.

*   *   *

The next morning, with the sun rising slowly across the field as if it, too, found the thought of another day hard to take, Liberty was woken by a call from Evelyn. 'Could you be a dear and bring me some breakfast? A bacon sandwich or two and some coffee would do.'

Liberty looked at the clock by her bed; seven-thirty on Friday morning. As recently as a month ago she would have been at her desk by now, to use up the best hours, the quietest

94

hours, when the phone stays silent and the gas man doesn't call, to write. She was not by nature an early riser, but she had grown to love those morning hours when the world seemed to shrink for a time to the size of a computer screen.

'I haven't got any bacon, I'm afraid,' she said, 'but I'll fry you an egg both sides and put it in a sandwich. I might have some tomatoes, too.'

Twenty minutes later she was hurrying across the field with her basket of food like an over-age Red Riding Hood. She could see a crowd surrounding the oak, but she could not see Evelyn. As she came closer, half running half stumbling across the dry furrows, she recognized the reporter and photographer from the day before, and a few mothers and children from the village, but the rest of the twenty or so people were strangers. Two children separated from the crowd, running off and leaving a gap through which Liberty finally glimpsed Evelyn. 'Is everything all right?' she called out, and got a wave from Evelyn in return.

'The power of the press never fails,' the reporter grinned at her, raising his hand in a fisted salute that was more Soweto than Tollymead, Liberty could not help thinking. Just then a Land Rover revved into view, moving towards them like a ship at sea, up and down the ploughed and frost-hardened furrows. It stopped some twenty yards away, and Tim Haville-Jones jumped out followed by Bob and Clive, who was once again brandishing his chain-saw. The crowd jeered. Tim strode up to the circle closing in round Evelyn, his colour rising with every step. 'This has gone on long enough.' He tried to push closer to Evelyn. 'Now get off my field or I'll call the police.'

The crowd booed.

'Mr Haville hyphen Jones's cows produce the milk supplied by Daisy Dairy,' Evelyn's honeyed voice came from the back of the crowd. 'I'm sure many of you get your milk from your local Daisy Dairy milkman.' There was a general nodding as she continued, 'Of course, the Co-op also supplies milk in our area, so we do have a choice.'

'You're going to regret this.' Tim shook his fist at Evelyn.

Liberty looked closely at him. She had never allowed any of the characters in her novels to shake their fists, because until now she had believed that it was something people in real life never actually did, and here was Tim Haville-Jones shaking away. She made a mental note of exactly how the gesture was done and of the expression on the farmer's face, before remembering that such things were of no more use to her than a view of the Taj Mahal to a blind man. This mental refuse collecting had become a habit, the gathering up of bits and pieces of conversation and expressions, the storing away of tastes of other people's lives. She forgot, sometimes, that it was all surplus to requirements now, just like all those little black-bound notebooks she had carried around everywhere. The same thing had happened when she was four and new at school. They were all selecting bits of cloth for a Mother's Day card, rummaging round in the large box of materials given to them by the teacher. Carried away by the excitement, Liberty had joined in, digging her hand deep inside the box and pulling out the prettiest piece of all; it even had a sequin, like the eye of a bird, still attached to it. She was holding it high above her head for everyone to see and envy, before it hit her that she alone had no use for it, no mother to make a card for. She had handed it to the child at the next table, a girl she did not even like.

Evelyn, swaddled in several blankets, called her name and extended a mittened hand, beckoning Liberty towards her as if she had just spotted a favourite guest at a drinks party.

'Liberty dear, how nice, and you've brought my breakfast.'

The crowd parted to let Liberty through with her basket of food, when Tim said, quite calmly, to Clive, 'You can begin now.' Then he called out to Evelyn, 'I suggest you un-chain yourself, unless you want Clive to cut you loose. Of course we don't want any nasty accidents.'

'Could you hold the saw up please sir,' the photographer shouted to Clive, raising her camera. 'Like that, that's right, thank you.'

'So I can say that there's already considerable support for a boycott of all Daisy Dairy products?' the reporter shouted.

'Yeah,' the crowd shouted back.

Tim Haville-Jones turned quite grey. His gestures and expressions were all so gratifying, Liberty thought. He would have had a great career in silent movies: 'Do fury Tim darling! Show us despair!'

Clive put the saw down and collected a pair of bolt cutters from the Land Rover before beginning to push his way through the crowd. Tim stopped him.

'It's all right boys,' he said. 'Let's call it a day.'

Village Diary

Tollymead: *There were celebrations in the village this week as Mr Tim Haville-Jones agreed to accept Miss Evelyn Brooke's offer to make the great oak in West Field safe again after the fire to its trunk. There had been huge support for Miss Brooke's attempts to save the ancient tree that has long been a favourite with local walkers.*

Miss Agnes Coulson, organizer of the Tollymead Walk Your Way to Fitness Club, especially welcomed the news of the reprieve. 'My fellow walkers and I each put a lantern in a tree in our gardens, to show solidarity. I put mine in my Dutch Elm, a survivor if ever there was one,' Miss Coulson told the Diary. 'That oak is a joy and an inspiration to us walkers. In the spring we watch out for the first buds on its branches, and we follow the progress of the seasons through its leaves until, back in winter, its branches are naked once more.'

Miss Coulson also tells me that walking is at last coming out from under the shadow of jogging as the way of keeping fit. Just forty minutes, four times a week, at a speed of three miles an hour will make you lose between 10lbs and 15lbs in a year without any changes to your diet. If you're walking at the right speed, you should perspire gently and be able to exchange the odd word with a companion. If you can have a good chat, you're too slow.

The American television writer, Anne Havesham, who had admired the lit-up trees on her evening walks, told me she saw them as a perfect illustration of the sort of community spirit she hoped to soak up by the gallon for her latest project, 'Atlantic Cousins', set in two small communities, one English, one East Coast American.

CHAPTER SIX

'Have you come across a woman called Anne Havesham?' Nancy demanded of Ted Brain as she stood in the vicarage porch, waiting to be given the keys to the church. It was her turn on the brass-cleaning roster.

'Who?' Ted shifted from one foot to the other, his slight frame barring the entrance to the hall.

'Anne Havesham. According to the Village Diary she's some American television person and she's just moved here. And then there's this Agnes Coulson. I didn't see any lanterns in the trees did you?'

'I don't take the local paper,' Ted said with an air of not listening. 'If you know where these people live, I'll pay them a visit. It does occur to me, sometimes, that the local estate agent sees more of my parishioners than I do.'

'Rubbish. It's just we've had quite a few people coming and going lately.'

'Rich commuters coming, and villagers going.'

'I do so hate that expression "rich",' Nancy snapped. 'It sounds so, so envious. Anyway, if you meet her, you do meet some of your parishioners occasionally I presume, do tell her I'd love her for the League.'

Ted, who, to Nancy's knowledge, never joked, quipped, 'Served up with two veg and mint sauce,' making Nancy wonder why he bothered now.

'Well then, if you'll excuse me...' he handed Nancy the keys to the church and with a little nod, closed the door in her face.

The vicar is getting more peculiar by the day, Nancy thought as she strode off towards the church. Her friend Pat had twittered something about comings and goings at night, but Nancy had not really listened; Pat's conversation was like drizzle on hard ground, it left little impression.

Later that evening Nancy, placing a starter of smoked trout in front of her husband and sitting down herself, said, 'For once I agree with the vicar. With all this infilling and redevelopment and all these city types moving in and out, one might as well live on Waterloo Station for all the sense of community one gets in this place.'

'I've told you that for years,' Andrew looked pleased with himself. 'You can run around doing your bit until you're blue in the face, but Tollymead is and will remain nothing but a collection of houses. All that rot about village life—'

'That's not true,' Nancy yelped. She felt as upset as a mother complaining about her child and finding everyone else agreeing with her.

After dinner Andrew picked up *The Tribune*. Being a major advertiser through his farm supply business, Sanderson's Seeds, he liked to check each edition for clarity of print and correctness of positioning. Nancy had left the paper open at the Diary section and, reading the entry for Tollymead, he suddenly banged his fist down on the arm of his chair. 'That bloody woman again!'

'Who?'

'Evelyn of course. There was no agreement from Tim about that tree. He had to give in to blackmail, simple as that. No, she's gone too far this time. She's never off my back about supplying pesticides. Times are hard enough without some unhinged old bag like her putting people off.'

Nancy winced. Somehow, when he got angry like this, Andrew's whole being coarsened alarmingly. Not only his words, but his face, always on the heavy side, reddened in a frown that turned his face into a messy jungle of features: bushy eyebrows, flaring nostrils sprouting black hair, grooves like dried-out river beds across the forehead. She looked hard at the *Telegraph*'s crossword puzzle as he carried on:

'The other day she actually tried to block one of my lorries trying to enter Campbell's Farm. She's got a bee in her bonnet about the insecticide we supply. The woman is unhinged, no doubt about it.' He gulped down some brandy, and seemed to calm down as he leant back in the chair, the colour subsiding from his face.

'Often happens apparently to spinsters, as they get older. Whatever these magazines you like to read say, you women need us to keep you on the straight and narrow, eh?' He gave his wife a little nod as their eyes met, the rescuer and the rescued, comfortable once more in their allotted roles.

Nancy had only to close her eyes to be Nancy Rogers once more, smelling the early climbing rose that spring morning years ago. Andrew's mother, who had extended her friendship to dear little Mrs Rogers for many a morning coffee and afternoon tea, was visiting and Nancy, Mrs Rogers's wide-boned, moon-faced daughter, had sat on the bench outside the open window, reading.

'She's so clever, your Nancy.' Those kind words that somehow managed to sound not so kind when coming from Mrs Sanderson, made Nancy put her book down.

'Such splendid news her making it to Oxford, and so lucky. She's always struck me as the sort of girl who will need to earn her living and what better start than that. Of course dear Andrew says he's really quite glad not to have made Oxbridge, Bath is quite the place now I believe. Charlotte, of course, isn't bothering with any of it, she doesn't need to, the lucky girl. Do you know, just the other day we had a call from Lady Hill saying that her son absolutely refused to leave for America and that they were all convinced it's because the poor boy can't bear being parted from my Charlotte. No, there will be a wedding before the year is out. I said to her, "Charlotte," I said, "leave the study to girls like dear clever Nancy; what do you need with it?"'

The words had dropped from Mrs Sanderson's lips like the poisonous pellets her husband manufactured, and all that could be heard from Nancy's poor fluffy rabbit of a mother were little mewls of agreement. What triumph, what bliss then, when the wedding at the end of the year had been between 'poor dear Nancy' and Mrs Sanderson's own son, Andrew.

Thirty years on, the memory still warmed her like the glow from a bonfire blackening your neighbour's washing. Charlotte, 'the dear unfortunate child', as she was referred to for ever more by Nancy's mother, in a silky voice that drove Mrs Sanderson to silent fury, got herself involved with a married man, and the least said about her the better.

Nancy would tell her own children, Piers and Louise, that she never regretted her wasted university place. She knew her achievements as a magistrate and member of the parish council were seen by Andrew as an indulgence, rather like a weakness for buying extravagant hats, and smiled upon as long as it did not interfere with her role as his wife. She did not mind; first and foremost, flirtatiously and wonderfully, she was Mrs Andrew Sanderson.

'My career will come first,' Louise had announced the day she left home for university. In a voice calculated to upset her mother she had added, 'And when I have children they'll come first. I don't know that I'll bother with a husband.' Nancy did not like to think of the expression on Louise's face that day.

'Poor old Evelyn,' she said now, and she got up from her chair and went across to Andrew, planting the lightest of kisses on his head.

Without looking up, Andrew said, 'Sounds an interesting woman, this Anne Havesham. Television, eh?'

* * *

'Get off my property!' Nancy heard Andrew's voice the second she got out of the car. It was Thursday, Nancy's day for doing the weekly shopping in Fairfield. She had forgotten to ask Andrew that morning if there was anything she could get for him on the way in to town, so she stopped off at Sanderson's Seeds. But something was wrong. There, on the tarmac forecourt in amongst a crowd of amused shoppers, Andrew stood shouting, his face red and his eyes bulging. Who was he yelling at? Nancy elbowed her way through the crowd.

'You evil old woman, I'll get you for this!' Andrew's voice soared so high that it broke and it was Evelyn Brooke he was shouting at. Evelyn, wrapped up against the autumn wind in a floor-length astrakhan coat with a huge velvet shawl collar, was carrying a placard saying 'A £ spent at Sanderson's—a £ spent on the Death of Our Planet!'

'Do stop shouting, Andrew,' Evelyn said, as she paused momentarily in her march up and down the forecourt.

'I'm telling you for the last time, get off my property or I'll hurl you off myself!' Andrew screamed, taking a step towards her. Another step and his left foot hit a multi-coloured circle of spilt motor oil. His leg went up in the air as if pulled by a bad-tempered puppet master, making him fall flat on his back at Evelyn's feet. As Nancy rushed to his side, the laughter started, a bit nervously at first but, as Andrew sat up, apparently unharmed, it erupted all around from the customers and onlookers and, worst of all, from the sales staff inside,

106

watching from the windows. Even Miss Trent, Andrew's secretary whom Nancy had long pitied in the belief that the poor woman was hopelessly in love with Andrew, even she could be seen through the panorama window of the little office, doubled up over her desk in helpless laughter.

'Time to go home I think,' Evelyn smiled graciously at Nancy. 'Must be tea time.'

Close to tears, Nancy blinked up at her. 'You've made a fool out of him, Evelyn. You've gone too far this time, really you have.'

* * *

Autumn: pretty, decaying autumn. Evelyn shivered in her woollen tartan dressing-gown, as she scraped the toast crumbs from her plate onto the bird table. The short days allowed for too much thinking. Until Evelyn herself had grown old, she had assumed that with age came an acceptance of mortality, a gentle resignation to the inevitable; but not a bit of it. Life was just as endlessly fascinating as it had always been and Evelyn, looking round her sleeping garden, was not ready to leave.

'You're just resting,' she murmured, running her hand down the rough bark of the copper beech that spread its naked branches across the top lawn. 'But for me it's terminal. Autumn leads to winter, but there will be no spring. Your life is a circle, mine is a line.

Lucky you.' She shook herself and, wrapping the worn dressing-gown closer, she padded back inside.

As soon as she had dressed in her tweed gardening skirt and her mother's old cashmere jersey (Evelyn had no truck with wastefulness, and her mother had worn out and died well before the excellent two-ply knit) she was on her way outside again. A few hours' digging would put a stop to morbid thoughts. In the hall she paused to fetch her post. She had become quite a celebrity in the weeks since her sit-in over at the Haville-Joneses field and the protest outside Sanderson's Seeds. There had been an appearance on local radio that, Evelyn had to admit, had gone very well, (although that twit Sanderson had threatened to sue) and almost daily a whole heap of fan letters arrived.

Normally Evelyn did not get much post. In the past she had carried on long and stimulating correspondences with other environmentalists, but most of her old colleagues were dead now, or as good as; too feeble in body and spirit to write. That was the worst of growing old: your world, as defined by the people you shared it with, shrank before your eyes, until there was no-one left of your time but you. Family, friends, colleagues, hacked-off crumb by crumb, your references fading, so in the end you bumbled round life like a blind person in a strange house. No wonder such worship was accorded to people

108

like Bob Hope and the Queen Mother; after all, they were still there.

But the garden, that was different. It never died, it just slept; even in its winter sleep it stirred and muttered, with buds and winter blooms appearing like contented dreams. Evelyn was smiling as she opened her mail. There were five letters today; three were from people saying they had stopped buying their milk from Daisy Dairies. One was from a young mother thanking her for making a stand on behalf of future generations. The last was unsigned. Evelyn stopped smiling. Her hands, holding the letter, began to tremble.

'People have had enough of your shenanigans,' the letter said, and it ended with a warning not to meddle in legitimate country business, or she would get her interfering fingers badly burnt. Evelyn dropped the letter as if it were already singeing her flesh. After a few moments thought, she went to the telephone and, hands still shaking, dialled the number of Home Farm.

'That was a very ugly thing to do.' Her voice, too, was unsteady.

'What are you talking about Miss Brooke?' Tim Haville-Jones sounded weary. 'You're not on about that damn tree again? You got your way didn't you?'

'I'm talking about the letter.'

'What letter? I don't know anything about a letter. Now if you'll excuse me, I've got things

109

to do.' He hung up, leaving Evelyn standing, the dead receiver still to her ear, the letter in her free hand. Next she called Sanderson's Seeds. 'I wish I'd thought of it,' Andrew Sanderson said quite calmly, 'but I didn't, so don't you go and cause more trouble or an unpleasant letter will be the least of your worries.'

When Liberty called round half an hour later, she found Evelyn by the stream, digging, like a giant mole in her shiny black-brown oilskins.

'The artery carrying blood to my creation.' Evelyn leant against the shovel, waving towards the slow-running water and the tiny pump-house by the wooden fence. 'Irrigation, the new Messiah.' She grinned and slipped off her heavy-duty gloves. 'So what can I do for you?'

'Nothing really, I'm just here to waste your time. I'm supposed to be on a walk.' Liberty perched on a tree stump, feeling the slimy moss against the palm of her hand. 'I've got time to kill and I'm out searching for a weapon: slow strangulation? Death by television?' She wiped her hand absent-mindedly on her jeans. 'You know, I used to get up at five in the morning, pottering down to my word-processor with a feeling in my stomach as if I was meeting my lover. Three hours of exquisite agony interspersed by cups of coffee ... it's not that I like coffee all that much, it's more that cosy "I'm an artist working away in my garret, this

110

is all that keeps me going" feeling. Thursdays I would be especially busy, with Tom coming down and Johnny too every other week-end as well.'

'What you need is shape,' Evelyn said.

'I do exercise. A bit,' Liberty said, hurt.

'To your day, silly child.'

'Oh. Well I have drawn up a kind of schedule: three hours translation work after breakfast, then a long walk (that's the point I'm at now) followed by more translation, then the day finished with an imaginative candlelit dinner for one; to show I care.'

'Why isn't that Tom fellow here?'

'Oh, we broke up. He was right to go. As my friend Penny said, I wept more for my rejected book than for him. I miss him, though. It's funny, but it's things like his toothbrush being gone that upset me most. There's something rather sad about a single toothbrush in a mug where there used to be two. But he left his shaving foam; he knows I like using it for my legs.'

'Come inside and have a cup of coffee.' Evelyn propped the shovel carefully against the tree. 'I'd like to have your opinion on something.' She led the way through the french windows, not stopping to take her boots off, but leaving little deposits of black soil across the sun-bleached oriental carpet. 'Here,' she handed Liberty the letter with a muddy hand. 'Someone educated, good grammar and

111

spelling,' Liberty frowned. 'Could be Tim Haville-Jones.'

'Says he knows nothing about a letter.'

'What about Nancy Sanderson's husband? Didn't you picket his store the other day? And then there was the radio. I heard you. You were very good, I thought.'

A small, smug smile spread across Evelyn's face. 'Thank you dear. But I don't know that I think it was him either. He sounded genuine enough when I confronted him. Anyway it was only a small protest, more of a gesture really. It wasn't my fault that he went and fell flat on his behind. And as you said, I was very fair on the radio.'

'I didn't say you were fair. Anyone else you've upset?'

Evelyn, looking offended, shook her head. 'My dear girl you make it sound as if I make a habit of upsetting people.'

Liberty allowed the remark to pass. 'What about that business with the delivery truck?'

'Oh that was nothing.' Evelyn's voice held the bravado of a guilty child. 'One of Sanderson's lorries was delivering its poison to Campbell's Farm. I just persuaded the driver to turn back, that's all.' She dropped her coat on the crested chair in the hall and stomped through to the kitchen. Liberty watched, amused, while she battled, cursing, with the gleaming chrome espresso machine that made such momentous sounds as it worked that

Liberty thought it ought to produce a Booker-prize winner at the end, not just a tiny cup of sour-tasting coffee.

'Are you taking it to the police—the letter I mean?' Liberty put her cup on the table.

'I don't think so,' Evelyn shook her head so hard that her chins quivered.

'I think you should.'

When they finished their coffee Evelyn walked Liberty back out along the path to the gate. She stopped to point out to Liberty the solitary purple rose that flowered amongst the dying leaves of the Rosa rugosa. Burying her nose in the moist petals with a clumsy gesture and inhaling noisily she said, 'It hasn't got a rose scent as such of course, but,' she sniffed hard again, 'it has a lovely freshness, like the skin of a new baby.'

Liberty looked a little surprised at such a comparison from Evelyn. She was about to bend down to the flower herself when she spotted something hanging from the gatepost. 'What's that?' She put her hand on Evelyn's arm. 'Look!'

Evelyn had straightened up and now she walked closer, treading carefully as if on a slippery surface. 'Rabbits,' she said finally. 'Tied together and strung up like a brace of pheasants. Looks like myxi ones, too. No good for eating.'

Liberty followed behind, then she stopped again, staring at the little animals dangling upside down in a deathly embrace, their eyes pussed over and half closed bulging from their emaciated faces. She slapped her hand across her mouth and bent double.

'Poor little mites,' Evelyn was saying. 'Lots of people around here can't stand them, and that's not just the farmers. Amateur gardeners are the worst. Say they eat things. Of course they do, but there's plenty of other stuff you can grow besides roses and pinks.'

'I think you should call the police.'

'Why on earth should I do that? Someone probably shot them and dropped them on the road.'

'So how did they end up strung up on your gate?'

Evelyn seemed unconcerned. 'Don't know. Postman probably thought they were mine. You fuss too much. Run along now, busy day ahead.' She held the gate open and Liberty went through, her eyes fixed straight ahead, away from the bodies on the gate.

*   *   *

That evening, as on so many others, Oscar lingered in his small office at *The Tribune*. When the phone rang at eight, he knew it would be Victoria.

'Supper's ready and waiting,' her voice coiled towards him like a silk lasso.

'Sorry darling. Got held up. I'm on my way.'

114

He hung up, but instead of switching off the light and getting up from his desk, he sat back in the chair and began reading the article sent in by a freelance contributor, about a local surrogate mother. As he read, guilt at not leaving, at not hurrying home as promised, crept up like marching ants, making him angry. He finished the article and reached for the pile in his In-tray. He could see Victoria pacing back and forth between the kitchen and the hall window, and still he went through his post, getting the same, slow satisfaction he did as a boy, playing just out of sight, listening to his mother calling and calling him to come inside. He picked up the contributions to Village Diary. There was a piece from Tollymead most weeks now. Nice little entries about life in the village, coming right on time for the Friday edition. Like the entries from the other villages, the ones from Tollymead were not signed, but he was pretty sure they were sent in by the same person. Maybe it was old Neville Pyke who had finally decided to take matters into his own hands. The Tollymead entries were chattier than the pieces from the other villages; whoever it was writing seemed to know more about what went on than anyone else. He had put a reporter on to finding out more about this American television writer, but so far without success.

Oscar sat back in his chair and began to read the neatly typed page.

The Reverend Brain has asked if visits to the vicarage could be kept to 'surgery hours', 2.00 p.m.–4.00 p.m. and 6.00 p.m.–7.00 p.m. Monday to Friday, as he is especially busy at the moment. If this is not possible, could you please phone to make an appointment. 'These are crucial times for all of us,' the Reverend Brain told me outside church on Sunday, but I could not draw him further on the subject. So keep going to church and I'm sure all will be revealed, eventually.

Bonfire Night is approaching and as usual an uneven battle is fought to get there before the first Father Christmas of the year is sighted. Doesn't the Bible tell us that for each thing there is a season?

In the meantime, following appeals from Sam and Gertie Cook, the owners of Tigger the prize-winning gun dog, Tollymead residents have agreed to fireworks being confined to the recreation ground.

Tigger, four, on a walk with his owner through the village during last year's celebrations, was so traumatized when a squib exploded by his tail that he has not been able to work since.

Discussing the matter, Hester Scott OBE said, 'Quite apart from the fact that Sam has lost a hunting companion, it's the matter of Tigger's professional pride.' Remembering back to her days on stage, Miss Scott added that, in her experience, once you'd lost your nerve, it could take years to get it back.

Several residents then spoke up about the suffering caused to their pets by exploding rockets, and Agnes Coulson reminded us of the plight of wild animals who have not got a voice. 'Just think if you're a rabbit whilst all that is going on,' she said.

So this year, Tollymead is looking forward to a cruelty-free November Fifth. Such an event, I can't help thinking, would have greatly pleased Guy Fawkes in the final hours of his life.

CHAPTER SEVEN

Oscar smiled to himself as he put the A4 page in his Out-tray. It did not sound much like Neville Pyke. No, the correspondent was a woman, probably elderly. Looking at his watch, it was eight-thirty, he made a mental note to ask Evelyn who this Hester Scott was. He got up from his desk. By now Victoria would be tearful, but bravely resigned to a ruined supper. No doubt several of her friends would have heard by now, about this latest manifestation of his callous disregard for her feelings. It was not that she would directly complain about him, but her voice would tremble as she called up for a 'quick chat', and

117

when asked what the matter was, she would say it was nothing, she was probably silly worrying about Oscar...

He had heard her once or twice, across the table during a dinner party, or curled up on the bed with the phone.

'It's not his fault. He's been a bachelor so long he just isn't used to thinking of anyone's feelings but his own. And something definitely happened in Colombia...' As he grabbed his coat, Oscar winced at the thought of his private nightmares being tittle-tattled around her girlfriends.

With a sigh, he locked his office and walked outside, turning his collar up against the drizzle. So what was wrong with him? Sometimes he thought he was the only man he knew who was not in love with his wife. Like a rich man with the tastes of a Franciscan monk, he had what everyone envied and he alone could not treasure.

He had first met Victoria on his return from Colombia. He had arrived at his newspaper's office, the returning hero with a briefcase full of explosive material for a projected series of articles. Victoria had just started as secretary to the political editor, and he found that looking at her was like having his eyes bathed in Optrex. Frank, Victoria's boss, had put his hand on Oscar's shoulder. 'We're all desperately sorry about Rachel. Dreadful thing to happen, dreadful.'

118

Oscar had blinked hard and looked away as Victoria's face gave way to the picture of the jeep with Rachel's body held upright against the back of the seat by the safety-belt still fastened across her chest. He was always telling her to fasten her seat-belt.

When he had looked up again, Frank's beautiful secretary was still smiling at him, but asking no questions. She had not said much at any time during the afternoon, but whatever she did say sounded somehow special when uttered in that deep, sweet voice. No, he was a lucky man he thought, aiming a kick at the front tyre of his car, to be loved by a woman like Victoria.

Back home, those sloe eyes were brimming with tears as they gazed at him across the dried remains of the Ginger Chicken. She had laid the table as usual in the 'dining hall' as the estate agents had called the space that he would never have thought of putting a dining-table in, unless so helpfully shown the way. People knocked estate agents, Oscar thought sourly, but one had to admire their creativity.

'You don't need to go to so much trouble,' he said now to Victoria. 'You know I'm happy to eat in the kitchen.' He looked at her across the table she had set in co-ordinated pinks and greens, with lighted candles and the arrangement of dried flowers, and felt like a nasty big brother gate-crashing a dolls' tea party. 'I'm sorry I was so late.'

'It's all right.' Victoria's smile was moist but brave. Then, in one graceful movement she was out of the chair and walked across to his side, perching on the arm of his chair. 'Did you have a rotten day?'

Now she'll ruffle my hair. Oscar tensed, then he felt the long, cool fingers descending on his scalp like the rain outside.

'Let's have an early night.' Victoria pressed her tear-drenched cheek against his. The phone rang. Oscar shot up from the chair, almost toppling Victoria.

He answered, and an anxious voice said, 'It's Liberty, Liberty Turner. I'm sorry to trouble you so late, but I've been worrying about your aunt. I didn't know if she had told you. About the letter. And the rabbits?'

'Letter? Rabbits? No she hasn't.'

Liberty explained.

'I expect it's that farmer, Haville-Jones,' Oscar said.

'I don't know. He absolutely denies it. And there's Andrew Sanderson; she's had quite a few goes at him. And that other farmer, Campbell; she stopped a delivery lorry from Sanderson's Seeds coming into his farm. She opened the gate to the cattle field and shooed all the cows off into the yard. There was actually a very funny picture in your paper, before your time, though, of them all practically drowning in heifers.' She paused for a moment before saying, 'The thing is, there're

120

so many people who'd like to throttle Evelyn, and I don't know half of them.'

'She doesn't let up does she? Has she called the police?'

'She doesn't want to. She says the rabbit thing is nothing, just someone leaving them there by mistake. Hardly likely in my view. I mean, "Sorry to bother you but did I leave two myxomatosis rabbits strung up on your gate by any chance, about fifteen inches long, scruffy fur, pussie eyes." Anyway, she's had the odd quarrel with the police too over the years.'

'Well, I'm very grateful that you called,' Oscar said, following Victoria with his eyes as she came past, blowing him a kiss on her way upstairs. Turning his attention back to the phone he said, his voice lightening, 'Maybe I should go over and see how she is? Now I mean.'

'There's no need, really there isn't. I'm only a few yards away. I shouldn't really have bothered you, but I knew you'd want to know what was going on so you could keep an eye on her, too. I mean, I'd hate it if I was kept in the dark over my aunt, that is if I had an aunt, an authentic aunt I mean, not one that's just married to an uncle ... Sorry, I'm burbling...'

There was a goodbye to her voice and Oscar realized he did not want her to hang up. Above, on the first floor, Victoria was preparing for bed; flushing the loo, running the water for the basin and the bidet. Soon she'd be in bed, warm and smelling faintly of Lily of the Valley; waiting.

'How's your dog bite?' he asked Liberty quickly.

'Oh that. Fine. The scar has sort of puckered, so it's pulling down the corner of my eye when I smile, but as I'm such a miserable bastard that's not really a problem.' There was a small pause before she went on, 'I haven't told my son anything about the accident. He's away, working in Sweden and I wouldn't want him to worry.'

The way she said that to him, all of a sudden over the phone, made Oscar think she wanted to tell her son very badly. 'That's noble of you,' he said.

She sounded as if she was smiling when she answered. 'Well you see, I used to nurture this dream of being a Good Writer, but one way or another, times being hard and all that, like so many people, I've had to cut down. So I'm left with just Good. It doesn't come naturally to me, but you have to make the most of what you've got, so I'm practising. Helping old ladies across the street and such-like is child's play, but anything more advanced, that's where the hard work comes in.'

Oscar started to laugh. He leant against the doorway and he laughed out loud. Why, he did not really know, she was not that funny. He said, 'Is Johnny an only child?'

'Yes, and he's so old now.' Oscar could hear

the groan in her voice. 'It's not exactly a secret that children grow up, but still, when it happens to yours, it seems to take you by surprise. One minute you're the sun and star in their firmament. You only have to give a little of your time, build a Lego tower or bake a cake with them and it's like you're on stage being Dame Judi Dench and Madonna rolled into one. The next day you wake up and find you're a lovable nuisance, a bit like the itchy sweaters your Aunt Jessie insists on giving you every Christmas. Are you thinking of having children?'

'Oscar! Darling are you coming up?' Victoria's voice called, soft but insistent.

'No, not at this precise moment.' Oscar turned his face away from the receiver, 'Coming!'

'You must go,' Liberty said. 'Goodbye.' And, just like that, she hung up, leaving him standing there with the receiver still to his ear.

Oscar remained by the phone for a couple of minutes. Finally, with a sigh, he turned the lights off and walked, lead-soled, up the stairs. Victoria lay waiting for him, naked amongst the froth of the oyster-coloured, lace-trimmed sheets, like a delectable chocolate in a presentation box. She did not ask who it had been on the phone, but just smiled and stretched her arms out towards him.

For Christ's sake get excited, he told himself desperately, you owe her that much. Think

123

about it; how many men do you know who wouldn't swap places with you right now? He undressed slowly: shoes, socks, shirt, trousers, pants before going into the bathroom and showering; a hot shower. He brushed his teeth.

'Oscar,' the honeyed voice beckoned him and, with a doleful look at his limp penis, he came out of the bathroom. Her eyes, fixed on him the moment he stepped through the door, were reproachful and expectant all at once, and he attempted a loving smile, feeling his dry lips stretch across his teeth. Once in bed, he made much of setting the alarm clock and choosing a book, a big hard-back, pretending not to notice the wounded glances and restless little sighs. Finally, she turned noisily right away from him and he felt her hurt, and hated himself. He turned pages without caring what he read and then he put the book away and folded his glasses. Switching off the light, he leant across and kissed her cheek.

'Goodnight, sleep tight.' What a bloody stupid thing to say. He lay in the dark, listening to her stifled sobs until he could stand it no longer. Sitting up, he pulled her over into his arms.

'There, there my little love. It's all right now. It's not you, you know that, don't you? You're beautiful and sweet. Much more so than I deserve, and I'm just a washed-up old wreck who doesn't know how to appreciate you.' He kept on holding her and whispering to her in

124

the dark until the sobbing had turned into little snuffles and then stopped altogether. At last she was asleep, her breath coming light and even from her lips, blowing little puffs against his shoulder as he lay, eyes wide open, in the dark room.

'Why can't I love you? Why the hell can't I love you?' Restless, he turned on his stomach, then back on his side. Each night it was the same: he would fight the sleep he needed so badly, terrified of his own dreams. As he drifted off Rachel would come to him, her eyes staring out at him in death from a face still pink and so soft he wanted to put out his hand and caress it. The next moment that same face would be grinning, decomposed with dried eyeballs and dissolving lips. He groaned and pressed his face down hard against the pillow.

'I can't even fuck myself senseless,' he whispered, teeth clenched. 'I'm lying in bed next to a beautiful young woman who wants me, and I can't even do that.' He grabbed the frilled sides of the pillow, smothering his face with its softness.

*   *   *

It was late the next day and Liberty had finished the translation into Swedish of a guide to English country houses. She switched off the computer and brought out the leather writing case which had been a present from her

125

grandfather. She began her letter to Johnny, wondering if it was right to miss an adult child as much as she missed him. She had thought of joining him in Australia over Christmas, but there just was not the money. With the last of her books out of print, there were no royalty cheques coming in and the money from her translation work and the teaching was only just enough to pay Johnny a small allowance and to keep herself in modest comfort.

'The great thing is that one can live cheaply in the country,' she wrote to him now, 'mainly because, as you know, there's so little to tempt you. It's a challenge, living on just enough and no more, baking my own bread, preserving fruit, pickling the odd horse you come across in the hedgerow. I look forward to the spring, when I can make nettle soup; I never have quite believed it doesn't sting your mouth and now I'll find out.'

She finished the letter, having tried to achieve just the right balance of missing him, while still being happy for him to be away having a good time. Leaning back in the kitchen chair, she looked out across the sodden lawns and the empty flower beds. She shuddered: they looked just like fresh graves.

Until recently, Liberty had felt barely a twinge of interest in gardening. She wished she could be more enthusiastic. Just look at Evelyn, greeting each day like a child running towards the entrance to Disney World. That,

126

of course, was how she herself had felt when she was writing. But now it was as if her life had been taken away, to be filleted by a trainee waiter and returned to her a shapeless, spineless helping of years.

Maybe she could work herself into a passion for her garden? After all, constant exposure made addicts. It worked with soap operas and radio presenters and Kit-Kats with your mid-morning coffee, so why not with gardening? Drip, drip, growing and weeding, mucking and mulching, picking and pickling, and bingo! She would be hooked. Contented, serene, she would spend her days within the coloured, scented world that was every bit as much her own creation as her stories, and probably a good deal more lasting.

She got up and rooted out one of her stash of small black notebooks she had bought from an artist's shop in Paris, on a side street close to the Bastille. The pages were edged in red, and crackled as if they had been soaked in water before drying out again.

Garden, she wrote, then she messed about some more in her desk drawer until she found a red biro to underline with. She might end up a sort of mix between Evelyn and Penny. It would be a bit late in the day, but Johnny would like it. All that time while she had been working his childhood away, writing, typing and translating other people's manuscripts, filling in at the local bookstore, teaching, writing some more, he had probably nurtured a dream of an apron-clad, bread-and-butter-pudding mother with flour, instead of ink stains, on her fingers. So he was grown-up. What a grandmother she would be! She buried her head in the crook of her arm and wept.

Minutes later, with an irritated swipe at the tears, she began a plan of the garden. She sketched in a small rectangle close to the back door, for vegetables, before fetching a book on plants called *A Gardener's Calendar* that Hamish had given her when she first moved to the cottage. With its help she began making notes, filling page after page in her sprawling, slanted hand, getting pleasure from the act of catching words and pinning them down, like moths, to the paper. When she had finished, she sat back and looked out again across the garden, blinking when she saw, not the richness of fruit and flowers bathed in golden summer sunshine, but an unkempt lawn boarded by naked rosebushes and hydrangeas whose heads, dried to the colour of dead leaves, remained on the shrubs like the memories of a faded beauty queen.

She was stretching and yawning at her desk when the doorbell went. Oscar apologized for disturbing her.

'I should have phoned first, but I've just been across to see Evelyn.' He looked tired and seemed glad of the offer of coffee. 'I wanted to have another word, if you've got the time.' He

128

followed her into the kitchen, and as they passed the hall mirror Liberty tried to catch a glimpse of her face, but failed. Her hand went up to her cheek, fingering the scar.

Oscar looked hard at her for a moment, then he said, 'It was good of you to call last night. The old girl's more rattled than she lets on.'

In the kitchen Liberty offered him a chair. She moved round him in the small kitchen, filling the kettle, spooning instant coffee into the mugs, pouring milk into a small china jug with painted pink roses and a chipped handle. Oscar leant back in the white-painted chair. With a gunshot sound, one of the wooden ribs snapped in two. He leapt up, spouting apologies in every direction.

'Don't worry,' she smiled. 'It happens all the time. Here.' She pulled out another chair and, with a suspicious look at it, he sat down again.

'Have you called the police?' she asked, putting the mug of coffee down in front of him.

'No. Evelyn told me to stop behaving like a demented hen and keep my beak out of her business.' As he spoke, Oscar pointed to the black notebook Liberty had left on the kitchen table. 'Writing again, that's good.' He smiled, a nice open smile, Liberty thought. A nice smile on a sad face.

'No, I'm not. That really is all over. I've...' She paused, pleased at how light her voice sounded. She imagined it soaring through the sky like an air balloon that had ditched its passengers and every ounce of bagged-up sand. Noticing that Oscar was waiting for her to continue, she hastily carried on. 'I've wasted enough time flogging a dead horse.' She added as an afterthought, 'It makes your arm hurt. No, those are my gardening notes.' Without thinking, she picked up the notebook and put the open page right up to her nose, closing her eyes and sniffing the ink-filled paper. She opened her eyes again, pulling a little face of embarrassment. Oscar grinned back. He looked nice in her kitchen, she thought, rather big, with those long legs stretched out, but comforting somehow, and calm where Tom had been restless, given to pacing and picking things up, returning them always to the wrong place. There was a stillness about Oscar as he sat in her chair. Maybe he was just scared to break it again. She realized she was staring at him. 'Do you like it down here, running *The Tribune*?' she asked. 'It must be very different from the way you lived before.'

'It is different, but that was what I wanted. Had there been a newspaper on Mars, I would have gone there.' He was quiet for a moment. 'There are things I miss, of course, bound to be when you leave one kind of life for another.' He fell silent and stared morosely into his coffee.

Liberty looked at him, her head a little to one side. 'Funny things sometimes, I bet,' she said. When Oscar said nothing she continued,

'I know, the other day when I was in the Sports Centre, this group of lissom young bodies entered from the changing rooms just as I emerged from the water, and I remembered how I used to be able to tell myself, "All right, so you have cellulite, but at least you're an *author* with cellulite."'

'Why don't you write just for yourself?'

'I ask myself that.'

'And what do you answer?'

Oh dear, she thought, the problem is to make sense of an answer you know too well. She looked thoughtfully at him, resting her arms on the table.

'Do you not sometimes think that whoever or whatever created us installed a fail-safe mechanism in our brains?' she asked him instead. 'You know—something to stop us really comprehending that we are actually just on one long, forced march to the grave, that we'll grow old and surplus to requirements one day, that none of us actually matters two hoots, that sort of thing? I mean if we did understand, we'd dig our little feet into our mother's womb and refuse to budge.'

'I only asked why you couldn't write just for your own pleasure,' Oscar said mildly. 'You can solve the meaning of life tomorrow.'

Liberty blushed. 'Sorry. Well, it's a bit like cooking really.'

'Really,' Oscar smiled politely.

'Well, think if, night after night you put your

131

soul into preparing dinner, using all the most precious and wonderful ingredients you could find. You'd lay the table, light the candles, pour the wine and then you'd wait, and each night your children would rush through the kitchen saying could they please just have a sandwich, and your husband would switch on the television and say thanks, but he had eaten already. Eventually you'd decide to hell with it and take up stamp collecting or wind surfing or something. Well, that's how it was with me.'

'So now you're going to garden instead?'

'Absolutely,' Liberty said without much enthusiasm. 'And I'm sorry. You came here to talk about Evelyn.' She looked down at her hands, embarrassed. She had a habit she herself deplored, of breaking her long periods of silence with reams of speech, as if she were paid handsomely by the word. As a child she had always hoped to find a book where the heroine had the same problem, but invariably the only girls who did were the heroine's silly friend, or the comic nurse. The exception, of course, was Anne of Green Gables, but she, on the other hand, was unbearably winsome and never drew breath at all.

'You know these people, Haville-Jones and Sanderson?' Oscar said.

'Not that well, but I find it hard to believe they'd behave in such a nasty, childish way.'

'I know what you mean,' Oscar agreed. 'But she's been carrying on these mini-crusades for

132

years. I remember she asked me to put her on to a printer some while ago. She wanted to distribute a pamphlet about a company she said was dumping toxic waste. As you say, there must be dozens of people gunning for her. You've lived next door to her for years; you can't think of anyone in particular?'

'I haven't had very much to do with her work, other than admiring it from a safe distance, I'm afraid.' She felt unhelpful with Oscar looking up at her, with those blue eyes fixed on her with such intensity; it was as if she carried the power of life and death in her answers.

Disconcerted, she went on, 'I do worry about her, and I felt you should be told about what happened, but I didn't really think there was anything very serious behind these incidents.'

'I don't really think it's anything much either,' Oscar agreed, getting up suddenly. 'I just want to keep an eye on things, that's all.' He gave her a quick smile, his face relaxed again. 'If anything else unpleasant happens, will you let me know?'

As she saw him out, Liberty assured him that she would.

In the door, Oscar turned. 'That scar, it doesn't matter you know. Not in the slightest.'

Scar or no scar, Oscar thought as he drove off home, it was an odd sort of face, Liberty's. Dimpled and creamy-skinned, framed by all those blond curls, she looked like a doll but for those long, green eyes; a hospital doll, like the one they had given Victoria's little sister, that came ready injured for you to bandage and make better.

CHAPTER EIGHT

'I must say it will be a great relief, not having those rockets going up all over the place, scaring man and beast.' Neville Pyke was speaking ostensibly to his wife, but he had long given up believing she listened. But silence disconcerted Neville, and directing his flow of words towards her at least saved him from the ignominy of talking to himself. Neville was sitting at the G-plan dining-table, working on the broken Chinese pot which Nancy Sanderson had let him have. When he was done it would go down a treat at the jumble sale, together with that old push-chair he had rescued from a skip. A bit of attention to the brake, some rust remover and a good clean, and it would be as good as new. Neville placed the last-but-one piece in its place along the rim of the pot, wiping the glue carefully from the edges and holding it in place with a stained thumb and finger.

Gladys was watching *Knot's Landing* on television. Before *Knot's Landing* there had been *Neighbours*, and later on she would settle down to *Home and Away* and *Eldorado*, before switching sides to *Coronation Street*. She had never been much of a talker, Gladys, and when they first met he had believed her the perfect listener. That was until he realized that the polite little half smile on her face remained the same whatever he said, leaving Gladys's mind free to wander as it wished between Ealing and Hollywood. This morning the only thing she had said apart from, 'Your dinner is in the freezer,' was, 'I don't care what anyone says, I like *Eldorado*.'

Still Neville chatted on stubbornly. 'It's very heartening, the village getting together and acting for the best. People complaining about this place don't know what they're talking about, that's what I say. They should read the paper.' He waved *The Tribune* at his wife. Neville always had to read it on a Monday; his pension did not seem to stretch as far as it used to, so he relied on Nancy Sanderson passing on her copy to him.

Gladys sighed and leant closer to the set. She was wearing her smart pistachio green suit, bought for a nephew's wedding three years earlier. Neville liked the suit, it brought happy memories of when they used to go out together. Nowadays Gladys hardly ever went out, not even at week-ends; week-ends there were the omnibus episodes, but she still wore the suit, every Monday, for *Knot's Landing*. She painted her nails, too, on Sunday evenings. She'd sit up in their queen-size bed, an old copy of *Hello!* to protect the sheets, and she'd paint her nails bright scarlet. Neville liked to watch her. When they first met it was her hands he'd noticed; small and so white, it was as if she'd taken off her gloves for the first time just for him.

'Although I must say, there never seems to be that much going on here on Bonfire Night anyway. Now you mention it, I can't think when we last had a proper Bonfire Night party in Tollymead. You remember me saying it was a crying shame people had to travel to Everton for a display. Still, the kiddies should at least have a proper bonfire, seeing they're so good about the rockets. I think I'll go and pay Nancy a visit, see what she has to say.' He heaved himself up from the armchair and stomped off towards the door. In the doorway he stopped for a moment to give his wife a little wave. 'Don't worry if I'm late dear,' he said unnecessarily. 'Nancy might ask me in.' He lingered in the doorway for a moment then, as Gladys turned the sound up on the remote control, he hurried off.

*   *   *

Andrew had come back late for lunch that afternoon. He always came home for lunch, something that both pleased and irritated

136

Nancy. It showed that she knew how to look after a husband. Not like poor Charlotte going through her second divorce and pretending she liked living on her own. But it did tie Nancy down. She could not just take off for the day, go up to London for a matinee or a gallery or a day's shopping, and on court days it meant getting up extra early to prepare something ready for him to heat up in the microwave. Andrew did not like the microwave. 'It's the last refuge of the sloppy housewife,' he had said when she first bought it, but for once Nancy had ignored him. She did not use it more than she had to, and the steak and kidney pudding for his lunch today had stewed slowly on a low setting in the gas cooker.

'I think I saw that American writer woman this morning, outside the Post Office,' Andrew said.

'It's not open Mondays.'

'I expect she didn't know that. She hasn't been here very long. Good-looking woman actually; redhead. Big, in that way American women are. Can't think who else it could have been.'

Nancy tipped a large helping of steak and kidney on to Andrew's plate, for once not bothering to make it look appetizing. Then she served herself.

'You still haven't managed to find out where she lives?' Andrew shovelled a huge forkful of pie into his mouth.

'I can't say that I have particularly tried,' Nancy snapped. She patted her hair nervously with her square-fingered hand. What was the matter with her, carrying on like that. He'd always liked looking at pretty women, flirting at parties when dinner carried on late and there was plenty of wine and port. She never worried. He always came home with her. She even got a funny sort of pleasure from watching him, enjoying the hot colour rise in his face, the excited glances and the little squeezes, as if they had been directed at her. Then she would choose her moment to rein him in, walking up and putting her arm through his, listening with a little smile as he introduced her as his wife. So why was she snappy now? All he'd done was say the woman was handsome. She forced herself to smile while she waited for him to finish.

'No-one seems to know anything about her,' she said, 'but then that's not unusual for Tollymead, not these days. I mean, how come we've never met Hester Scott? I mean, we would expect to have been introduced to someone like her.'

There was a loud knock on the door. 'It's bound to be for you,' Andrew said, settling back in the chair and picking up his pipe.

Nancy opened the door to Neville. With ill-concealed impatience she asked what it was he wanted. 'We're just finishing lunch.'

'It's about Bonfire Night,' Neville said, his

watery grey eyes beseeching her to share his excitement as he took a step closer to the door, peering inside the hall with a hopeful smile. 'Seeing the kiddies are being so responsible about the rockets, I thought we should reward them, so to speak, with a really good old-fashioned Bonfire Night celebration over at the recreation ground, with a Guy and everything.'

Nancy did not ask Neville in but she said, 'I saw that piece in the Diary too, but there's no mention of who these paragons amongst us are.' She guffawed, 'No-one's asked me whether or not I am likely to want to fire off a rocket or two from my back garden.' Neville laughed at the joke, loudly. 'Still,' Nancy said, 'a Bonfire Night party is a good idea. I'm for anything that brings the village together as you know. I'll talk to the school, I'm sure the children could get a morning off to help. I'll give the headmaster of Tollymead Manor a call too.'

Neville smiled delightedly at her, and the smile was still there as Nancy closed the door on him. Andrew was waiting for his coffee as she returned to the kitchen. She made some Nescafé for them both, weak with sugar and milk, neither of them cared for that strong continental stuff everyone raved about, and as she came up behind him she had to bend down to brush a kiss against his neck that was brown still from last year's summer sun. Andrew shrugged her off with a little flinch, as he

139

always did, good-humoured or irritated, depending on his mood that moment. She did not really mind the way she had when they were first married. Instead, she repeated like a mantra her well-used phrases of comfort: I'm his wife; I'm the woman who shares his bed; only I know the expression on his face when he's making love; only I know the little sounds he makes in his sleep. Nancy stood poised over her husband, the mug in her hand, a rapt look on her big, weather-beaten face. As he turned to reach for the coffee she rearranged her features until they were back to their usual expression of capable good sense.

'Thanks old thing,' Andrew said, his eyes still on the paper.

Tollymead: *We still need more fireworks for Bonfire Night, so if anyone would like to help, Neville Pyke has set up a collection point at his home, 'Wee Nooke', The Street, Tollymead.*

A suggestion for how we could all help to make our village a more beautiful place has come from Miss Agnes Coulson, who tells me, 'My walkers and I never go anywhere in the autumn without a bulb or two in our pockets. Then when we pass a dull spot we bung one in. Now if every gardener in Tollymead would do the same, we'd have a village that would make the poet Wordsworth sit up in his grave.'

Miss Coulson's idea is bound to find favour with many Tollymead residents. Mrs Laura Brown, who recently moved down from London with her four young children, says, 'It's just the sort of community action that makes taking a break from the rat race and moving down here so worth while.'

Mrs Brown, who was an advertising executive, tells the Diary that she finally took the decision to leave London when, after a week-end visit to the country, her three-year-old son asked where the cows worked during the week.

There are whispers around the village that the vicar is planning something special for us all. I have not been able to find out exactly what, but I'm sure that a visit to Sunday's Family Service will reveal all.

CHAPTER NINE

When Liberty arrived in church on Sunday morning she could hardly find a spare seat. Looking around, pleased for poor old Ted, she caught Neville Pyke's eye.

'A little bird whispered to you too, eh?' he winked at her from across the aisle.

'Whispered what?' Liberty asked.

'You mean you don't know?' Neville hissed. 'We're on *Songs of Praise*! That lot in Everton with their lens-louse vicar will be eating their hearts out.' Looking round, craning his thin neck on which his big head seemed a heavy burden, he carried on talking. 'I wonder where they've hidden the equipment—cameras and lights and the like?'

Gladys, seated next to him, smart in her pistachio suit and cream blouse with pussycat bow, looked around too, her large eyes swivelling in their sockets, focusing on nothing for longer than a second.

'Maybe they're just scouting this week, making sure there's a good congregation, that

142

sort of thing,' her husband soothed her.

'I don't think we should count on this being televised. It's just nice to see so many people in church,' Liberty said, a little anxiously. 'By the way, I don't think we've met, have we Mrs Pyke? Not properly. Your husband comes to my writing class.'

Gladys Pyke turned her gaze reluctantly on Liberty. 'Oh yes. You're the lady what can't get her books done no more, so Neville tells me. I can't say I'm surprised. What with the telly I don't see the use for books myself. You should write for the telly, like that American woman.'

'A lot of people prefer books,' Liberty said, stung. 'I mean, you can't take a television to bed with you—'

'Lots of people have a telly in their bedroom these days.'

'—or sit with it under a flowering apple tree.' Liberty glared at Gladys. 'You can't bring it with you on a picnic by the river or take it on holiday. A book is so much more than—'

'Don't need to. They've got that Sky in the airport lounges nowadays and on board plane. And then there's your own set in the hotel room when you arrive.' Gladys resumed her scanning of the church, leaving Liberty to ponder the truth of her words.

'A book is quiet,' she muttered, 'and you can have your favourite bit any time. And it doesn't have Terry Wogan in it.'

'Terry Wogan!' a woman sitting behind
143

Liberty hissed, craning her neck. Liberty turned round and gave a regretful shake of her head.

'False alarm,' she whispered.

'I like Terry Wogan,' Neville said with a stubborn look to his round face.

'So do I,' Liberty hastened to assure him. 'I was merely speaking of choice.' Then the organ struck up.

Normally on a Sunday the small but regular congregation stood and sat, kneeled and bowed, with the timing and precision of a ballet, their singing modest and the muttered responses audible without being showy. But this Sunday Liberty thought, it was more like a class of five year olds on their first day at school; everyone looking sideways at their neighbour to see how it was done, nudging, whispering. Nevertheless the singing was lusty, particularly the chorus, and everyone, it seemed, managed to smile right through each hymn, even when their mouths were wide open in song. Ted Brain looked like someone who had been given a present he had dreamt of for so long that he was not sure anymore that he wanted it.

'This isn't *Challenge Anneka* is it?' he greeted them to uneasy titters. The uneasiness grew as the service went on, until it covered the congregation like an itch. No-one seemed to be able to sit still, everyone was twisting and turning and rubbing against their pews.

144

Embarrassed for them all, Liberty kept her eyes downcast.

In order not to turn up to church on Christmas Day feeling like a day-tripper, she usually increased her church-going in the run-up to Christmas. This autumn she went almost every Sunday. Church gave structure to her week-ends, now she was on her own. Tom might not have been the love of her life, but he had been her friend and her companion. She felt lonely when Friday afternoon came, but in church even strangers seemed glad to see you. And God did not have it all his own way either. His readership was falling away in ever increasing numbers too, and in some quarters He was even denied title to His creation.

The service was over. The members of the congregation hurried out into the dank morning air, like a dispersing lynch mob, eyes lowered, chatting nervously to each other about everything other than what they had just been up to. Evelyn waited for Liberty at the side gate. She, too, was a church-goer. As she said once to Liberty, 'There's a lot of it I don't believe, but from time to time I feel the need to pay homage to the greatest naturalist of them all.'

They had been invited to lunch by Victoria and Oscar and, as they were early, they decided to walk the mile or so to the house. Oscar opened the door; his smile was as strained as the fit of his new-looking jeans. Liberty

145

imagined he'd put it on that morning, together with the trousers and the pale blue sweater, and told not to change any of it.

Victoria would not be long, he told them as he showed them in, she was in the kitchen putting the finishing touches to lunch. He offered them a seat, he got their drinks, whisky on the rocks for Evelyn and Stone's ginger wine for Liberty, but he moved around the room like a visitor who'd been asked to make himself at home, bumping into the vast, frilled sofas and peering inside cupboards for glasses and bottles. Handing Liberty the wine he said again, 'She won't be long,' and sat down in a worn, high-backed armchair that looked as if it had gone underground while the rest of the furniture was being done over. 'His' chair, Liberty thought. What was it with men that they seemed to need a special chair? Maybe it was a big boy's equivalent of a security blanket.

Victoria emerged from the kitchen. Her dark hair shone, framing her pale face, and her simple cream wool dress hugged the elongated elegance of her body, stopping short just above her knees. Those knees, Liberty thought, so round and smooth under the sheer tights. Liberty's knees were like her grandfather's, and he had been a great athlete, not a great beauty. She looked from Victoria's legs to Oscar's face, waiting for his eyes to light up with pride and sheer pleasure that such delights

146

were his; but Oscar was not looking at his wife.

'Now Evelyn,' he said after a while, 'you've had another letter.'

Liberty looked at her. 'You never told me.'

'Seeing you made such an appalling fuss last time, I didn't want to worry you any further.'

'But I'm your friend.' Liberty was upset. 'I'm supposed to be a person to whom you turn for support.'

'But you're not family,' Victoria said. 'In times of crisis one tends to turn to one's family.'

People, Liberty thought, who went about giving their honest opinion were very difficult to live with as they goose-stepped all over the moral high ground. It was especially disconcerting to be flattened by someone so young. In the silence that followed Victoria stood up with a warm smile. 'Lunch everybody.'

They all admired the table, set in blue and white, with a parade of tiny vases along the centre, each filled with heather and dried lavender.

'I believe in making every aspect of my life special,' Victoria said.

Had Evelyn and Liberty been visiting judges of the Best Wife competition, Victoria could not have tried harder. All through the delicious meal of lamb noisettes and crisp, glazed carrots, she shot adoring looks across the table at Oscar, asking his opinion on every topic, about everything on which he could possibly have an opinion, and when she passed his chair she would touch him with her shoulder or plant a little kiss on his cheek or the top of his fair head. He was not allowed to help either, other than with the wine. When he stood up to clear the plates, she told him to stay right there. Liberty had always asked Tom to help with the chores. Through it all, Oscar behaved with an uneasy friendliness, which was puzzling.

'I'm looking forward to class on Wednesday,' Victoria said, as she brought in the pudding. 'Peach Roulade,' she placed the dish on the table. 'Oscar loves his gooey puds, don't you darling?'

'Yes, yes I do,' darling said, while Liberty noticed a tiny frown appearing between his eyebrows.

'I've written a little piece that I'd like to read out.' Victoria paused on her way to the sideboard. 'Quite a serious piece actually. I really wanted to say something with my writing this time. It's about this woman giving up her career for her family and how it changes everything. I've got this moving scene at the end when Cosima ... Actually,' she picked up a jug of cream and returned to the table, 'I think I'll make you wait till Wednesday. It won't have the same impact if you already know the story. I know Romance is easier to get published, but this story just begged me to get written. Actually, have you tried Romance,

148

Liberty?'

'Romance!' Evelyn scoffed, taking her plate.

But Liberty nodded. 'Oh yes, I have, but I wasn't any good at that either. I always seemed to feel too much or too little. It was all either totally embarrassing or plain cold. And my heroines were bullies.'

Oscar, who had leapt up to get the bottle of wine, began to laugh.

'He never laughs at my jokes.' Victoria's eyes were accusing.

'But I wasn't joking,' Liberty smiled at her. 'If it's any comfort, people only laugh at me when I'm serious, my jokes, on the other hand, tend to fall flat.'

Oscar refilled their glasses before sitting down again. 'I don't think we should publish your article,' he said to Evelyn. 'Not until we've found out who this nutcase is.'

'The question of harmful pesticides is bigger than all of us,' Evelyn replied pompously, but she looked old and a little frightened.

'Please Evelyn,' Liberty said, reaching across the table and putting her hand across Evelyn's permanently grubby, liver-spotted one. 'There are a lot of crazy people out there, each satisfying every low grade whim as if it was their democratic right. It's as well to be careful.'

'I have to keep on with my work,' Evelyn said. 'It's what keeps me sane.'

'Oh, you're just saying that. We all have to

retire some time,' Victoria's voice was coaxing. 'You deserve a rest.'

'I deserve a rest like I deserve being skinned and popped into a vat of boiling oil,' Evelyn said coldly. 'To me, life is work, contributing. I know because once I was stuck like a growth to my chair for months, convalescing after a very nasty case of hepatitis—oysters by the way, not sex. In the end I didn't know who I was. I remember feeling like being a permanent guest, controlling nothing, contributing nothing, achieving nothing. I'd rather be dead than spend the rest of my days like that.'

Liberty nodded. 'That's just how I feel, now I'm not writing; like a permanent guest in someone else's creation.'

'Cream with your roulade?' Victoria asked brightly. 'I have to warn you, it's double double.'

They all had some. When Victoria passed Oscar his plate, she put her long fingers on his head, ruffling his blond hair. Oscar put his hand up to take hers, giving it a little squeeze. Looking at them made Liberty feel lonelier than ever. Then she saw the look in Oscar's eyes, a resigned look, as if Victoria had just marched into the room with curlers in her hair and a fag-end hanging from the corner of her mouth and slammed down a plate of baked beans on the table.

*   *   *

After their guests had left, Oscar cleared the table and put the glasses and plates in the dishwasher. Victoria washed the silver by hand. All those shiny knives and forks and spoons had been presents to her from her grandmother, one piece each Christmas and birthday. Seeing Victoria caress the cutlery with the tea towel, Oscar thought of how she'd told him that even as a young child she had appreciated the gift, never, like her sister, pushing it aside with a disappointed little shove because it was not a Sindy Doll or shiny pointed shoes. Victoria, even then, had relished the thought of the precious possessions accruing in the strong box in the cellar.

They had sandwiches made with the left-over lamb, and the rest of the Peach Roulade, for supper. They ate in front of the television. They were watching *Poirot*, but Victoria said she'd much rather watch the documentary on Jackson Pollock.

'Watch it,' Oscar said. 'I really don't mind.'

Victoria, curled up in the sofa, said, 'No, it's all right. I know you like this sort of thing.' After a moment she added, 'I know who did it. Don't ask me to tell you, but I know who did it.'

As the credits rolled she switched off with the remote control. 'I hate these cheating endings.'

'You were wrong were you?' Oscar smiled

at her.

'Well you didn't guess either.'

'Didn't have to. I read the book.' He reached for the Sunday paper.

With a sideways glance at him, Victoria yawned loudly, stretching her arms high over her head. Oscar put the paper down and, folding away his spectacles, pushed himself out of the chair.

'Hi there,' he said. He took her by the hand and led her upstairs. As he pushed her gently down on the bed, Victoria wriggled out of the dress, lying back, waiting for him to release her from the silk knickers and lace-tipped bra.

I should say how beautiful she is, Oscar thought. There isn't a man alive who wouldn't gasp in admiration. He opened his mouth to speak, but before all that unblemished beauty laid out like the Peach Roulade, he felt only sated. Victoria looked up at him, her eyes full of expectation and, closing his eyes, he let himself sink down on top of her. As she sighed and rubbed against him he desperately conjured up pictures in his mind of every actress he had ever thought attractive, of strip joints in Bangkok and past loves, anything to stop his tenuous erection from fading. An image altogether different appeared unasked, long green eyes in a doll-like face with an ugly scar breaking the white skin, and with a rush of confused excitement he made love to his wife.

152

Village Diary

Tollymead: *With the help of our two local schools, Tollymead Church of England Primary School and Tollymead Manor, a successful Bonfire Night seems assured this year. The bonfire will be lit on the recreation ground at 6.30 p.m. and everyone is welcome, especially our neighbours in Everton who won't, I hear, be putting on a display of their own this year.*

There has been a last-minute appeal to refrain from burning the Guy, posted on the parish notice-board. Explaining the reasons for the appeal, the author of the notice, Mr Terry Pearson of the Fairfield Branch of 'Action For Penal Reform', said, 'The cause for more humane treatment of offenders is not advanced by encouraging our kids to burn effigies of past victims of a brutal penal system.'

There does not seem to be much sympathy for his views in Tollymead, however. Walking past the notice with her three pugs, Larry, John and Ralph, Miss Hester Scott exclaimed, 'I've had it up to here with these do-gooder types—there, darling, you lift your leg up and show that silly man what we think of him—and if it was up to me it would be one of these bleeding heart liberals placed on the bonfire, sandals, beard and all.'

153

Oliver Bliss, lecturer at Southampton University's renowned department of Marine Biology, sat sketching a few yards away and as I stopped to admire his work we agreed that few things caused as much belligerence as the preaching of non violence.

Finally, with Thanksgiving coming up, the Diary called on our American resident, Anne Havesham, for her special recipe for Sweet Potato Bake.

2lb sweet potatoes
$\frac{1}{2}$ a cup of light brown sugar
2 tbsp of butter
$\frac{2}{3}$ of a cup of milk
a pinch each of cinnamon, cloves, nutmeg and salt

Cook the sweet potatoes in simmering water until soft. Peel and mash. Stir in all the remaining ingredients except for 2 tsp of the sugar. Turn mixture into a generously sized casserole dish and sprinkle with the remaining sugar. Bake at 400°F for approximately thirty minutes.

Delicious served with roast turkey!

CHAPTER TEN

When Nancy Sanderson returned home from the magistrate's court the day before Bonfire Night, the sight of a small group of children huddled in a ditch outside the entrance to Campbell's Farm made her brake sharply. Winding down the window she asked, 'Everything all right?'

The children, five of them, looked up for a moment but said nothing. Hoping I'll go away and mind my own business, Nancy smiled grimly as she tightened the handbrake and got out. 'Now what's going on children?' She leant over the muddy ditch and peered down at them. 'And what have we got here? Fireworks ... and matches ... Do you children realize that you are less than five yards from an open barn full of dry hay?' Nancy used her magistrate's voice.

'So what if we are?' A fat boy, older than the others, with a single strand of hair like a limp snake hanging down his back, stared back at her.

'Yeah, so what if we are?' the others chorused, but their voices were uncertain and they kept their eyes to the ground.

'If that barn catches fire, which it easily could, through your irresponsible games, you and your parents would have to pay Mr

Campbell many thousands of pounds; that's "so what". Now give me those fireworks and the matches, and I might not tell Mr Campbell.'

'They're ours,' the fat boy said.

Nancy felt her face redden. She took a step down into the ditch, her new Ecco lace-ups sinking into the mud. 'Give them to me now, or I will alert the police, and Mr Campbell's three rottweilers.' She held out her hand.

'Cow,' the fat boy hissed. 'Stupid old cow.' Then without warning he picked up the rockets and the box of matches and threw them at her before scrambling out of the ditch and running off. The other children followed and when at a safe distance one of them, a small girl with bruised-looking eyes in a pale face, turned and repeated in a shrill voice, 'Stupid old cow!'

Nancy stood staring after them, surprised at the intense dislike she felt for those small, unkempt people. With a sigh she bent down and picked up the rockets before climbing up back onto the road and into the car.

When she got home, Andrew was already there, sitting in the tall-backed armchair, a glass of whisky in one hand, reading the paper. He looked up at her over the top of the page. 'You're late. Where have you been? You're absolutely filthy.'

Under his gaze Nancy felt the heat rise in her cheeks and she turned her head away. He had no right to speak to her, to look at her, like

156

that. She was tired. In the kitchen there was fish waiting to be skinned and boned, potatoes to be peeled. And there was Andrew looking at her with much the same expression as her own when she had looked at those unappealing children. Close to tears she lowered her gaze to the mud-splattered hem of her shapeless blue skirt and her thick ankles disappearing into the mucky lace-ups that had left a trail of mud on the carpet. Where, she thought, was her friend? Where were the comforting arms waiting to envelop her?

Suddenly angry she said, 'I suppose you'd prefer it if I sashayed round the village in a mini skirt and stiletto heels like that American woman?'

Andrew lowered the paper, a look of interest replacing the frown for a brief moment. 'You've seen her, have you?'

Nancy pulled off her shoes, slamming each one down on the blue carpet. 'No, no I haven't.'

'So how the hell do you know how she dresses?' The frown was back in place, fitting as snugly as if it had never left.

'Oh do stop frowning, just for once!' Nancy shouted, swinging round in her stocking feet off towards the kitchen.

She filleted the fish and put it in an oven-proof dish, and was turning her attention to the potatoes when the hard set to her jaw began to soften. Poor Andrew, she thought, he was under a lot of pressure. It was not long before she was asking herself what kind of a wife she was, attacking her husband when he was worried and tired and most needed her understanding and support? She picked up his napkin from the dresser and smoothed it out before rolling it up again and pushing it into his napkin ring. How hard he worked to keep her in their lovely home. Of course he got snappy from time to time, it was only natural. She shook her head. Poor Andrew.

The fish was poaching in the oven and the potatoes were on, and in her stocking feet she padded into the sitting-room and up to the armchair where Andrew was sitting, still reading the paper.

'Had a bad day?' She was bending down to kiss him when he passed the paper to her with such violence it almost hit her face. She flinched but took it. 'Whatever is the matter?'

'I would have told you when you got home but you were obviously in a foul mood,' Andrew said, and the unfairness of it all brought her close to tears once more. But she said nothing and Andrew carried on, 'Read it and see for yourself what your chum Evelyn has cooked up this time. Old cow.'

'Andrew please don't use that expression, it's so coarse. There was this dreadful boy over at Campbell's farm.' She told him about the children. 'I can't stand that expression, it's so ... so ugly.'

158

'Oh don't become the Lady Magistrate with me. I should have known you'd stick up for the old bat.'

A fat tear rolled down Nancy's cheek and she wiped her eyes with the back of the hand, smearing the layer of Max Factor concealer stick. 'I'm not siding with Evelyn,' she said tiredly, then, pulling herself together she added, 'I'm very cross with her.' And suddenly she *was* angry. It was Evelyn's persecution of him that had made Andrew so out of sorts lately. It was damaging his business, too. As she read on, fury swelled up from the pit of her stomach, clawing its way up through her chest.

'The Killer In Our Midst' Evelyn's article was headed, and what followed were two columns about the dangers to the community of pesticides, some of them known carcinogenics, entering the food chain. These pesticides, Evelyn's article said, were of the kind supplied by well-known local companies, and used by local farmers.

Nancy sat down on the window seat close to Andrew. Struggling to remain calm, the way Andrew preferred, she said, 'You can sue you know. She doesn't mention Sanderson's Seeds by name, but you should talk to Nick Hudson, or maybe a London solicitor, for something like this. I'm sure if I asked one of the other magistrates—'

'Let me handle this, will you.' Andrew seemed almost cheerful as he heaved himself out of the chair. 'Dragging us all through the courts with her bleating on about the safety of future generations. The papers would have a field day and before we knew it, every greeny lefty trendy in the country would be on our backs. No, for once, Nancy, let me handle things my own way.'

'Have you spoken to Oscar Brooke?' Nancy asked, in a voice that tip-toed around the words. 'You know best of course dear, but—'

'I have. He tells me the article was taken on its merits as a valuable input to their debate on environmental issues.' Andrew made his voice all minced and sleek. 'Not because bloody Evelyn is his aunt. Now could we *please* have supper.'

'Maybe if I called Evelyn, appealed to her.' Nancy got up, too, putting her hand on his arm. 'If I tell her how much distress she's causing and—'

'I said let me handle this.' Andrew shook her hand off and strode off towards the kitchen.

'I'm sure she'd see sense.' Nancy hurried after him.

In the hall Andrew stopped. With something close to glee on his face he said slowly, 'You obviously have no intention of serving any supper, so I'm going out. I don't know when I'll be back, so don't bother waiting up.'

'But Andrew, darling, I've got it all prepared. It won't be two minutes.'

Andrew looked at her for a second before

slamming the door, leaving Nancy alone in the hall. 'It isn't fair,' she whispered. Andrew was not fair. It was Evelyn he was angry with, but he was punishing Nancy, as if she were an old dog to kick whenever he felt small. It wasn't right. She should not be treated like this.

CHAPTER ELEVEN

Two buses had been laid on by Tollymead Manor to transport the boys to the recreation ground at the northern end of the village where the bonfire, as tall as a one-storey building, held centre stage. Liberty spotted her father stepping off the bus behind the tumble of boys, each carrying a torch. Hamish carried a lantern which he directed on the large, white painted sign telling dog owners not to let their pets foul the playing fields. Underneath the sign curled a large defiant turd.

'Robert you clumsy boy, watch where you put those big feet of yours!' Hamish barked. Robert's brown lace-up squelched down on the mess, and Hamish closed his eyes and shook his head.

'Long grass boy, go and find some long grass.' As Liberty came up to him, Hamish smiled delightedly and kissed her on the cheek. 'It's as I suspected,' he said, 'literacy amongst the canine population is at an all-time low. I

161

blame television.

'Hey, Dominic.' Hamish left Liberty, to hurry after another small boy who was walking slowly off across the field with his torch turned straight back into his eyes.

Looking around the crowded playing field, Liberty could put a name to only a handful of faces. With a small estate erected here, a couple of cottages infilled there, a family going, another coming, even Ted Brain had given up trying to call on every new resident. With the shop gone, too, and most of the children bussed to the school from nearby villages, there were times when Liberty felt as if each villager were moving round the place in his own plastic bubble. It had not always been like that of course. For the few days following the great storm in 1987, when most of the village was cut off from power and phone lines and even water, the spirit of the Blitz had come to Tollymead. Waiting outside the Post Office for the water van, names were exchanged, help was given and there was much talk of how splendid it was that at last people were getting to know each other. There were even plans for starting a weekly meeting point in the village hall, like the one they had in Everton. Then each house got back their power and water and now, Liberty thought, Tollymead could well be a haven for Nazi war criminals for all she knew.

'Your lips are moving but nothing is coming forth.' Hamish had returned, putting his large,

162

shapely hand on her shoulder.

'Just hankering back to the days when it was not just the smell that alerted you to your neighbour's death.'

'Gruesome girl.' Hamish smiled, but in the light of the torch she could see his eyes flicking across the crowd, like a restless guest at a cocktail party.

Who was Hamish today? Liberty wondered. He was wearing heavy, worn-in tweeds and a deer-stalker, but in a way that was more old-world gent than Sherlock Holmes. When a small group of boys came rushing towards him and Hamish shifted his hand from Liberty's shoulder to the tousled head of the nearest child, her face brightened; that was it, Edwardian *pater familias*.

'Sir, are they setting off the rockets?' one of the boys asked. 'I'm bloody freezing,' he added before the admiring glances of his friends.

'Language, you little wart,' Hamish said. 'At break tomorrow you can write, "Swearing shows a sad lack of vocabulary" a hundred times.'

'Can you still give people lines?' Liberty asked, awed.

'Certainly.' Hamish lit his pipe. 'I can't beat the little so-and-sos, but I most certainly can still give them lines. By the way, Penny sent her love. Little Fred or whatever the youngest one is called—'

'Edward.'

163

'Edward, well anyway, he's got a bug, nothing serious, so they won't be coming tonight.'

'I can't see Oscar Brooke either.' Liberty, searching the crowd, was surprised at how disappointed she was. 'I wanted you to meet him. His wife's very sweet too.'

'Are you saying Oscar Brooke is sweet and that so is his wife, or is the wife alone in this nauseating attribute?' Hamish puffed at his pipe.

Liberty gave him an evil look. What a posturing old sod he was. Parents had a trigger, no doubt about it, that, when pressed, set off the memories of a thousand past injustices and irritations that lodged like delayed-action poison pellets in the minds of their children. And who else but a posturing old sod would name his daughter Liberty Bell? As for his explanation ... Liberty glared at her father who was smoking his pipe so contentedly, surveying his charges, as if there were no daughter standing at his side wanting nothing better than to kick him in the balls.

She could hear her father now, his voice close to breaking as he told the tragic story to yet another table full of sympathetic guests. 'She was named in honour of dear Sofia's final words, "Liberty, Liberty at last!" I'll never forget it. Everything had happened at once, nurses calling out, doctors running, machines, tubes. At the end I stood there, bending over

164

my newborn daughter's cot and I looked at her and whispered, "Welcome little Liberty, welcome."'

'Why didn't you go the whole hog and call me Last?' Liberty had shouted once, upsetting the whole party. '"Last Bell", that really would have satisfied your instinct for the theatrical.' She had been eighteen and she had had enough.

Now she looked at Hamish, trying to quell her rising irritation. 'Don't bear grudges,' she told herself. 'It's ugly and takes up valuable space.'

A rocket shot into the sky from between two Roman candles, then Ted Brain stepped out from the crowd and up to the bonfire, lighting a petrol-soaked rag at the base. Within minutes the fire was licking the feet of the Guy. Liberty turned away. She never did have a taste for burning Guys. The scarecrow figure in his borrowed clothes seemed to take on such human qualities just as the flames engulfed him. Anyway, she was frightened of fire. There was nothing like it to remind you of the fragility of life. One moment you could be cruising along the motorway, chatting to a friend or listening to the radio, thinking of your dental appointment or the wedding reception you thought lay ahead at the end of the journey, then Bingo, you were screaming in agony as you burnt to death, a picture of your twisted metal torture chamber ending up as breakfast news.

The fire crackled and spat as Liberty made her way back towards the cricket pavilion at the edge of the playing field. She spotted Evelyn and, as she came closer, Oscar standing a little way off, his arm round his wife's shoulders. He was looking at Liberty. She gave a little wave, embarrassed. Realizing you were being watched was like finding a silent queue waiting as you stepped out of a public loo still doing up your trousers. Had she been absent-mindedly picking her nose, or been stooping, chest and stomach sagging?

She was only feet away when there was a sharp whistle, followed by a bang and a fountain of multi-coloured lights, not in the sky above the field, but half a mile away, out by River Lane.

The crowd let out surprised oohs and aahs as heads turned away from the bonfire in one long movement as if a single thread connected them all. Then another rocket shrieked its way into the night sky above the river.

Oscar pulled his arm away from around Victoria. 'It looks like it's coming from your garden,' he said to Evelyn. 'I'd better go and see what the hell's going on.' He disappeared off towards the cars parked at the entrance to the grounds.

'Typical,' Victoria complained. 'He was the one who wanted to come tonight, he's got an absolute thing about fireworks, and now he's going to miss it all.'

'He's right, it is coming from my garden.' Evelyn grabbed Liberty's arm. 'Some little so-and-so is firing rockets in my garden.'

'We'll take my car,' Liberty said. Turning to Victoria she asked, 'Coming?' But Victoria decided she'd wait for them where she was.

*   *   *

A cascade of stars rose through the shattered glass of Evelyn's workshop, as flames took hold on the far side gable.

'My papers, the seedlings...' Evelyn's voice was a whisper as they rounded the corner of River Lane and approached the house. Two minutes later, Liberty turned the car up the drive, skidding to a halt on the gravel courtyard.

Oscar came running from the workshop and flung open the car door on Evelyn's side. 'I've got some of your stuff out and I've called the fire brigade, they should be here any moment.' His eyes were streaming and his face was streaked with soot and sweat. 'Make sure both gates are open, will you,' he shouted as he ran back towards the fire.

Liberty stared after him and then at Evelyn who sat, grey-faced and silent, at Liberty's side. Then, as sirens reached them from a distance, she hurried from the car and up to the gate, opening both sides right back against the

167

hedge. Within seconds the fire engine was through, the men running towards the blazing building with giant hoses dripping water like salivating sea snakes. Evelyn appeared. For a moment she stared at the flames then, before anyone could stop her, she ran towards the burning building and disappeared into the smoke.

*   *   *

CHAPTER TWELVE

'The police seem to think it was just children playing,' Victoria said. They were sitting in Evelyn's kitchen, looking out at the drive and the blackened corner of the workshop. 'You're so lucky the house itself didn't catch fire.'

Oscar had tried to run in after Evelyn, but he had been held back. 'It's only a small fire, but there could be a lot more smoke inside, and then there's that bit of glass roof,' he was told as two firemen with masks went instead. The flames were put out within minutes, but it was another long moment before Evelyn came out. Oscar had taken Liberty's hand, giving it a small squeeze as they waited. Finally, Evelyn emerged, pulled along by one of the firemen. With a grin on her blackened face she had hurried across to Oscar, passing him the bundle in her hands as carefully as if it had been a newborn baby.

Now she sat at the kitchen table, wrapped in her tartan dressing-gown and two wool blankets, her hair singed and her bandaged hands clasped round a mug of warm milk. The police had come and left again with a bag full of shrivelled cardboard from a cluster of used fireworks. 'One thing we know for sure,' one of them said, 'is that someone chose to set this little lot off inside that building.'

'There was a lifetime's worth of work in there,' Evelyn said, her voice trembling. 'I could have lost it all. Those seed trays I brought out, there was more than ten years of research riding in them.'

'Of course it could just be irresponsible children,' Oscar said, 'but coming after those letters and that very nasty little gift of two dead rabbits, I wonder...'

'It's really terrible, what's happened,' Victoria's sloe eyes were expressionless, 'but Oscar did warn you about writing that article after everything else you've done.'

'What are you saying, Victoria?' Evelyn looked coldly at her, but she clasped the mug harder.

Liberty felt herself going pink. She loathed scenes and here was one about to happen. Hamish created scenes: all her childhood, at airports and in department stores, in restaurants and in front of her friends, happy scenes, angry scenes, noisy scenes, quiet scenes, it did not really matter. He made himself

169

conspicuous, that was enough. Once, at Heathrow, he had goose-stepped through a crowd of elderly German-speaking tourists he decided were queue-barging, his hand raised in a Nazi salute, only to find they were a group of travellers from Haifa being ushered through first because of the special security precautions. These days Liberty could not even bear to watch someone cause a fuss on television without switching off, or at least putting her hands over her ears and singing very loudly; and here was Victoria, chin jutting and her eyes, as yielding as one-way mirrors, looking straight out at nothing as she said, 'Well you must admit you've caused a lot of people a lot of trouble lately.'

Oscar looked tiredly at his wife. 'Come on Victoria, that's not very helpful just now. Anyway, it was most likely a childish prank gone wrong.'

'I know who it is you remind me of Oscar,' Liberty exclaimed. 'Peter O'Toole, that's who. When he was younger of course. Don't you think so Victoria?'

Oscar looked up at her, surprised, then he smiled, a sudden smile that made Liberty's throat constrict; beautiful things had that effect on her.

'I don't think so at all,' Victoria said.

'I'm going to bed.' Evelyn tried to get up, but fell back onto the chair again with a little thud. Oscar leapt up and helped her to her feet. 'We'll stay the night.'

Victoria stood up too. 'I'm sure Evelyn would like to be left in peace. Anyway, you know the cats give me the sneezes.'

Oscar turned round to look at her. 'All right,' he said slowly, 'I'll take you home first, then I'll come back and spend the night here.'

Liberty smiled a large smile right round the table. 'I'll stay,' she offered, making another and, she hoped, more successful attempt to ease the tension. 'It's so easy for me, being next door. It'll only take me a minute to get my stuff. I'd like to stay. To be honest, I sometimes get a bit lonely at week-ends.'

'Thank you, Liberty,' Evelyn said from the doorway. 'You run along home Oscar. I'll be fine here with Liberty.'

Oscar opened his mouth to speak but then, obviously thinking the better of it, he just nodded. At the front door he said to Liberty, 'I'll go with you to get your things, Victoria won't mind waiting.' Victoria gave a small smile and said of course not.

'You're a very nice person, Liberty,' he said, as he dropped her off back at Evelyn's front door. He bent down and kissed her lightly on the cheek, right on the scar. It must have felt like kissing an alligator, Liberty thought as she watched him join Victoria who was waiting in the car. She closed the door behind him, double locking and fastening the chain.

'I can't stand the woman.' Evelyn had come

downstairs again. 'That cutesy little-girl act fools no-one.'

'It must have fooled Oscar,' Liberty said, adding quickly, 'She's very nice, though. You know, she comes to my classes sometimes. She's always very sweet.'

'She is nothing of the sort and you know it. Why do you always have to be so damned nice about everything?' Evelyn pottered into the kitchen.

Sitting down at the kitchen table, Liberty said, 'I'm glad you've noticed my increasing goodness. I was afraid no-one would.'

Evelyn sighed and fixed her with those blue eyes so like her nephew's. 'Dare I ask why you are trying to be especially nice?'

Liberty pulled an apologetic face. 'I've been giving these things a lot of thought, and I've come to realize that whether I do what is right or what is wrong, is one of the few decisions that are truly mine. Even just being mildly pleasant can be a struggle for me, but at least it's wholly in my power to succeed. Of course you have to separate being actively good from instinct. I mean, like most mothers I would gladly give my life for Johnny, but I don't stand around patting myself on the back for that. It's no more than, say, a mother hyena would do for her offspring. But being nice to Victoria, now that goes against all my instincts, so if I succeed I have shown I have some control, and that I'm just not some pre-programmed thing toddling along my pre-ordained path.'

'I like hyenas,' Evelyn said companionably. 'They get a bad press, but they're quite nice little things once you get to know them.'

'Are they really?'

Evelyn nodded.

Liberty smiled at her. 'Would you like some more warm milk?'

'Please.'

The milk heated slowly on the red-hot spiral cooker plate, and while she waited Liberty said, 'I'm very fond of animals and all that, and I'd like to think I respect their rights, but Evelyn, doesn't it worry you that you are one?' Seeing Evelyn's expression of polite surprise, she added quickly, 'Of course I don't mean you in particular, but all of us.'

'I like it,' Evelyn said. 'Puts things in perspective when you know you're just a link in the evolutionary chain.'

Liberty sighed. 'I wish I could see it that way, but it makes me feel that life is even more random and pointless. I've decided that if I have to be an animal, at least I'll be an animal with a difference. That's why I've been brushing up on my Latin and Greek; a knowledge of the classics instantly gets you one-up on the average chimpanzee. And that's why it's so important to have a good soul, not just a quiver of nerve ends and electrical impulses, but a nice big soul that gets even bigger with exercise. Being nice about Victoria

173

is tremendous exercise.'

'And there, in one small sentence, you fail.' Evelyn grinned at her. 'Anyway, what makes you so sure hyenas don't have souls?'

'I'm not,' Liberty said. 'It's just a suspicion.'

'Well it certainly wasn't his soul Oscar listened to when he married that girl, nor his brain.'

'When I was a rather plain little girl being told that I shouldn't worry, the boys would get to like me for my jolly personality, I used to pray for someone to want me just for my body. I especially wanted enormous breasts,' Liberty added dreamily. She placed the mug of milk in front of Evelyn, having first tested the temperature with the knuckle of her little finger. She did it automatically with milk.

'What happened to all that soul?'

Liberty sat down, perching on the edge of her chair. 'Oh, I hadn't thought of a soul then, I needed breasts first.' She looked hard at Evelyn's pinched face. 'Why don't you let me take that upstairs for you?' She nodded towards the mug. 'You must be exhausted.' She gave Evelyn her hand and helped her from her chair. 'Tomorrow we'll start sorting out your papers and things in the workshop.'

'Large breasts are a nuisance, take it from me,' Evelyn said. 'Get in the way in the garden.'

Liberty's eyes were drawn to Evelyn's ample bosom wrapped in tartan wool and she smiled. But as she walked upstairs she noticed the

174

small bandaged hand trembling as it clasped the banister, and she grew serious. She kissed Evelyn goodnight at the top of the stairs and then wandered down again, checking all the doors and windows. Back in the hall she stopped, staring into the darkness and thinking how nice it would be to see the twinkling of street lights. If the council did not put some up soon, she would bung a couple in herself: one each for her and Evelyn. With a little shiver, she drew the curtains. If the fire was not an accident, a childish prank gone wrong, Evelyn would need more protection than a mere street lamp.

CHAPTER THIRTEEN

'Look at that. I told you she was mad.' Andrew Sanderson waved *The Tribune* at his wife across the kitchen table. They were having supper, cottage pie and garden peas, and the sight of Evelyn posing in front of the damaged building, hair singed and her bandaged hands aloft as she clutched at what looked like a fish tank, made Nancy choke on her mashed potato. 'Not while we're eating *please*, Andrew.'

'Still, the old bat's got guts, I'll say that.' Andrew held out his plate for more. 'It'll certainly make good copy for that American television writer.' He drew a caption in the air. '"Crazy English Woman Risks Life to Rescue Seed Tray."' He chuckled as he put his full plate back on the table.

'I don't see what all the fuss is about,' Nancy said. 'It was the tiniest fire. Trust Evelyn to get her face in the paper over something like that.'

'Well, the whole incident might serve to quieten her down. I hope it does, or next time someone might be tempted to put a rocket up a more sensitive part than her workshop.' Andrew's face turned brick red as he laughed out loud at his own joke.

'Don't be coarse, Andrew,' Nancy said, but with none of her usual playfulness as she stood up to clear the plates.

'Hang on, I haven't finished my food.'

'Well then it's about time you did. I don't want to stand around all night doing those dishes. I don't suppose you remember, but I've got a meeting of the trustees of the village hall tonight and an early session in court tomorrow.' She pulled the plate away, leaving him gaping over the last mouthful, fork in hand.

As she cleared the table Nancy looked critically at her husband. He wasn't, in his middle years, much like the demi-god on whose altar Nancy had felt any woman would gladly worship. His complexion was not fresh, it was brick red, and his neck, which once had looked touching, fragile almost, was thick, as he leant

176

over the table. And why did he care so much for his own opinion and so little for hers? Nancy stared at Andrew. Was this how others saw him? All those friends who never seemed to envy Nancy the way she felt they ought to. Friends who had never cared over-much for Andrew's opinions, and whose eyes had begun to wander as he gave them his views on the state of the nation's defence or the handling of the economy or the mounting price of diesel. Friends she had thought foolish and undeserving and who kept making little remarks like, 'Why don't you let him get his own lunch for once, it wouldn't hurt him,' or, 'He does like the sound of his own voice, doesn't he?'

She filled the sink with hot water, adding a dash of Fairy Liquid, and stood watching the bubbles form and grow like her anger. She shook herself, but the feeling didn't go, it got worse, bubbling up her chest and into her head, making it fuzzy, itchy inside, as if her brain were wrapped in an angora rug.

It had happened when she was a little girl, suddenly and without warning. Nancy's little moods, her parents had called them, but Nancy knew she had frightened her fluffy bunny of a mother. Like the time when she had insisted Nancy wore her plaid wool skirt to a party when Nancy had set her heart on going in her best summer frock with tiny sprigs of yellow flowers all over the brushed cotton.

177

'Nancy you just can't and that's that,' her mother had said with unusual firmness. Then at the sight of what she called, 'that look', she had added, 'It's not just that it's wrong for the season. Look at you, a great big girl trying to squeeze yourself into a pretty little dress like that. Your friends will laugh at you.' Vicious, fluffy white bunny. Nancy had glared her mother from the room. There had been the most tremendous fuss later when Nancy's mother discovered her silk frock, the one she had saved two years' worth of coupons for, draped across her bed like a huge doily; there was not a foot of that silk that did not have a perfect little circle or triangle cut through it.

Nancy plunged the plates into the hot washing-up water until they were covered with white froth, then she began scrubbing at them with the nylon brush, its bristles splayed and grubby like an old toothbrush. By the time the dishes were sitting draining on the sink, she was able to turn round and offer Andrew coffee in an almost normal voice.

Ten minutes later she set off for the vicarage, where the evening's meeting was being held. As she drove the short distance along the dark main street, she still felt out of sorts, disconnected, as if she were a dinghy drifting further and further from its moorings. Relax, she told herself, you're not yourself tonight, it'll pass. She relaxed her grip on the steering wheel, and the single diamond in her engagement ring flashed in the lights of a passing car. She had wept when Andrew first put that on her finger.

She began harnessing pretty images to her mind. Like a doubting nun surrounding herself with the trappings of her faith—bible, crucifix, rosary, a hairshirt maybe—she called up the memory of Andrew on the rugby field, the day of their engagement, scoring a try. She remembered how, as he passed her on the way to the dressing-room, sweaty and exhilarated, he had grabbed her round the waist in front of everyone and kissed her. She thought of his distress when their first child died within hours of being born. Like whispers from the devil, Andrew's words as good as blaming Nancy for the child's deformed head and weak heart pushed into her memory, but she whacked them off again with the picture of Andrew on their wedding day. Nervous, grinning, handsome, marrying her, plain awkward Nancy Roberts, and making love to her that night, his hands wandering across her body as if it were a journey worth making. 'Darling Andrew.' Hot and flushed, she smiled to herself as she parked the little Fiat in the vicarage drive. 'Darling Andrew, I do love you so.' She climbed out of the car, taking a couple of deep breaths and smoothing down her check wool skirt before ringing the doorbell.

As she stepped inside the narrow hall she was met by a strong smell of frying onions and some spices she recognized but could not put a name to. 'I didn't know you were a cook Ted,' she said, looking towards the closed kitchen door.

Ted, receiving in his clerical shirt sleeves and with a tea towel slung across his shoulder, hustled her through into the sitting-room, saying he'd always had an interest in ethnic food. 'You're the first to arrive, but the others should be along any minute. If you'll excuse me for a moment,' Ted pushed a chair towards her and disappeared from the room.

'Our local magistrate and busybody,' Ted smiled at Veena, who was clearing away the last of the supper dishes. 'We need to stay well clear of her.' As she reached for the last of the dirty plates on the table, he put his hand lightly on hers. 'Better leave that. She could hear.'

Veena looked up at him and he pulled his hand away as if stung. 'Right then,' he said, clearing his throat. 'Now you're sure you are going to be all right, stuck in here all evening?'

Veena smiled at him. 'Of course I am. Thanks for getting all these,' she nodded towards the heap of magazines that lay in front of her on the table: *Company, Just Seventeen, Hello!* and *Bella*.

Ted had felt a right fool going into Smith's in Fairfield for them, but he had been touched when Veena explained to him that they had been the favourite reading of her English pen pal.

'Then you must promise me to read some of my favourite books,' he had said to her. 'Your English is well up to it.' In fact, he thought, her English was remarkably good. She was obviously intelligent, already knowledgeable on current affairs and politics, although, he had noticed, strangely awkward when it came to even the most basic household chores. She had become quite agitated at first when he had asked her to cook a traditional meal from her home region. Her older sister, it turned out, had jealously guarded her position as lady of the house after their mother died, hardly allowing her younger sister inside the kitchen. So Ted cooked for them both, and he had put a lot of effort into tonight's meal, prepared from a recipe he had cut from a newspaper. 'Does it taste like home?' he had asked and she, with her mouth full, had nodded and smiled.

'You have fun then, with your magazines,' Ted said a little awkwardly, before disappearing into the sitting-room.

By eight the other two trustees had arrived. Ted tried to look relaxed, crossing and uncrossing his legs as he leant back in the hard chair. The woollen upholstery scratched right through his thin polyester trousers as Derek Campbell read out the list of events that had been held in the village hall since their last meeting back in July. Now and then, through the drone of voices, Ted thought he could hear Veena moving round the kitchen; he even

181

imagined he heard her turn the pages of one of those ridiculous magazines, and he looked sharply at the others. But they carried on, seemingly having heard nothing.

'Let me make the coffee tonight,' Nancy offered halfway through the meeting.

He had forgotten to offer them coffee. They expected coffee, with biscuits. He shot out of the chair. 'I'll go, I'm sorry, so engrossed...' Ted hurried from the room.

Veena seemed not to have moved from her place at the kitchen table, and she barely lifted her head from the magazine. 'Coffee. They all want coffee.' Ted muttered.

By ten o'clock the meeting was over, with a formal proposal for the next one to be held at the same place three months hence.

'Now let me help with those,' Nancy was up and gathering the cups and saucers before Ted had time to stop her. 'We can't go on meeting at the vicarage if we can't do our little bit. And I'll bring the biscuits next time.' Nancy headed for the door with the tray.

'No, wait!' Ted leapt in front of her blocking her way. Nancy took a step back, her lips opening up into a cyclamen O.

'What I mean is, there's no need.' Ted bared his teeth in a smile. 'Here let me.' He snatched the tray from Nancy. 'Now where did you leave your coats?' He felt their eyes on him as he bumbled round the narrow hall, the cups on the tray rattling with every step.

'Well 'bye then, Vicar,' Derek Campbell said as he, Nancy Sanderson and Ron Brown formed a mini stampede to get out of the front door and into the clear, sane air.

As the front door closed, Ted leant against it with his full weight, half expecting it to spring open and Nancy Sanderson to bob up like the indestructible monster in a horror film. He stayed with his back against the door for a good five minutes and then, when his pulse rate had returned to normal, he put the tray down on the hall table and locked the door, before going into the kitchen.

'Everything OK?' Veena asked, with one eye still on the story she was reading.

'Yes, yes fine.' Ted decided not to let on how close they'd been to discovery. The poor girl had been through enough. There was no need to alarm her. In fact, Ted thought, as he watched her tuck into another chocolate chip cookie from the blue-and-white Paddington Bear biscuit tin in front of her, Veena was remarkably stable for someone with her appalling history. Naturally she did not like to dwell on her past. Even now, weeks after she first arrived on his doorstep, he knew precious little of what suffering had led her to leave her home and family to try her luck as an illegal immigrant in Britain. When he asked her, her face closed and she changed the subject. Ted gazed across the room at her as he plunged the cups and saucers in the basin. She was putting on weight, he was sure of it. Her face was rounder for a start, and he had noticed that she undid the top button of her jeans when she sat down. He smiled delightedly as the girl helped herself to yet another biscuit. Chocolate chip and those little round things with a dollop of jam in the middle were her favourites. She could demolish a whole packet at a time. He dried the cups one by one before switching the kettle back on. 'Tea?'

Veena stretched and yawned. 'I think I'll go out for a bit.'

Ted turned to her, frowning. 'Again? What do you do on these night walks? I've told you, even Tollymead isn't safe for a young girl on her own. We've got our own dangers here in Britain you know. Violence and poverty are not confined to—'

Veena got up and planted a kiss on Ted's thinning hair. 'You're sweet, but I'm OK. I just like to get out of the house, get some fresh air.'

Ted sighed. 'I suppose I can't stop you. But I really would prefer it if you'd let me come along too.'

'I've told you, I enjoy being on my own.' Veena got a far-away look in her eyes. 'Being alone, not always surrounded by relatives, was one of the things I longed for back home. I even shared my bed with my two little brothers.' She turned her eyes on him. 'You don't know what it's like to be watched all the time, how one longs to just be left alone.' She smiled. 'So

184

don't worry. Besides, you shouldn't be seen with me. It's dangerous enough for you with all the people coming and going in this place. Who'd ever be a vicar?'

'Who?' Ted thought bitterly as the door slammed shut behind her. Since Veena had arrived in his life he had grown even more disenchanted with his work as Vicar of Tollymead and Greenway. His two years had made absolutely no difference to life in the parish. The congregation in the two churches had neither increased nor fallen off, the same faces met him at each service, their expressions suggesting placid forbearance. Vicars came and vicars went, he felt them thinking, but Sunday morning was for church. But now at last he was doing something. For the first time since he came to Tollymead, he was doing more than waste his time and the church's money. He had got in touch with the Organization through a Methodist minister friend, and they had written back with a list of clergy sympathetic to the cause. They had suggested the girl be moved as soon as possible, as no-one should stay in the same safe house for more than a month. By then the risk of discovery increased dramatically. In the meantime, the Organization's legal advisers would start looking into her chances of being allowed to remain in the country. But Veena had become so distressed at the suggestion of moving that, not unwillingly, Ted had said she could stay for a little while longer. Dismissal from the church, prison, what did he care? He was at last doing God's work.

*   *   *

Veena hurried down Vicarage Lane and up to the car that was parked on the curb. With a quick look round to check that she was not watched, she opened the passenger door and stepped into the front seat, slamming the door closed as the car started up its engine.

Tollymead: *Police believe that children playing with fireworks were responsible for the fire at one of the outbuildings at Glebe House on Bonfire Night. Luckily the fire brigade arrived within minutes, saving much of the building, used as a workshop, and its contents.*

True to form, Tollymead residents have already begun the task of restoration. Filing away a freshly typed document, American scriptwriter Anne Havesham told the Diary:

'A fire destroyed my father's career. A brilliant man, an academic, he had been working for five years on his thesis on "The Influence of the Digestive System in the Lives and Works of American Artists", (apparently Henry James was but one of many great writers suffering from chronic constipation). The thesis, which would have led to a university post, was only days from completion when a fire in his study destroyed his only copy. After that he was a broken man, remaining for the rest of his life a teacher in a small town high school.'

With the memory of her father still haunting her, Ms Havesham, once news of the fire reached her, wasted no time in offering her help. There is still work to be done, copying notes from damaged files and

*sorting seed trays, so anyone who can spare
some time will be most welcome.*

CHAPTER FOURTEEN

Liberty had been helping Evelyn clear up after
the fire, but when she arrived on Saturday
afternoon she found several people already
assembled in the sitting-room, working away
like over-grown Santa's helpers, typing,
sorting, cutting. Evelyn herself was perched on
top of some steps, in the adjoining library, a
box file in her hand. Seeing Liberty, she gave
her a wave with a paper, its edges blackened
like a slice of burnt toast. 'I'm afraid some of
Father's books will have to go to make room
for my stuff. Isn't this marvellous though? All
these kind people turning up out of the blue to
give me a hand, and I thought it would have to
be just us and Oscar struggling on. Whoever
would have thought it of Tollymead?'

'I don't know why you should say that.'
Nancy Sanderson, who had arrived with the
vicar in tow, looked annoyed.

'Pardon me,' Neville Pyke, carrying a stack
of box files, brushed past.

'I came straight over from court,' Nancy
said to Liberty. 'But I see that after all this, the
Havesham woman herself hasn't bothered to
turn up.'

188

'What about the Havesham woman?' Evelyn called from the top of the steps.

'It was in the Village Diary.' As Evelyn looked blank, Nancy continued in an exaggerated clear voice, 'You know, in *The Tribune*, your nephew's paper. Didn't you see? Some sort of appeal on your behalf.'

Evelyn climbed down gingerly from the steps, a stack of paperbacks clutched to her chest. 'I only take the paper because Oscar's editing it, but I can't say I read it cover to cover.' Remembering Victoria, who sat at the other end of the sitting-room, leafing through a copy of *The National Geographic*, she added quickly, 'It's got a darn sight better since he took over though, I must say.'

Victoria turned and looked up. 'Hi Liberty,' then she turned to Evelyn.

'You should read the Diary. I wouldn't know half the things that go on in this village without it. It was quite sweet, actually. Whoever it is had put in a whole piece about how Oscar saved the day, being first at the scene of the fire, and all that. Of course he made them edit it out, you know what he's like, Evelyn.' She uncoiled from the seat. 'Anyone for coffee? How many are we? One, two, three, four, five...' She counted them out with her red-tipped index finger in the air, '...nine,' and sauntered out to the kitchen.

Liberty looked round for somewhere to put her portable typewriter, as Evelyn stomped across the room to her with a heap of papers.

'Could you be a brick and save what you can of these notes, and these too if you've got time. I literally pulled them from the flames.' The second pile of papers looked as if they had donned combat fatigue, the white paper mottled with parchment-yellow and brown. Most of the writing was visible, however, and Liberty began to copy down Evelyn's wayward hand, turning the damaged pages carefully; the heat had made them as fragile as dried flowers. Victoria returned with a tray. Liberty took a mug commemorating, rather optimistically she thought, the Coronation of Edward VIII. 'Where did you get this?' She raised it above her head for Evelyn to see.

Evelyn looked up from a stack of books. 'Oh that, I got it years ago. A local pottery was flogging them off cheap. They had rather miscalculated on that one. I'm not sure it's not the last, though, all the others seem to have got broken.'

Victoria looked sharply at Evelyn. 'They could be worth something, you know. It's a shame you broke them. I have to say, my mother positively imprinted on me that you can't be too careful with your things.'

'Oh yes,' Evelyn said, 'you can.'

'Oscar's very interested in memorabilia,' Victoria carried on, undeterred.

'Hideous word that: memorabilia,' Evelyn said dreamily. 'Like authorization, or implementation, which always makes me think of something rather intimate you do to cows.'

Victoria was not really listening, Liberty thought, and her lovely face seemed oddly vacant in repose, as if it were a photograph rather than the woman herself. She stopped typing and asked quietly, 'Victoria, what made Oscar leave Fleet Street or Wapping or whatever and come down here?'

Victoria did not seem to mind being asked, just surprised. 'I don't really know. He had some sort of a crisis,' she lowered her voice to a whisper. 'He was in a terrible state, crying and everything. You wouldn't think that, looking at him, would you? I mean he seems so in control.'

'Oh absolutely,' Liberty said, feeling uncomfortably like she was betraying a confidence just by listening.

'Anyway,' Victoria continued, 'he said he needed a change. I didn't mind. I was fed up with London anyway. And the house prices in town ... I mean, the difference between what you get for your money down here and up there. Anyway he's fine now. I expect it was some sort of mid-life crisis. I told him at the time, "don't look back." I mean you can't change anything, so what's the good? Live for today, that's my motto.'

Victoria, Liberty thought, lacked curiosity.

'So where is *Ms* Havesham?' Nancy asked.

'She's no doubt busy with her television

show,' Neville said. 'Who knows, we might all end up on telly ourselves. Mrs Pyke is very excited about it all. She's very keen on television, Mrs Pyke. No, a busy lady like Miss Havesham, we must make allowances.'

Evelyn didn't seem to be listening, but she nodded agreement all the same. Liberty nodded too. For some reason that she could not understand, she saw Oscar before her, naked, about to lie down on top of her in bed, as she nodded. Maybe that was what head banging was all about: inducing erotic fantasies. She thought she might ask Johnny next time he called.

Ted Brain, who had worked diligently on a stack of water-damaged papers, got up to leave. 'Busy evening ahead,' he muttered nervously to the room in general as he made his way sideways through the room. Someone said, 'It's getting dark,' and as the light was switched on, Oscar's naked body evaporated. Liberty sighed and carried on with her typing. Shortly after that a couple of the ladies began to leave, muttering about tea and supper to prepare. No-one would say they did not care to walk through the village in the dark. Ever since Liberty moved back down to Tollymead, she had been waiting for someone to admit to being frightened of being alone in their house at night, or worried about a late walk home from a party or Evensong, the way everyone did in London. But no-one ever did. 'This is the country dear!' In fact, Liberty thought sourly, they would step over a battered corpse in their sturdy walking shoes to proclaim how safe it was. To really shine, you should say you never locked your back door.

'Street lights,' Liberty said now. 'That's what we need, good, bright street lights.'

Several outraged faces turned on her. 'Street lights!' repeated one of the ladies, a woman whose name Liberty did not know, but who always ran the White Elephant stall at the Summer Fête. 'This is the country, dear.'

Liberty looked around her with a contented smile, she liked predictability. 'I take the same view on roads as I do on Christmas trees,' she said, 'the brighter the better. Refinement should only be carried so far.'

Neville put down a stack of neatly copied notes. 'Mrs Pyke would like street lights. It's comforting when you lie awake at night, to look out and see a light outside your window.' No-one took any notice of him. Then poor Neville did not really belong, Liberty thought, he was just indispensable, like an expatriate worker in Kuwait.

'You know, that's just how I feel,' she said to him. 'I'd love to have a light outside my window at night.'

'Well then you should live in a town,' Nancy said. ''Bye Evelyn. I hope I've been of some help.' She turned round again in the doorway. 'Maybe you should take this accident as a sign

193

to slow down. You've done your bit. And more...' Liberty heard her mutter.

Liberty was the last to leave. She stood with Evelyn in the middle of the room, surveying the afternoon's work. Freshly typed pages lay stacked on the large, round table by the window. By the bookcase stood ten box files, each containing notes and news clips that had been rescued from the flames and from the water, all sorted through and filed. 'I'm touched,' Evelyn said. 'Damn it, I'm touched.'

There was a knock on the door and Liberty went to answer. It was Oscar.

'Victoria said she was going to come here to help,' he said stepping inside. 'I thought I'd pick her up.'

'Oh I'm sorry, she will be upset to have missed you. She got a lift with Nancy Sanderson. She was worried she wouldn't have supper ready for you.'

'Oh.' Oscar did not move for the door. 'She's lovely isn't she?' he said suddenly. He could as well have been saying he had a bit of a cold, Liberty thought, if one was listening just to the tone of his voice.

'Yes, yes, she really is,' Liberty nodded, adding so as not to disappoint him, 'And so nice too.' She would have liked to ask his opinion about how far one should go in lying to spare someone's feelings, but this of course, was not the moment.

'Yes, she really is a very nice person. I don't

194

know what I've done to deserve someone like her.' Oscar sounded as if he took exception to such preferential treatment.

Evelyn called from upstairs, 'Come inside and help yourself to a drink, you know where everything is. I'll be down in a minute.'

In the kitchen, Oscar poured them both a gin and tonic. 'I mustn't stay,' he said, promptly sitting down at the kitchen table.

'No, no of course not.' Liberty sidled onto the chair opposite.

Oscar stared down into his glass, then with a small smile he looked across at her. He really had such sad eyes—beautiful, sad, cornflower blue eyes. If I didn't know better, she thought, I'd say he is as unhappy as I am.

'Thank you for helping Evelyn,' he said. 'Sunday tomorrow, so I'll be able to come and do some carrying.'

'There were about ten of us here today, would you believe it?'

'I noticed the call for help in the Village Diary,' Oscar said. 'I didn't think Tollymead went in for this sort of neighbourly act.'

'Well it doesn't,' Liberty said. 'You get to read the Diary, do you?'

'I see everything that goes into the paper,' Oscar said with a small smile.

'Don't you get bored?' The question slipped out, and she regretted it as soon as it was said. 'What I mean is, it's all very different from being foreign editor of a big national paper.'

Feeling the heat in the puckered skin on her cheek, she said quickly, 'Of course it must be enormously rewarding, running your own paper. Local papers perform an invaluable service to the community and you are right at the heart of it—'

Oscar seemed amused by her embarrassment. 'I enjoy the work. I needed the change.' He looked up at her with those bright blue eyes, leaving Liberty wondering if he really was as unaware of his looks as he seemed to be. She realized he was speaking to her again.

'Sorry, what was that?' She pulled a little face. Oscar's grin got wider.

'I asked,' he repeated mildly, 'if you thought we might yet turn Tollymead into "Ambridge"?'

Liberty thought for a moment. 'I don't know that it's not just a last stand,' she said finally. 'Like a family of grazing microwavers solemnly munching their way through the Sunday roast with the telly silenced in a corner. Just death throes.'

'It's always easier to create a new set of values than to retrieve old ones,' Oscar said. 'Your average punter probably thinks the nice piece of Brazilian rain forest mahogany in the sitting-room is a worse crime than a spot of Saturday-night-and-nothing-to-do granny bashing.' He grinned at her. 'Can't you just see some smart bastard in court: "I beg you to consider, m'lud, that rape does less damage to the ozone layer than farting."'

He made Liberty laugh, and as he drained his glass and stood up, she said, 'Don't go.' Looking down, she muttered, 'I mean, would you like another drink?'

He put his hand briefly on her shoulder. 'I'm driving.' In the hall he called up to Evelyn, 'I'm off, but I'll be over tomorrow.' He turned to Liberty and said quietly, 'Will you be here?'

'Yes,' Liberty smiled at him. 'I'll be here.'

She stood looking after him, feeling as if she had just missed the marching band, as, brasses gleaming and flags waving, they turned the corner out of sight. Calling goodbye to Evelyn, she walked the few yards home. She boiled herself an egg and sat down to read a book of interviews with famous authors. She needed to cry.

* * *

Victoria greeted Oscar in the doorway, dressed in an ankle-length fur coat she had acquired long before she even met him. One of the first things she had said to him was how unfair it was that now she finally owned a fur coat, wearing it had become as antisocial as dishing up under-cooked chicken at a dinner party. Then, he had thought her complaint charming. Now he just hated the coat. 'Going out?' he asked, trying to sound as if he cared.

197

Victoria smiled, a slow, long smile as she opened the coat, letting it slip off her shoulders and down on to the floor so that she stood there, naked but for her high-heeled pumps.

CHAPTER FIFTEEN

'It'll be "Jennifer's Diary" before we know it,' Alistair Partridge, the assistant editor of *The Tribune* handed the latest Diary entry from Tollymead to Oscar.

It was heart-warming to see so many people turning up to help Evelyn Brooke restore her files and work notes. Decades of research, much of it to be used in Miss Brooke's forthcoming book on organic farming, is now saved and in good order.

Are we dipping into the past and retrieving old community values, or are we waking up to the future of a new, caring decade? Are we looping the loop? No matter, what counts is that in Tollymead we care.

That happiness can come through helping others is not a new notion, but is one that seems increasingly forgotten these days. But newly-arrived advertising executive Laura Brown, one of Miss Brooke's helpers, found love across a stack of singed documents. At the opposite end of the large rosewood table

198

sat Oliver Bliss, marine biologist and amateur artist. By the end of the afternoon, Oliver was so taken by Laura that he begged to be allowed to paint her portrait.

'She looked like a land-locked mermaid, with her rippling hair and sea-green dress. I just had to paint her,' Oliver said. Now, just two weeks later, Laura and Oliver have announced their engagement. Everyone in Tollymead is delighted, including the two ladies of the village's Neighbourhood Watch scheme who almost made a citizen's arrest on the couple as they enjoyed a romantic walk together.

Phyllida Medley invited fifteen small boys and girls from the village into her kitchen on Saturday to show them the basics of baking. When I popped in for a cup of tea, they were just taking trays of Chelsea buns from the oven. Outside, it was one of those still, grey winter days, when the world seems wrapped in mist and you feel any sound could carry to the next county. While I warmed my hands by the Aga, Phyllida told me she feels quite evangelical about teaching young people to cook.

'Cooking and eating well is an art form, and like all art it adds another dimension to our lives. Now just compare an individually prepared TV-dinner with a proper family meal: some vegetables roasted with garlic and *oil, a bowl of pasta with a tuna, black olive and tomato sauce and a nice glass of Chianti for the grown-ups.'*

When I objected that working mothers don't have time to prepare that kind of meal, Phyllida replied sensibly that that was exactly the reason why she was teaching the children to cook.

While we are on the subject of tea and buns, if you like to use loose leaves but don't like to use your teeth as a strainer for the disposal of the tea leaves afterwards, using a metal spice ball is the answer. You'll find them in most good kitchen shops and a certain well known kitchen mail-order firm.

Oscar was smiling as he handed the neatly typed page back to Alistair. 'It's different. Let's see how it goes for the next few weeks. There's a lot of interest in village life and in my experience, the more personal the information, the better. You know better than I the problems of finding decent contributors with the money we can offer them, so we're in no position to turn down free copy. No, let it run for now.'

His phone rang. It was Victoria saying she was going to her writing class so could he pick up some cold roast beef and potato salad from the delicatessen.

The class had been discussing Neville's *DIY*

Manual For the Senior Citizen, and the use of dialogue in fiction. 'Anyone got anything they'd like to read out?' Liberty asked.

'I've got a little piece.' Victoria waved a black-and-silver striped folder at Liberty.

'Go ahead,' Liberty nodded and smiled.

One thing that united the eleven members of Liberty's class was their self-consciousness when reading out their work. The words stumbled from their lips, bumping into each other in their eagerness to get away, but Victoria, reading her story about a teenager on her first date, seemed to taste every word and find it to her liking. She paused at artful intervals and led the class in laughter at appropriate places. It was a story revelling in period pains and untimely zits, with everyone drinking a lot of black coffee, but it was an effective story, holding the attention of the class. Even Neville listened with obvious interest and almost no embarrassment.

Victoria finished reading. The consensus was that it was a lovely story. Liberty said she thought it was very good too, but maybe it was worth looking again at one or two of the characters who were just a little bit stock-in-trade.

'Oh I can't change anything,' Victoria said, 'it's been taken by "Blue Jeans" already. It'll be out in next month's issue.'

Liberty took a deep breath, getting pumped up with envy. 'Right,' she said. 'Excellent, congratulations.'

'She'll be taking over the class next, won't she Liberty?' Melanie, the solicitor's secretary, giggled.

'Yes, absolutely, why not,' Liberty nodded manically. Keep laughing, she told herself, envy is so ugly. Soar above your baser instincts on a gale of mirth, ha ruddy ha. She finished laughing and told Victoria how proud they all were of her. 'Now get cracking and produce some more. You'll have a career in writing before you know it.'

'I'm not sure,' Victoria shrugged her shoulders. 'There's so much else I like to do. I quite enjoy writing but I can't really see myself spending all my time on it the way you used to. Life is for living, you know; for doing.'

Liberty remained at her desk as the class packed up and trickled out into the late November gloom. Dear God, she thought, how could you? How could you give me running shoes and no feet? How could you fill me with passion and coat me with incompetence? She shook herself and rose from the chair, assembling her books and notes, not really looking at what she was doing.

By the time she got back home it was dark, but she grabbed a torch and, switching on the small lantern by the back door, she went outside. Shivering in her thin black jumper and short skirt, she stared across the large square that was to be her vegetable garden, staked out already, waiting to be dug. She stepped out of the circle of lantern light, her stubby heels sinking into the lawn. Switching on the torch, she pointed it at the ground like Johnny had shown her long ago, to see it alive with worms out for the night, diving into holes for cover as they were hit by the light. It was winter now, but there was nothing dead about the garden. It was full of life and movement, just like a decomposing body.

Annoyed with herself, she turned and hurried inside. There was something wrong with her imagery. Her garden was supposed to be a thing of beauty and solace, not a corpse. Enjoying the trail of mud (clay with a bit of green sand running through it, according to Evelyn) that she left behind on the carpet, she threw herself down on the sofa. Her mind was cluttered with ballast these days, unused pictures and scraps of conversations that had been snatched from their context and stored. Stored but not used, shaken but not stirred, mumbled, jumbled, scrambled. She pressed her hands against her temples. Her head felt weighed down, like the pockets of a small boy who couldn't stop picking up all those useful things like chalky stones and bits of string and the rings from coke cans.

She closed her eyes, but after a while she opened them again to look at her watch. It was a quarter to six. At six o'clock she could pour herself a glass of wine. She had begun to look forward to that glass in the evening, but at six, not before. Before would be sluttish. She lay back down on the sofa, looking at her feet in their muddy lace-ups dangling over the armrests. She was so ridiculous she might as well have bought those red Dr Martens she had liked since she saw a friend of Johnny's wear them in the summer. The ones that laced right up the ankles. She looked at her watch, and she kept on looking every few minutes. The moment six o'clock came, she was up and into the kitchen, grabbing the bottle of Australian burgundy that she had left on top of the cupboard by the kitchen table. She skewered the cork with the opener, and managed as usual to leave a deposit of crumbs round the neck of the bottle. She fetched the dishcloth and wiped them off before pouring herself a glass. Everyone knew you had to watch out once you started drinking on your own, and without even the excuse of a meal, so after a moment's thought she fetched an open packet of stale peanuts and tipped what was left into a small bowl.

Sitting down at the table, she could hear Victoria's treacly voice reading her soon-to-be-published story. She splashed some more wine into her glass. 'Supper,' she said. She had some more wine. It was not a very good wine, but after a while she got to like it. She gave the bottle an affectionate look and heaved herself out of the kitchen chair. She peered inside the fridge. Tinned herring: out of date. She put it back on the shelf. Ah, ham! No, that too was past its sell-by date and dark-edged, like a card of condolence. Right at the back she found a lone egg. 'Right you little bugger,' she reached in and grabbed it. She decided to fry the egg. Once that was done she splatted it down on a limp piece of ready-sliced bread. She brought the plate over to the table and sat down. She looked at the egg. The egg seemed to look back at her. Liberty raised her knife and fork. She shook her head. 'No? You'd rather I didn't? OK.' She grabbed the wine bottle instead, about to pour herself some more, but stopped, bottle in mid-air. She was meant to limit herself to two glasses a night, three on special occasions. Then this was a special occasion. How often, after all, did she corrode with envy? Holding the bottle up against the light she saw there was only a glass or so left. She got tearful. It was so sad, so very like life itself; no sooner had you got into your stride when suddenly the end was in sight. Bloody typical. She buried her head in her hands, but after a while she got bored with that. She squinted at the bottle. Maybe there was more left than she thought. There was only one way of finding out. She managed to fill the glass and drank it quickly before she had time to change her mind.

She smiled. There was a silver lining, indeed there was, she had just spotted it, a little sliver of glitter at the edge of the dirty great black cloud: Victoria could not appear on *Wogan*, no siree, *Wogan* had finished its run, stopped, ceased to transmit. Then she got sad again; there was still *Pebble Mill at One*. The thought upset her so that she had to pour herself some more wine. She emptied the last of the bottle into her glass and wandered through to the sitting-room. She had the oddest sensation, as if she were walking on a giant marshmallow. She peered down at the carpet, just to make sure. No, it was the same old green carpet.

She put on some music. 'Sing along with Placido,' she crooned, waltzing round the room. What an artist, old Placido! Puccini too. So why not me? She stopped in the middle of the room. Her mind seemed to clear like a summer's day, with brilliant thoughts breaking through like rays of sunshine. What had she been thinking of, giving up her passion, turning her back on the very purpose of her existence simply because of a few years of rejection? Crazy! She hurried back into the kitchen and on her way to the desk she stopped and picked up the empty bottle. Giving it a disapproving look, she turned it upside down over her head, feeling the last drops scatter in her hair. With a slow grin spreading across her face she sauntered over to the computer and switched it on. The faint humming of the machine was like the whisperings of a lover, and she caressed the grainy plastic, letting her fingers run down to the keyboard. She had the germ of a story already in her head. The first sentence came swiftly, without effort: "I always was an ugly little batard..." correction, "bastard".

She worked well into the morning. At around midnight she had pulled the cork from an already open bottle of white wine in the fridge. It was all right to have some, she told herself sternly, after all, today already was the next day. A new, hitherto wine-free day. Now and then she would get up to stretch her legs and change the music that was on so loud, it reached into the kitchen.

At four o'clock in the morning she had finished the first chapter—the speed of it! Peering at the keyboard, she pressed the Save button. There were many people, she thought, as she plopped the empty bottle into the wastepaper basket, who would go to bed after so many hours of intensive work, forgetting to Save. But not she. No way. She gave the computer a little pat before switching it off. Upstairs she crept into bed and fell instantly asleep, vaguely aware that apart from a broad smile that refused to leave her lips, she was still wearing her socks.

CHAPTER SIXTEEN

'Start the day with a song,' Liberty croaked, avoiding her face in the bathroom mirror. She poured herself some dank-tasting water from the tap and drank it greedily.

For two weeks her routine had not varied. She got up late, her mouth dry, her head pounding, and made herself a pot of tea and a slice of toast. At around eleven she began work on the translation of a series of three children's books, stopping only for a quick lunch. At six she slumped in front of the television with a glass of wine and some bread and cheese or an egg. Around nine she got up and went into the kitchen, settling down at the computer with a bottle of wine at her side, ready for the real day to begin.

She had never worked so well, with such ease and fluency. It was as if a huge funnel hung above her, its point right on top of the keyboard. Men and women, houses and gardens, love and sacrifice, all came tumbling through the giant funnel in a stream of flowing sentences, down to the tips of her fingers. Sometimes the excitement of creation was so acute that it felt like a pain in her gut and she would have to get up from the desk and pace the floor, taking deep breaths, before she could settle down again. She never printed out and never read the previous night's work. Nothing was allowed to break the flow. Around four in the morning she would turn off the computer and fall into bed, her last thought often being that there was no-one now on God's earth she would rather be than herself.

In the bathroom she brushed her teeth until her gums bled. She had gone to bed without washing again and woken up with a mouth that felt as if one of Tollymead's protected belfry bats had died there during the night. She showered, and as she dressed the phone rang. Margaret, a friend from Everton, called and wanted to know how she was. Liberty had no sooner assured her that she was well and hung up, when the doorbell rang. It was Evelyn wanting to know if she had some good beef dripping for the birds.

'You look awful.' Evelyn pushed her face close to Liberty's. 'What's up?'

Liberty blinked in the clear December sunlight. 'Nothing. Nothing is up.' She stood aside to let Evelyn in. 'In fact, things couldn't be less up.' She paused for a moment, having confused even herself. 'Which isn't to say that things are down, because they're not, in fact they're quite the opp—'

'Do stop twittering dear.'

'Oh. Right. Of course.'

'Victoria said your class was cancelled last week and the week before.'

'Ahh that.' Liberty shifted her weight from

one foot to another. 'Just a cold that's all, two colds really, one after the other. Or maybe it was the same cold returning...' Catching Evelyn's eye she said quickly, 'I'll be there tomorrow.' But the days seemed to come round like the baskets in a Ferris Wheel and until Evelyn reminded her, she had completely forgotten that it was Wednesday's turn again.

'Well, as I said, you look dreadful. Come and have dinner with me tonight.'

'Can't,' Liberty shook her head, knowing Evelyn was far too polite to ask why not.

*   *   *

In class, the next day, Neville Pyke peered at her over his reading glasses. 'Oh dear, you really have been under the weather haven't you? Flu was it?'

Liberty nodded. Settling at her desk she asked the class, 'Anyone brought a piece to discuss?'

Tobias Fry, who had lost his job as manager of an electrical shop, waved his hand in the air. He had started off wanting to write spy stories in the mode of Frederick Forsyth, but with no Berlin Wall or Soviet Union he had problems with his plots. Instead he had decided to try his hand at comic articles. He read out a story set in a supermarket; all the characters other than the un-named hero were called after their style of dress. 'As the Pink Shell Suit disappeared

210

round the next aisle I grabbed my trolley and hurried off in pursuit, almost knocking over a Green Puffa on my way...'

Liberty's head ached while through the pain came line after line of Tobias's story of droll happenings, all involving people with colourful clothes. With her eyes fixed on him in an interested manner, Liberty poured herself some water from a flask at her side. The story came to an end.

'Good use of your visual senses. You've remembered my advice about using active verbs, always active verbs,' Liberty intoned. She wondered why, with these virtues, Tobias's work was so excruciating. She stifled a sigh and turned to Victoria. 'Have you got anything new you'd like to show us?'

Victoria shook her head. 'No, nothing new I'm afraid. Sorry.' She gave a regretful shrug of her shoulders. 'I've been really busy lately. I just don't think it's in my nature to sit cooped up on my own for hours on end.' She smiled. 'I remember when I was small and in hospital with scarlet fever, all the staff called me Little Miss Sunshine...' catching Liberty's look she added, 'after the Mr Men and Little Misses books, you know.'

'Little Miss sodding Sunshine,' Liberty muttered, 'I don't believe it.' Aloud she said, 'Anyone else?'

*   *   *

Later that day, Hamish looked at her in much the same way as Evelyn and her class had earlier, as if he didn't know whether to pity her or hose her down. 'You should go and have yourself checked out,' he said. 'Your eyes are puffy and you've put on weight as well.'

He had called in unannounced at six o'clock and now he sat in the kitchen, a mug of tea clasped between his liver-spotted hands.

'I'm fine,' Liberty said, 'seldom been finer actually.' She was about to say she did not like the look of Hamish much either. For the first time in his life he seemed his age, nearly seventy. 'I've just been working rather hard,' she added. But she did not tell him about the novel, not yet. 'What about you?' she asked instead.

Hamish looked up from fiddling with his un-lit pipe. 'They're getting rid of the old man. Falling numbers, unpaid fees. They're letting younger staff go, so I won't escape, not this time. The headmaster told me as much himself the other day.' He sighed and shook his head. 'And at my age, I won't even have the satisfaction of adding to the unemployment figures.'

Her father retiring? He had been teaching on borrowed time for the last five years, but still ... Tollymead Manor without Hamish— worse, Hamish without Tollymead Manor. 'Surely not,' she said weakly. 'They couldn't do without you.'

212

It was Hamish's turn to smile. 'There are very few people in this world who are indispensable; I'm not one of them,' he said. He was supervising prep that evening and he left before Liberty had a chance to work out how best to deal with her father's sudden inclination to face the truth. She was sure that his unfailing good humour and positive outlook on life were possible only because he never saw things for what they were, but for what he wanted them to be. But if he was going to start facing the truth all of a sudden, what would happen to him then? Liberty sighed and wandered across to the looking-glass on the wall behind the aspidistra. Hamish was right; she looked disgusting. She peered at the pale face that looked back at her with blood-shot eyes. The whites of her eyes had little yellow lumps on them, and her hair looked as if it had been rinsed in paint stripper. No matter. She bared her teeth in a grimace and turned away. By the end of the night she would have completed the first half of her story. Only a couple of hours' work, and she would at last allow herself to print out and read. If it was as good as she thought it was, maybe she would let her old agent see it.

She went upstairs to run a bath, a bottle of wine and a glass in her hand, and while she waited for the tub to fill, she brought out her cuttings book. Her young, smooth-skinned self smiled back at her from the cut-out articles and publicity material. She smiled back a little sadly. Young, unscarred, sleek-thighed, and a writer; maybe it had all been a bit too good to last. On the other hand, she thought, pouring herself a second glass, middle-aged, scarred, dimple-thighed and a failure, was that not too bad to last? She turned the tap off and was about to put the cuttings book back on the top shelf of the wardrobe where she had found it, when she changed her mind and put it instead on her mother's old dressing-table by the window. She undressed and got into the bath, lying back in the hot water. She closed her eyes and allowed herself to dream of having happiness restored to her like a stolen wallet with an apologetic note from the thief.

'Dear Liberty' the letter would say,

'I can't thank you enough for giving me the opportunity once more to see your work. There is no doubt that you have emerged from your period of silence, a great writer...'

CHAPTER SEVENTEEN

At the Oast House Oscar lay awake next to his wife, every muscle tense as if he were trying to levitate from a bed of nails.

They had been out to dinner and Victoria had laughed a lot and drank a lot and when she got inside she had kicked off her shoes and put on music. 'I want to dance.' With her eyes half closed, she had moved to the rhythm, arms raised and clasped behind her neck, hips snaking. Oscar had opened his eyes wide and bitten his lips to stop himself from bursting out laughing and Victoria had mistaken his vacant look for desire. Letting her arms drop, she unbuttoned her blouse and grasped his hand, putting it on her breast. 'Come,' she had given him a slow smile before disappearing up the stairs. Oscar had thrown himself down on the sofa and, burying his head in the soft cushion, he had let the laugh rip. Then to his horror he was crying. Furious with himself, he grabbed the cushion and threw it across the room, hitting the music stack. The music, Victoria's music, carried on playing. He sat up. In the good old days, he thought bitterly, the needle on the gramophone would have slid and scraped its way across the record until it stopped, but a bloody CD just went on and on. He heaved himself out of the sofa and went across to turn the music off. Next to the stack lay a book in a spine-breaking attitude, and out of habit he picked it up and closed it. He noticed the title: *The Secrets of the Eternal Honeymoon*, written by a nearly famous actress. He leant back against the wall and opened the book again, flipping through the pages. His eyes stuck on a passage entitled: 'The Secrets of Mid-week Sex'. He read on, 'The man in your life's coming home late, he's tired, you're tired. So don't just sit yourself down in front of the telly. I know, it's what millions do, but you are different.' The next paragraph suggested that a wonderful way of injecting that honeymoon feeling into the man in your life was to greet him at the door when he arrived home, dressed only in high-heeled shoes and a fur coat. There followed some comforting words for the readers of a squeamish nature: 'Fake is fine these days, in fact many of the most glamorous women in my circle won't be seen in anything but.'

Oscar smiled and shook his head; even Victoria's daring burst of originality the other day had been borrowed from someone else. He closed the book and put it back where he had found it before going upstairs to bed.

Now he lay staring at the small crack between the curtains, waiting for the first shaft of morning light to break through and rescue him like an outstretched hand across an abyss. He turned and raised himself on one elbow, looking at Victoria sleeping at his side, innocent of everything but being herself.

He had met her when he was at the lowest point of his life and he had imbued her with a rare and beautiful mind to match her rare and beautiful face. He had been amazed that such a creature as she would be interested in him.

'For one, I'm so much older than her,' he had told a GP friend. 'I have absolutely no idea what people her age like or do.'

'It's my guess that blue eyes and a few appearances on the box more than make up for that. Physically you're in good shape. And there's no need to worry about sex. There's no reason why you shouldn't go on happily bonking away until you're in your nineties.'

'Well you were bloody wrong there,' Oscar whispered, rolling over on his back. He lay, eyes wide open, staring up into the darkness. Suddenly, staring back at him from the ceiling, were two green eyes in a cherubic face. Smiling, he stretched his arm out and stroked the air as if he was running his finger down the pale, scarred cheek. The vision vanished and he sighed fretfully. Next to him Victoria stirred and woke. He felt her hand on his arm.

'What's the matter, can't you sleep?' Her hand moved on to his chest and then down to his stomach. She giggled softly. 'No wonder you can't settle. You naughty boy.' She slithered across, lowering herself down on top of him. 'You naughty boy.'

*　　　*　　　*

On his way to work the next morning Oscar stopped at his aunt's. It was only eight o'clock, but he knew Evelyn was an early riser. 'By getting up at five,' she had boasted the other day, 'I'm prolonging my conscious life by two to three hours each day. Even if I only have one year left, that would still be a gain of at least

217

seven hundred and thirty hours.'

Oscar had agreed it was an irresistible argument; if one cared for conscious life, that is. This morning he wanted to talk to her about the latest in her series of articles on local footpaths. Evelyn had become something of a local celebrity. Her nature columns were hugely popular, but they were also increasingly controversial. Evelyn was spreading it on ever more thickly: insinuations about pesticides in the river, damage done to wildlife through cutting down hedgerows, stubble-burning, more and more each time until this week, when she pointed the finger straight at Derek Campbell.

'You can't name him like that. He'll sue and *The Tribune* can't afford it. I'll get the sack for a start,' Oscar said, sitting down at the kitchen table and accepting a cup of coffee and a burnt croissant. 'If an actor can be awarded fifty thousand pounds for being called boring, what do you think the going rate will be for being told you're responsible for the birth of a two-headed sheep?'

Evelyn, dressed, but wearing her tartan dressing-gown on top for extra warmth, shrugged her shoulders. 'Every word is true.'

'I doubt you can prove it. I'm sorry, but you'll have to tone it down a bit.' He handed her the article feeling old, older than Evelyn, and gutless. And was that not what he had come down here for, to be old and gutless in peace? 'I've marked the places.' He put his hand over hers that was rutted like a dried-out river bed and stained inky-blue by permanent bruising. 'I think you've made enough enemies, you know. I worry about you.'

Getting up to leave, he asked her, 'You haven't had any more of those letters have you?'

Evelyn looked away, scuffing her small, square men's trainers against the flagstone floor. Finally she said, 'Just one.'

'Why on earth didn't you tell me?' Oscar slammed his fist down on the kitchen table.

Evelyn smiled impishly at him, giving Oscar a glimpse of the young Evelyn that lived just under the surface of the skin. 'Because if I had, you would have stopped my articles. And you're wrong, you know. If papers like *The Tribune* won't stand up to be counted on local issues, who will?'

'I'm sorry,' Oscar said.

'Very well.' Evelyn stood up too. 'Now we both have things to do.' She pushed him off towards the back door. 'I want to call in on Liberty in a minute. There is something the matter with that girl. I've hardly seen her in the last couple of weeks and when I have, she's looked dreadful.'

Oscar wandered off to his car and had already put the key in the lock when he looked across to Laburnum Terrace. What sort of name was that for a country cottage? He smiled

219

to himself, then, putting the key back in his pocket, he strode across to Liberty's front door and rang the bell. It was half past eight now, she should be up. He rang the bell a second time, thinking that if he had woken her the damage would already be done. Shifting from one foot to another, feeling cold in only his tweed jacket, he pulled his woollen scarf up round his neck, and thrust his hands in his pockets. Morning mist hung across the sun like a net curtain, the still air carried only silence once the bell had stopped. It was the kind of morning he had dreamed of during that year in South America, an English winter morning. He looked round. Her car was in the drive. He rang the bell again. Evelyn had said Liberty had not been looking well. He felt the door. It was locked. He was about to leave but changed his mind, and walked round to the back. He put his hand up to knock, then he paused, moving closer to the door and peering inside the kitchen, his hands framing his eyes.

Sheets of typed paper lay strewn across the black-and-white tiled floor and an empty wine bottle had rolled under the table. Liberty lay slumped across the desk in the alcove, her hair fanning out across her arms. The desk, too, was strewn with paper, as if someone had dropped a stack of it from a height, and across the pages blood was splattered like red ink from an exploding fountain pen. Oscar rattled the door but it too was locked so, taking a step back, he grabbed one of the large stones that edged the flower bed and wrapped his scarf round it. Raising his arm, he smashed the stone against the door, breaking the glass just above the handle. He reached in through the jagged pane, praying the key would be in the lock. Grappling round he felt the metal against his fingertips. As he turned the key, his wrist scraped against the broken glass and for a moment he looked down as his own blood, thick and stagey-looking, dripping down the glass and onto the white-painted wood beneath.

CHAPTER EIGHTEEN

The cold air sweeping in from outside rustled the pages on the floor. In moments Oscar was at Liberty's side. He took her arm to feel for a pulse.

'Liberty, come on, wake up.' He was so scared that his voice came out harsher than he had intended.

'My God, Liberty.' The blood caked in neat horizontal lines where she had sliced her arm right up to the elbow, making the grey-tinged flesh look as if it had been pressed against a griddle. Standing up, he slipped his arm under her chest, raising her up against him. He felt her forehead with his free hand, letting it run down her face. The skin felt clammy. Resting his cheek on the top of her head for a moment he grabbed the phone by his side. He felt a lump in his throat and swallowed hard. With only one hand free, he put the receiver down on the desk and put his finger to the dial when suddenly Liberty stirred, rolled her eyes and smiled up at him as sweetly as if she had just woken up from a good sleep.

His heart was thumping so hard he thought the noise alone would have been enough to wake her. He swung the chair gently round so that she was facing him. Kneeling down again, he picked up her hand and put it to his cheek. 'My God, why?' he whispered.

Again, Liberty smiled that sweet, disconnected smile. 'It was no bloody good. No bloody good at all.' She closed her eyes again, resting her head against the back of the chair.

Oscar looked at the empty wine bottles, then he got up, fetched a clean tea towel and dampened it in tepid water. Returning to Liberty, he picked up her limp arm and rolled up the sleeve of her dressing-gown. Making his touch as light as he could, he washed the cuts. They weren't deep cuts, he saw that now. Liberty looked as if she was sleeping, a still, soundless sleep. Oscar paused with the blood-stained towel in his hand, lifting her arm to take her pulse again; it was almost normal.

'Liberty, Liberty, can you hear me? Can you

stand up?'

She stirred and her eyes opened with a blank stare. He pulled her to her feet and picked her up in his arms, carrying her upstairs. He looked into the first bedroom he came to. Her son's, he decided, judging from the posters on the wall and the teenage mix of old toys and accoutrements of adulthood. The room opposite had to be the spare room, neat with uncluttered oak furniture that looked as if it had once belonged to a much grander room, and no signs of occupancy. As his arms tired, he reached the last bedroom, her room. Smaller than her son's and not much larger than the spare room, it was pretty, and a little worn-looking, just like its owner. He hurried over to the double bed in the centre of the room and laid her down. Liberty stirred and mumbled but she did not open her eyes. For a moment Oscar stayed looking at her. He put his hand out, touching her cheek with the tips of his fingers, then he turned and walked out of the room.

The bathroom was just across the landing, a tiny room, more like a walk-in cupboard, the ceiling pitched. Inside, he turned the taps on to run the bath, looking round until he found some bottles of scented bath oil. He took the top off the first, smelling it then replacing the cap. The second had a sharper, lemony scent and he chose that, measuring out two capfuls into the running water. When the foam reached almost to the edge of the tub, he turned the taps off and went back into the bedroom. Liberty was awake now, smiling up at him with fuzzy eyes. Smiling back, he perched on the edge of the bed.

'Can you sit up?'

Liberty arched her back, a look of intense concentration on her face, then with a half groan, half giggle, she fell back against the pillows.

'What shall I do with you?' Oscar murmured. After a moment's hesitation he loosened the belt of her dressing-gown and lifted her up against his arm. He pulled off the dressing-gown and she winced as the cloth rubbed against the cuts on her arm. She was wearing a bra and pants underneath, and after a moment's pause he pulled them off too, quickly, keeping his eyes fixed on her face. Draping the dressing-gown over her, he picked her up and carried her across to the bathroom. Letting the dressing-gown slip to the floor, he lowered her into the tepid bath.

'It's cold,' Liberty mumbled, opening her eyes and raising her arms up to him.

'It's meant to be.' He sat silently on the edge of the bath while Liberty closed her eyes and rested her head against the hard edge of the tub. The dried blood on her arms coloured the foam pink and the tips of her hair curling down into the water turned pink too as if dipped in strawberry ice-cream. After a while Oscar reached for a bottle of shampoo. Pouring a little into the palm of his hand, he reached down into the water and began to wash her hair, just the ends, and then he scooped handfuls of water up over her arms to rinse away the last of the caked-in blood. When he had finished, he lifted her out of the bath and, steadying her with one arm, wrapped her in the large blue towel he had grabbed from a hook at the back of the door.

'Put your arm round my shoulder,' he said, but he was too tall and her arm slid down round his waist. So he put his arm under hers instead and, almost lifting her off the floor, he led her back into the bedroom. Sitting her down on the small upholstered chair by the window he asked, 'Where do you keep your sheets? You should have clean sheets with all those cuts.'

Liberty had kept her eyes fixed on his face as if there were an invisible rope between them keeping her upright. Still looking at him she said, 'Over there, in the blanket chest.' She tried to raise her finger to point but the hand was too heavy.

The chest was almost empty but for a set of worn and mended white linen sheets and a lace pillow case. A white cotton night-dress fell out from amongst the sheets and he picked it up. When he had finished making up the bed, he brought the night-dress across to her and gently lifting her arms above her head, slipped

225

it on her as the towel crumpled round her waist. He helped her in between the cool sheets, then he left her to telephone the office to tell them he would not be in until later.

Before going back upstairs, he tidied away the bloodstained papers from the desk, wiping the veneer top with a cloth rinsed in cold water. He picked up the papers from the floor, putting them with the others in a heap on the kitchen table. He swept up the broken glass by the door and wrapped it in newspaper before throwing it in the bin together with the empty wine bottles. In the Yellow Pages he found the number of a glazier, and made an appointment to have the broken window pane fixed and then, before going back upstairs, he taped some cardboard across the window frame to keep out the cold.

Liberty was asleep. There was no colour in her face other than the scar, even her lips were pale. He stood looking down at her, listening to the light, steady breaths. Then he kicked off his shoes and lay down by her side, carefully, so as not to disturb her. He turned sideways to face her, allowing his fingers to touch the damp tips of her hair across the pillow.

Liberty opened her eyes wide, then she smiled, nudging closer to him. 'Thank you,' she whispered. 'You're very kind.'

CHAPTER NINETEEN

Liberty woke, dry-mouthed and tender-headed, to find Oscar gone and Evelyn sitting, like a poor substitute, on the chair by the window. Disappointed, she sat up too quickly, making her feel as if her brain had dropped out of her skull and on to the floor. Groaning softly, her hands cradling her face she asked, 'How long have you been here?' Feeling ungrateful she added weakly, 'It's just that it's all a bit of a muddle.'

'If you mean was Oscar here getting you out of trouble? Yes he was. When he had to leave, he asked me to sit with you. I haven't called your father.'

'Thank goodness for that.' Liberty sank back down on to the pillows.

'Oscar says you didn't lose very much blood.'

'I was very drunk.' Liberty was apologetic.

'I thought you had turned your back on all that suicide nonsense.' Evelyn looked annoyed.

'I did too. I just had rather a shock.'

Evelyn stopped frowning. 'Not Johnny?'

Liberty smiled for the first time. 'No, no thank God, nothing like that.' She paused for a moment, allowing herself to dwell on the great good fortune contained in that statement. 'No,

227

Johnny is fine, touch wood.' Suddenly her despair seemed petty now that it was about to be aired before Evelyn's clear gaze.

'You see, I didn't really believe it myself when I said I was useless at writing,' she pressed her forehead against the palms of her hands, trying to force some sense from the aching lump that was her head. She looked up again. 'Deep down, I still couldn't really believe that all that desire wasn't matched by at least some ability.' She looked pleadingly at Evelyn. 'It was an easy mistake to make, don't you think?' Turning grey, she put her hand up to her mouth. 'If you'll excuse me. Feeling a bit sick.' She hurried off unsteadily, reaching the loo just in time. After brushing her teeth and splashing cold water on her face, she returned to the bedroom. Evelyn had not moved from the chair.

'Sorry about that.' Liberty crept in between the sheets and leant back against the pillow.

'I myself never found that drinking did anything for my research,' Evelyn said, making Liberty open her eyes wide. 'I can't think it would have done much for your writing, either.'

'Well no, it didn't.' Liberty pulled a face. 'But oh, Evelyn, I was happy. I know I looked like shit from all the booze and sleepless nights, but I was happy. I really believed that at last I was working on something first rate, and boy, did it feel good. You know, for a couple of weeks I got all my dreams back.' A small burp made her slap her hand across her mouth and with a muffled, 'Please do excuse me,' she hurried off into the bathroom again.

'I'll make us a cup of tea,' Evelyn said when Liberty returned.

The tea was weak and very sweet, but Liberty drank it gratefully. She put the empty cup down on the floor by the bed and closed her eyes. After a while she looked up and asked Evelyn, 'Have you ever had your hair permed?'

'No,' Evelyn said slurping her tea.

'Well I did once, to try to straighten it actually. I remember I was about fifteen and wanted to look like Mary Hopkin. Anyway, you spend all this time sitting with rollers in your hair and perm lotion dripping down your face. Then, just when you think it's all done, they put what they call a stabilizer on, and it's very boring and uncomfortable because by that time you're sitting by the basin with your neck about to break as it's pressed against the porcelain edge. But without that stabilizer being applied, the rest of the procedure would have been for nothing, your time and your shillings, as it was then, wasted, because the curls would just drop out.' Exhausted she stopped.

'That's fascinating, Liberty dear,' Evelyn said without conviction. 'I never knew that.'

Liberty laughed, then instantly felt sick again. This time it passed before she had any need to rush off. She tried to explain. 'That's how my writing was for me: my stabilizer. Life flutters past; an experience here, a happening there, but it was only through writing that it got any sort of shape and meaning...' Tears filled her eyes and, burying her face in the pillows, she sobbed. 'Oh what shall I do? Just look at me, I'm nothing but a contradiction in terms: a castrated Casanova, a peg-legged mountaineer, a pregnant nun—'

'I'll get us another cup, shall I?' Evelyn stomped up to the bed and took the half-empty cup from Liberty's side.

* * *

At the offices of *The Tribune*, Alistair Partridge popped his head through Oscar's door. 'Quiet down your way is it? Nothing stirring in old Tollymead?'

Oscar looked up at him. 'No, no I wouldn't say it had been particularly quiet. Why?'

Alistair sloped in and perched on Oscar's desk. 'Still no Diary. Third week running.'

'Yea, I know.' Oscar took off his glasses and rubbed his eyes. 'Sorry, I've had a bit of a day. I'll ask around, try to find out who is doing it, or not doing it, as it happens. It would be a pity if they stopped. The other villages have livened up their entries since Tollymead began to appear as the Mecca of village life, Everton in particular.' He gave a little laugh. 'Their entries

230

seem to lengthen by the week. More importantly, the whole section is changing tone, getting a little more personal, not so dry. It's more like a community meeting point than a notice-board.'

Alistair stroked his beard. 'I've been thinking. Maybe we should sponsor one of those inter-village competitions. Best Kept Hampshire Village, that kind of thing.' He crossed and uncrossed his legs. 'What about, Most Caring Village? Very much with the times, very nineties.'

Oscar smiled. 'Not a bad idea. "The Most Caring Village in the *Tribune* Area". Yeah, I like it. Give it some more thought over the week-end and we'll talk on Monday.'

Alistair was on his way out when Oscar stopped him. 'Oh, and what about that appeal from the parents of the missing girl? Have we got it on the front page?'

Alistair nodded. 'Yeah, it's all there. The police think she might just have decided to disappear. There was that bit of boyfriend trouble, nothing very much, but when it comes to teenagers, who knows, it might have been enough. We've got the latest sightings too. One old bat in Ambrose Lane is convinced the girl stayed the night in her attic; said the mice had been disturbed.'

'Her parents must be going through hell. If she ran away, why didn't she leave a note? For all they know, she could be lying dead in some

231

ditch.' Oscar looked up at Alistair's untroubled grey eyes. 'Anyway, I'll see you on Monday morning.'

He waited for Alistair to leave before phoning Victoria to say not to wait with supper for him. It was half past eight when he finally got into the car to start the drive home.

Once in Tollymead he turned into River Lane, telling himself it was his duty to check on Liberty, to make sure she was all right. The outside light was not on and the curtains were open. The pit of his stomach churned as he stumbled up the unlit path. He rang the doorbell as he had early that morning, but this time when there was no reply he threw himself against the door only to find it unlocked.

'Liberty! Liberty are you in there!' he strode through the hall, cursing Evelyn for leaving her alone.

'In the kitchen! I'm in the kitchen.' There was a brief pause. 'Hanging from the rafters.'

'What the hell—' Oscar began to run, then stopped short by the door. 'Ha ha, very funny,' he said as he sauntered through, his heart thumping.

Liberty sat at the kitchen table wrapping Christmas presents. She looked up. 'A wet-suit for Johnny. He'll need it in Australia.' She turned over the large parcel on the table in front of her and stuck down the sides of the glossy pine-green paper with sellotape.

'You shouldn't leave the front door

232

unlocked,' Oscar said.

'You mean in case someone should burst in and cut me up.' She gave him a big smile.

Oscar frowned at her. 'How's the arm?' he picked up her hand and rolled the sleeve of her jersey back.

'I look like a zebra crossing,' Liberty pulled a face. 'But you were right, none of the cuts are very deep, just scratches really.' She looked him straight in the eyes. 'I feel very embarrassed. I was pissed, you see.'

He looked back at her and she could see he was making an effort not to laugh. 'You don't say. I never would have guessed.'

'I'm sort of fatter without my clothes on,' she blurted out. 'Did you notice?'

'No,' Oscar shook his head. 'I never looked,' and they both burst out laughing. He sat down opposite her at the table and almost absent-mindedly took her hand in his, turning it palm up. 'I picked up a whole pile of papers from the floor.'

She looked away and nodded. 'I have to thank you for tidying up, too. You really have been terribly kind.'

He shook his head. 'Don't mention it. But was it a book I swept up with the broken glass?'

Liberty nodded again.

He traced a line on her palm with the tip of his index finger. 'That bad, was it?'

'Hm,' she nodded. 'Worse.' She looked into his blue eyes and thought he was really quite beautiful. Hardly aware of what she was doing she freed her hand from his and raised it to his face, gently removing his glasses. With a quick movement he caught it again, putting it to his lips.

Liberty closed her eyes leaning back in her chair, her head still fuzzled from the night before. Then as nothing else happened, she opened them again. Oscar was sitting looking at her, eyes glazed. Lust she thought, God I hope that's lust.

'I must go,' Oscar sprang up from the chair, dropping her hand. 'I just wanted to make sure all was well.'

Liberty stood up too. I never should have brought God into it, she thought sadly, handing him his glasses with an embarrassed little smile.

'Will you be all right? You won't...' he paused.

She shook her head and smiled. 'No, I won't. If I feel bad I'll call a friend, or even my father. But really, I'm fine now.' She walked Oscar to the door and, closing it behind him, she went into the sitting-room. She curled up on the sofa and switched on the television with the remote control. There was nothing on that she wanted to watch, but it was some sound, some company. She laid her head on the armrest.

If I was married to Oscar, she thought sleepily, how lovely it would be. Whenever I was tortured by ambition I could just look into those blue eyes and we could bonk each other silly, or we could talk. Even that would be lovely.

Tollymead: The Christmas Bazaar is being held, as usual, in the village hall on the second Saturday of December between 2 p.m. and 5 p.m. There will be more stalls than ever this year and there has been a suggestion from Oliver Bliss that we should add an exhibition of paintings by local artists to the attractions. The idea is that thirty per cent of proceeds goes to the fête and the remainder to the artist. Anyone wishing to exhibit should leave their work in the vicarage porch, (back door, it's always open) together with name, address and a proposed price. There's no need to ring the door bell.

Everyone is welcome. As the poet Keats said, 'Beauty is truth, truth beauty—that is all Ye know on earth, and all ye need to know.'

Ms Anne Havesham has asked the Diary to pass on her most sincere thanks to all the kind neighbours who visited with food and flowers during her recent illness. She especially appreciated the Italian pink-and-gold covered notebook with matching pen, brought by Laura Brown from a recent trip to Tuscany. 'It was especially welcome,' Anne says, 'because just the other day, I started the last page of my "Writer's

Notebook", and Laura's gift will be a perfect replacement.'

The beautifully bound, crisp white pages might soon be filled, as Ms Havesham has announced that the winning village of the Tribune *Area's Most Caring Village Competition will be chosen for the filming of her projected series, 'Atlantic Cousins', with many villagers picked as extras.*

Now, a tip from Phyllida Medley on how to give your Christmas cake a bit of a kick: just substitute your normal spoonful of brandy or sherry with a good glass or two of dark Jamaican rum.

CHAPTER TWENTY

Neville was helping the vicar to deliver the Christmas News Letter. As he approached each house he walked slowly, whistling a tune, so that if there were anyone at home they would hear and maybe come out for a chat. He had hoped to be delivering over at the new estate, but it was the vicar's patch, and Neville's was across the river. It was Saturday, but it might as well have been the middle of the week with everyone out at work, for all the people he saw. Three years he and Gladys had been in Tollymead and still they only really

237

knew a handful of people, he thought sadly, as he stomped past the three grey pebble-dash cottages on the corner of River Lane. He brightened. Things were changing in Tollymead, he was sure of it. A car rounded the corner, splashing Neville's polyester twill trousers with mud. No, there was no doubt about it, Tollymead was becoming a really neighbourly sort of a place.

As he approached Evelyn Brooke's house he heard loud voices. Peering over the hedgerow, Neville spotted Andrew Sanderson standing by Evelyn's gate. Even viewed through a hedge he looked upset, and Neville telescoped his thin neck another half inch.

'You call me across on a Saturday morning for what you call a "friendly talk", and this is what you've got to tell me!' Andrew's voice, guttural with outrage, carried right over to Neville. Feeling guilty for listening in, Neville whistled his tune ever so softly whilst taking a couple of steps towards them, but Andrew did not notice, nor did Evelyn, whom Neville could now clearly see on the other side of the gate. Now Evelyn was speaking, but Neville could not hear what she actually said. Then Andrew started up again. Dreadful temper on the man, Neville thought. And Evelyn such a nice lady too.

'You arrange for the Ministry of Agriculture to send someone down to check on Sanderson's Seeds and you expect me to be pleased? You must be battier than I thought—'

Again Neville could hear Evelyn's voice but not her words.

'No thank you I don't want any bloody broad bean plants!' Andrew Sanderson yelled his reply as if Evelyn had not only suggested he go off and die, but offered him a choice of poison as well. 'I want you and your bloody green chums off my back, that's what I want.

'And no, I do not want a sample of your bug-resistant beetroot seedlings, no, no, no!'

Moments later, Andrew stormed down the lane, past Neville without a word of greeting. Neville stopped whistling and looked after Andrew until he disappeared round the corner. Shaking his head, he stepped back onto the road from the grass verge and pottered off towards the gate, but by the time he got there, Evelyn had gone. He continued up the path and round to the back door, making a business of pulling the magazine from the brown imitation leather satchel hanging at his hip, whilst giving a breathy rendition of 'Colonel Bogey'. Evelyn was not in the kitchen, he saw, as he peered through the window, but he pretended not to notice the letter-box and gave a knock on the door. There was a doorbell but he preferred to knock, feeling that pressing the bell was somehow overstating his arrival. He knocked again, a little louder, and presently Evelyn came through into the kitchen and up to the door, opening it.

239

'Evelyn, you're there.' He beamed at her.

'If I said no, would you go away?' Evelyn glared back.

'You don't frighten me,' Neville twinkled on her doorstep. 'I brought you your News Letter.' He handed it to her, planting both feet inside the hall before she had a chance to shut the door. 'Have you seen this?'

'Seen what?'

'This.' Neville shoved a page from *The Tribune* under her nose.

'That's last week's paper.'

'But have you seen?' He pointed at the headline, reading out loud, '"Most Caring Village in the *Tribune* Area, does that sound like your village? If it does, we would like to hear about it."'

Evelyn sighed. 'What have you come to ask me to care about, Neville?'

Neville giggled nervously, wiping his bald head with his hand. 'There will be inspectors from the paper doing the rounds of the villages. Incognito, I assume.' He tasted the word and decided he liked it. 'Incognito, I wouldn't be surprised.'

'Like undercover policemen?'

'No, no nothing like that. More like one of those Egon Ronays, I should say. All very nice and friendly.' He paused for a moment before saying a little anxiously, 'I should think that lot over at Everton are up to all sorts already.'

'What do you have in mind?' Evelyn asked.

'Old ladies being chased out of their beds at all hours so they can be helped over the road by marauding gangs of boy scouts, neighbours force-feeding each other with nourishing casseroles?'

Neville giggled again. 'Come come, we all have our own little stories and successes to tell,' he said. 'We can cite the help given to you after the fire, to take but one example.'

'Oh yes,' Evelyn gave him a dirty look. 'And I can nominate the kind Samaritan who set fire to the barn in the first place.'

Neville took a step backwards, out of the door. 'Oh Evelyn, Evelyn you wouldn't? And we don't know it wasn't simply an awful accident, after all. We have the wedding too, between Mrs Brown, well the paper calls her Ms, and Mr Bliss. That all came out of the same neighbourly act.'

'My dear man, what are you rabbiting on about?'

Neville pulled out a torn page from the inside pocket of his jacket. 'I saved this one,' he said proudly. 'I thought there would be interest.' He unfolded the paper and held it up for Evelyn to see.

Evelyn bent close, peering at the text. 'Never heard of them,' she said finally, straightening up. 'And they most certainly haven't been here.'

Neville decided not to argue. A certain forgetfulness was to be expected in the elderly.

'I know I missed them when I was over...' Neville scratched the bit behind his ear where the arm of his spectacles rubbed. 'It makes a lovely story, anyhow.'

Evelyn gave him a pat on the shoulder with a grubby hand. 'You live in a very nice world, Neville. Stay there.'

As he wandered back down the path Neville pondered Evelyn's words. It was as if one had a choice. Funny old stick, Evelyn.

* * *

'I don't believe this!' Andrew was shouting down the telephone to Tim Haville-Jones so loudly he might as well have saved himself the cost of a call and just opened the window. 'Bloody Evelyn Brooke!' He slammed his fist down on the table, creating a squall in Nancy's cup so that the coffee spilt over the edge onto the saucer. When she lifted the cup to drink, the coffee dripped from the bottom of the cup down onto her new, cream-coloured cardigan.

'Now look what you made me do,' she snapped.

Andrew looked at her surprised, losing the thread of what he was saying. 'Sorry Tim. Where were we? Oh yes, an inspector from the Ministry of Ag, yes, absolutely.' Andrew gave a joyless laugh. 'You'd better hide any two-headed calves you might have hanging around the place.'

242

He finished the conversation and turned on Nancy. 'I don't want to see this fucking paper in my house, do you understand!'

Nancy stared at him. Who are you? she asked silently, you with your coarse tongue and face like a beetroot. Who are you? Without a word she took *The Tribune* from Andrew and pushed it into the bin under the sink. The doorbell rang.

'Oh, Neville. What can I do for you?' Nancy gave a mechanical smile.

'I've got your Christmas News Letter,' Neville handed the last copy over. Nancy gave a meaningful look in the direction of the letter-box. 'I especially wanted to talk to you,' Neville said quickly.

Knowing it would annoy Andrew, Nancy asked Neville in. 'It was Mrs Pyke, she had this idea.' Neville sounded as if the news surprised him as much as it did Nancy. '"Why don't you do up the vicarage?"' she said. '"It's ever so gloomy and the vicar'll never do anything about it." And I said, "Gladys," I said, "that's a first class idea." Some of us parishioners getting together and decorating the place for him, cheer it up a bit. I don't know that that lot over in Everton have ever done anything for their clergy, we'd have heard about it soon enough if they had. No, they can fancy their chances as Most Caring Village for all they might, but I know where I'd put my money.'

'Why not?' Nancy said. 'The vicarage is

243

rather gloomy with all that brown and beige wallpaper. Mr Brain takes absolutely no interest in how the place looks. Yes, why not?'

'Well, it would show we care, that's what I say.' Neville beamed at Nancy.

'I'll tell that inspector where he can get off,' Andrew stormed past on his way out of the front door.

'Inspector?' Neville's watery blue eyes bulged.

'That's what I said: inspector,' Andrew slammed the door behind him.

'I'm afraid poor Andrew is a little out of sorts,' Nancy explained, astonishing herself as well as Neville by adding, 'to tell the truth, he has absolutely no self-control, never has had.' To hide her confusion she offered Neville a cup of coffee, something normally to be avoided at all costs. 'Now for your idea. I will speak to a few friends in the Women's League. It should be just their thing.' She ushered Neville into the kitchen. 'Let's try to keep this a surprise from the vicar.'

* * *

Liberty was constantly surprised at how much she enjoyed Sunday lunch at her father's. He had always been a good host, focusing all his energies on the job of making his guests adore being his guests. Today he had met her at the door with a glass of his special apéritif, the juice

244

of a fresh peach topped up with dry German Sekt.

She sat back in the kitchen chair, sipping her drink and watching as he hammered at the turkey escalopes with a wooden mallet, before dipping them in egg and flour and fresh white breadcrumbs.

'There,' he beamed at Liberty. 'In the pan they go. The secret is to keep the fat hot.' He chucked the escalopes into the sizzling pan so that the brown butter splashed across the enamel top of the old-fashioned gas cooker.

Hamish was an excellent cook, one of the by-products from an earlier relationship with a home economics teacher who thought men in the kitchen, 'absolutely adorable'. Liberty had not liked the woman much, but Hamish's cooking had improved immeasurably, and the improvement had long outlasted the affair. If only he could take up with someone who believed in housework, Liberty thought, looking round the tiny kitchen. Weeks' worth of crumbs and dirty footprints covered the floor and the rug that Hamish had painted on the lino. The china-blue-and-white painted pattern was chipped here and there, but the frill lay as carefully dishevelled as always; it had to, it was painted that way. The blue-and-white tiles above the cooker were speckled with dried-in fat, and there were cobwebs dangling from the strip lighting.

'I won't be here for long,' Hamish said as if

he could read her thoughts. He fished out the escalopes from the pan and put them on two warm plates together with potatoes and garden peas. Carefully, he placed first a slice of lemon, then a curl of anchovies, on top of each escalope. 'The question is, where can the old man go?'

Liberty hated the way he referred to himself as 'the old man', coming as it did with an inbuilt expected response of, 'Oh, you're not old.'

'But you have enough saved at the building society for a small house, haven't you?' she said instead. 'I always thought you had.'

Hamish poured them both some Chianti and sat down. 'I don't know,' he shook his head. 'I've made some investments, not all of them wise, I fear. Black Mondays and Wednesdays and what not. No, I might have to come and stay with my little girl for a while. You won't mind, will you Liberty? You won't mind your old father coming to stay a while?'

Liberty cut into the crisp escalope. 'How long did you have in mind?'

'Oh a couple of months, no more.'

'A couple of months? I don't—'

'Do you know what I dread the most?' Hamish looked up at her with green eyes which she always feared were very much like hers. 'It's walking out of this place for the last time. Not just the flat, but the whole place. Teaching that last lesson and then leaving, knowing that

I'm no longer part of it. I'll walk down those corridors, past the classrooms and the common-room, past colleagues and boys; an outsider.'

'But Daddy...' Liberty put her glass down and put her hand on top of Hamish's. 'You'll always be welcomed back. You know they'll always want to see you.'

'"A guest in reality",' Hamish quoted. 'Being a visitor where you were once essential, or thought you were, whilst all round you the real business of life goes on without you.' He shook his head. 'Oh no, that's not for me.' He poured some more wine. 'I'll have to hand over my keys, do you know that? Like a disgraced officer handing over his sword.' He scrambled in his pocket and turned up the bunch of keys hanging from the little copper viking that Liberty's mother had once given him.

'Flat, labs, Chapel, San.' He chucked the keys on the table in front of Liberty then, with a quick smile, he got to his feet. 'More wine I think.'

With a sigh, Liberty put down her knife and fork. 'Of course you can stay. Just give me a couple of days' warning.'

'Thank you darling. What a lucky man I am to have a daughter like you.' He sat back in his chair with a delighted grin.

'Indeed you are. I could have been a hyena and then you would have had to ask in vain.'

Hamish looked at her. 'Eat your escalope

247

Liberty, or I'll think you don't like it.'

'Of course a hyena would eat its escalope,' Liberty said, feeling just as childish as she sounded.

Hamish frowned then, pushing away the strand of hair that fell in a carefully arranged lock across his forehead, he smiled. 'All this talk of hyenas, is it a new kind of slang? It's a movie isn't it?'

It was always the same, he just could not bear to be out of things. He had been a nightmare in the sixties. 'Yeah, sure,' she said, 'haven't you seen it? French. At the Curzon Mayfair. "Do Hyenas have souls too?" or to be precise, "Hyenas ont ils souls aussi?"'

Hamish gave her a long look. 'Pud,' he said standing up. 'It's a very good one.'

*　　　*　　　*

On the way home Liberty drove up behind a car with a sticker in the window saying, 'Open Your Heart to Jesus!' The car was driving slowly on the narrow winding road and Liberty stared at the sign mumbling over and over, 'Open Your Heart to Jesus.' If only she could. It was obvious that doing that was a bit like opening the door of your home to Mary Poppins. Before you could blink, the innermost corners of your soul were tidied spit-spot and cosily lit, and you were launched on some purposeful activity. Liberty's friend

248

Margaret was Born Again. She lived in a large Victorian villa in Everton that overflowed with family and friends and spent her holidays with her family in Butlins on special off-season Christian Weeks. Margaret radiated such fulfilment that, though a plain woman, her skin glowed and her eyes sparkled. She had stopped being scared, stopped wondering where she was going. She said she was being led through life by a strong hand and a comforting voice. For me, Liberty thought as she came to a clear stretch of road and overtook, life is like a deserted freeway leading to somewhere I don't particularly want to go. 'Open Your Heart to Jesus!' She drove into Tollymead, but instead of turning right into River Lane, she continued straight on, across the bridge and up towards the church. At this time on a Sunday afternoon it would be empty. Liberty parked in the small car park and hurried across in the twilight. Once inside she sat down in a side pew. Looking round her to make sure she was alone, she knelt on the stone floor. It felt as if she was kneeling on ice, so she quickly unhooked a prayer cushion and slid it between her and the floor.

She prayed with her eyes shut tight. 'I'm opening my heart, I really am. Do please come in.' And she imagined Jesus swooping like a giant cuckoo, filling every available space, pushing out all the doubts and fears and unfulfilled yearnings.

'Please come,' she mumbled.

Before her closed eyes came a picture of Oscar sitting on her sofa, his blue eyes fixed on her, all misted over with desire. With one step he crossed the room to her and swept her up in his arms. 'Oh Liberty, Liberty.'

'Damn!'

Liberty opened her eyes wide and shocked. Had she really said that, here, in God's house? She sighed and got up from the floor. She looked across at the altar apologetically. But she felt let down. She had opened her heart to Jesus, but it was Oscar who had crept in.

CHAPTER TWENTY-ONE

'Goodness and beauty were inextricably linked in the classic fairy tales,' Liberty was telling her class. And, she thought, I have neither as I sit here gracelessly lusting after my pupil's husband.

'Even Beast in "Beauty and the Beast", to take a topical story, was only ugly as a result of a spell given as a punishment. Once he redeems his character, he becomes physically beautiful as well. An actual physical flaw, like this scar for example,' she pointed to her cheek, 'is as sure a way of signalling a correspondingly nasty flaw in the figure's character as a sign saying "This way for a princess with a nasty character flaw". Not very subtle, but effective in its day. Now for next week, I'd like you all to write a modern fairy tale, using your own symbolic language.'

Liberty dismissed the class and began clearing up her desk, when she looked up to see Victoria still in the room—And the poor beggar girl gazed in awe at the beautiful Queen. 'I want your husband,' the beggar girl spoke, upon which she was immediately struck by lightning—

'Hi, Victoria, I didn't see you there.' Liberty tidied her features into a friendly grin.

'I just wanted to ask if you would like to come over one night for supper.'

Don't be nice to me, Liberty thought, I don't deserve it, you should know that from the scar on my face. She smiled up at Victoria. 'It's kind of you to ask but—'

'Oh come on. It can't be much fun sitting around on your own every evening. I can't stand the mentality of some couples who never mix with single people. It doesn't take much effort to share yourself around a bit, does it? It's a very eighties thing, that sort of cliquiness. Totally uncaring really. No, honestly, I like to mix with everyone.'

Maybe not so nice after all, Liberty thought, but she said, 'How very nice. Yes, thank you. I'd love to.'

* * *

251

What is the required dress for husband-stealing? A tasteful covering of tar and chicken feathers? Liberty stood in front of the full-length looking-glass the next evening, regretting the impulse that led her to accept Victoria's invitation. What would Oscar think of her following him into the sanctuary of his own home with her zebra-crossing arm and failed hopes? She peered at her face in the glass. The concealer she had smeared over the scar was like a plaster on a spot, it only drew attention to the problem. She rubbed some off and turned her attention back to her clothes. She could wear the short black skirt and her treasured ten-year-old black cashmere jumper, oozing 'classic chic', then again, it could just say, 'please forgive me, but I've just come from a funeral.' Of course there was the new, deeply fashionable long, straight grey skirt that made her look dumpy and ten years older. In the end she settled for the black skirt and a white long-sleeved blouse made of lace. She put a vest on underneath; that way she could offend no-one.

* * *

Oscar opened the door for her, giving her a big grin. He seemed genuinely glad to see her, but it took Liberty no more than five seconds to decide that his obvious pleasure in seeing her was nothing but the relief of a concerned acquaintance glad to see her back on form.

Still, that was how it should be, of course it was.

She followed him into the sitting-room, trying not to look at his bottom. But bottoms were important, of course they were. She had always found slack-bottomed men hard to trust. A slack soul in a slack-bottomed body. But what did it matter to her if he was a man to trust? And a man to be trusted by whom, his wife? If he was, there was even less point in her worrying about the slackness or otherwise of his bottom and soul.

'I said, what would you like to drink?' Oscar had stopped by the drinks tray standing on a small table by the window.

'Oh ... sherry, please. Dryish.' It was not that she particularly liked sherry, but it was a bit like taking visitors from abroad to an Andrew Lloyd Webber musical; the safe option when you did not have the energy to think.

'Here I am,' Victoria sauntered in from the kitchen. On her way to sit down next to Liberty she paused to riffle her fingers through Oscar's fair hair. A little later she got up again to refill the bowl of Japanese rice biscuits that Liberty particularly disliked, but ate several of, so as not to give any cause for annoyance. She left to make a phone call and twice she went to check on the food. Each time as she passed Oscar she rubbed against him or planted a kiss on the top of his head and once she sat down on his knee, rubbing her nose playfully against his.

She's like a dog marking out its territory, Liberty thought sourly, accepting a second glass of sherry. Oscar kept smiling, but there seemed to Liberty to be an irritated look, like an itch, at the back of his eyes. Now Victoria wanted Oscar to come with her out into the kitchen to help with a heavy saucepan.

He'll probably return with a tag in his ear like a Steiff bear. Liberty got up from the chair and walked round the sitting-room. It seemed more than ever to be Victoria's room she decided, with little bits of Oscar here and there as conciliatory gestures. There were the sporting trophies crowding a small shelf in the bookcase, the political biographies amongst the blockbusters and prize-winning novels by fashionable authors. On the wall by the door—you could see it if the door was closed—hung three framed awards, two American and one British, earned for reporting conflicts as far apart as the Falklands, Afghanistan and East Timor. So what on earth had brought this man to Tollymead?

As if summoned by her thoughts, Oscar appeared at her elbow. 'That's pretty impressive,' Liberty said nodding to the wall. 'You're a certified clever clogs.'

Oscar laughed, but then he said, 'It really isn't my idea to have them displayed like that, but at least they're hidden most of the time.'

'She's proud of you, that's lovely.' Liberty

turned round to face him.

'Yes, yes isn't it,' Oscar said without conviction. He did not move, nor did Liberty.

We've got a minute or so before your wife comes back into the room, so use it, take me in your arms, kiss me, press your body against mine . . . Looking into Oscar's melancholy blue eyes she said, 'It's nice to be here.'

His eyes brightened. 'It's nice to have you here.'

'Come through!' Victoria called from the dining hall.

Liberty admired the pale green candles that floated in a large bowl at the centre of the table. Touched, and ashamed of her earlier thoughts, she said, 'You shouldn't have gone to so much trouble.'

'Oh don't worry. I did them for a dinner party the other day and they didn't quite burn out.' Victoria looked pleased as she sat down. Then she looked across at Oscar. 'What's the matter?' She gave a little laugh. 'What did I say?'

'Nothing,' Oscar frowned. 'I'll get the bread.' He got up again.

He walked past Liberty's chair on his way out to the kitchen and she had to grab her left hand with her right to stop herself from reaching out and touching him. If he was Victoria's dog or child, she thought, a caress would be perfectly in order. Liberty smiled inanely across the table at her hostess.

'You'll be glad to hear I'm working on another story after all,' Victoria said. 'Actually I was thinking that I should probably get an agent. Maybe you could introduce me to your old one. If you recommend him, that is.'

Liberty's smile remained on her face like a guest who did not know when it was time to leave. 'Would I recommend my old agent? Well yes, I would, he is very highly thought of.'

Oscar returned and Victoria looked at him pleased. 'Liberty thinks I should try her old agent.'

Oscar looked surprised. 'That's very generous of you.'

'Why?' Victoria asked. 'Just because you can't make use of an opportunity yourself there's no reason you shouldn't help someone else to do so, is there Liberty?'

'No, no of course not. I see it rather like a dying woman passing on her clothes to her friend. I mean, what use are they to her?'

'There you see,' Victoria said to Oscar. Oscar looked ill at ease.

Dinner was over and after two cups of coffee Liberty stood up to leave. 'Do you mind if I leave my car in your drive overnight?' she asked. 'I've had a bit too much to drink.'

'I think I have too,' Oscar said, 'but I'll walk you back.'

'It's all right, I've got a torch in the car. Please don't worry.'

But Oscar insisted. It was a fine cold night

256

and the air was as high as a cathedral ceiling. It was not a long walk, a little over ten minutes, that was all.

Back home, Liberty paused on the doorstep. 'Thank you for everything.' She went inside and turned, about to close the door, when Oscar said, 'Can I come in?'

She nodded and held the door for him. In the hall he stopped and stood for a moment looking down at her, smiling. She looked back up at him uneasily, feeling sick to the stomach with nerves and excitement. It would be wrong to speak now, that much she knew.

He took a step towards her and, bending down, he cradled her face with his hands, tilting her chin upwards, then he kissed her, a long kiss. He took her by the hand and led her upstairs into her bedroom and gently pushed her down on the bed. He knelt over her, straddling her waist and as he began to unbutton her blouse she closed her eyes: hear no evil, see no evil, say nothing. But I love him, she thought, how can it be evil when I love him? She looked up at him, smiling, and lifted her hands to his face, taking off his glasses. Oscar smiled back lazily as her fingers travelled down his shirt, undoing buttons as they went. He lowered himself gently down on to her, taking his weight on his palms for long enough to kiss her, then he pressed down on her whispering, half laughing half sobbing, 'Oh God, Liberty, at last.'

Village Diary

Tollymead: *As the date of the Christmas Bazaar approaches, all seems set for a record fund-raising success. The vicar is thrilled with the pictures he's received for the exhibition so far, and we seem set to have more stalls than ever before. Mrs Sanderson and Mrs Smedley still need more clothes for the Dressed Dolls Stall.*

Phyllida Medley, popping in for a cup of camomile tea (made from the flower rather than the leaf, it's much nicer that way) mentioned that several residents had asked her about resurrecting the carol singing in Tollymead this Christmas. We both agreed we missed hearing the sound of familiar carols coming towards us in the winter night, and Phyllida admitted to keeping a bottle of Stone's ginger wine in a cupboard for years, just in case. You don't need to be a brilliant singer to take part, although we all hope, of course, that Miss Hester Scott, OBE, described once by a critic as Britain's answer to Ethel Merman, will join us. So anyone interested should be outside the church this coming Sunday at 7 p.m. Ask the vicar for song sheets. The money raised will go towards providing a minibus service into Fairfield for those of our residents without cars.

And finally, Oliver Bliss and Laura Brown have set a date, the Saturday after Christmas, for their wedding. As Oliver said, 'Getting to know each other first is for cissies.'

Maybe he's got a point. How is it that while the number of couples living together before marriage is going up, so is the divorce rate?

CHAPTER TWENTY-TWO

Ted Brain could not make it out. Yet again he had opened the back door to find a painting in the porch. He picked up the latest offering, a ghastly-looking thing in purple and black, and brought it inside. Turning it this way and that, Ted could not make out if it was a high-rise building or a triffid. Then he saw written on a card at the back: 'Winter 2, by George Tennant, Greensleeves, Well Road, Tollymead.' Shaking his head, Ted put it with the other four pictures in the hall.

'It was another one of these pictures!' he called up to Veena. 'I haven't got a clue what this is all about.'

'Let me look.' Veena came running barefoot down the stairs. She dreamt of going to art school, she had confided to Ted, and spent a lot of her time sketching with some materials he

259

had bought her in Fairfield.

'It's awful.' Veena burst out into that throaty laughter that sent a little shiver of excitement through Ted. 'And look at you, you should see your face. You look really sweet.'

Ted glanced at himself in the small hall mirror and then he laughed, too.

'Anyway, what is this all about?' she asked. 'Why are all your parishioners leaving bad pictures on your doorstep?'

Ted shook his head, but his eyes were on the girl's face. He knew it was irresponsible of him to allow her to stay on like this. It was almost two months now since she had first arrived. He knew he should have moved her on. He even had a couple of addresses of safe places for her to go. But each time he had suggested she move on, the girl had wept and clung to him and begged to stay. What could he do? He loved her.

* * *

Nancy was meeting Neville Pyke outside the vicarage at three. She was glad to have a project on her hands. Back home, lately, she had felt as if she was walking across a frozen lake, at every moment risking the ice breaking and sending her down into the freezing water. Sanderson's Seeds was close to collapse and Andrew blamed everyone and everything but himself for the firm's trouble. Most of all, he

260

blamed Evelyn Brooke. He blamed her even more than he blamed the government and the recession. Day after day Nancy watched as every one of his faults became as pronounced as if they had been read out in court by a disapproving judge. He seemed to have lost his strength too, that forcefulness she had so admired in the past. Now he whinged and whined as the layers of worry and frustration descended on him with every bit of bad news from work.

'We're losing Tim now,' he had said the night before. 'He cancelled his last order. Says he can't pay. His business still suffers from all the bad publicity over that damn oak. And then there was that ridiculous piece on television the other day, about those children with birth defects. Nothing to do with us here, but it really put the wind up Tim. He says he's going organic. Who can blame him, eh? All the supermarkets are clamouring for the stuff.' For once he was not shouting and he had a confused look in his eyes. He kept rubbing the back of his neck with his broad hand that was covered in red hair. A paw like a werewolf at full moon, Nancy used to say in the days when it had wandered over her sturdy body at night.

'Surely there is no question of legal pesticides causing the damage to those babies?' Nancy had asked. 'Not any of the kind we supply?'

Andrew had not answered. He just clenched

his teeth and looked away.

'Oh what can we do?' she had whispered.

'I don't know, I really don't know. We lost another big export order this week. If we lose our local business as well ...'

Nancy's fingers tightened around the wheel of the car. Andrew would never cope with the loss of his father's business. She spotted Neville in the vicarage drive and gave him a little wave. Concentrate on the project in hand, that was the thing. If Tollymead won the Most Caring Village Competition, a little more business could come Sanderson's Seeds' way, especially if Andrew's wife had been prominent in winning the award. Her spirits lifted. Maybe Sanderson's Seeds could sponsor some community project? She smiled to herself. It was not a bad idea. She had always wanted to be more involved in the business but Andrew had always resented any attempts she made at getting involved, reminding her of a child refusing to share a toy, 'No, it's mine.' Maybe now he would realize he needed her.

Neville waved back at her, the vicarage keys in his hand. They had roped Ned Smedley, who was church-warden, into their plan, and he had told them when Ted Brain was out of the parish for the day and lent them his set of keys.

'We'll have it all measured up and ordered so that when we tell the vicar, he can't argue,' Neville said delightedly to Nancy as he let them in through the front door.

262

'Now look at that dreary paper,' he pointed a stubby finger at the wall, 'and great big chunks of it coming off the...' he stopped in mid-sentence. 'What was that?' He cocked his head to one side, placing his hand behind his ear. 'I thought I heard someone upstairs.'

Nancy, who had been leafing through the stack of paintings that leant against the wall by the stairs, listened, but she could hear nothing. 'Most probably a mouse,' she said. 'The vicarage has always had a problem with mice. Now, Honeysuckle White in here, I think, to make the place seem larger.'

'Maybe the vicar didn't go out after all,' Neville said.

'Ted! Ted are you up there?' Nancy called. There was no answer, no sound at all. 'Mice,' she said again. 'Now, the sitting-room.' She strode off.

'I don't think the man has any taste at all, good or bad.' She looked around as she hauled a notebook up from the pocket of her voluminous navy blue skirt. Always when Nancy had been there before, the small rectangular room had been brimming with people obscuring the waiting-room meanness of the place. Brown upholstered chairs and a sofa with its moss green cover torn like fashionable jeans, lined the grey-painted walls; the floor was covered in a patterned carpet of rust and brown. Then, surprisingly, on the small teak veneer table under the window stood a crystal vase with a single yellow rose.

Neville hauled out a tape measure from the pocket of his anorak. Nancy made notes as he called out the measurements.

'He does have some rather unpleasant pictures, doesn't he?' Nancy said, looking at the charcoal drawings above the small gas fire.

Neville paused from his measuring and glanced at the trees whose gnarled branches caught at the flowing hair of the woman passer-by like greedy hands and at the second picture where a giant dove rode the back of the same girl, naked now between the bird's claws. 'He told me they're mostly by a friend of his,' Neville said. 'They're very skilfully drawn I must say, very skilfully drawn.'

'Well that one is a very poor copy of Dali's Leda and the Swan,' Nancy said, pointing at the leering dove.

'Oh really, you don't say,' Neville blinked.

'No I'd say the pictures in here are as bad as any of the ones stacked in the hall. I suppose, heaven help us, that they're destined for the Christmas Bazaar.' She wandered through the room, making notes of the colours of the room and when she looked at her watch, it was almost three o'clock. 'When did the vicar say he was expected back?'

'Oh not until four. I'm all done here. Shall we have a peek at the kitchen?' Neville's voice trailed off as the first-floor boards creaked overhead.

264

'You're right, there definitely is something up there,' Nancy said.

Neville scratched his ear, his pale blue eyes fixed to the ceiling. 'You don't think the vicar is hiding from us?'

'Of course not, don't be an idiot, Neville. I'm going upstairs.' She walked as quietly as she could back into the hall and up the stairs with Neville following behind, his breath noisy like wind coming through a window crack. Other than that, there was no sound but Neville's and Nancy's feet on the thin stair carpet. It was most probably mice, Nancy thought as she reached the landing. She stepped firmly across to the first door which opened to reveal nothing more exciting then Ted Brain's bedroom that was so bare it could have belonged to a monk. Neville peered in across her shoulder and with an irritated shrug Nancy hurried across the landing to the next door. She began to feel ridiculous as she flung open the door to an empty bathroom and then the door next to that. 'Well what did I—' She paused in the doorway.

'Good God!' She took a step back as she saw the reflection in the mirror on the wall by the unmade bed.

'Come out of there, do you hear, come out at once!'

A boy and girl stepped out from their hiding place behind the wardrobe. Nancy had not seen either of them before.

'Why are you hiding like this? Are you friends of the vicar?'

The girl, slight and dark-skinned nodded, her eyes huge and frightened.

'We startled them.' Neville had squeezed in between Nancy and the door. 'Did you think we were burglars maybe?'

'Using a key and speaking of a new colour scheme for the sitting-room? Hardly, Neville,' Nancy snapped.

'Anita lives here,' the boy mumbled, his blond head turned away.

'You live here? Well...' Nancy said, 'that certainly explains a lot of things.'

Neville had been staring, goggle-eyed at the girl and now his face brightened. 'I know where I've seen you. You're the young lady that went missing a couple of months ago. Your picture was all over *The Tribune*.'

Nancy turned to Neville. 'This is the missing Fairfield teenager? I don't believe it.' She looked hard at the girl. 'Are you saying that all this time you've been here, at the vicarage?'

The girl nodded.

'The vicar allowed this, knowing what your parents must be going through?'

The girl lifted her head. 'No, he didn't know who I was. I pretended to be someone else.' The last was said in a voice no louder than a whisper.

'Who?'

'I told him I was looking for asylum.'

266

'Asylum!' Nancy snorted. 'I always thought he was a fool, but this ...!'

'Don't talk about him like that,' the girl narrowed her eyes at Nancy. 'He's a very brave man. He really thought he was hiding a helpless refugee.'

Nancy took no notice of the protest. 'But two months ... what sort of a community is this when our own vicar can have a young woman living with him for two months and no-one even noticing? I never did like this new vicarage, stuck half-way up a field.' She looked hard at the girl. 'I'll give you, you look quite different from your picture, but still ... I find it very difficult to believe that the vicar hasn't recognized you.'

'He doesn't take the local paper!' the girl shouted.

Nancy raised her eyebrows. 'Well we can't stand around here. Now you come with me downstairs. We must call your poor parents before we do anything else.'

The girl hurried forward and grabbed Nancy by the arm. 'Don't interfere. You shouldn't be here anyway. Ted didn't say you could come bursting in to his house like this.'

'I beg your pardon young lady, we were not bursting anywhere.'

'It was meant to be a surprise,' Neville looking unhappy, tried to explain, annoying Nancy by retreating from the room with apologetic little phrases. 'A caring gesture towards our vicar.'

'Hello, what's going on up there?' Nancy turned round as Ted's voice reached them from downstairs. 'Veena, are you all right?' They heard Ted's feet running up the narrow staircase.

'Mrs Sanderson, Neville, what are you doing here? What's going on? Veena, who is this boy?'

CHAPTER TWENTY-THREE

Ted Brain knelt in front of the altar in Tollymead church, his chest and arms resting on the red velvet railings, his head hanging like a broken-necked bird's.

'It was my pride, wasn't it, Lord?' he whispered. 'My sinful pride and my lack of love for the people here?' He stifled a sob. Light footsteps against the stone floor made him straighten up and turn round. 'Oh, it's you.' He heaved himself up from the floor.

Anita stopped a little distance away, not quite looking at him. 'I don't know what to say other than I'm sorry.'

Ted sank back down on to the altar steps, hugging his knees with his arms. 'All of it, the whole charade just so you could be with this, this young lout you believe you're in love with.'

'You sound like my parents.'

'Oh, I don't feel like your father I can assure you.' Ted buried his face in his arms. The girl said nothing and after a while he looked up at her. 'How could you do it to me? I loved you.'

'Why did you make it so easy for me?' All accent had gone from her voice. 'Why were you so ready to believe my ridiculous story? I never really thought you would. It was all done on a whim. I had to get away for a while, to think and to see Paul without my parents breathing down my neck. You see,' she paused, 'I'm pregnant.'

Ted gave a choked snuffle and a tear, then another one rolled down his pink cheek.

'Oh Ted please,' Anita put her hand out to him but he turned away, shaking his head like a child.

'I saw this article in the paper about clergy running safe houses for asylum seekers threatened with deportation.' She looked down at her feet. 'It started off as a bit of a joke really. Paul lives over at the new estate.' She gave him a small smile. 'You didn't know, but he's one of your parishioners. He said you were just the sort of person who would be involved in that kind of thing. "That's our vicar all right," he said. "He's one of those trendy types, always going on about some cause or another with about as much of an idea of what's really going on as you could fit on a gnat's—"' She hesitated.

'Gnat's?'

'Arse,' the girl mumbled.

Ted groaned, his face hidden once more in his arms.

Anita took a step towards him, putting her hand out, then letting it fall back to her side. 'One night I just couldn't take it any more, all of them going on and on at me, arguing with each other, wanting to decide for us. "You have to get married. Don't get married. Go and live with your aunt. Stay and finish school. Have the baby adopted. Let us look after it." On and on. I thought I was going to faint. All I could see was their mouths opening and closing, opening and closing.' Her voice shook. 'I just couldn't take it, so I grabbed some things and ran out of the house. But I couldn't stay at Paul's place. His parents don't approve of me any more than mine do of him. We're still at school. We have no money. None of our friends' parents would put me up. I couldn't live on the streets, not with a baby to think of. That's when Paul said, "Go on. Go across to the vicarage. Tell him you're a refugee or something. He'll believe you. He'll get you somewhere to stay, some nice cosy vicarage." It was almost like a joke.' She took a step closer. 'Please Ted. Forgive me. It just all sort of happened. I never thought you'd believe me. Then when you did, it was all so easy, so restful. I just floated along, no school, no hassles, no-one telling me what to do. I could even see Paul. Ted please, can't you try to understand?'

Ted pressed his face harder against the sleeves of his jumper.

'You believed everything I said because of my colour.' The girl sounded suddenly cross. 'In your own way you're just as prejudiced as the people you fight against. And in case you should ask, I didn't think my parents were going to force me into an arranged marriage, nor are they planning to stone me. They just don't like Paul because he's got a record. And I know they'd just take over. I had to have time to think, to decide what I wanted. I didn't even know if I wanted to keep the baby.'

'I thought it was all those biscuits you kept eating.' Ted's voice came muffled. 'All those long walks I could never join you on. That's when you were ... seeing that boy?'

Anita nodded. 'I'm sorry,' she whispered, taking another step closer, holding out her hand again. Ted remained still. She touched his shoulder lightly. 'I'm keeping the baby. My parents are going to help look after him, provided I stay on and finish my A-levels.' With a sudden flush of pride she added, 'My projection is two As and a B.' She lowered her eyes. 'They've agreed to me seeing Paul too. It's all worked out really well for us.'

'I should have seen through it. That phoney accent for a start. You kept losing it. Your story was full of holes.' Ted looked up at her, his eyes prickling with held-back tears. 'You're right, I wanted nothing more than to be deceived, to be confirmed in all my beliefs and prejudices. Veena the refugee was as much my creation as yours.' He got up clumsily from the steps and walked, head bent, into the vestry.

'Ted, don't leave like that,' Anita called after him, but he closed the door and turned the key in the lock.

$$*\qquad*\qquad*$$

Liberty stretched in her upholstered desk chair, pushing the back of her head against the padded head-rest. Love was truly the opium of womankind. Nowadays when she thought of Hemingway shooting himself, she wondered if he would have gone through with it if he had had a love like hers. Then again, men were great pigeon-holers, stashing away the different components of their existence into the neat little compartments that made up their beings. With women it was messier. Women's minds and hearts were like an intricate construction of sluices and canals, each flowing into the other. Love invariably flooded the whole system. Now was that bad or good? She stretched out her legs in front of her, pointing and flexing her feet. 'Good toes and naughty toes,' she crooned in the carefully enunciated tones of Miss Dubois, her childhood dance teacher. 'Good toes and naughty toes.'

272

Every evening other than Wednesday this week, Oscar had come over on his way home from work. He had not been able to stay very long, just long enough for them to make love and talk a little. Oscar was unusual amongst the men she had known in that he seemed actually to enjoy conversation. He liked to find out what she thought about things and why.

'I don't want to be sexist or anything,' she had said to him the other night, 'but in my experience most men view conversation rather like the application of deodorant; something they do to keep the peace, although they can't for the life of them see what all the fuss is about.'

Each evening after he had gone she would return for a little while to the bed, lying down on his side, her arms round the pillow where his head had been just minutes earlier, going over each word he had said, trying to recapture each caress and the expression on his face when they made love.

Today, like every day for the last week or so, she was working on the translation of a two-part fantasy novel for teenagers, work rejected by a fellow translator as too much for the tight dead-line. It had been offered to Liberty with a bonus payment if it was finished by the second week in January. Liberty thought you can get through an awful lot of work if you're broke enough, so she worked hard in five-hour stints with only a short break for lunch. The moment seven o'clock came though, she would switch off the computer and begin her wait for Oscar.

She could not concentrate on reading or even on television. Always given to dreaming, both in her sleep and when wide awake in the middle of the day, she dreamed away the waiting time instead, drifting round the rooms, polishing and polishing again, every piece of wooden furniture in the house until it shone, until she could see the outline of her face in the wooden surfaces and the rooms smelt of beeswax. Always mindful of her grandmother's advice, 'As long as your good furniture is polished and there are flowers in every room, there's no need to go on cleaning,' she gave no time to tidying or washing floors, but she bought flowers from the supermarket, and found some in the garden where white hydrangeas still flowered amongst dying leaves.

She finished a chapter just as the old kitchen wall clock struck seven and, setting the computer to Print, she got up to make herself a cup of tea before sitting down again to write to Johnny. She could see that it was a letter daubed with happiness, but she did not tell Johnny the reason for it, he would only worry about her getting hurt again. She licked the stamp and was about to stick it down when the doorbell rang, one short signal. She jumped up from the chair and hurried to the front door. As she opened it, a gust of icy wind almost blew her off her feet.

'Oscar,' she put her hand out and pulled him inside, burying her face in his thick coat, teasing herself by putting off the moment when she could look up at him.

'Hey,' Oscar pushed her out to arm's length. 'Is everything all right?'

She smiled. 'You know you're so gorgeous that if I had invented you, you wouldn't be believed.'

Oscar was taking his coat and scarf off, but now he turned back to her with a surprised look in his blue eyes.

'Well let's not argue about it,' Liberty said, standing on tip-toe to kiss him.

In the middle of their love-making that evening, there was music. Liberty opened her eyes. That was not supposed to happen in life, only in bad films. She closed her eyes again, clasping Oscar's back and burying her face in his shoulder.

'Ding Dong Merrily on High, In Heav'n the Bells are Ringing. Ding Dong...'

Oscar relaxed his grip round her waist. 'Glor or or or or or ia, Hosanna in Excelsis.'

That was it! They both sat up, misty-eyed, hair tumbled.

'Aah a hahaha aah, Aah a hahahahaha...' the song rose into the night sky outside the open bedroom window.

'Carol singers.' Liberty scrambled from the bed, and pulled on jeans and a sweatshirt. 'You

275

wait here,' she whispered before hurrying downstairs.

The carol singers were hammering away on 'We Three Kings' when Liberty opened the front door, dishevelled but smiling. 'Sherry?' she called to them. 'I'm sure you'd like some sherry.'

The singers, lead by Neville Pyke and a self-conscious looking Ted Brain, crowded into the hall where Liberty had hastily assembled every glass she owned and a full bottle. She disappeared out to the kitchen to find some juice for the three children in the choir and as she came back, she stopped in the hallway to look with satisfaction at the singers that crowded in her hall, red-cheeked and wrapped up against the cold December night.

'This is so nice,' she muttered as she walked around pouring drinks, 'so very nice.' She thought of Oscar waiting for her upstairs like a half unwrapped present and she gave a little shudder of excitement. It was moments like these that made life worth the effort.

'Oh dear,' Neville peered at her. 'We've let the cold in, haven't we?'

Liberty just shook her head and smiled. The glasses were empty and the singers donned their gloves and hats and bustled off once more into the night, singing 'Jingle Bells' as they went. Liberty stayed a moment in the doorway looking after them, before locking the door and hurrying back upstairs to Oscar.

Tollymead: *The carol singing around the village last week was a great success with everyone, singers and householders alike, having an excellent time raising £165 towards the minibus. Miss Scott had to rush back to London as a burst pipe flooded her Knightsbridge mews house, but Pat Simpson, who is also acting as treasurer for the Minibus Fund, kindly took over the arrangements.*

So, the unkind person who suggested there was more community spirit in the Serbo-Croat district of New York than in Tollymead can go eat his hat.

When does pornography become art, and vice versa? The question is vexing the artistic community (yes, there is one) in Tollymead, as well as chucking a spanner in the workings of true love. Oliver Bliss was so pleased with his portrait of his fiancée, Laura Brown, that he decided to exhibit it at the forthcoming Christmas Bazaar and Art Exhibition. However, Laura, who posed with little else than her long hair and a fishtail constructed from plain and coloured tin foil—the kind they wrap those little chocolate sardines in—feels the painting is too revealing and should not be seen in public.

Personally I feel that as the painting is quite beautiful, it should be exhibited, but then again, I never understood all the fuss about Sharon Stone parting her knees during a police interview when her habit of killing people seemed so much more offensive.

CHAPTER TWENTY-FOUR

On the twelfth day of Christmas, Liberty sat in Evelyn's kitchen drinking coffee from a chipped butterfly-painted mug. The January sun came straight and low through the window, showing up the dirt on the leaded panes and forming a pattern on the Formica table.

'I can't stand it,' Evelyn complained. 'Kindness is spreading like a damn rash through the place; nothing is sacred. The other day I was coming back from town and this woman, a complete stranger although she said she knew me, rushed up and offered to help me carry my shopping inside. It was like some terrible scene from an Australian soap opera.'

Liberty laughed. 'So village spirit is rising like the good old phoenix from the ashes?'

'I don't know,' Evelyn snapped, taking a noisy gulp of coffee. 'What I do want to know is, do I look decrepit?'

'No, of course not,' Liberty said, 'but it's nice to be helped.'

'It's only nice when you know you don't need it. Of course I blame this blasted competition. I can't think what Oscar can have been thinking of.' She looked sternly at Liberty. 'Let me rephrase that. I know exactly what he has been thinking of ... and you can stop smirking, he's not yours.' She reached across the table and put her hand over Liberty's. 'My dear child, you do understand he isn't yours?'

'I spent Christmas on my own, didn't I?' Liberty answered, sounding even to herself like a cross child. 'Well, not completely on my own. I had Hamish. It wasn't much fun actually. The people I loved and liked were not there and I was left with someone I love but can't stand.'

'Oh, your father isn't that bad. How is he anyway?'

Liberty thought for a moment. 'You could say that he's searching for his true self, which in his case could take up the rest of his life. He's retiring at the end of the summer term and he's devastated. He's like Mr Chips on speed. Without Tollymead Manor he's nothing, or that's what he suspects. I've tried to make him take up some hobby, but he always flits from interest to interest, the only thing that's been solid is his teaching. He's quite a good amateur artist, so I encouraged him to take part in the Christmas Bazaar Art Exhibition. I even put a

279

picture in myself. It wasn't very good, but his was bought.'

'I know, nice water-colour of the bridge. So which was yours? I don't remember seeing it.'

'Oh, quite a big canvas with an awful lot of little people doing different things and in the centre an old man seated at a table with a huge matchstick model of Winchester Cathedral in front of him.'

'Oh, that one.'

'It didn't sell.'

'No, I expect it didn't.'

'It was wrong to imagine you can slip out of one passion and into another like a snake changing skins.'

'Well I don't know,' Evelyn said. 'Some great writers have become great painters.'

'Ah, but only when they were great writers already, that's the snag.' She sat back in the chair and with a sigh undid the top button of her black jeans. 'I'm getting fat.'

'Oh my dear girl, you're pregnant.'

Liberty smiled. 'Nice thought, but I'm not. It's just that I'm happier. Happiness makes me hungry.'

Evelyn had a compassionate look in her eyes when she said, 'And to think that you were always such a scrawny little thing. You've got this round face, so one forgets.'

Liberty was thinking of Oscar. He was thin—strong but thin. There was something touching about his body, just as Johnny's had

280

seemed to her infinitely touching, when he had hovered on the brink of adulthood, tall, with huge feet but a child's face. With Oscar it was the other way, a body full of power, hovering on the brink of decline; the beginnings of a tummy, the muscular arms that softened in repose, the slight thickening of the jawline.

'And what about when Victoria finds out?'

'She won't.'

'I have no time for that girl, but I don't approve of adultery.'

'I know,' Liberty sighed. 'I do agree with you in principle, it's just that some of my best relationships have been adulterous.' She looked into Evelyn's eyes that were sad and disapproving both at once. 'I'm sorry,' she mumbled. 'I didn't mean to be flippant.' She looked down at her hands, scratching at the scar. Then she looked up again. 'Oh Evelyn, what do you want me to do? Flee the country from some channel port under cover of darkness, my golden curls hidden beneath an unbecoming scarf, one of those with a pattern of stirrups all over it to add to my sufferings, my sacrifice misunderstood by everyone due to a complete and selfless absence of any form of explanation?'

'You don't need me to tell you what would be right,' Evelyn said. 'You know very well.'

Liberty threw herself back in the chair as if Evelyn had slapped her face. 'No, no I don't know and I won't do it, whatever it is. No-one

281

can ask me that.'

* * *

Liberty had not seen Oscar since Christmas Eve. He and Victoria had gone skiing, as they did each winter, and Liberty had got a postcard with a picture of snow-covered Alps and a small chapel with a tall spire surrounded by pine trees in the foreground. There was not much scope for intimacies on a postcard, but sometimes at night she would look at it and wonder if all those erect images of Alps and trees and church spires carried a special message to her.

When Oscar did come, the first evening he was back, she asked him, making him laugh before he'd even had time to remove his coat.

'I can't say, my darling, that I thought of it in those terms.' He put his arms round her and pulled her close. 'But now you mention it, it was most probably subconscious. Very Freudian indeed.'

Liberty was laughing too, but she was pressing so close to him it was as if she was trying to disappear into him like a disembodied soul into a new body.

In bed, sitting with her back against Oscar's arm she asked, 'Why did you marry Victoria? Why did you wait so long and then marry the wrong woman?'

Oscar stared out at the room in silence and

finally he said, 'I needed someone to fall in love with.' He kissed the top of Liberty's head and she could feel his breath on her hair.

'Victoria always looked as if she might be everything you are but she is not. Everyone told me what a lucky dog I was and there wasn't a man I knew who wasn't half in love with her. That sort of thing is very seductive.'

'It can't be easy being Victoria. I mean apart from me sleeping with her husband, she walks through life wrapped up all wrong. I like Belgian chocolates but if I found some inside a box from Tiffany's, I'd be disappointed. It doesn't make the chocolate any less delicious.'

'You're kinder than I am,' Oscar said.

'No I'm not. I'm just used to seeing the other person's point of view. That's why I'm no good at arguing and why I should have been a good writer. By the time I get a chance to put my views across, I've already come round to the other person's way of thinking.' She paused. 'Do you think I'm self-centred?'

Oscar turned round, one leg on either side of her hips, facing her. 'Yes, yes I do.'

'Oh. Right.'

'But I forgive you.'

'I'd forgive myself that and much more besides if I was a good writer.'

'Well I forgive you because you're so wonderful in bed.' He bent down and kissed her.

'"Oscar kissed her expertly but tenderly, his
283

firm lips covering hers,"' she smirked.

'Piss off.' Oscar straightened up. Suddenly serious, he said, 'We can't go on like this you know.'

'"Liberty steeled herself against what was to come, her small pointed chin set."'

He looked at her unsmiling. 'I want us to be together all the time, not just in secretive little snatches, however delightful those snatches are.'

Liberty looked into his eyes and said only half joking, 'Let's run away to a crofter's cottage in the Hebrides and live for each other, two giant valiums in each other's troubled lives.'

Oscar let go of her shoulders. 'Is that how you see me, like a giant tranquillizer?'

Liberty smiled sweetly up at him. 'That's right; a valium with a willy.'

'Bloody charming.'

Liberty kept looking into his eyes that seemed a darker shade of blue all of a sudden.

'You know it's not true,' she said, stroking his hair away from his forehead. 'After I stopped writing, before you loved me, my life was like a bad painting: the kind in which you find a landscape and you know it's meant to be of hills and valleys and shades and light, but all you can actually see is flat. When I was writing everything had a point, even if it was just the point of being put into words. Every sight and sound was flavoursome and full of

284

possibilities. I could cut and paste and polish before putting them back together again in shapes that pleased me. It didn't make me see the meaning of life, but it stopped me worrying about there being none. Your love has given that back to me.' She shook him gently by the shoulders. 'Do you understand that you've given shape and substance to the flat landscape that was my life?'

The doorbell rang, once, twice, and with a sigh Liberty slipped off the bed and, throwing on a long sweater, ran downstairs. Opening the door on the chain she asked, 'Who is it?'

'It's me, Evelyn. If Oscar is there that's fine, I wanted to catch him, too.'

Liberty opened the door and Evelyn stomped in, depositing little puddles of slush from her flat-heeled sheepskin boots onto the blue carpet. 'Now you're always complaining you have no purpose in life, well you can shovel compost. I'm going away for a week or two. I've brought a list of things I'd like you to do for me. If you don't mind,' she added as an afterthought.

Oscar came downstairs, a pink bath towel wrapped round his waist.

God he was beautiful, Liberty thought, middle-aged but beautiful. A grin grabbed at the corner of her mouth.

'Liberty stop leering at Oscar!' Evelyn snapped. 'Here's the list.' She handed Liberty a grubby piece of paper covered in huge, spindly

285

writing lurching across the page.

'Come and sit down.' Liberty gesticulated towards the sitting-room.

'Why this sudden departure?' Oscar asked.

Evelyn glared at him. 'You, dear boy, have no business asking questions dressed like that. Anyway, I've simply decided to pay a visit to my friend Mary Cotterell in Yorkshire.'

Oscar gave her a long look.

'All right,' Evelyn capitulated. 'I thought it might be a good idea to lie low for a bit.' She inspected the muddy tip of her boot.

'Evelyn, what have you done?' Liberty asked.

Evelyn looked up from her inspection of the boots. 'I've only done what any self-respecting, upright individual would do in my—'

'What have you done, Evelyn?' Oscar sat down on the sofa facing Evelyn, who looked small in the generous armchair.

'I've reported Campbell for illegal use of pesticides—'

'Bloody hell!' Oscar threw his hands in the air before having to grab the towel which fell open at the hip.

'—and old Andrew Sanderson for supplying them.' Evelyn looked carefully past the sofa and across to an oil-painting of a ship. 'Well I mean, the Ministry of Ag sent down an inspector to check on the farming practices in the area and nothing came of it. Someone had to act.' When there was no reply she went on, 'I

286

don't suppose you two are aware that the common bumble-bee might be extinct before the millennium.' Her chins wobbled with outrage. 'Yes, extinct.'

Oscar shook his head slowly. Liberty asked herself if she was wholly in favour of Evelyn's actions this time.

Looking from one to the other of them, Evelyn said, 'Well I must off. Got an early start tomorrow.' She hoisted herself up from the armchair.

As soon as she had gone, Oscar hurried upstairs to dress. Five minutes later he, too, was gone, and the house seemed to have grown. Empty room led into empty room, no noise, not much light. With a sigh, Liberty went into the kitchen and dished herself up a large bowl of chocolate fudge ice-cream. She took the bowl back to bed with her; as a sex substitute it would do, but as a conversationalist, she thought, it was lousy.

Tollymead: *The Tollymead Christmas Bazaar and Art Exhibition raised the astounding amount of £2,354.50p, to be divided between the Church Fabric Fund and the Minibus Fund.*

Anne Havesham returned from Christmas in New England topped up with new ideas for her planned television series, 'Atlantic Cousins'.

'My home town, Maryville, is not unlike Tollymead,' she told me. 'It's got the same old-fashioned friendliness and neighbourliness. I miss the store, though. It's housed in a brown clapperboard house and stocks everything from Salsa to needles and thread on its wooden shelves.

'Of course a store like that is not only a cosy and convenient place to get one's groceries, but a meeting place as well. As it says on a sign inside the Maryville store, "People who shop together, talk together".'

'If I see that woman mentioned once more I'll cancel my subscription to that damn paper,' Nancy said out loud as she turned the page of *The Tribune*. She had returned from shopping too exhausted to bother unpacking the groceries. A cup of tea and a rest first she had decided, but now, as she flitted through the pages of the paper, she felt only irritation. They all missed the old shop in Tollymead. Ms Havesham had been making eyes at Andrew too, she was sure of it, you just had to look at his smug expression when the woman's name came up. She drained the mug of tea and got to her feet.

'Well, he has no money,' she said. 'Not a bean.' Picking up the carrier bag closest to her, she thought grimly that the way things were going at least there wasn't such a mountain of stuff to put away. She brought the tins of crushed tomatoes and the tins of tuna fish into the larder and placed them on different shelves, one for the tomatoes, another for the fish. Nancy loved her large, old-fashioned larder with its papered shelves and cold marble slab; it was one of the things that had made her fall for the house. She thanked God every day that they did not have a mortgage. Andrew had paid it off during the years since the children left school. He would do anything to save the business, but he knew better than to try to persuade her to agree to selling the house. The other day, though, they had agreed to sell the half-acre of paddock at the bottom of the garden. She did not mind that so much. They had had planning permission to build on it since the days when Andrew's mother had talked of moving close to her dear boy. Mrs Sanderson had died before her plans came to fruition, but the planning permission for a two-bedroom bungalow with loft space and a single car porch remained.

Nancy reached for a packet of Earl Grey tea and her eyes fell on the octagonal boxes of Turkish Delight and Chinese figs and the net bags of pecans and hazel-nuts. It had all been a waste, she thought, and wiped a tear from her eye with an angry gesture; no-one would eat them now. It was the first Christmas that neither of the children had been home. She could not blame Piers for going off to Greece with the new girlfriend they had never met, or Louise for going skiing with a group of friends. Christmas at home had always been subordinated to Andrew's needs and desires, like everything else, and Andrew had never had much time for Christmas.

Nancy leant back against the larder door, hardly feeling the cold of the small, marble-shelved room. Oh, if she could do it all again, recreate the moments she had squandered: Christmas shopping with a small excited person at her side, a tiny hand thrust in hers, hiding presents, filling a stocking, decorating the house. She stood there and realized that she would gladly give ten years of her life for just one day back when her children were small and it was still within her power to make them happy; one day to do everything so very much better.

With a deep sigh she kicked off her new

shoes that grabbed at her toes like crabs, before unpacking the rest of the bags. She paused by the replenished biscuit tin, picking it up and bringing it in with her to the sitting-room. She settled herself on the sofa and with a little sigh, curled her legs under her and picked out a chocolate Hob-nob. She leant her head back, closing her eyes, filling her mouth with the taste of chocolate.

A loud snore made her open her eyes wide. She placed the tin on the floor and got up. Another snore led her into the study and to Andrew who lay open-mouthed in his armchair, his lower lip sucked into his mouth with every noisy breath. The study smelt bad. She walked right up to him, not caring if she woke him or not. Bending over him, it was as she had thought: he'd been drinking. And it was only three o'clock. The first time this had happened she had pitied him and raged with him against the times and the people who were conspiring against him and the firm. But now she had had enough. His breath smelt permanently sour these days, and his face seemed coarse and foreign to her feelings. With longing so strong that it hurt, she remembered the soft flushed cheeks and wide smile of a small boy standing up in his cot, arms stretched towards her, and that baby's breath as sweet as sugared tea, even first thing in the morning. What had been her response to all that love so freely given? 'Chop chop, up we get. Now don't be silly, there'll be time for cuddles later but now Mummy's got to get on. Chop chop, daddy is waiting, chop chop...'

She turned away from the snoring Andrew and left the room, closing the door behind her.

She sat down, counting to ten and then as she had expected, the door opened again, letting out the bellow, 'What the hell did you have to do that for?'

'Do what Andrew?' she called back, eyes closed.

'You slammed that door deliberately, didn't you? It's all right for you, you can laze around in bed half the day but the rest of the world has to work.'

Her eyes still closed, Nancy could feel rather than see that he was coming into the room. Then she leapt up and stood before him. 'It's three o'clock, so don't talk to me about working. Look at you, you're not even sober. You disgust me.'

Andrew grabbed her arm and pushed his red face close, howling into hers, 'So I disgust you do I? That's not how it seemed the other night when you begged me to—'

'No, Andrew please no.' She put her hand across his mouth. 'I'm sorry Andrew. I don't know what got into me. I'm tired, that's all. Come and sit down and I'll make some fresh tea.' She hurried out into the kitchen and by the time she returned with the tea Andrew was slumped on the sofa, his head in his hands.

Nancy kneeled in front of him, pouring out the tea. Handing the cup to him she whispered, 'We're losing everything else, we can't lose each other.'

Andrew did not seem to hear her and she got up from the floor and sat down next to him. He turned and looked at her with bloodshot eyes. 'They're taking us to court. The bastards will fine us, I know they will, and we just can't afford it. They're out to close me down, do you hear. They're making an example of us. It's over. The blood, sweat and tears of three generations brought to nothing, and by me.'

Nancy watched the tears welling up in his eyes as he said, his voice breaking, 'I've got nothing now. It's all gone and whose fault is it? Eh? Whose fault is it?'

Nancy just shook her head.

'It's Evelyn. You know that, don't you?' Andrew went on. 'Your friend Evelyn.' With a grin that was almost a grimace he added, 'I thought Campbell was going to take a shot-gun to her this morning.'

'She's away,' Nancy said tonelessly. 'When you told me this inspector was finally coming down I went to call on her but Liberty Turner, you know, the woman who lives next door, said she'd gone away to stay with a friend for a week or so.' Nancy was not looking at Andrew as she spoke. She heard him snuffling and she heard, rather than saw, the shiver going through his massive chest, and she despised

293

him. She felt it in every part of her, this contempt, as if some latent disease had finally taken hold of her. Was it for that blubbering, disintegrating figure she had sacrificed everything? Nancy's world was falling apart and whose fault was that? Evelyn's, that's whose. Nancy felt cold all of a sudden, and her head ached. She got clumsily to her feet and went across to the drinks tray to pour herself some sherry.

*   *   *

Coming back from her friend Mary's a week later Evelyn barely stopped to put her suitcase down before hurrying out into the garden. Late January was almost her favourite time of year, with the earth and the trees and shrubs barely containing the new life waiting to burst forth, and each morning like a birthday holding a new surprise.

'You're a lucky woman, Evelyn Brooke,' she said to herself as she unlocked the back door. Two steps out and she stopped dead.

Next door, Liberty thought she heard the howl of a fox.

CHAPTER TWENTY-FIVE

Liberty stared out across the wasteland that had been Evelyn's garden. Every perennial, every small shrub, every rare and beautiful plant, all shrivelled yellow and brown like late autumn leaves. It was as if a vampire had flitted from plant to plant, sucking the sap from each, leaving just the desiccated shell. She put her arm round Evelyn's shoulders.

'What on earth has happened?'

Evelyn did not answer. She kept staring out over the devastated garden.

Liberty knelt down stroking the grass as if it were the pelt of some dying animal.

'I don't know what's happened,' Evelyn said at last, her voice trembling. 'I only know that it's gone. The greenhouse too. My seedlings, all destroyed.' And suddenly she sank to the ground by Liberty's side, kneeling, and burying her face in her grubby, chubby hands, she wept.

'Oh Evelyn, don't, please don't.' Liberty put her arm round Evelyn's hunched back. 'Please don't. Come with me inside. I'll call Oscar.'

Evelyn swung round, looking at her. 'Can't you stop thinking about your fancy man for one minute?' Then she clasped her hands over her mouth and turned away.

'It's all right,' Liberty whispered. She

managed to get Evelyn to stand up and walk with her back inside the house. She led her through into the kitchen, seating her at the table, before switching on the electric kettle.

'What are you doing? I shouldn't be in here,' Evelyn levered herself out of the chair. 'I have to go out there, why did you make me come inside?' As Liberty took a step over to the phone, lifting the receiver to dial, Evelyn shrieked, 'Who are you calling?'

'I'm calling Oscar, but not because he is my, my fancy man, but because he's your nephew and he loves you ... as do I.' Dialling the number of *The Tribune*, she looked sternly at Evelyn as if to stave off any further protest.

*   *   *

'Nurture nurture, water water,' Nancy chanted to herself as she pranced round her garden, a fanfare of smoky breath streaming from her lips, her bare feet glistening with melted frost. Every so often she would pause by a particularly healthy-looking shrub or plant and give it a good soaking from one of the two watering cans in her hands. 'Nurture nurture, water water,' she stood on tip-toe, dousing the clematis and passion-flower that climbed up the old brick wall. She stopped for a moment to watch the poisoned water trickle down on to the plants. 'Have a little of Mr Andrew Sanderson's life-removing mixture, and a bit more.' She gave an extra splash to the evergreen leaves of the passion-flower. 'What a brave little plant,' she mumbled, 'attempting to stay green through winter.' She hurried on. 'Lots to do, lots to do for Jack Frost and his trusty Speed Weed,' she sang.

* * *

The next afternoon, when Andrew came back from work, Nancy was sitting in the armchair by the window, his armchair, her naked feet comfortably high on the footstool his mother had lovingly embroidered with roses and violets. She glanced up at him from her magazine, *For Women Only*.

'Look what I've missed all these years,' she said. She gave a last loving glance at the centre-fold picture of the dark-haired young man whose taut, muscular body glistened as if it had been rubbed with oil, before holding it up for Andrew to see.

Andrew seemed scarcely to have noticed her as he entered the room, heavy shoulders hunched, eyes down. Now he flinched as if Nancy had flicked the magazine in his face instead of just holding it up for him to look at. 'What the hell is that?' But his voice was expressionless.

'I'm not surprised you have to ask,' Nancy looked Andrew up and down appraisingly. 'I mean looking at you both, one would hardly think you belonged to the same species.'

Andrew just kept staring straight at the picture, not really seeing it at all. 'I don't know what you're on about,' he said in the same even voice, 'but I've just paid off my work force.' His voice suddenly trembled. 'I've just put on the street people who have been working for me all their adult life. There's nothing left now.' He gave a vague gesture with his hands before turning and walking out of the room. 'Nothing left at all,' Nancy heard him repeat as he disappeared from sight.

She sat back in the chair and continued flicking through the pages of the magazine. Five minutes later, she heard the anguished roar from the garden.

'God what's this? What's happened?'

Nancy took one last look at the centre-fold, turning it this way and that, before putting the magazine away and getting up from the chair. She wandered across to the french windows, looking out. It was a garden made of straw, she thought. Andrew stood right outside and as he turned round she gave him a little wave, pretending not to notice his shouted questions and furious gesticulating.

'To build Jerusalem...' she sang to herself like she had when she was little and spoken to by her father ... 'Really Nancy, there are times when I just don't know you. Tell me child, what gets in to you?'

'... on England's...' Nancy moved away

298

from the french windows, her hands still clasped over her ears. '... green and pleasant land.' It was not many minutes, maybe about five again, Nancy calculated, until Andrew steamed back into the sitting-room.

'Fee Fi Fo Fum, I smell the flesh of an Englishman,' Nancy said. And she did smell him. She had never told Andrew, but the truth was, he always had been smelly. His feet smelt and his breath smelt and the suits he never allowed her to take to the cleaner often enough, they smelt too. Maybe she should have told him about it earlier. She decided to tell him now. 'You smell. I can smell your feet from here.'

'What the hell has got into you? Have you gone quite mad? You've been home all day. You must have seen what's happened out there.' Suddenly his voice rose to a shout. 'Have you not seen?'

Nancy joined Andrew by the window. 'You mean that?' She lifted a lazy hand, pointing to the devastation outside. 'I did that. Yesterday actually. Of course you wouldn't have noticed this morning. It was dark when you left. Anyway, it takes a little time to work, but you know that.' She felt tired all of a sudden and, not bothering to suppress the yawn, she said, 'I think I'll go and lie down.'

Andrew barred her way, his hand raised, then he let it drop to his side, stepping back to let her pass.

'Middle-class country dwellers have souls too, souls and all the problems they bring.' Wasn't that what Liberty Turner had said to him once, Ted Brain thought as he drove along River Lane towards Evelyn Brooke's house. Well he had not cared much whether they did or not, creating instead a worthy cause from a child's lies. Not only that, he had fallen in love. He still could not bear to dwell on the afternoon when he had been exposed, not only to himself but to everyone else, as a credulous fool. Just the memory of the expression on the policeman's face, when they had come to interview him after Anita's return home, made him unable to meet his own gaze in the mirror.

'You mean to say, sir, that you never suspected? Not in all those weeks. You didn't wonder at her command of the English language or her familiarity with things British? You didn't at any point make the connection between the missing Fairfield girl and the girl in your care? Really sir.'

Ted felt the heat rise in his cheeks. But he was determined to turn this episode into something ultimately good, determined to reach out to his parishioners without the veil of prejudice over his eyes. He felt a twinge of excitement at the thought of rebuilding his dwindling congregation. He had already spoken to Nancy Sanderson about starting

300

Sunday School. He remembered an old teacher at his college saying, 'It's a simple truth that there is less crime amongst regular church-goers.'

Ted had assumed that the kind of youth club he ran in Liverpool would never get off the ground in Tollymead. Maybe he had assumed wrong. In Tollymead the young people didn't have to steal a car, they just borrowed their father's, but that did not mean they did not need him. Ted pulled up at the entrance to Evelyn's drive and got out of the car. He did not know, from Liberty Turner's telephone call some half an hour earlier, what was wrong, only that something had happened that had left old Evelyn Brooke in a state of collapse.

In spite of the icy January wind, the front door stood open and he walked inside. He followed the voices into the sitting-room, where he found the curtains drawn and the lights on as if it was night already. Evelyn sat slumped in a small, hard chair and Liberty and a man he recognized as Oscar Brooke, the local newspaper editor, were kneeling by her side. Oscar sprang up from the floor, looking relieved to be doing something, even if it was just shaking hands.

'Thank you for coming,' Liberty said, looking up at Ted. 'We couldn't think who else to call.'

'I'm glad you did call me,' Ted said. 'That's what I'm here for, to help if I can.' Excited by his own words, he carried on, 'I wish more people would call on me. After all I . . . What is the trouble?' he followed Oscar who was beckoning him to the other side of the room.

'It's her garden,' Oscar spoke quietly. 'You know what that garden means to her. It's wrecked. She's hardly spoken since she discovered it this morning.'

'What do you mean wrecked? Animals, weather? There've been no storms or anything like that.'

'Come with me. See for yourself.' Oscar led him outside.

'Great heavens!' Ted stopped dead on the back doorstep. 'I see what you mean. It's all . . . dead.'

'She's just come back home from ten days away to find this. The extraordinary thing is that Liberty, Mrs Turner, had been over only yesterday morning to turn the heating up, that sort of thing, and everything looked fine then.'

'What about the neighbours' gardens?'

'They're all OK as far as I can tell. That's Liberty's cottage over there.' Oscar nodded towards the house next door, visible through a gap in the yew hedge. 'I don't know who lives the other side.' He turned and pointed to the gabled roof of the house across the narrow lane. 'I don't think Evelyn does either. Their drive comes out on the main road the other side, they keep themselves pretty well to themselves.'

'Tollymead people in other words,' Ted couldn't help saying.

Oscar frowned at him. 'Well anyway, no-one seems to have seen anything.' He stepped out on the dying grass. 'It's some kind of weedkiller you know. It must be.'

'Weedkiller?' Ted followed him towards the first flower bed, careful to step only on the green patches of the grass as if the poison could seep up the thick rubber soles of his shoes. 'How?'

Oscar just shook his head. 'I don't know. Evelyn uses the stream for irrigation, but the pump has been turned off most of the winter. Still, I'll take some water for testing.'

The garden shed down by the stream looked more like a gazebo than a shed, tall and octangular in shape. Inside, it was as clean and tidy as it was messy and dusty in the house. Polished tools hung like trophies on the walls and clay pots were stacked on the wooden shelves that lined the walls. Oscar found a small jar on a shelf and brought it outside, filling it with clean-looking water from the stream. Back inside the house he went to put away the jar of river water, Ted joined the others in the sitting-room.

As if they were actors in an interminable Edwardian tableau, Evelyn Brooke had remained hunched and silent in her chair and Liberty was still kneeling by her side.

Ted did not care for gardening, or gardens

either, for that matter. When his father had joked about concreting over the family's neat handkerchief garden in Wimbledon, Ted had secretly thought it a perfectly sound idea. Only weeks ago he might have judged Evelyn's grief unworthy of sympathy, the champagne tears of an over-privileged old woman. But then would he not also have scoffed at the idea of a deluded vicar who played at being the Scarlet Pimpernel and fell in love with his own creation?

'Miss Brooke, Evelyn.' He squatted by her chair, his knees creaking. 'Can something be done?'

Evelyn did not look at him but she did answer. 'Nothing. Nothing can be done. That garden is dead, and even you, vicar, can't resurrect it.'

Ted shifted his weight from one leg to the other. Liberty squeezed Evelyn's hand, turning her vivid green eyes on him. She gave a little shake of her head, blinking back tears, and he flinched as he pictured for a second those eyes opening up dead and colourless like the leaves and grass outside. But her eyes opened up clear and green still as she smiled weakly at him.

'Have I had breakfast?' Evelyn asked suddenly, her voice strong.

Liberty nodded. 'I would think so, before you left Mary's?'

Evelyn nodded back, but slowly. 'Oh yes, so I did.'

Ted sat down on the sofa. Evelyn freed her hand from Liberty's clasp and struggled to her feet. 'I would like to talk to you vicar.'

Liberty got clumsily to her feet, grabbing at the chair for support.

'No you stay. We'll go into the library.'

Ted got up and put his hand out to Evelyn who took it, using it to lever herself out of the chair. Liberty sat down again, following Evelyn with worried eyes as she stuttered across the worn carpet with Ted following behind. They closed the door behind them. Moments later Oscar came in from the kitchen with a tray of mugs and a gleaming glass-and-chrome jug.

'I made coffee,' Oscar said unnecessarily as he put the tray on the low table, after first removing the heap of seed catalogues that lay scattered across the ink-stained and scratched mahogany.

'Modern machine monstrosity,' Liberty nodded towards the jug from Evelyn's cappuccino maker, but the sight of the polished chrome, incongruous amongst the shabby comfort of the room, made her feel tearful again. 'Evelyn has gone into the library to talk to Ted. I offered to leave,' she added hastily in case Oscar thought she had no tact, 'but Evelyn wanted me to stay.' She looked at him longingly, badly wanting to snuggle up close to him and forget the misery around them, but she stayed put. Touching would be

305

unfeeling.

But Oscar took a step closer and put both his arms round her. 'No-one has died,' he said.

So touching was all right. She buried her face in his shoulder and then she looked up again. 'It will take years to restore that garden. Some of those plants were grown from seeds she had collected from all across the world. Not to mention the amount of plants she smuggled into this country. There was even a plant from Tibet. How do you collect plants from Tibet when you're almost eighty years old? No, it's over Oscar, as surely as if that garden had been parcelled up in a publisher's padded brown envelope and stuffed through her letter box.'

VILLAGE DIARY

Tollymead: *Miss Evelyn Brooke regrets that her 'Winter Garden' will not now be open to the public as planned these next four Sundays.*

Yesterday afternoon I went to tea with Sam and Gertie Cook, and was met by the sad news that Tigger, Sam's gun dog, has been killed in a hit-and-run accident.

Unable to hide his tears Sam told me, 'Tigger didn't come in for his dinner and his toys were all over the place. You see, normally when he goes out for any length of time he collects them all up and puts them by his bean bag, so he can't have meant to be gone very long. Then this little lad comes running and tells us that a dog looking like our Tigger was lying injured up by the rec.'

Apparently poor Tigger died just minutes after Sam and Gertie arrived. 'He must have been waiting for us to get there,' Gertie told me, her voice choking, 'but how he managed to hold on, we'll never know, every bone in his little body was broken. When he heard us come he struggled to lift his head, and there was a tiny waggle of the tail, but within seconds of Sam reaching him, he was gone.'

'Maybe the person who did this thought that because Tigger was a dog, it didn't

307

really matter,' Sam said, 'but that little dog meant the world to Gertie and me. We had no children, so Tigger was the closest thing to it. Gill, that's Gertie's sister, she told us we were making a ridiculous fuss over an animal, but I can't see it myself, really I can't.'

I'm sure the vicar would tell them that there are no scales on which to weigh your loss. No-one has the right to judge what is worthy of grief and what is not. 'You've lost an arm and a leg and a mother, you may weep and wail for two hours a day for months but you sir, you over there with the dead dog, you can't have a tear over half an hour.' Hardly.

I am glad to say that Agnes Coulson and Phyllida Medley came across just as I was leaving, bringing flowers and best of all, sympathy and understanding. At least they're lucky to live in a place like Tollymead, surrounded by friends and neighbours.

CHAPTER TWENTY-SIX

Nancy was washing the brick imitation kitchen floor with the Handy Mop. Sweeping as she went, she backed out of the kitchen, away from the large Brother gas cooker, like a courtier

308

taking leave of the monarch, she thought, giggling. She paused for a moment in the doorway, the broom in one hand, the other on the china door handle. Her whole life seemed to have been confined to that room: cleaning, washing, cooking, always cooking, vast pies, enormous roasts, high-smelling, bloody lumps of meat, the way Andrew liked it. 'We don't want any of that rabbit food,' he always said, so the children had said it too. 'None of that rabbit food, Mummy.' Now Louise was a vegetarian, another excuse for not coming home.

Suddenly she burst into tears. Louise, Piers, squandered gifts, chubby babies, endearing toddlers, awkward teenagers, hostile young adults, second fiddles always, to Andrew. She sank to the floor sobbing, and that was how Andrew found her some time later, crying her heart out in the kitchen doorway.

She looked up when she heard his steps.

'Get up please Nancy. We need to talk.'

'Why? We've never talked before.'

'Don't be silly Nancy,' but he said it quietly, gently almost and she searched the face for signs of the usual irritation. But Andrew just looked tired, tired and old. He put his hand out. 'Up you get,' he said.

Feeling stupid, she scrambled to her feet, stumbling as her foot got caught in the hem of her skirt.

'Let's go and sit down shall we?' Andrew

made a move towards the kitchen table.

'No, not in there.'

Andrew peered anxiously into the room. 'What do you mean, what have you done in there?'

Nancy frowned then she understood, 'Oh, nothing, nothing at all. I just hate that kitchen.'

With a sigh as heavy as a rock sinking to the bottom of a pond, Andrew turned and led the way to the sitting-room. He walked towards the sofa, not his armchair, and he put his hand out and took hers, pulling her down beside him.

'I want to read you something.'

'Oh make it Kipling,' Nancy said, 'I haven't read any poetry for such an age.' She remembered Andrew reading to her, on a long-ago picnic on a wintry Devon beach: 'If you can fill the unforgiving minute with sixty seconds' worth of distance run, Yours is the Earth and everything that's in it, And—which is more—you'll be a Man, my son!'

'Do you feel you've done that?'

'Done what, Nancy?'

'Filled each unforgiving minute with sixty seconds' worth of distance run?'

Again that heavy sigh. 'Now why do you ask that?'

Nancy sighed too. 'Because I'd like to know of course. Why else?'

Andrew shifted in his seat. 'Well no, I suppose I haven't. I suppose I always meant to

310

though. We all do, don't we?'

'And you thought selling farm supplies and pesticides was a good way to go about it,' Nancy stated rather than asked. 'Well, why not. I thought being the perfect wife for you was a life.' The wild plans that had been forming in her mind during the last week suddenly seemed not only possible, but her salvation.

'I'm going to Italy,' she declared.

Andrew opened *The Tribune*. 'Yes, yes why not. You should go away for a while. Have a break. Use the money in the holiday account, you might as well. I'll manage. If you just label the meals for me and leave them in the freezer, I shall be quite all right.'

'I'm not going there for a holiday. I'm going there to have a baby. They are good with older mothers in Italy. Besides, I've always wanted to go to Italy. You know how I used to beg you to take me—'

Andrew leapt from the sofa. 'What do you mean you're going to Italy to have a baby. You can't. We haven't—'

'Slept together for over a year.'

Andrew looked away as he paced the room. 'You can't anyway, you're too old.'

'I'm only forty-eight. Anyway, I told you, in Italy women of sixty have babies. I want a baby.'

Andrew crossed the carpet and sat down next to her again. When he spoke again, his

311

voice was reasoned, level.

'I bumped into Oscar Brooke in town. He told me Evelyn's garden had been vandalized, hardly a plant untouched. He says it was almost certainly poison of some kind.' Andrew sighed. 'He obviously was wondering whether I had anything to do with it. Look at me Nancy.' He took her by the shoulders and swung her round so that their eyes met. 'But it wasn't me, was it Nancy?'

Nancy frowned, trying to concentrate her fanning thoughts into one direction. 'No,' she admitted finally. 'No, it wasn't you.'

'You did it for me, didn't you?'

Nancy looked up at him, surprised. 'No, no not really.'

'You didn't do it for me?' He stared at her. 'But why then?'

Nancy's brow cleared. 'Because she made me see you for what you really are.'

The colour rose in Andrew's stolid face, but his voice remained calm. 'And was that so terrible?'

'Not terrible, just not worth it all.'

'All what?'

'Everything, Andrew. Everything that could have made my life count for something. I turned down my university place and we both know I was the clever one. I squandered Piers's and Louise's childhood, putting your needs always before theirs, and they have never forgiven me. I want some of it back, some of

312

those squandered minutes. That's why I'm going to Italy.' She was silent and in the silence she heard Andrew crying.

*   *   *

Liberty sat in the worn grey-and-white striped sofa in the sitting-room of Laburnum Terrace, flicking through the papers. They had been over to see Evelyn. Now Oscar lay stretched out, his legs over the armrest, his head in her lap. She dropped the paper over the back of the sofa and it fell to the carpet. Oscar did not stir, he must have fallen asleep. She could look at his face as closely as she liked. Without actually touching him, she outlined each feature with her finger, lightly, in the air. She leant forward, and knowing she had not long ago brushed her teeth, felt free to blow a puff of breath across his forehead, moving the lock of hair that had flopped down across the pale skin. Oscar smiled, his eyes still closed, and suddenly his arm shot up and he grabbed her wrist, pulling her down so he could kiss her.

'Oh God, I love you,' Liberty said.

Oscar opened his eyes, dark in the evening light, and serious. 'I love you too. I wonder if you know how much.' He kissed her again.

Liberty thought of the article she had just read in the paper. 'When I'm older I will keep your love by becoming immaculate, lacquered, scented, stockinged, bedecked and bejewelled.

313

It's the way to go when you get older. Only youth can afford to be careless of their appearance.'

'Is this original thought or something you've just read?'

'Something I've just read.' Liberty wriggled onto her knees and tipped herself over the sofa-back, fishing up the paper. 'Here,' she pointed at the elderly but newly engaged countess pictured immaculately in love in a large photo on page five.

Oscar propped himself up on one elbow, looking first at the paper, then at Liberty. 'Well, for the moment I like you fine all tousle-haired and pink-cheeked and,' he poked her leg with the toe of his shoe, 'dimple-thighed. But who's to say in a few years ... Immaculate can be very restful. I had an immaculate great aunt. On my mother's side, not Evelyn's mother, you understand. I could sit for hours when I was a small boy, just listening to her and looking at her. I still remember her scent—gardenia and face powder. Face powder had a scent in those days.'

'Hypo-allergenic,' Liberty said. 'That's what stopped things smelling.' She got up from the sofa. 'Hang on a moment.' She disappeared upstairs to the bathroom and rummaged through her cupboard, overflowing with years' worth of oils and soaps and shampoos and more packets of Tampax than anyone could decently need in a year. Right at the back was a round box with rose-tinted loose powder, topped with a velvet puff. She undressed swiftly and grabbing the box, she powdered herself until she stood like a great, floury rose-scented bun on the bathroom floor. Then she dressed again and ran downstairs.

'I like that you discuss these things seriously,' Liberty said as she plumped herself down on the sofa. 'Appearance probably influences people's lives more than most things. I mean it's so obvious, yet we're all supposed to think it's frivolous to worry about it. "You've just been selected the Most Beautiful Face of the Nineties, and will be paid four million dollars a year for sticking that face on our posters, but remember, it's what's on the inside that counts." Sure thing.' She knelt up beside him, putting her hands on his shoulders. 'Smell me,' she said. 'Do I smell like your immaculate great aunt?'

'Better,' he said.

She stretched her arms up in the air and she felt the tips of his fingers hot against her naked back as he pulled her jumper over her head. Pushing her down against the cushions, he lowered himself down on top of her, kissing her. She opened her eyes and looked into his face. Some men, like opera singers performing their arias, contorted their faces when making love so that you got a fright if you looked up at them, but Oscar looked back at her with a half smile and hazy eyes, and just the faintest frown

315

of concentration.

Later he said, 'I don't want to go,' sounding like a child, pleading and truculent both at once. Normally it was he who was strong and Liberty who clung to him, thinking up new things to say to keep him with her a little bit longer.

This time it was she who got up first. He followed her reluctantly, standing in front of her. Then he clasped his hands behind her neck, and just stood there looking at her.

She smiled. 'Oscar, is it possible that you are beginning to need me the way I need you?'

'Well Liberty, it sure looks like it.'

They kissed again and it was another ten minutes before Liberty freed herself and whispered, 'You must go now. Victoria will be worrying.' She felt wicked as she said it, like when she was small and had watched Hamish pot the rabbits on the school lawn moments after she had admired them playing in the twilight. She shuddered, clutching him to her, trying to kiss away her thoughts.

After he had gone, before popping over to say goodnight to Evelyn, she went upstairs. She splashed her face with cold water and put on some lipstick, making sure she did not look like someone who had, only minutes earlier, cried out with ecstasy in her lover's arms.

*   *   *

'Can you believe it?' Evelyn asked her the moment she opened the door. 'It was that Sanderson woman who destroyed my garden.'

'I know,' Liberty said gently. 'Remember I was here when you talked to Oscar.'

'Yes, of course, so you were. Well don't stand about in the hall, dear, come on in.' Evelyn gesticulated aimlessly.

'Have you eaten?' Liberty asked.

'Eaten, yes of course. I had fish fingers.'

'You had fish fingers yesterday.'

'Did I? Well maybe it was an egg I had. That's right, an egg.' Evelyn hurried, stiff-legged, ahead to the kitchen. 'Have some coffee.'

In the sink Liberty could see at least two days' worth of dirty dishes; Evelyn herself was still wearing the same shabby tweed skirt and moth-eaten green jumper that she had worn on her return home five days earlier.

'Are you sleeping all right?' Liberty asked.

'Yes, of course I am, like a log,' Evelyn said, but when they went into the sitting-room Liberty saw the blankets in the armchair and she said, 'You weren't going to sleep down here?'

Evelyn shrugged her shoulders. 'I like it.' She pushed the blankets onto the floor and sank down on the chair. 'Did I tell you it was Nancy Sanderson who destroyed the garden?'

'I know, you told me. You really should let us call the police, as Oscar said.'

317

'She shovelled a couple of sackfuls of salt into the inlet to the pump and switched it on. Simple really. It killed the garden and destroyed the pump.' Evelyn gave a hoarse laugh. 'Organically too; the irony wasn't lost on me.'

'I'd like to kill *her*,' Liberty said quietly. 'Please let me contact the police.'

'It won't bring my garden back and I couldn't stand the fuss, going to court, and who's to say the Sandersons don't just deny it all? There's no proof. There could be counter claims: libel, defamation. They've got nothing to lose now; he blames me for his business going to the dogs. And I don't want any talk from you either, you must promise me that.' Her voice shook. 'I'm too old, I'm tired, I just want to be left in peace.'

Liberty said nothing, but took Evelyn's mug of coffee across to the drinks tray. She found the brandy bottle, sticky and covered in dust, and splashed a good couple of spoonfuls into the coffee. 'Here,' she said, 'drink this.' She watched as Evelyn gulped the drink down in noisy mouthfuls, then she picked up the blankets and spread them across Evelyn's legs and waist, half expecting to be told not to fuss. Evelyn did not protest, allowing herself to be tucked in like a child.

Liberty stayed until Evelyn was asleep and snoring open-mouthed in the chair, then she tip-toed from the room, unlatched the front

318

door and closed it softly behind her.

She slept in the next morning. When, swollen-eyed and heavy-headed, she ventured out to post a letter to Johnny, she was hailed from across the main street by Neville Pyke. Crossing the road just in front of a builder's van that screeched to a halt inches away from him, Neville grabbed her by the elbow, panting, 'It's dreadful, really dreadful.'

'I know, they drive round here as if it was the M25.' Liberty smiled at him.

Neville looked uncomprehendingly at her for a moment. 'Oh the van, I wasn't thinking of that. No, I was referring to Miss Brooke's garden.'

'Yes, that is dreadful.'

'I wouldn't be at all surprised if this has all but ruined our chances. I hope whoever it was who did it, is thoroughly ashamed. I mean to say, that sort of thing is hardly likely to make us the most caring village in Hampshire, now, is it?'

'I hadn't actually thought of it in that light, but now you mention it, no, I suppose not. It's broken Evelyn's heart. It was a life-time's creation, that garden, her passion. Life's no good without a passion.'

Neville looked confused so she added briskly, 'Well that's how I feel anyway.'

Neville rubbed the tip of his nose with a forefinger. 'I wonder if a special plea to Miss Havesham would do any good. I know she isn't

319

judging, but she is planning to base her new series on the winning village. So if she puts a word in, explains how this sort of thing is not at all like Tollymead...'

'I agree there,' Liberty said, feeling unkind, 'it takes a certain amount of interest in your fellow man to poison his garden. Not like Tollymead at all.'

Neville looked confused, making Liberty feel guilty. 'Have you met Miss Havesham then?' she asked quickly.

'I wouldn't say I had exactly met her. But I've seen her a couple of times. Pretty young woman I thought. Tiny wee bit of a thing, with hair cut like a boy's. I'll catch her attention next time I see her.' He was turning to leave when he stopped and added, 'A very pretty lady she is, I must say.' He crossed the road once more, looking as he went this time.

Liberty, deep in thought, wandered up to the mail box and giving Johnny's letter a quick kiss for luck, popped it in.

* * *

Back home again, she opened the latest parcel of translation work. Could they, the publishers asked in their letter, have the translation into English by Easter? Liberty looked with distaste at the glossy proofs which accompanied the manuscript. On the front they sported a picture of the author who was young, female and theatrical-looking, with dark, square-cut hair and black-fringed, bedroom eyes. 'Birgitta Jungman,' the cover said on the back, 'has, although still only twenty-three, written a novel of hypnotic power.' Liberty glared at the photo and then, slamming the book down on the table, she hissed, 'And what have the British public done to deserve you?' After that she did what she always did when she had a new deadline: she emptied the wash-basket and did the ironing, then she cleaned the kitchen, wiping down the back of the work surfaces and underneath the jars of coffee and tea. She polished the Aga lids, on top and on the inside, and finally she weeded the flower bed by the back door. Then at last, she sat down and began work. After a while she stopped to make herself a cup of coffee and as she returned to the desk, she asked herself for the hundredth time why it was that she, who could translate as well from English into Swedish as from Swedish into English, an unusual talent she had been told, she who gave chapter headings to every incident in her life and titles to her daydreams, why she could not write one acceptable novel? 'Birgitta Jungman, how I hate you,' she sighed, then she spent the next hour practising writing simultaneously in Swedish and English, a pencil in each hand.

Tollymead: What a sight! Daffodils, everywhere daffodils; along the river and up the path to the recreation ground, in the hedgerows and on road verges. Residents of the village must have followed Agnes Coulson's advice and popped their spare bulbs into the ground all across Tollymead. The main street, hitherto immune to any attempts to make it picturesque, looks as different and as pretty as a woman in one of those Before and After make-overs. Better probably because, have you noticed, half the time these women looked better before all those professionals got to them.

Love, too, must be in the air, judging by the 'No Canoodling' that has been added to the 'Dogs Not Allowed' sign on the playing field.

Miss Hester Scott's weekly card nights are a great success with young and old alike. 'I told the vicar that I don't believe God would object one little bit to us playing cards on Sunday,' Miss Scott told me, 'and it gives a nice family feeling to the day: church in the morning, a family game of cards in the evening.'

Vanishing Whist and Racing Demon are current favourites. 'The children love playing with their parents,' Miss Scott tells me. 'It makes such a nice change from watching television or playing computers all alone in your bedroom.'

CHAPTER TWENTY-SEVEN

It was warm for early April. Liberty was outside on the road, white-washing her gate. Now and then she paused, turning away from the paint and breathing in the mellow air.

'It's a grand sight, isn't it?' She felt a heavy hand on her shoulder. 'I don't think I've seen a display like it, not since Mrs Pyke and I went to the very home of the bulb, Holland that is.'

'Oh, Mr Pyke,' she turned round. 'You mean the daffodils? Yes, they're gorgeous.'

'Yes, Mrs Pyke and I were quite the travellers in our day, but as I say, this is in a class of its own. Very good idea of hers, this Miss Coulson, that is. There's a bit there you've missed, I think.'

'Right, absolutely.' Liberty smiled, hoping the words covered everything.

'There's a piece about it in this week's Diary,' Neville stopped to pull out a crumpled paper from the large pocket of his tweed jacket. 'Here.'

'Yes I've seen it, thanks,' Liberty kept smiling as she painted round the black wrought iron handle.

'I just hope those judges see it too, better still, make their way over here. That's the thing with them, you just don't know when they're here, just like those Egon—'

'Ronays,' Liberty could not help filling in.

'That's it, that's it. I don't know that I like this bit about the carrying on, though.' Neville pointed a paint-stained finger at the column. 'I've been up there just now, you know. I was going to rub it away, but the sign was as clean as a whistle. Mind, I've noticed before that the Diary isn't always very accurate. In fact,' he looked around him as if he was half expecting the writer to be lurking behind a hedge somewhere, 'nice as the entries are, and useful too, I sometimes feel as if I'm reading about another village altogether.'

Liberty nodded. 'I know what you mean,' she said. 'I know exactly what you mean.'

'Well,' Neville said, 'I must hurry. I'm on my way over to mow the little that's left of old Miss Brooke's lawn.' Neville's pop eyes shone with satisfaction at the thought of his good deed. 'I know for the rest of us the garden isn't of such importance, but what right have we to say what's worth grieving over and what isn't?' He nodded goodbye and left Liberty at her gate. A few yards down the road he turned and called, 'See you in class this afternoon.'

'"Old Miss Brooke",' Liberty repeated sadly to herself. It was true though. It was no longer splendidly 'Bloody Evelyn', or 'that menace', let alone, 'the owner of that wonderful garden'. No, it was 'old Miss Brooke', and that, Liberty thought, was truly the end.

* * *

Her melancholy mood did not improve when she greeted her class later in the day. Have I no more soul than a hyena after all? she asked herself. No wonder I fail to thrill and move readers. Loving a man and teaching his wife to write romantic stories, were those the actions of a being with a soul?

'Theme versus plot,' she said hastily, noticing the expectant faces turned towards her. 'Any thoughts on the subject?' Blank looks. 'Think of a life,' Liberty said. 'Is parenthood the theme of yours? Then the fun and the slog of bringing those children up, the pitfalls and the high points, that's your plot. Maybe you're dedicated to good works in a selfish world, or single-mindedly pursuing fame or material wealth? Sometimes you might think your life's theme is one thing but as the plot unfolds you realize you're out of control, the plot has run away with your life, and your theme is destroyed. Then, in life as in a novel, you've got problems. Now, for next week, I would like you to write down a theme you would like for a story, in no more than five words.'

'I don't agree with that,' Victoria said.

'Sorry, with what?'

'This theme business. You're too focused. I think it kills the spark. Sort of imprisons you.' Encouraged by approving nods from some of the other students, she went on, 'You should allow things to develop, it should be more organic, you know what I mean? I think that's right for life as well. I like to live for the moment,' she added as if no-one had ever said it before.

'Oh well...' Liberty said wondering why that was all she ever found to say to Victoria's statements. Making an effort she added, 'That's very interesting.'

Victoria looked as if that went without saying, leaving Liberty to ponder another dilemma: which was worse, deceiving a woman you liked or disliking the woman you were already deceiving? Looking at Victoria's smug beauty she felt she did not really have much choice in the matter.

*   *   *

Later that day Oscar rang the doorbell at Laburnum Terrace. As Liberty opened the door he almost fell into her arms. 'I had to see you for a couple of minutes,' he whispered holding on to her tight, moving her along with him into the sitting-room and down onto the sofa, where he kissed her as if he needed her

326

breath inside him to go on living.

'Oi, what's going on here?' Liberty said softly when finally he let her go.

He pushed his glasses up on his forehead and rubbed his eyes so hard she half expected they'd come off on his knuckles. 'I don't know any more. I'm almost afraid to see you, because I hate leaving you so much. I don't love Victoria, I love you.'

Liberty felt her face contorting the way it did sometimes when she heard a particularly beautiful piece of music and she blinked away a tear.

'Whoa there, what did I say?' Oscar asked.

'Well the exact truth is that your words were like music to my ears, but that's an awful cliché of course so—'

'Don't burble my love.'

She smiled weakly. 'You can't bring yourself to tell Victoria, can you?'

'No, no I can't. It's not her fault that I don't love her. She hasn't changed. Two years ago I promised before God and a congregation to love and cherish her for the rest of my life. How can I just abandon her? In fact,' he threw himself back against the cushions, 'I'm an all-round rat.'

'It's all right, rat,' she said. 'Don't worry about me.' She twisted round, smiling at him. 'This is new. How long have we known each other? A few months, that's all. You can't just walk away from your marriage. There's too much walking away in this world. We need time to think.' She stroked his cheek, then, pulling his glasses off and putting them on the table, she kissed him lightly on the lips. 'But I can't leave you either, not yet. I love you.'

He straightened up and held her at arms' length, then with a little groan he pulled her down again. She felt him searching for the buttons of her shirt and like a mirror image she unbuttoned his, bending her head to kiss every part of him she uncovered and stopping only for a second to undo the buttons and zip on his trousers.

It was half an hour later that Oscar looked at his watch. 'I must go.' He got up, searching for his clothes that Liberty had deliberately chucked as far away from the sofa as she could throw them. She watched as he moved round the room picking up his clothes, slipping them on. He pulled his pants and trousers on and, reaching for his shirt, he turned suddenly. 'I feel so damn shabby, coming here like some sneak thief, taking what I need before slinking off. I don't want to treat you like that.'

Liberty walked up to him, unconcerned for once by her nakedness. Standing on tiptoe she framed his face with her hands, looking deep into his eyes. 'You're my love and my heart's delight,' she whispered with a small smile. 'Now go home to your wife.' She gave him a little push towards the door.

Victoria greeted Oscar with silence and cottage pie. He ate his way through the huge helping that Victoria had insisted on giving him, in the conviction that it was his favourite food. His marriage, he could not help thinking, was founded on just such misunderstandings sustained by lazy little lies. Victoria had once said that she just knew he was the sort of man who liked good plain home cooking, and he had felt it churlish to contradict. After that, each time she placed another plate heaped with faggots or bangers and mash in front of him, he put on a pleased expression and he rubbed his hands together with false glee, 'Cottage pie; lovely,' he'd say, or 'Sausages; just the job.'

He pushed another forkful of mince and mashed potato into his mouth. It was the same with her surprises, he thought. He had once told Victoria soon after their first meeting that he loved the way she seemed to live in the present, relaxed and willing to grab any opportunity of pleasure. Now he never knew when Victoria was about to turn every day into a feast. He could be sitting reading, tired and sleepy from a long day's uninspiring slog and she would appear with a rug and their supper in a basket lined with red and white check cloth. 'A picnic in our own sitting-room, that's great,' he'd say because this fun-filled monster was his creation. But this evening, apart from pointing out that as it was such a gloomy day, she had cooked his favourite food, Victoria was quiet. In bed he found out why.

'You're so cold towards me these days,' she said with a snuffle. She snuggled closer and with her voice choked with emotion, her hands busy across his body, she said, 'Make love to me Oscar. Don't reject me. I can't stand it if you reject me.' Her hands, small and strong continued their work expertly, rubbing, squeezing, caressing. 'Please Oscar, what's wrong with me? Am I so disgusting?' She wept openly now, as she slithered on top of him, her naked body soft and light against his. 'Hold me please Oscar. I'm your wife. Don't reject me again.' She shook from all the weeping. 'If I'm so revolting to you I might as well kill myself.' She pressed against him, rubbing her knee up and down his thigh, and his body, a creature of habit, responded.

'Oscar love me,' Victoria whimpered, her legs clutching his waist. 'Love me.'

CHAPTER TWENTY-EIGHT

Nancy woke earlier than ever these spring mornings. She slept better, too. It was having her own room that did that, she thought. She had moved into the spare room straight away on her return from Italy the week before. From

330

the window she could see the bungalow being built on the plot of land at the bottom of the garden. She checked its progress every morning as she got up and then she looked with satisfaction at her stomach. The two went together. The baby had been bought with money from the sale of the land. She had simply cashed a cheque for half of the proceeds. Half of that, in its turn, she had put aside in a personal account for her future and the new baby's. It had been so easy, it made her laugh.

When she had first arrived home, she had pointed at the building works and said to Andrew, 'It's that erection, not yours, that's made my baby possible.'

Andrew, pale and set around the jaw, had flinched. 'Please don't be crude Nancy.'

Andrew had become much quieter since it all happened. The business was being wound up by the receivers and now Nancy had returned announcing she was pregnant with another man's child. 'A medical student most probably, they're always donating sperm. I told you I wasn't too old. Well I had a little bit of help, but nothing major.' She smirked. 'I've always been very fertile'.

Andrew had just stood there, taking it all. Never once had he ranted and raved, not once had he threatened. He just got quieter and quieter, and his normal ruddy colour seemed to have drained permanently from his cheeks.

He seemed too defeated even to ask her for a divorce. Last night he had looked past her out at the garden and said, 'I'll go along with the pretence that your child is mine, but don't expect me to be a real father to it.'

Nancy had smiled sweetly and answered, 'Of course not, you never were to the other two, so why start now?' But it suited her that they stay together. Single parenthood was all very well for actresses and the working classes, she thought, but not for her, not for this baby. Look at poor Liberty Turner. The boy by all accounts had turned out well, but at what price? The woman's life was a mess. No, Andrew could give his name to the child if nothing else. And she wanted the house, not a half share of the money from its sale that she would get if they divorced. In fact she wanted it all again, a baby there in that house, sleeping in the same nursery, playing in the same garden, having tea at that kitchen table, only this time, everything would be perfect.

Andrew kept out of her way, spending his days in Winchester. For two thousand pounds, he and five other unemployed business men had the use of a small office, a part-time secretary called Mia, a fax machine, a BBC computer and most important of all, somewhere to go each morning. As far as Nancy knew he used his time there to despatch job applications together with an increasingly imaginative *curriculum vitae*.

She had talked to Piers and Louise, too. She had not told them Andrew was not the father, but she did say, 'I'm having a baby, to give it all the attention and love I didn't give you.'

'Most people's embittered menopausal mothers go for the bottle or a new job,' Louise had said but not unkindly.

Piers had said, 'Oh God!' and put the phone down. Five minutes later he called back to say, 'Whatever turns you on Ma, honestly.'

Nancy was pleased that the children seemed to accept, even if they did not understand.

These fat, calm days of growing, her baby, the bungalow, its four walls erected already, the beginnings of a new garden that Andrew had planted while she was away, were contented ones. She was so calm she surprised even herself. Was she the same person who had set off fireworks inside Evelyn Brooke's barn and destroyed two gardens? She found it difficult to remember quite what happened that day when, with a throat raw from screaming, she drove across to Evelyn and pranced round her garden like the Angel of Death with her bags of salt. It had been so simple, that was the awful thing. A couple of sackfuls of coarse salt from Sanderson's Seeds dumped into the pump inlet, switch the system on, and that was that; two days later, no garden, no pump. It had pleased her at the time that she did not have to resort to using any of the chemicals Evelyn fussed over so much, just salt, totally organic, usually harmless, salt.

But she was truly sorry now. She had blamed the messenger for the message, blamed Evelyn for making her see how she had wasted her life on an unworthy cause. After all, it was Nancy who had created a God out of a thick-necked and ordinary young man and a life's work out of being his wife. 'Being Mrs Andrew Sanderson is all I want.' How many times had she heard herself saying that.

The same week that Nancy left for Italy, Andrew had gone over to Evelyn and told who it was that had ruined her garden. Nancy never asked what was said, enough to know that no official action was going to be taken beyond Andrew paying for the garden to be replanted and the irrigation system restored. But they had not received a bill yet, and when Nancy glimpsed Evelyn in her nephew's car or out walking with Liberty Turner she hardly recognized her. No, Nancy was sorry but she did not dwell on it. What was the point? All that mattered now was the baby.

She was having her mid-morning coffee when Neville Pyke called in. Poor old boy, still hoping that Tollymead be chosen as The Most Caring Village in the *Tribune* Area. Of course he, like everyone else, had no idea of Nancy's own contribution.

'The daffodils will be a great help,' he panted on her doorstep. 'But this time I've come about the fête.' He looked impishly at her, his big, bald head to one side. '"There he goes again, old Neville," I bet you're thinking, "with another of his schemes."'

'Not really Neville,' Nancy said, but she said it with a smile.

'You know it isn't many months ago that I wouldn't have felt I could come on a little neighbourly visit like this and be welcome.' Nancy said nothing and he shifted his weight from one foot to the other. 'What I mean to say is, we need a much bigger do this year. No offence to you and the other ladies, but earlier years' fêtes have been a bit of a disappointment to Mrs Pyke and myself.'

'Come in for a moment then,' Nancy stepped back to allow him in. As she led him into the kitchen she gave her stomach a surreptitious little pat. 'Wouldn't the silly old man be surprised if he knew about you,' she mumbled. To Neville she said, 'There certainly is room for improvement. Now we haven't set a date yet, but we talked about the first Saturday in July.'

Neville nodded. 'But then we have no time to waste. I am more than happy to serve on the committee.' He spoke the words as if tasting his favourite dish. 'The committee is most important. And of course with all that talk of inspectors going round judging the different villages, I can't say I have seen any, but maybe they are incognito—'

'Like the man from Egon Ronay.'

'Now that's just what Mrs Turner said the other day. So we have to be prepared at all times, that's what I'm trying to tell everyone.'

'What about a bonniest baby competition? They're such fun. I'll judge if you like,' Nancy offered brightly.

*   *   *

Saturday sun shining, benign breeze blowing beautiful ...? Liberty looked up at Oscar sitting next to her in the old hammock under the apple tree, and smiled beatifically. 'If my name was printed down your spine and £5.99 stamped on your bottom, I couldn't love you more,' she said, and the words rolled up in her mind: blond blue-eyed blessed boy. She put her arms round his neck and whispered, 'Blessed boy.'

Oscar gently loosened her arms and looked quizzically at her. 'What did you call me?'

'Blessed boy,' Liberty mumbled. 'Man didn't fit in.'

'Ah,' Oscar said. 'I don't think I shall ask what it did not fit with.' He pulled her towards him resting his chin on the top of her head.

'It's a blessing too,' Liberty said, 'that we are capable of such limited compassion and understanding. A total lack of insight and an inability to use what brains we have, are probably God's greatest gifts to mankind. Here we sit, perfectly happy, throbbing with

336

barely-contained lust—'

Oscar raised an eyebrow and was rewarded with a slap across his back.

'—revelling in each other's presence, whilst all round us people are having a tough time: Evelyn, and that prat Sanderson, poor old Ted Brain, the Haville-Joneses, last I heard, he was off demonstrating in Brussels, my father, even Penny, her husband is threatened with redundancy as well, and that would mean losing her house and, you know, she's created a whole world around that house. There are thousands and thousands like them, what's more, and yet I'm happier than I've been for eight years.'

'You're sure it's not nine, or seven?'

Liberty looked up at his laughing face. She smiled back not bothering to answer. After a few minutes she shook herself and said, 'I'm getting cold. Shall we go inside?'

She made some tea and while she moved round the small kitchen, filling the kettle, warming the pot, putting out mugs and sugar and milk, she kept looking at him. When the tea was ready to pour she sat down opposite him and said, 'You're so beautiful you should be on television. I know you used to be, but you're even more beautiful now. I suit you.' To her delight Oscar's cheeks coloured. 'You're clever too. So why do you bury yourself here?' She was serious suddenly.

Oscar put his mug down with a precise little

337

slam. 'I've told you, I wanted a change. Anyway, I know you mean well but I wish you'd stop going on about how I look.'

'I'm sorry.' She was hurt. 'Personally I would find it very gratifying if someone carried on about how gorgeous I was. In fact, I spent many an hour when I was a plain but clever young girl, wishing someone would love me for my looks alone.' She turned away.

'Hey,' Oscar put his hand over hers, 'I'm sorry.'

Liberty got up and went across and plumped herself down on his lap. 'I want to know why you're here. I want to devour every grubby little detail of your life and absorb it into mine, so it grows all thick and glistening like a first-rate sauce.'

'Look Liberty can we change the subject?'

Know when to stop. Why do I never know when to stop? 'You should see your eyes,' she insisted instead. 'They're troubled and I want to know why.'

Oscar bounced up from the chair pushing her off his lap. 'I'm off. I should have been home ages ago.' He was out of the kitchen with three big steps and then the front door slammed shut behind him.

Liberty sat dry-eyed, staring out at the road as the sun set behind the gabled roof of the house opposite. After a while she got up with a sigh to get paper and pen to continue her letter to Johnny.

'I'm on top of the world,' she had written earlier that day, 'but I can hardly wait until you're home again. It never ceases to amaze me that each generation has to have babies of their own before they get any sympathy for their worrying, bleating, loving parents. When you get home, there's someone I'd like you to meet.'

She looked at that last line now, wondering if she should cross it out. In the end she decided not to and she finished the letter describing Hamish's impending retirement and friends she'd seen who had asked after Johnny. She put the letter in an envelope and sat down to work. At ten she cleaned her face and changed into her dressing-gown before going downstairs again to continue with the translation of the Jungman novel. She never liked splitting her time between two manuscripts, but she still had not finished the teenage fantasy novel. Her eyes grew sore from looking at the computer screen, and she rested her head against the desk. She must have fallen asleep, because she woke with a start to the sound of the doorbell. Her heart thumping, she jumped up and hurried to the door.

'Who is it?' she squeaked.

'It's me.' She heard Oscar's voice.

She opened the door so quickly that Oscar, who had leant against the door, almost fell inside. He was sorry. Thank goodness, he was terribly sorry. And to her embarrassment, she began to cry.

'Come and sit down.' Oscar took her hand and led her into the sitting-room. He sat down on the sofa, pulling her down next to him.

'What have you told Victoria?' Liberty asked before pulling a handkerchief from the pocket of her dressing-gown and giving a loud blow.

'I said I was taking the dog for a walk.'

'You haven't got a dog. Sooner or later she'll spot that.'

Oscar laughed. 'She's asleep. I didn't have to tell her anything.' He put his arm round Liberty's shoulders and pulled her close, resting his cheek against the top of her head. 'You asked me about why I moved down here.'

Liberty waited, snuggling closer, feeling his grip on her arm tightening. After a long moment Liberty eased herself free and stood up. 'I'll put on a record,' she said. 'Music brings things to the surface I've noticed.' She padded across to the CD player and brought out the new recording of 'Unchained Melody'. She turned to Oscar with a smile. 'Music is good for the soul,' she said. 'Even simple stuff like this. Sometimes when I fear I'm just a tangle of nervous impulses, I put music on and up it pops, the elusive little devil.'

'I lost my soul in Colombia.' Oscar smiled back but his eyes were sad. 'How about that for a song title?'

'Don't you make his blue eyes blue,' Liberty

sang softly. 'No, that's wrong.' She walked back and sat down on his knees, her arms round his neck, her face buried against his shoulder. 'You're a good man,' she whispered. 'So what happened?'

For a long time Oscar said nothing and Liberty, itching to prompt him, kept quiet and still. At last he began to speak. He spoke for a long time and Liberty understood from the way he picked his words so carefully that he had not talked much of this before, but that he had thought about it all the more often.

It had all happened two years earlier. He had been living in Colombia with his girlfriend, a photographer, researching a series of major articles on the drug trade. 'I really cared about this one,' he said almost apologetically. 'There's a direct link between children dying in squats in London and Glasgow and some businessman sitting down for lunch with his family down on a ranch two hundred miles south of Cartagena. We all know about it, but he and hundreds like him still get away with it.'

After months of tracking through the jungles and mountain villages, bribing and threatening, he had found a man prepared to act as intermediary. The young man had been frightened. 'All the time he was working to set up a meeting with the local drug cartel he was frightened, but he carried on for reasons of his own. I never even asked what those reasons were. I was too busy chasing my story. A rendezvous was arranged.' He paused.

Again Liberty said nothing, waiting.

'The man I was meeting was a boastful bastard. Full of bull and bravado, a survivor of countless assassination attempts, too used to evading the authorities. I think he had begun to fall a victim of his own publicity as an indestructible folk hero. Anyway, he told me too much, a lot of it on the understanding that it was off the record. I put it all in my article. I felt it was the right thing to do. Several members of the drugs cartel, including a government official, were arrested as a result.' Oscar rubbed his chin back and forth against his fists.

'The boy who had set up the meeting was beaten to death and his body strung up from the spire of his village church. Rachel was shot through the head as we drove to the airport. I survived.'

Liberty leant across and took his hand. 'So you married Victoria, thinking you could drown your memories in those great shallow eyes. You left the work you loved and took a job you couldn't care less about down here. I can understand that.' She paused, treading carefully around the broken bits of his past. 'But I've never been a great believer in self-flagellation. Who does it help? It might ease your pain to know that although you're still alive, at least you're bloody miserable, but it doesn't really do a lot for anyone else.'

Oscar did not answer but sat looking straight ahead across the untidy sitting-room with its heap of books, unread, half read and read, in piles on the floor along with a huge unfinished jigsaw that spread across the hearth rug. Liberty did not want to badger him. Carefully, so as not to disturb his thoughts, she got up from the sofa and picked an apple-core from a corner of the room, chucking it into the wastepaper basket by the window. As she returned to him, he put his hand out and, smiling, pulled her down towards him.

'We should say to hell with everything,' he said. 'Go away somewhere. I've got contacts in the States. I could get a job over there. Just think about it.'

CHAPTER TWENTY-NINE

'I've been thinking,' Alistair Partridge had settled his corduroy-clad bottom on Oscar's desk and showed no signs of moving.

Oscar sighed and put away the unopened letter he knew was from his friend Larry in Boston.

'Why don't we do one of those Everyday Stories of Country Folk that's so popular? We could keep the Village Diary for announcements, and put the new column on, say, page two. Base it on Tollymead. It seems

343

the right sort of cosy village, but mixing in a bit of make-believe to pep it up.'

'I think whoever it is writing in now, has done that already,' Oscar said.

'We needed to tighten up on our news coverage and the arts,' Alistair said, 'I'm with you all the way there, but people like a bit of light stuff, too, gossip, that sort of thing.' He chucked an A4 page at Oscar. 'This is this week's.'

Oscar picked it up and scanned the page.

Plans for the forthcoming Fête and Flower Show are progressing well, but we still need more helpers and some more ideas for stalls and attractions too. Details of the next meeting will be posted on the Parish Notice-board. Please turn up and help to make this year's show one to remember.

Yesterday as I was out walking, enjoying the sunshine, I bumped into Laura Brown and her youngest daughter Polly. Laura had that glowing, replenished look not fully explained by her just having had tea at Phyllida Medley's. I remarked on how well she was looking and she told me that Oliver Bliss and she had settled their differences over the painting and set a new wedding date.

'I'll put Staffordshire figurines on top of the wedding list,' Laura told me. 'It was last night; I was having a glass of sherry with

Hester Scott. I kept looking at those funny little china figures she's got all over the sitting-room, most of them real people, dead real people of course. It made me think, especially the one of Nelson. I mean, one day a man bursting with life and power, hero of Trafalgar, the next a faintly comical ornament on someone's mantelpiece. So I thought, life's too short to waste arguing, and I went straight home and called Oliver.'

Carried away by the good news and the spring warmth, I told Agnes Coulson on our walk the next morning that although power walking was excellent in its way, for a really glowing complexion, love was the thing. Agnes, reasonably, pointed out that at sixty-eight she didn't have all that much choice.

For optimum well-being, I include a recipe for Nettle Soup:
   4 grip-sized bunches of young nettles
   1 medium onion, chopped
   1 parsnip, peeled and boiled until soft
   ½ pint good chicken stock
   ½ pint single cream
   salt and pepper to taste

Blanch the nettles and soften the onion in some fat in a frying pan. Put the nettles, parsnip and onion together with the chicken stock into a food processor. Process until *blended. Pour into a thick-based saucepan and add cream and seasoning. Heat gently while stirring all the time. Serve piping hot with crusty wholemeal or granary bread and butter.*

Oscar finished reading and gave the page back to Alistair.

'My wife quite likes the recipes, actually,' Alistair said. 'We could have more of those: Phyllida Medley's chocolate cake, Anne Havesham's Thanksgiving dinner.'

Oscar nodded. 'What we want is a sort of soap in print. See if you can think of anyone to do it. Otherwise, put an ad in, asking whoever it is writing in from Tollymead to come to the office. We can talk a few ideas through, take it from there.' He gave Alistair a quick smile before reaching for Larry's letter, tearing it open the second Alistair was out of the room.

Larry was delighted, he wrote, to hear of Oscar's plans to come over and he was pretty sure a certain foreign editor on a rival paper was for the chop. 'Watch this space,' was how the letter ended and with a little sigh of contentment Oscar leant back in the chair and allowed himself to dream. A new start, a new life just when he thought there was nothing left but bare existence. A life with Liberty, of waking up to find that dimpled cherub's face next to him and those long eyes, those amazing green eyes, smiling at him. The small room with its battleship-grey walls and standard office furniture, the piles of newspapers and clippings, disappeared and instead he was at home, wherever that home was, with Liberty.

* * *

It was love that did it, Liberty thought on her walk. No doubt it was love that made her smile when waking in the morning, the way she had when she was still writing, and love that made her really quite kind to others, ready to help and take an interest. Of course it was possible those hyenas felt the same when meeting their mates. Maybe it was just another lot of instincts clubbing together to make an effect. But there again, maybe it was her soul working up towards immortality. All that love could not possibly just vanish with her disposable body. Of course the whole idea of immortality is very un-green, she thought, as she passed the new bottle bank at the top of the road. Recycling was the thing these days, everyone agreed, so were immortal souls that hung around the atmosphere for ever really such a good thing, or ecologically unsound? And did the yellow eyes of a hyena light up with the same spark as hers did when it saw the object of its affections? Was it ready to die for its mate?

She had just posted some letters and was on her way across to see Evelyn. It was only a while ago that Evelyn would have entered into that argument with spirit and knowledge. But not now. Liberty let herself in with the key Evelyn had handed to her months ago. She tried to visit every day, but it felt more and more like visiting a burial vault. There was decay in the air. Before, there had been a fresh, outdoor feel to the rooms, with the doors and windows flung open to the garden. Now the windows and doors remained shut and the dust and grime from years of neglected upholstery and furniture, the dirt from countless muddy steps, loitered in the still air of the rooms. And Evelyn, Evelyn herself was old. It was passion that had kept her young, passion for her work and for her garden. With her garden gone, she was going too. It was as simple as that, Liberty thought, and as sad.

Downstairs, Evelyn was nowhere to be found, so Liberty hurried up the stairs calling her name. When there was no answer she got worried and reaching Evelyn's bedroom, she knocked on the closed door.

'Yes,' the voice sounded unsure.

Liberty opened the door and stepped inside. Evelyn was in bed, leaning back against a wad of pillows in her tartan dressing-gown. Liberty checked her watch again. It was ten o'clock, just as she had thought. Normally by this time Evelyn would be coming in from the workshop or the garden for mid-morning coffee, but here she was in bed with her dressing-gown so mucky and crumpled that it looked as if she had slept in it.

'Are you not feeling well?' Liberty asked her.

Evelyn gave her an irritated look that somehow cheered Liberty up. 'Of course I'm well, why shouldn't I be? I'm always well.'

'Of course you are. I'm sorry. I shouldn't have come barging in like this. It's just that I got worried. You're usually up so early.'

'I don't know what you're talking about. This is my usual time for getting up.' Evelyn looked angry but frightened too. 'What do you mean I'm always up early? What time do you make it?' Suddenly she sounded pleading.

Liberty shifted her weight from one foot to the other. 'Tennish,' she said finally.

'I make it seven,' Evelyn said glaring at her small gold wristwatch.

'I think you'll find it's ten,' Liberty said gently.

But Evelyn seemed to have lost interest in the whole question of time. 'I'm tired,' she said. 'A day in bed will do me good. Be sure to close the door properly when you leave. I don't want Linnaeus to get out.'

Liberty's mouth dropped. Linnaeus, Evelyn's cat, had been dead for two years.

CHAPTER THIRTY

Liberty, wandering across her own neglected garden, thought her plants were downright tropical in their overgrown lushness, now the sun had finally come out. The first flowers on the mock orange by the back door were opening white and purple at the heart, sending wafts of fragrance half-way down the lawn, and fat drops of rain dripped down on her head from the branches of the maple tree. Maybe she should plant a laburnum at last, right there, next to the maple, now there was no little boy waiting to poison himself with the pea-like pods. It would be nice to think that, long after she was gone, some new owner might point out the yellow-flowering splendour and say, 'Of course that's what the house took its name from, that wonderful laburnum over there.' And he would be wrong.

She could easily afford a tree. She had finished both her translations ahead of time and had been well paid for what were major pieces of work. She in turn had paid off her overdraft, with some money to spare for a welcome-home present for Johnny, who was returning at last, at the end of July. But before then she was going to Sweden with Oscar.

'We should go away together,' he had exclaimed a few days earlier, looking all boyish and excited. 'Get a chance to talk everything through, make plans.'

She had gone straight out and booked two plane tickets to Gothenburg. From there, she planned, they would travel the short distance to the island where her mother's family still had a house. None of the cousins had planned to stay that week, so the house was hers. Still, the most difficult part of the arrangements remained: how to hoodwink and deceive, how to fool poor Victoria.

To Liberty's relief, Victoria had stopped coming to the classes. She had phoned, sounding relaxed and friendly, to say that she had other things to take up her time and interest now, but she had not said what. Liberty had put the phone down with a sense of wonder that someone who had a talent for getting into print, however slight, could turn her back on that gift with no more thought than you discarded a broken umbrella. Yet Liberty, who would have hugged such a gift to her chest and never let it go, who would have nurtured it and polished it, she had not received it. It was difficult to accept, but she was learning. She was no more suitable for the work she had so desperately wanted to do, than a chimpanzee, or, seeing that a chimpanzee was supposed to be able to write the plays of Shakespeare if left with a typewriter for long enough, perhaps marginally less suited.

Later, when Oscar came over, she told him

about the trip.

'That's great, it really is.' He wandered back and forth in her kitchen pulling his glasses on and off, reminding her of Tom in the way he was picking things up, an apple, the tea caddie, oven gloves, and looking at them absentmindedly before putting them down again, mostly in the wrong place.

'But . . .?'

'Oh to hell with it. We have to go.' He stopped in front of her, looking down at her as she was sitting sipping her tea. 'Do you realize we've never had more than three hours together at any one time? You can't plan a life that way.' He pulled a face. 'I'll tell Victoria I'm off to do an article on the decline of Swedish shipyards or something.'

Liberty got up and put her arms round him and because she was feeling guilty, because she too had had a husband snatched from her, she rested her face against his shoulder and mumbled her excitement, as if by being really quiet about it, she could somehow avoid retribution.

* * *

They were having five days away, and on the first, they stood on the small passenger ferry that was bringing them the short distance across the harbour to the island of Carlskil. Pastel clapper-board houses lined the promenade and climbed up the hill towards the old fort which dominated every view and every photo of the island, like an ageing starlet at a première. Liberty turned to Oscar, as proud as if the island were her own creation. Oscar, his arm round her shoulders, was gazing across the water, but when he said nothing about what he saw she gave him a nudge with her elbow.

'Well?'

He gave her arm a little squeeze. 'Well what, my cherub?'

'I suppose that's because of my thighs?' She looked up at him and he looked calmly down.

'No, because of your face.' He said nothing more, but continued to gaze across the teal-coloured sea.

Liberty breathed in the salty air and wondered how she had managed so long without it. Overhead the gulls circled, screeching at a returning fisherman whose catch lay exposed on the deck of his small boat.

They walked the short way from the ferry landing to the house, Oscar insisting on carrying both their bags.

'All these flag poles,' he said nodding upwards.

'One for every house,' Liberty made a sweeping movement with her arm. 'Even the houses that haven't got a garden have one, like that.' She pointed to a bright yellow house with a short pole rigged from the wall, as if from the stern of a ship.

The last hundred yards were up the cobbled hill towards the fort. As they turned in the narrow lane that led to the gate, Liberty stopped and, making Oscar put down the cases, she put her arms round him and hugged him out of pure happiness at the thought that he was hers for every moment of five days.

Oscar smiled at her as if he had forgotten how to stop, but he did not ask her what the latest display of affection in the middle of a sandy lane was all about. A few yards further on they stood by the gate to the house. Liberty sighed with satisfaction; it was almost five years since she had been there last, but she had not exaggerated the charm of the white wooden house with its glass-fronted verandah turned towards the sea. The short gravel path, lined with rose bushes that were barely in bud, led straight to the front door. From the window, an emerald green parrot perched in his wrought iron cage peered at them with sapphire blue eyes. Like the frilled roller-blind, he was painted onto the glass panes.

'My grandfather did that, and he helped us paint the rug in my father's flat,' Liberty said, putting the key in the lock. 'Grandfather was very keen on painting, but strictly in an amateur sense. He'd always wanted a parrot but my grandmother wouldn't hear of it. "Nasty dirty things spreading seed and psittacosis."'

'Psitta what?'

'Now that's exactly what my grandfather said.'

They dumped the cases in the hall and went up the steep wooden staircase. The sun shone through the skylight and onto the pictures of boats and the sea that lined the wall.

'I've always loved that one,' Liberty pointed at a painting of a red sail disappearing round the point of a small peninsula. 'It really annoyed me that I couldn't disappear into it the way children always managed to do in books. I would stand for ages at all hours of the night and early morning, eyes closed, hands stretched out, but it never happened. Of course,' she added as if she still hoped.

After they had unpacked, Liberty made some tea and Oscar lit a fire in the tiled stove in the corner of the verandah.

As she lolled in the armchair next to Oscar seated on the sofa, she said smugly, 'You look comfortable here. Patrick never did. He always had the air of an Englishman indulging the natives. "Wicker chairs ... well I suppose it's all right if you're a Swede."' She took a long gulp of the hot tea, choking as it burnt her throat.

Oscar put his own mug down on the wooden floor next to him and got up, pulling Liberty out of her chair. Tilting her chin, he bent down to kiss her, and still kissing her, he knelt down, making her kneel with him. He tore his shirt off before unbuttoning the top of her brown cotton dress and slipping it off her shoulders, kissing her neck as he gently pushed her down on the floor.

*   *   *

Liberty lay naked on the rug, her head resting on Oscar's chest. 'Do you think,' she said, 'that God made making love so good just because He wanted us to procreate, or do you think He was actually being nice?'

'Oh, He was being nice, definitely. He probably thought we needed some reward for putting up with living.'

'You know when I was writing my books, what I had most difficulties with: showing the hero and heroine as they fall more and more deeply in love. I always felt I should have them say deep and meaningful things to each other, to show what soul-mates they were becoming, but the truth is, when you're first in love, all you do is bonk and talk rot. Well almost anyway.'

'It's not a bad way of life, bonking and talking rot,' Oscar said.

*   *   *

On the island in May there was only one store open mid-week, the others stayed closed until the week-end, when trippers and summer residents flocked across to the island from their homes in the nearby towns. It was a good store, stocking all kinds of different things from muesli to school stationery. Moving through the narrow aisles with Oscar, Liberty picked out frozen peas and meatballs, dried macaroni and fat bars of Marabou chocolate with nuts and raisins. They got loo paper and washing-up liquid as well, and matches and charcoal for the tiled stove. For wine or spirits you had to put in an order in advance at the Monopoly that looked more like a dispensary with its brown-panelled walls and long counter.

On the way back up the cobbled hill they met the man who had run the fruit and vegetable stall when Liberty had been a child. Liberty stopped and chatted, although she knew he could not hear a word she said. He appreciated the courtesy though, and they parted with big smiles.

'His wife was deaf too,' Liberty told Oscar as they lugged the bags up the hill. 'But both of them made it clear that they viewed it as a slight if anyone referred to it. "How much for the bananas today Albert?" you'd ask. "The pears are three kronor for the half kilo," he'd answer, but you generally left with what you had come to buy.'

Later that night Oscar found an old flag in a cupboard outside the bathroom. Liberty, who had been asleep, woke to find him outside in only his jeans, hoisting it. Naked, she leant out of the window and called softly, 'You could get arrested for that. Flags come down at sunset,' but she was grinning.

Oscar just laughed and waved before securing the line. Liberty waved back, looking out at the floodlit façade of the fort and the blue-and-yellow flag stiff in the sea breeze. 'You'll be feeding the parrot next,' she whispered before padding across the wooden floor and back into bed.

CHAPTER THIRTY-ONE

When she woke the next morning Oscar was already gone. His side of the bed was straightened and his clothes were gone from the chair. She threw off the duvet, shivering in the morning air, put on her dressing-gown and closed the window. He had had a shower. She picked up his damp towel from the chair and covered her face with it, inhaling the smell of soapy skin. She walked down the steep wooden staircase and into the kitchen. No Oscar.

She went back up to the bedroom to put on jeans and a big checked shirt under a ribbed fisherman's sweater that had once belonged to her grandfather, then she ran out into the garden and up to the gate. A woman, dressed already in her pastel summer clothes and a pale blue cotton hat, walked past with her dachshund. Liberty nodded as she crossed their path on her way up the last bit of the hill to the fort. The woman nodded back, and the wind made the ears of the little dog rise like spinnakers.

Liberty found Oscar sitting on a rock, looking out across the sea. As she sat down quietly by his side he turned with a small smile, putting his arm round her shoulders. The sky was blue, turquoise really. Liberty squinted up at the sky, watching the white clouds racing along, crossing the sun's path, one after the other. It struck her how odd it was that she had once wanted to kill herself through despair, when it was so obvious that now was the time to die, now when she was happy. She closed her eyes and saw herself rising from Oscar's side and running to the edge of the cliff. She jumped . . . and there: a happy ending.

The wind dropped so it was warm enough to have breakfast outside on the wooden terrace. Liberty was pouring the tea when Oscar put his hand on her arm, making her put the teapot down.

'We should get married,' he said. 'Being with you like this, I've realized I could never go back to how things were before.' He pulled her down on his knee and murmured, 'I knew that would happen. That's why I almost chickened out of going.' Clasping his hands round her waist he asked, 'Could you consider leaving Tollymead and moving abroad with me? I think there's a

359

job for me in the States, on a weekly news magazine in Boston.'

Liberty stared hard at the blue-and-white pattern of her cup, then she blew her nose noisily into her paper napkin.

'I'm sorry,' she muttered. She cleared her throat and said in her normal voice, 'I'd love to. I'll have to ask Johnny about his plans of course but ... Oh my God, I'd love to.'

Oscar handed her his paper napkin and she used that too. Giving her a look that was half amused, half concerned, he disappeared into the kitchen only to appear moments later with a bottle of champagne and two glasses. 'I brought this with me,' he lifted the bottle in the air, 'just in case.' The cork popped and flew across the table, and his face broke into a grin as he poured out the wine.

*   *   *

Victoria kept a trunk filled with baby clothes in the attic of the Oast House. The little knitted jackets and smocked dresses had once been worn by Victoria and her sister, and ever since had been lovingly kept, safe from moths, in the camphor wood chest. Victoria smiled as she picked out the red-and-white dress she had worn for her first birthday. She held it up to the sunlight that filtered through the dusty attic window and marvelled at the hundreds of tiny stitches that criss-crossed the gingham checks.

There was no yellowing of the white collar and cuffs; the dress could have been made yesterday.

She placed it back amongst the tissue paper in the chest and closed the lid. Only two more days and Oscar would be back from his trip. Walking back downstairs she took extra care with the steep attic stairs. She made herself a cup of decaffeinated coffee and settled down on the sitting-room sofa, picking up a copy of *Marie Claire*. Leaning back against the cushions she sighed with contentment; she was getting everything she wanted.

CHAPTER THIRTY-TWO

It was eight-thirty in the evening and dusk was settling as Oscar dropped Liberty off at Laburnum Terrace. She entered her house feeling like a bride, carried over the threshold, not by Oscar, not yet, but by the promise of a new life. She stood in the narrow hall, beaming as he followed her inside with her suitcase. He put the case down and put his arms round her, kissing her.

Pulling free reluctantly, he said, 'I must go. Really I must,' he added more to himself than to Liberty. He took a step towards the door and as she stood there, still grinning, he laughed and shook his head before coming back for one more kiss.

After he had gone, Liberty resisted going into the sitting-room to dream. She had work to do, another dead-line to meet. She went into the kitchen and made herself a cup of tea, taking it over to her desk and switching on the computer, telling herself she was lucky to get the work. In their accompanying letter the publishers wrote, 'Maria Grip's prose is of an especially sensitive and poetic nature, so we would ask that particular care is taken not to lose any of these qualities in the translation.'

'Other people's perfect prose.' Liberty buried her head in her hands. 'It's a living,' she mumbled to herself, 'it's a living.' She stayed with her head in her hands bashing it slowly and rhythmically against her palms. What was wrong with her, her and Maria Grip, what was wrong with people, that they could not be content with God's creation but insisted on trying to set up like rival stallholders, flogging their own? What was it with people?

Her head began to hurt, so she sat up straight and began reading. '*Den tysta sommar natten penetrerade min nakna kropp*'. She sighed and shook her head; it sounded no better in English: 'The silent summer night penetrated my naked body...' filling me with hot air, she added in her mind. She scratched her head with the biro, itchy with boredom. She continued reading until late into the morning. She needed the money. She had no

362

intention of coming to Oscar a pauper.

*   *   *

Nancy was sitting up in bed in her newly decorated bedroom. By her side, on the little chest of drawers, stood a plate of chocolate Hob-nobs and a mug of warm milk. As she bit into her biscuit and turned another page of *The Tribune*, she sighed at the thought of all those years sharing a bed with Andrew, of being told not to be a pig and eat in bed, being told not to rustle the pages of her magazine or newspaper, being ordered to switch off the light. She loved her new room. Her eyes slid contentedly across the page and fixed on the Village Diary.

> *Tollymead: Laura and Oliver Bliss returned this week to their new home on the outskirts of the village after their surprise wedding at the British Embassy in Paris. It had rained in Paris on their wedding day, Laura told me, but the sight of the flowering chestnut trees flanking the broad avenues of the Champs Elysées, leading up to L'Arc de Triomphe lost nothing of its magic in the light mist of the afternoon.*
>
> *So that their friends would not feel sidelined, Laura and Oliver gave a party on their return and Laura looked beautiful in the pale pink linen dress and pink-and-white check jacket that she had worn on her wedding*

363

*day. Our vicar, the Reverend Ted Brain, was
also at the party, and there was talk of a
service of blessing to be held at St Saviour's
church at a later date.*

*It was a warm, starlit night and the party
ended with dancing outside on the terrace as
more people from around the village joined in,
lured by the music and the light.*

*'I'll pinch all this for my series,' Anne
Havesham told me as we watched the scene
together, 'and I would just love to set it in
Tollymead.'*

For once, Nancy could not care less about
that Havesham woman being mentioned, but
she did think, a little sadly, that maybe she and
Andrew would still be sharing a bedroom if
there had been dancing under the stars in
Tollymead years ago.

*   *   *

'I just had a call from the Reverend Brain,'
Alistair Partridge pottered in through Oscar's
open door at the *Tribune* offices. 'He's the
Vicar of Tollymead,' he added helpfully.

Oscar looked up at him, red-eyed and wild-
haired. 'I know that Alistair. Christ I know
that.'

Alistair stroked his beard. 'You don't look
as if you've had a holiday.'

Oscar glared at him. 'So what did the man

364

want?'

'He wondered who it was who was responsible for the Diary. Said he'd never even heard of an all-night do in Tollymead with dancing under the stars, and that he had most certainly not taken part in anything of that nature. Sounded like he'd been accused of being the life and soul of the local orgy.'

'What did you tell him?' Oscar asked tiredly.

'I apologized and all that. Said we'd check our facts extra carefully next time.'

'I think it's about time we found out whoever it is writing in. Have you run that ad?'

'It'll be in Friday.'

'Good. We might or might not be able to use her, but either way, we need to ask her to get right back to basics with the Diary entries.'

'Might be a bloke.'

'Don't think so somehow,' Oscar said. 'Anyway, have you thought of someone for the new column?'

Alistair shook his head. 'I had a chat with young Robert, but he's not keen. He rather fancies himself as the hard-nosed reporter. Sally and David are stretched as it is, and we shed most of our outside contributors when we reorganized.'

Oscar nodded. 'I think what we want is something entirely fictional, but in a diary style. It's been done before, but not here, and it's always popular. Anchor it in a fictional village too, a sort of mix of the ones around

365

here. Call it "Miss X's Country Diary", that sort of thing. We'll talk to whoever it is doing the Tollymead contribution and take it from there. Oh, and the entries for the Most Caring Village competition will be judged soon. Get Robert and Sally to go out and interview locals from the different villages, and keep running the ad for nominations for kind neighbours. And get everything verified.'

When Alistair had gone Oscar continued going through the stack of mail in front of him, although half the time he was not noticing what he was reading. Almost at the bottom of the pile he found the letter with a US postmark. The job on the east coast weekly was his if he wanted it. There it was: a new start. Sighing, he put his head in his hands. After a moment, trying out his voice to make sure it was steady, he lifted the phone and dialled Liberty's number. When she answered she sounded in a hurry but she slowed down with pleasure as she said, 'Oh it's you.'

'Going out?'

'Just across to Evelyn.'

'I need to talk to you. Can I pop over tonight, on my way from work?'

'Of course. Can't you tell me now?'

'I'd rather not. See you tonight then.'

Liberty put the phone down, feeling curious and a little annoyed at Oscar hanging up so quickly. She shrugged off her unease and, picking up the small watercolour of the island she had brought for Evelyn, she hurried across to Glebe House and knocked on the door. She waited a couple of minutes then knocked again. Again she waited until finally she heard the rattling of keys and muttered swearing. At last the door opened and Evelyn blinked at her in the morning light.

'It's me,' Liberty said unnecessarily.

'Hello dear.' Evelyn stood aside to let her in. 'I'm sorry, I haven't had time to dress this morning.' She was wearing her tartan dressing-gown and her hair was a mess. 'I've been very busy,' she gesticulated aimlessly.

'You've started back on the garden?'

'No, not really. Correspondence, that sort of thing.'

Liberty felt suddenly furious. 'You should sue that woman.'

'What woman?'

'Nancy bloody Sanderson of course.' Evelyn did not move from the hall so Liberty moved towards the kitchen, hoping Evelyn would follow. 'She's back you know, from wherever it was she's been, looking fat and contented. Maybe she is a vampire. That ghastly Andrew seems to have halved in size. He's all pale too; I saw him in Fairfield the other day.'

'I'm getting some money.' Evelyn came into the kitchen with her, plumping herself down on a battered oak chair. 'I've got the letter somewhere. I told Oscar I didn't want any fuss. I'm too old for all this fuss.'

Liberty's heart gave a jolt. Evelyn was always talking about her age now. She never had before. It had been the least interesting subject in the world. Evelyn had taught her that it was not being old that made you pitiful, only talking about wanting to be younger, as if that was all you wanted to be in life. No, the trick was to behave as if you were completely at ease with your age, and everyone else would be too. But Evelyn of course did not even want to be young.

Liberty looked away from Evelyn's defeated face, down to the floor where balls of dust sat like mice in the corners under the cupboards. She was about to say the money would help to get the garden re-stocked but, looking across at Evelyn's hunched figure on the chair, she changed her mind. Evelyn was right; it was too late. She made polite small talk instead about her trip and then, unable to keep down her own happiness any longer she said, 'Don't tell anyone, but Oscar and I are getting married.'

Evelyn turned tired eyes on her. 'My dear child, Oscar's already got a wife.'

Liberty looked away, blushing. 'I'm sorry. That sounded awful.' Dutifully she added, 'Poor Victoria.' Her face brightened again. 'But you know he doesn't love her. The whole marriage was a mistake.'

'He made a lot of promises in church. I know, I was there.'

'Well I love him,' Liberty muttered.

*   *   *

Neville sat writing at the desk that he had been allowed to purchase at a very good price from British Rail when he had retired.

Dear Sir,

I'm writing in response to your request for readers to send in nominations for Most Caring Village. To me Tollymead is the obvious choice for the coveted award. Quite apart from countless instances of neighbourliness chronicled in your own pages through the Village Diary, some of which I cannot, of course, personally vouch for, I can relate to you many other incidents . . .

Neville Pyke wrote in his small, neat hand that made the most of every inch of the paper. He paused and thought, turning round and looking hopefully at his wife for inspiration. Gladys was watching *A Country Practice* and offered none. Neville scratched his bald head with the top of the roller ball pen. Then his face brightened.

For one, folk from the village banded together to re-decorate the vicarage as a surprise for their vicar. And after the accidental . . .

here Neville underlined accidental,

. . . fire at Miss Evelyn Brooke's farmhouse,
369

countless residents of our village turned out to help her restore her possessions to order...

Fifteen minutes later he had finished his letter and sealed it inside a neatly addressed envelope. On his way to post it, he was happy to be able to offer a stranded motorist the use of his telephone and, once the call was over, a cup of tea while they waited for the AA. The motorist thanked Neville profusely as he left and Neville waved and called out, 'Just remember to tell your friends what a caring place this is.'

* * *

At seven-thirty Oscar rang Liberty's doorbell. Liberty, who had been sitting reading through the manuscript she was translating, making notes, hurried to the door and flung it open.

'I'm nominating your kindness in making love to a poor divorced woman, as a typically caring Tollymead act!' she called out.

Oscar did not smile back. He looked tired.

'Sorry,' Liberty took his hand, 'was that tacky? It was tacky wasn't it?'

'What? No, no of course not.' Oscar went straight into the sitting-room and threw himself down into the armchair by the window.

'I love you, you know that, don't you?' He looked up at her in an agony of frustration.

She knelt down in front of him, resting her

hands on his knees. 'Yes. Yes I do know.'

Oscar looked away, bashing his fist against the armrest of the chair. 'Victoria is pregnant. She told me last night.'

For one insane moment Liberty wanted to congratulate him, after all, congratulate was what one did when someone was about to become a father. Instead she just stared. She could feel her mouth falling open and she clamped it shut, still staring at him.

Oscar gave a helpless shrug of the shoulder. 'It only happened once since you and I—got together. Just once.'

CHAPTER THIRTY-THREE

'It will be a beautiful baby,' Liberty said to Oscar, her eyes open wide with her effort not to cry.

'Oh God,' Oscar groaned.

'Are you fond of babies? Had you planned to have children before you met me?'

'No, well yes. In the beginning Victoria kept saying she wasn't ready. After a while I was relieved. I could kick myself, just assuming that she was looking after that side of things. Anyway,' he shook his head, 'I should never have slept with her after you and I became lovers.'

Still facing him, she pulled herself up and

clasped her arms round his neck. With a snuffle she said, 'There's no point carrying on like that. Lovemaking happens even in the best regulated families. You don't owe me an explanation, the woman is your wife, for heaven's sake.'

'Yes I do.' He loosened her grip and slid down from the chair so that he too was kneeling. He put his hands on her shoulders. 'I won't give you up.'

She couldn't help smiling. 'You say that now because you don't know the baby.'

Oscar let his arms fall to his side. After a moment he got up, easing her gently up with him.

'Talk tomorrow?' he said.

'Talk tomorrow,' she said, trying to smile again and failing.

She went to bed soon afterwards, praying for sleep so that she could arrive at the next day with the minimum of pain.

And she did sleep, waking only when her doorbell rang at eight o'clock. A woman she had never met before stood beaming on the threshold.

'Sorry to ring your bell at this hour, but I've been keeping an eye on your house while you've been away.' The woman put out her hand. 'Beryl Morgan, I live just up the road. Neville, Neville Pyke that is, told me you were away and asked me to keep a weather eye open.'

'Thank you,' Liberty said, unwilling to let the woman in as she herself was still in her dressing-gown with her hair and her thoughts in a mess.

'So when I saw the curtains left undrawn overnight, although you were meant to be back, I thought to myself, Beryl I thought, you be a caring neighbour and get yourself straight over there. She'll thank you for it, that's what Les, my husband said, that's us, Les and Beryl.'

As Liberty looked questioningly at her, she carried on, 'I mean in case you want to send in a little mention. You know, caring neighbours.' She winked. 'Most Caring Village. Every little helps you know, that's what Neville says.'

Liberty's face brightened. 'Right, of course, thank you.' She smiled at the woman and then closed the door before running round the whole ground floor drawing the curtains at every window. 'Frankenstein's monster,' she mumbled, 'that's what. Frankenstein's monster.'

* * *

When Neville arrived at the Sandersons' house, Andrew was just leaving.

'Going out?' Neville enquired politely. Andrew gave him a withering glance and marched off. As he had left the front door open, Neville took a step inside calling, 'It's only me—Neville.'

'I'm in the drawing-room. Come on through!' Nancy called back.

Nancy was sitting in a chair by the window, knitting. She smiled at Neville who beamed back, thinking how much friendlier Nancy had become since her trip abroad.

'I've come about the fête,' he said as he fixed his watery eyes on the flashing knitting needles. He liked to see a woman knitting, or sewing too, for that matter. When he and Gladys were first married, her small soft hands were always occupied. She would sew the tiniest little stitches you ever did see, and he had not owned a jumper that she had not knitted. Neville's mother used to say that their baby would be the best dressed infant in Fulham. But no baby came; and it wasn't for lack of trying either.

'I've talked to the vicar,' Nancy said, as she added yellow wool to the strand of white. 'We agreed on the third of July as a good date. It's a little early for some of the vegetable show entries, but we want to avoid clashing with Everton. They've got theirs scheduled for the tenth, and Abbotslea is on the seventeenth.'

'That trophy displayed in the hall, that would be something, wouldn't it?' Neville said dreamily.

'Trophy?'

'Most Caring Village. You haven't forgotten we're in the running, Nancy, have you now? And if we triumph, there might be that American television show to follow. Mrs Pyke would be excited at that.'

'That Havesham woman again! I'm sick and tired of hearing about her as if she was some kind of royalty, although to be fair,' Nancy added, 'there hasn't been any scandal concerning her, not yet.'

'What do you mean, not yet?' Neville's eyes bulged at her.

Nancy looked up at him coolly. 'I've had my suspicions for some time now that she's been trying to get her manicured claws into Andrew. Nothing concrete you know, just a feeling. You develop an instinct over the years.' She switched between the yellow and the white yarn, creating a pattern of little stars.

Neville wriggled from a mix of embarrassment and excitement. 'I'm sure. So you've met her then, I take it.'

'No, no I haven't. And I'm not sure that I'd care to now either.' She paused with the needles in her hand, and her eyes lit up, making her quite a good-looking woman, Neville thought.

'I've got other fish to fry,' Nancy said, needles clicking once again.

Neville badly wanted to know what those fish were, but he sensed it would be a mistake to ask. Nancy might have mellowed, but she could still turn a chap to stone with that magistrate's look. 'A theme fair,' he said hastily, 'and maybe a treasure hunt.'

'Well you get on with that,' Nancy said, 'I'm doing White Elephant, Pat is books, and

Joan's doing Gourmet Cooking. The vicar is in charge of ice-creams. Oh, and before you go,' she said to Neville who had had no intention of leaving, 'here's *The Tribune*, I've finished with it.' She nodded at the open paper on the coffee table. 'There's a bit about the fête in the Diary. And the usual talk about people one's never met.'

VILLAGE DIARY

Tollymead: *Mrs Smedley, The Old Smithy, Well Road, Tollymead, would like your old costume jewellery for her stall at the Summer Fête. It doesn't have to be in mint condition, clasps in particular can be mended or changed, and beads can be cannibalized. If you think you've got anything, please bring it to the house, or if that's difficult, give Mrs Smedley a ring and she'll collect.*

Also on the subject of the fête, Miss Hester Scott went against her principles in a good cause the other night, and played for money at her weekly cards night. She has kindly donated her winnings to the fête committee, as she herself will be in the South of France at the time of the fête.

Miss Scott will be back in August and she has already promised that if we ever do decide to form our own amateur dramatics society, she will tread the boards once again. Now the Everton Players have folded, there's more reason than ever not to let the arts die in our area.

We're proud to announce that a resident of Tollymead, Oliver Bliss, has been invited to join the Anglo-French expedition to the Arctic Ocean, taking off next month. His wife Laura tells me that although she

dreads the separation, she is proudest of all.
We both agreed that at least she won't have
to worry about being lonely as the village is
sure to rally round with visits and
invitations.

'Well this is excellent, excellent,' Neville exclaimed as he finished reading. 'I hope the powers that be at *The Tribune* take note of what's before their eyes.'

*   *   *

'None of these places are any too friendly once you look into it,' Alistair Partridge complained to Oscar as they left the offices together. 'It's easier to find teenage thugs than good neighbours in most of the villages around here. It's bad enough that I can't let my daughter out after dark in Fairfield, now it seems the same sort of thing is beginning to happen all around. One old lady in Everton called in to nominate her village as the most caring for the sole reason that after her little cottage was knocked off three times, a neighbour installed an alarm for her at a twenty per cent discount. That's the new morality for you.'

Oscar's laugh was hollow. 'Morality,' he mumbled. Aloud he said, 'Well do what you can. This competition is your...' he blinked, '... your baby now.'

'Time for a beer?' Alistair asked as they

378

passed the pub on the way to the car park.

'Thanks, no. I'd better get home.'

'Well, give my best to your lovely wife.'

Oscar smiled mechanically and gave him a quick wave before hurrying across to his car.

Fifteen minutes later he pulled up in front of Liberty's cottage.

'I'm going to paint furniture at the fête,' Liberty said almost the second he came through the door. She had green paint under her fingernails and a pale blue streak, like a bruise, across her forehead. 'I'll invite people to bring old wooden furniture and mirrors and stuff and I'll paint flowers and children's names on hairbrushes. Of course that will just be the beginning. Who knows? I might become a great painter.' She began to cry.

Oscar had stood watching her in silence, but now he took a step towards her and pulled her into his arms. 'I'm so sorry,' he whispered. 'Oh God I'm so sorry.'

'You're going to be a father and I can never have any more children, not yours, not anyone's. It's killing me, don't you understand? I just can't do anything right.'

Oscar led Liberty into the kitchen and he sat her down by the table before going across to the sink and filling the kettle.

'It isn't as if the child won't have a father,' he said, his back turned. 'Lots of children grow up perfectly well and happy with divorced parents. I mean, look at Johnny.'

The kettle boiled and he warmed the pot with some of the water before putting in three pinches of tea and bringing it right up to the kettle, to fill.

'You see how it is,' Liberty tried to smile. 'I find a man who is tall enough for me to have to stand on tip-toe to kiss him, a man who knows how to make a proper cup of tea, and then, then I lose him.'

CHAPTER THIRTY-FOUR

It was still early in the morning, just gone nine, when Ted called in at Laburnum Terrace with a request. 'Kids,' he said, standing on the doorstep, his face a little pinker even than usual.

Liberty flinched. 'Kids?'

'I've talked with a friend of mine who's a social worker in Liverpool, in my old parish. Can I come in?'

'Yes, yes of course. Oh and sorry about these,' she patted the pink curlers that clung to her hair like huge burdocks. 'I was just taking them out. I'm trying to achieve the hippy look one more time before it's too late. You know the kind of thing: straight hair parted down the middle, floaty dresses ... I tried to make a garland of daisies earlier but the stems kept coming off.' She fluttered around waving her arms a lot, guiding him into the kitchen that was hot from the Aga and the sun beating through the windows. She opened the back door to let in some air.

'Don't take them out on my account, please. My mother always wore curlers round the house.' He smiled soothingly.

Liberty thought that was probably all the more reason for her to take hers out, but she smiled back and said instead, 'I'll make us some coffee.'

Ted sat down at the table. 'I thought it would be great to bring some of the kids down here for a holiday. I never gave this place a proper chance, I'm the first to admit it, but things are happening, I can feel it.' Ted turned pinker than ever. Excitement, rather than the heat from the Aga, Liberty thought.

'You know,' Ted said, 'some of those kids have never been out of the city. So I thought of you.'

'Of me?' She felt a demand creeping towards her, and clutching her arms to her chest she just wanted to escape, hide her head under a pillow, like an ostrich. No, ostrich was wrong. Had she not heard Evelyn say that it was a myth, ostriches burying their heads in the sand to hide?

Ted cleared his throat. 'I have a list of young people here.' He fished out a crumpled piece of paper from his pocket. 'Keith, that's my friend, and I drew it up together. There's a girl here,

Karen English, solvent abuser since she was ten; she's fifteen now, one abortion. You could have Karen.'

'I could have Karen?'

'We thought two weeks at the beginning of the school holidays.'

'You'd like me to have this girl here for two weeks?'

'That's it.' Ted took the cup and saucer Liberty handed him. 'Cheers.'

Liberty sat down herself, with a heavy thud. Prodding her feelings carefully she said, 'I don't think I'm that nice really, Ted. I mean, do you think anyone in Tollymead is that nice. I know there's been a lot of things written about Caring and Neighbourliness and stuff, but you shouldn't believe everything you see in the paper. In fact I sometimes think you shouldn't believe anything you see—'

'You'd like Karen,' Ted said.

'You think so?' Liberty looked doubtful. 'It's just that I've led rather a sheltered life in some ways. I'm not proud of it or anything, but the fact is, I'm more pony club than glue sniffing, if you see what I mean.'

'I'm sure Karen would be too, if she had the choice,' Ted said calmly.

Liberty felt her cheeks turning pink like Ted's. 'Yes, yes of course. Silly of me. Who else are you going to ask?'

'I talked to Nancy but she has some private reasons for not being able to help this time

382

around. She suggested I ask this American woman, Anne Havesham. I'm ashamed to say I haven't met her yet—'

'Oh don't be,' Liberty said quickly. 'I mean you can't be everywhere. You think it's a good idea asking her?'

'Sure, why not?'

'Well...' Liberty took a deep breath. 'No, why not?'

'So you'll have Karen?' Ted drained his cup. Feeling trapped, Liberty wished childishly that she had given him a mug, a chipped mug, instead of that pretty rose-covered cup and saucer.

She thought of all the times she had cruised past some drenched teenager hitch-hiking on a wet night and how she had driven on, with her three empty seats. Fear was a great enemy of good deeds. What, she wondered as she fiddled with her cup, running the tip of her finger round and round the smooth edge, what would a hyena do about Karen the substance abuser? Not a lot, was probably the answer, not unless she was a nice, toothsome corpse.

'When do you want her to come? You see, Johnny's back home at the end of July.'

'I know Karen quite well. I'm sure they'll become great friends.'

And that is supposed to make me feel better. Liberty took a huge gulp of coffee, swallowing it down the wrong way. 'OK. I'll have her,' she said. 'Give me her address and I'll write to her.'

Ted stood up, looking so relieved she felt ashamed. Walking him round to the gate, she said, 'It's a very good idea, Ted. I hope lots of people will end up helping.' She bent down, sniffing a deep, red rose. 'She'll like the garden, don't you think, if she's from the city? It's messy and all that, but it's peaceful.'

'She'll love it,' Ted beamed at her. 'I knew I could count on you.'

After Ted had left, Liberty was so worried by her promise that the only thing she could do was take a long walk. It was hot and the birds were singing, one of the best sounds. She walked fast. She might as well do herself some good whilst she fretted.

Would not the girl be bored in Tollymead? At fifteen she most probably would not like the steam railway that ran between Alton and Alresford. Jane Austen's house too, was far from a safe bet. Did children read Jane Austen in schools these days? She did not think Johnny had, but if they did, were they impressed enough to want to see her house? Karen and she could read *Pride and Prejudice* together and then they could go and see the house.

Liberty marched on down River Lane, out of breath, fists pounding the air. Of course, Jane Austen's concerns would seem miles away from an inner city child of fifteen, they seemed miles away from most people's concerns, but that was part of the point of books, to give you a helping of other lives to enrich the staple diet of your own.

She was walking so fast that she was beginning to sweat and her heart was thumping. She slowed down as a car passed and she noticed the driver, a woman, grinning at her. Liberty grinned back. By the church she met a man with a retriever. The man, too, grinned. The birds were still singing. She hoped many people would agree to take in Ted's children. If Tollymead was really changing it meant it was possible to turn the clock back and make a smash-and-grab raid on the virtues of the past, instead of just hanging round dinner parties bemoaning their demise. Who knows, Liberty thought, emboldened by the hooting of the horn by another grinning driver, we might even be able to begin leaving the church unlocked again. She waved to the car.

On her way back she decided to call in on Evelyn. The back door of Glebe House stood open. Liberty paused on the doorstep, calling Evelyn's name. When there was no answer she stepped inside. She paused in the doorway to the sitting-room. A newspaper lay open on the sofa and several unwashed mugs stood on the small tables amongst the dust-covered seed catalogues. The french windows stood open, and Liberty stepped back into the sunshine. There was still no sign of Evelyn, so Liberty walked across the lawn towards the stream, which glittered like crumpled foil in the sun. The lawn was green once more and the first flowers were appearing on the clematis and the roses that Oscar had planted against the south-facing wall. A few yards from the edge of the water, she stopped. She knelt down, peering at the tangle of weeds. Sinking back on her heels she slapped her hand across her eyes. Then she forced herself to look at Evelyn, who floated face down against the small sluice, her grey hair tangling with the reeds. With a moan of distress Liberty jumped into the stream and with the water reaching up to her chest, half walked, half swam across to her friend, turning her on her back. Not stopping to look at her face, she gripped her under the arms and pulled her back and out of the stream. She tried to expel the water from Evelyn's lungs and all the while she called out, 'Help! Anyone help! Come quick!'

The murky river water dribbled from Evelyn's mouth, but her eyes were wide open and her breath had gone. Liberty bent low, exhaling into Evelyn's mouth. There was no response and with a whimper, Liberty scrambled to her feet and ran back to the house to telephone for an ambulance. Assured it was on its way, she chucked the telephone down and ran back to Evelyn. Throwing herself down on the ground by her side, she continued to apply every half-baked idea on resuscitation she had ever absorbed. She carried on until the ambulance men came to lift Evelyn on to the stretcher, then she got up and scrambled ahead of the men, opening each door to let them through.

Evelyn was carried through the front door and into the ambulance, leaving Liberty weeping by the door, thinking: is that all there is to it? Evelyn has left this house and this life, and still the birds carry on singing, the sun still shines, and today's newspaper lies open on the sofa. She watched the ambulance drive off towards the cross-roads and then she walked back into the house and called Oscar.

She tried to tell him as gently as she could that Evelyn had drowned in her own stream, floating face down amongst the reeds, with her spectacles left folded on a tree stump at the edge of the water. 'They've taken her to Basingstoke Hospital. I was going to follow the ambulance, but then I thought Victoria might want to come with you.'

'I'd like you to be there,' Oscar said.

'I'll come if Victoria doesn't want to be there,' she said tiredly. 'But I can't face her now, not just now. Death is bad enough.' Then she had to apologize. That was no way to speak to a man in mourning, the man you loved. 'Sorry darling. Sorry, sorry.'

After she had put the phone down she wandered round the sitting-room, touching the chair where Evelyn had sat when she last saw her, folding the papers, stroking the dust off the little china hedgehog on the mantelpiece. How could one fail to be materialistic, she thought angrily, when things were so much more permanent than people?

It was only when she got back home that she realized she had taken a walk through the village and discovered a dear friend drowned, all the time wearing a head full of pink curlers.

*   *   *

There was an inquest, at which Liberty gave her account of how she had found Evelyn and what had followed immediately afterwards. She tried not to look at Oscar. Officially he belonged to Victoria. On high days and death days and public holidays, he still belonged to Victoria. She gave Oscar a pale smile as she stepped down from the witness box. Oscar was solemn and red-eyed, and now and then he blew his nose loudly in a brown-and-white check handkerchief. Victoria was dressed in just enough black to show she was a certified mourner.

After the inquest was over and the judgement had been made that Evelyn's death had been accidental, for only the evidence of the neatly folded spectacles suggested anything else, Victoria went over to Liberty and asked if she would come back with them to the Oast House. 'We won't take no for an answer,' this mother of her lover's child said to Liberty, taking her firmly by the arm.

Liberty pulled an apologetic face at Oscar

over Victoria's shoulder as she allowed herself to be led out of the courtroom and into the car park. As she followed behind in her own car, Liberty found it difficult to concentrate on the driving. She kept seeing Oscar before her, his beautiful face and his body, strong, muscled, soft-skinned, with two greedy women pulling him apart: one whose greed was sanctioned by the courts, both earthly and divine; one whose desire was approved only by the devil, if there was such an unfashionable person. By the time she pulled up outside the Oast House, she was as exhausted as if her body was the battleground.

'Are you all right?' Oscar had time to whisper as they followed Victoria into the house. She could feel his eyes on her, but she did not dare to look back in case she threw herself into his arms kissing his lips, caressing his hair, whispering love, all while the balance of her mind was disturbed.

'What about a stiff drink?' Victoria said. 'For you, that is, Liberty. I mustn't now I've got Oscar Junior to think of.'

Oscar Junior! Coming into the sitting-room behind Victoria, Liberty rolled her eyes to the heavens. It was either that or breaking down in awful sobs. She rolled her eyes again before noticing Victoria looking at her with a curious little smile. Feeling the heat rise in her cheeks, she took the tumbler of whisky from Victoria's outstretched hand. The scar on her cheek was itching and she put her hand up to cover it.

'Don't worry about that scar,' Victoria said, 'we're all friends here. I promise you, after a while one hardly notices it. Isn't that right Oscar?'

'No, no of course one doesn't.' He looked furious, but Victoria just smiled serenely.

Liberty drank the whisky down in one, not really thinking about what she was doing in her miserable confusion. Then she burped.

'I'm most awfully sorry,' she said.

Victoria made much of not hearing, but Oscar grinned at her and winked, making her feel a bit better.

Serious once more, he asked her, 'Do you think her death was an accident?'

Liberty looked up at him and slowly shook her head.

'Well I for one can't understand why anyone would want to kill themselves over a garden, as you seem to suggest,' Victoria said, sitting down on the sofa. 'Can you Oscar?'

Oscar looked into his drink before answering. 'I think I can.'

Victoria looked annoyed. 'Well if you are right and she did kill herself, I think it was a very strange thing to do, don't you Liberty?'

Liberty did not want to seem as if she was ganging up with her lover against his wife, but nor could she deny Evelyn her reason. 'No, I don't really think it was strange,' she said.

'Quite frankly I think you're both being

melodramatic,' Victoria said. 'Old people slip and fall all the time.'

When it was time for Liberty to go, Oscar walked her out to the car, and as he held the door open for her, Victoria joined him in the soft drizzle, slipping her arm round his waist. He flinched and Liberty looked away as she started the engine. It was hard to leave Oscar with a woman like that.

CHAPTER THIRTY-FIVE

Oscar was not sure whether Evelyn's request to have 'An English Country Garden' played at her funeral was a joke. But there it was in black-and-white in her will, so what could he do?

'Play it,' Liberty said as she helped him go through the boxes of papers in the attic. 'If she meant it seriously, you've done what she wanted, if it was a joke, she would want us to fall for it.'

So the organist played it with due solemnity at Evelyn's funeral two days later. The church was almost full, as full as it had been when the parish thought it was featuring on *Songs of Praise*. Only a few pews at the back, on the right hand side behind a pillar, were empty.

Liberty did not go back to the Oast House for tea afterwards, but at seven o'clock Oscar

391

came to her. She opened the door for him, in her dressing-gown, with a large mug of tea in her hand.

'I'm sorry, were you in bed?'

'No,' Liberty shook her head, 'working. Anyway you know I'd interrupt an audience with the Pope to see you.' She stood aside to let him in, closing her eyes when he brushed against her. She shut the door and locked it. 'I suppose you could say, big deal, she's not even Catholic so of course—'

He smiled and put his finger up to her lips. Then he said, 'I'm not surprised you didn't come back with us after church. Not after the other day and all that "Oscar Junior" stuff. I'm so sorry.' Then he took his finger away and kissed her.

They sat down in the kitchen. Within moments Liberty had got up again. 'Tea, coffee, a drink?'

Oscar shook his head and put his hand out for her to come and sit down on his lap. 'I'm sure she suspects something,' he said, putting his arm round her waist. Automatically Liberty straightened up, sucking in her stomach and she could feel, rather than see, Oscar's quick smile.

Still sitting upright, her back to him, she asked, 'Have you got that job in the States?'

'Yes, if I want it.'

'If we go, you'll hardly ever see the baby.' She took a deep breath, then quickly as if it

392

would all hurt less that way, she said, 'I can't split you from your own child. If someone had done that to me and Johnny, I would have ended up hating them.' She twisted round and looked hard at him, forcing herself to carry on. 'I've brought up a child without a father, remember. I've seen what it does to a little boy to have all his friends bring out theirs for matches and Speech Days. I've made the most of week-end outings and lonely Christmases when the whole world, other than me, seems to be part of a shopping, decorating, loving parenthood. Do you know that for three years running, the only thing Johnny put on his Christmas list was: A Daddy. Have you ever heard anything so pathetic? And how do you think I felt? Maybe now it's quite easy for you to think of this baby as just an unwelcome appendage to a woman you don't love.' She framed his face with her hands, tilting it up towards her. 'But you see, when he comes along, you'll love him. He'll be tiny and helpless and yours and you'll love him. You won't be able to help yourself.' Letting her hands drop she sighed. 'Nor should you try.'

She got up with her mug and poured herself some more tea. It was cold by now, but no matter, it was something to do with her hands while she destroyed her life.

'He can come for holidays, lots of them. And I'll visit him.'

Liberty stayed by the Aga. 'Babies don't
393

have holidays,' she said. 'They hang loose.' She smiled suddenly at him. 'And don't you see, even if it's a little girl who looks just like her mother, you'll love her with a love that's stronger than anything else in the world, or at least you ought to.'

Oscar tipped himself back in the chair the way he had a long time ago when he had broken it. This time the wooden ribs held. 'All right. So we stay here in England.'

'And you'll be a man who walked out on his own child, a visitor to that child who'll grow up knowing you didn't love him enough to stay. And think what you would miss. I can never have another baby, have you thought of that? You'd all hate me one day.'

Oscar put his hand out again. 'Never. I could never hate you. I love you.'

'Well *I'd* hate me. How will it look on my CV when I apply for a soul, eh? "1973, failed attempt at husband-stealing, resulting in much-loved, fatherless son. 1993, second and successful attempt at husband-stealing, resulting in someone else's much-loved, fatherless child."' She took his outstretched hand pulling it up to her lips, kissing it, rubbing it against her eyes to wipe off the tears. 'Will I never learn, never get better? I can't write, I can't do what's right.' She smashed his hand down against her hip, shouting, 'What's wrong with me, Oscar, that I can never do what's right?'

Oscar got to his feet and grabbed her by the shoulders, forcing her to look into his eyes. 'To hell with your soul. What about me?'

She could see in his eyes that he was frightened. It was almost more than she could bear. Had he been a soft and sobbing kind of man, a velour-clad, leisure-time man, it would have been easier. She freed herself gently and sat down, pulling him down back onto his chair next to her. She took his hands and pressed them to her chest.

'Oscar, dearest, listen. We work hard, we write or paint, or build or garden, whatever, we try to carve out a life where we are in control and where what we do matters. Jesus, Oscar, don't I know it? It was the ultimate control trip when I was writing. I looked around me at God's creation and then sat down and rearranged it to my own satisfaction. Isn't that what all endeavour is about? Evelyn must have felt she was creating her own slice of paradise in her garden. But see what happens, God gets the last laugh. Ultimately we have no control. No-one wanted my creations, and a menopausal magistrate destroyed Evelyn's. So what's left?'

'Love,' Oscar said simply.

Liberty bent forward and kissed him lightly on the lips, her stomach knotting with desire. Pulling back, she shook her head slowly and said, 'Trying with all your heart to do the right thing, that's what's left. It's the only thing over which we have any control, any real say. We can't chuck that away. If we do, we could as well be hyenas.'

'What the hell have hyenas got to do with this? For Christ's sake Liberty, come off your hobby horse and listen to me. I love you. Get that in to your thick skull and stop being so damn analytical.'

She was so weak, she ended up begging him to make love to her.

Tollymead: *As you will have seen already in the pages of this paper, Tollymead has been chosen as The Most Caring Village in the* Tribune *area. And before any jealous voices are raised in protest, the editor of* The Tribune *might live in Tollymead, but the newspaper's owner is a resident of Abbotslea and the deputy editor lives in Everton.*

No, what matters is that Tollymead cares and what a tribute that is to all of us. The latest manifestation of this comes through the Revd Ted Brain's scheme to give inner city children a country holiday. Ten families have already volunteered to put a child up, and Tollymead is looking forward to welcoming its guests on 16 July.

A drink for those cool summer evenings when you are all alone and feel you can't put the heating on because it's the middle of the summer, is Anne Havesham's Boston Comfort.

Simply grate a bar of good plain chocolate, Belgian is lovely. Slowly melt it in half a pint of full cream milk. There's no need for a bain marie if you keep the heat low. While the chocolate is melting, cut some marshmallows in little chunks. When the chocolate is dissolved, pour into a mug and top with whipped cream and a sprinkle of marshmallows.

CHAPTER THIRTY-SIX

Liberty sat on a stool by her small stand, dressed like a jester with bells on the points of her soft, striped shoes and the three tips of her hat. High above her head, on top of the marquee, a chessboard-checked standard flapped in the breeze. It was two o'clock, and the visitors to the fête were only just beginning to arrive through the entrance to the recreation ground. Robin Hoods and Maid Marians manned stalls and sold ice-creams, while at the left-hand edge of the field a sturdy man in pea-green tights was preparing for the archery competition open to competitors over the age of ten.

*   *   *

It had all been Neville Pyke's idea. 'Sherwood Forest,' he said at the meeting of the newly formed Tollymead Summer Fête committee. 'We should have a theme for the fête, with everyone dressing up. They did that over at Everton last year and it was a great success: Wild West. That was what they did, The Wild Frontier.'

'Can you tell me why Davy Crockett had three ears?' Liberty asked.

'I can't see Andrew in a pair of green tights,' Nancy rolled her eyes.

'He had his right ear, his left ear, and the wild frontiear,' Liberty said.

'Maybe we should go for something a bit more contemporary,' Ted said.

'Acid House maybe,' Nancy said viciously. 'Not really Tollymead, I don't think.'

Liberty had thought how she disliked everything about Nancy: her speckled hair that she wore too long, her tights that were the colour of milky coffee, her way of adding, 'I don't think' to the end of a statement in an arch sort of way, her way of wrecking someone's life.

'No, not Acid House,' Ted said patiently.

'I like the idea of Sherwood Forest,' Pat Smedley said.

'We can have Robin Hood and Maid Marian and Friar Tuck.' Neville had spoken with such longing that Liberty had been moved to support him. 'We could be contemporary next year maybe,' she had suggested. 'And anyway, Robin Hood's ideals are very Now, aren't they?'

In the end Ted had agreed with good grace and it was decided that all the helpers would dress up and that the posters would announce that there would be a prize for the best-dressed visitor.

'The more Maid Marians the Merrier,' Liberty suggested. 'We could put that on the poster. You know—Maid Marian, merry men ... merrier ... no?'

*   *   *

Liberty wished she had not dressed up like that now. Everyone, the children especially, expected her to jest, not paint cornflowers and daisies on the backs of Fenwright and Mason hairbrushes, but she had seen the outfit in the costumiers in Fairfield and she had kept going back to look at it. Her bells jingled as she shifted on her stool, uncomfortable in the heat. With a small sigh she picked up her paints and a small hand mirror she was finishing off.

She got customers. 'You want "Pamela", circled with forget-me-nots?' Liberty confirmed with the couple who stood gazing over her shoulder with their small daughter between them. They had brought across a pink nursery chair.

'Look, Mum, there's a pony ride.' The child Pamela pulled at her mother's arm. 'C'mon Mum, I want a ride.' All three of them disappeared off towards the Shetland pony carrying children round the perimeter of the playing field.

Liberty picked up her brush once more. Now and then she looked up from her work, gazing across the field. The sun shone and there was just a faint breeze. There could not be a better day for the fête unless, that was, one was decked out in a woollen jester's suit. Behind her, from the marquee, she could hear the faint murmuring of voices and a steady buzzing of insects lured inside by the competition chocolate sponges. She squinted at the garland of forget-me-nots taking shape on the back of the tiny chair. Now and then people stopped to admire her work and Liberty smiled and mumbled her thanks. 'All proceeds going to the Elderly Persons' Minibus,' she reminded them. It was not long before she had another customer, wanting names and a sprinkling of ladybirds painted on the backs of two of the small wooden-backed mirrors Liberty had bought in as stock.

Deep in concentration, putting the finishing touches to the little pink chair, she was startled by a high pitched voice. 'P.a.m.e.l.l.a. Pamella has two Ls. You've done it all wrong.'

Liberty looked around and found the small owner of the chair standing at her shoulder, a dripping ice-cream in her hand and a sullen expression on her smudgy face.

'Are you sure?' Liberty looked around helplessly for the girl's parents.

'I told you,' the voice grew louder and more complaining. 'P.A.M.E.L.L...'

'Quite,' Liberty interrupted quickly, 'quite so.'

'What's the problem poppet?' the child's

father had appeared, an open can of Sprite in his hand. Liberty stared at his legs, wondering, not for the first time, what made overweight men so fond of wearing shiny little shorts cut high on their thighs. Even Neville Pyke in tights was a prettier sight.

'Now that's wrong,' the father said. 'I'm afraid you've got her name wrong. I'm sure we told you: P.A.M.E.L...'

'Right!' Liberty leapt from the deck chair, slamming the paintbrush down in the pot so that the white paint slopped over the edge, trickling down on to the grass. 'I'll see to it. I'll have a cup of tea and then I'll see to it.' Marching off she heard the man's voice: 'Don't look like no forget-me-nots to me.'

Although it was still early, there was a queue in the refreshment tent. When it was her turn, Liberty bought a cup of tea from one of Nancy's ladies who complimented Liberty on her outfit. Liberty said it was hot, especially the hat. She hovered over the slices of jam sponge and the fairy cakes, then bought one of each. She brought it all back to her stall and sat down on the grass. She ate every crumb of the jam sponge, although it was not nearly as nice as she imagined the winning chocolate sponge inside the produce tent would be. Munching on the pink-iced fairy cake, she gazed out across the field, idly counting the Friar Tucks. She made it eight: three very small ones, one very fat and appropriate and the remaining four pretty average. There was only one other jester, a child of about five who stared back at Liberty with startled recognition. Gazing out across the field crowded with people of all ages, Liberty quickly ate the last of the cakes. So she would get fat. The more unappetizing she became, the easier it would be for Oscar not to love her.

She had seen Oscar only twice since the night of Evelyn's funeral. Resting on her elbows in the grass, bells jingling, she squirmed and felt her face go all flushed, partly from shame, but also from remembered pleasure. To tear the clothes off your lover's back just after you had told him you were not going to see him again, to do that, and on the night of his aunt's funeral too, was nothing to be proud of. Then again, she had never been made love to like that before and she probably never would again. She closed her eyes and pictured his face above hers, his lips pressing down on hers. She gave a little moan and then, confused, opened her eyes to find a large fox staring down at her. She sat up, pushing her hair behind her ears, adjusting her costume as if she had risen from her lover's bed, not a piece of damp grass in the middle of the recreation ground.

'Oh, hello Daddy,' she said, blinking against the sunlight.

'How did you know it was me?' Hamish sounded annoyed, as he tore off the painted cardboard head.

'La Fontaine's Fables, last year's staff Christmas entertainment, remember?'

'Well I especially liked this costume,' Hamish said, seating himself gingerly on the grass next to his daughter. 'Great favourite with the boys.' He paused, looking out at the field. 'Only two more weeks until the end of term.'

Liberty clutched her knees, rocking gently back and forth as she looked sideways up at Hamish. 'I know,' she said quietly. 'It's good you can stay on in the flat a while, though.'

'Saves you having to put up with the old man.'

'That's not how I meant it,' Liberty said with the anger of someone found out. 'And don't keep referring to yourself as "the old man", it bugs me. Life is short and ghastly enough without everyone carrying on about age. We all get older, we all of us lose our precious pink plumpness, none of us like it, but for the life of me I can't understand why we all have to go on about it!'

A couple eating candy-floss stared at her as they passed. Liberty jingled her foot apologetically.

'Tut tut,' Hamish said, standing up and replacing his fox's head.

'I'm sorry,' Liberty put her hand up and took his. 'I'm not quite myself at the moment. And you know you can stay with me if you haven't found a place by next term. I've got

404

that young girl from Liverpool in July, and Johnny comes back soon, but there'll be room, of course there will be.'

'It'll be good to see Johnny,' Hamish said indistinctly through the cardboard head.

'I know,' Liberty nodded furiously making more noise than an ice-cream van. Then to her horror she started to cry.

'Look, Mum, that clown is crying.' A crew-cut boy of about eight tugged at his mother's arm, pointing at Liberty, a look of dispassionate interest on his ice-cream-smeared face.

Smiling sweetly through her tears, Liberty beckoned the boy towards her. 'I'm not a clown, little boy,' she hissed, as he came up close, 'and how would you like me to stuff my hat down your throat as far as it will go, bells and all.' She sat back looking with satisfaction as the boy fled howling to his mother.

'That was a little uncalled for don't you think?' Hamish said mildly.

Liberty dried her eyes with the back of her hand. 'I suppose so,' she sniffed, 'but I've had a bad day.'

She could sense Hamish retreat behind the mask. 'Isn't that Pat Smedley?' he trumpeted, 'I must say hello to old Pat.' He ambled off through the crowd and Liberty sat back up on the stool and began to paint again.

She finished a circle of ladybirds on the back of a mirror. After a while she took her hat off

405

and placed it on the grass by her stool. The wind through her hair felt good. An elderly woman pushing a buggy bought one of the hairbrushes and, after a moment's hesitation, a mirror to match, and a young mother carried across a tiny bookcase that she wanted Liberty to paint 'Mark' on in red with a navy blue border. After half an hour she had finished the bookcase and sold two more brushes. Sitting back down on the grass for a rest she saw Neville Pyke hustling towards her, his feathered cap resting at an angle on his large head.

'Well, well Mrs Turner, whoever would have thought it?' Neville beamed at her, rubbing his creosote-stained hands together.

Liberty beamed back, but her head was beginning to ache from the heat and the smell of the paints that hung round her like a drape in the still air, and the incessant jingle of her bells was getting on her nerves.

'No-one can say we haven't had our little difficulties here,' Neville went on, changing his smile to an expression of funereal dignity that sat badly, Liberty felt, with his green tights. Still who was she to talk? She gazed down at her own legs, one red, one yellow.

'No indeed, no indeed,' Neville said. 'But we came through it stronger than ever. I doubt that the Everton Fête and Flower Show will be anything like this, really I do.' He was beaming again, beads of sweat trickling down his forehead from under the brim of the tiny tricorn hat. 'And now we've got the Award. I never thought I'd live to see the day.' He nodded towards the wooden podium that had been erected in front of the Sports Pavilion.

'Neither did I,' Liberty agreed with complete honesty. 'And of course some of us didn't,' she added, not really meaning to.

Again Neville's face drooped into a suitable expression of sorrow. 'You're thinking of Miss Brooke, aren't you? A very sorry affair I don't mind telling you. But water is a dangerous thing, it can't be said often enough.' He cheered up. 'You do look nice all dressed up like that. Really entered into the spirit of the day.'

'There's a Swedish limerick about that,' Liberty said. 'About water being dangerous. It goes something like this, "There once were two brothers Montgomery who only ever drank Pommery, and if you gave them water they said..." It doesn't really work does it? Limericks never do translate. Goodness knows I've tried often enough.'

'You don't say, you don't say.' Neville rocked on his heels.

Over by the tea tent, Nancy Sanderson gave a wave and hurried across carrying a tiny white-painted toy chest. Liberty greeted her with the minimum politeness required and even then she felt a traitor. She wanted to give Nancy an icy stare and say, 'We were just talking about Evelyn,' but she lost her nerve and dithered about the weather instead.

'I brought you this. To paint.' Nancy plonked the tiny chest down by Liberty's feet.

'Grandchildren eh?' Neville beamed at Nancy who gave him a glacial look back.

'I'd like primroses,' she said to Liberty. 'I presume you've done this sort of thing before. It used to belong to my mother, so it's rather precious.' She grabbed one of the little mirrors that lay drying face down on the grass, inspecting the little ring of ladybirds. 'Very pretty, Liberty, I must say. So primroses then. I'll be back for it after the presentation.'

'I don't do primroses,' Liberty said.

Nancy, who had already started to leave, swung round. 'Really. Well I want something yellow, so what can you do?' She sounded impatient.

'Nothing yellow,' Liberty said.

Nancy looked hard at her. 'Well do your ladybirds then. I don't want pink or blue. The ladybirds will do.'

'Run out of red,' Liberty looked her straight in the eyes.

Nancy's sallow cheeks coloured. 'What can you do then Mrs Turner?'

'Moths,' Liberty said, 'and vampires. Vampires are very fashionable at the moment.'

Neville looked uneasily from one to the other. 'I don't know that moths and vampires are so suitable for—'

408

'I see,' Nancy said slowly, ignoring Neville. 'In that case I'll take my custom elsewhere.' She bent down with some difficulty, picking up the chest.

Liberty looked after her disappearing back, then closed her eyes and breathed in deep. When she opened her eyes she found Neville looking at her, puzzled.

'What do you make the time?' Liberty asked, not because she needed to know, she had just checked her watch, but to fend off any awkward questions.

Neville jerked his arm up, pushing at the sleeve of his sack-cloth tunic, to get at his watch. 'I make it half past three,' he said finally.

'That's what I thought,' Liberty smiled at him. 'Thank you.'

Neville pottered off and Liberty continued with her painting. Half an hour, she thought, and Oscar would be presenting the award to Ted Brain. He had probably arrived already. Somewhere in the throng of people was Oscar. The thought made her heart flutter like the tail of the tombola goldfish being carried past in a polythene bag. She crossed and uncrossed her ankles and each time the bells on her soft slippers jingled, so she stopped. Someone she did not recognize waved to her from the crowd and Liberty waved back. The sun stung her eyes as she scanned the playing field. She felt suddenly elated. She would see him again,

409

soon; maybe even touch him. It would be just a polite touch in passing as they said hello, but the thought of that moment grew until it filled her entire vision of the future.

Oh it was easy, she thought, to help old ladies load their shopping into the boots of their cars, or look after Penny's children so that she and Michael could go away together. It was child's play really, to agree to have Karen to stay, and she could even contemplate having Hamish coming to live for a couple of months. But letting Oscar go off with his wife and baby to America, now that was close to impossible.

She splashed the brush down in the old jam pot containing white spirit and picked up a wider one to paint over the first attempt at Pamella. She swept the paint across the letters, wondering if she would outlast the pain of losing him. Why was doing the right thing so hard? It was always the same, even with food. The more delicious it was, the more harm it did, but any baby knew that good food was hard to swallow. So it should not be a surprise to find that doing the right thing was as bitter and painful as a diet of cactus skin. But why did it have to be like that? She would not dream of giving advice to God, goodness no, but she would have done things the other way around. She looked up at the pale blue sky. Not that she expected an answer. As she straightened up she saw Oscar walking across the grass towards the wooden stand. She wanted to rush up to him but she stayed put.

'An answer would be nice,' she mumbled, gazing after him until he disappeared out of sight. She dashed off the rest of the letters on the little chair: M.E.L.L.A. 'Don't think an answer wouldn't be nice,' she whispered.

CHAPTER THIRTY-SEVEN

Ted Brain climbed up on the makeshift podium and picked up the microphone handed to him by the *Tribune* photographer.

'Parishioners! Fellow villagers, this is a great occasion and one, I don't mind telling you, that only a few months ago I would not have thought possible.' A murmur of approval rippled through the crowd surrounding the podium. Neville Pyke, standing a few feet away from Liberty, trumpeted into his handkerchief.

'Look at us, together like never before in my time as your vicar, young and old, home-owner and tenant, villager and commuter, all of us together, raising money for our community, enjoying a great day out at the Tollymead Fête and Flower Show. I'm proud of you.' Ted smiled. 'I'm even quite proud of myself. And to cap it all, we will today shortly receive the award for Most Caring Village from the *Tribune*'s...'

Oscar stood at the foot of the podium, Liberty could see him clearly now. She moved a couple of steps closer, just a couple. Victoria emerged from the throng, licking a large ice-cream with a chocolate flake. Liberty looked on as she nestled up to Oscar, putting her arm through his, offering up the ice-cream. It hurt her to watch, so Liberty turned her face away; but out of the corner of her eye she saw Oscar shaking his head impatiently before mounting the podium and taking the microphone handed to him by Ted. She blinked and sniffed and sniffed again, muttering about hay fever in case anyone was looking at her, but no-one was; all eyes were on Oscar.

'This is both a happy and a sad occasion for me,' he paused and smiled out at the crowd. 'In a couple of weeks' time my wife and I will be leaving Tollymead and moving overseas. It gives me special pleasure, therefore, to present to Tollymead the award for Most Caring Village in the *Tribune* area. Our three judges, Mrs Milton-Brown, Chairwoman of the Fairfield branch of the WI, the Reverend Blyth, Rector of All Saints Fairfield, and Tim Huggit, Chairman of the *Tribune* Group, discussed the merits of the different entries at some length, but in the end their decision to name Tollymead as Most Caring Village in the *Tribune* area was unanimous. On their many visits, they were impressed by the general helpfulness and kindness of the residents. To take just one example, when Mr Blyth pretended to have broken down in his car...'

As she stood in the crowd just some ten yards away from Oscar, Liberty knew your heart really could ache. There definitely was a dull pain on the left side of her chest that no amount of the pastel-coloured tablets Hamish was always sucking could relieve. Behind her a woman in a flower-sprigged summer frock was complaining to her husband about the tombola prizes and a baby was crying. A Friar Tuck put his elbow in Liberty's stomach and apologized profusely. Oscar spoke on and Liberty noticed the lightness and warmth of his voice more than his words. She wondered if having a soul really was all it was cracked up to be. It was rather like one of those 'pay-now-receive-later, you've been seen-off' deals that people were always writing about to 'That's Life'.

'Dear Esther, I bought this soul with every last bit of goodness and happiness I possessed, thinking I would do good on earth and be rewarded in heaven, but now as I stand at death's door, (I'm eighty-nine today and not as well as I was,) I am told there's real doubt that I'll ever get my reward, or even that this heaven exists at all. So Esther, what shall I do, and is there any chance I'll get my investment back?'

Maybe there were no rules and no order. Maybe right and wrong was just a passing fad in the overwhelming chaos of existence. Then she would feel jolly silly.

'Most of all, the judges were impressed with the vicar's scheme of inviting a group of young people from his last parish in Liverpool to come down here for a couple of weeks' holiday in the country,' Oscar went on. 'So, in a society that seems increasingly to have forgotten the concept of collective responsibility, where individuals seem ever more intent on self-gratification regardless of the cost to anybody else, and the Gospel According to the Lout is spreading through every section of society, it is good to have a Tollymead.' Oscar took a step forward. 'If the Reverend Brain would be so good as to step back up here, it's my great pleasure...'

In the distance came the sound of heavy vehicles grumbling across the ground and Liberty, ignoring it at first and keeping her eyes fixed on Oscar, eventually turned to look. A lorry, followed by a large multi-coloured caravan, came over the brow of the hill across the field that ran alongside the recreation ground. There were another couple of lorries and then an old bus, covered in huge rust spots like some notifiable disease, rumbled into view.

The children who had hovered, bored, on the edge of the crowd, whooped and ran towards the field and soon some of the adults followed. Oscar, after a quick glance, finished his speech and handed the trophy, a handsome silver rose bowl, to Ted. The applause was

414

drowned by the rumbling of the lorries. As the crowd around him thinned, Oscar spotted Liberty. Taking a long step off the platform, he came towards her. Liberty turned her back on the commotion and looked at him with such longing, she thought her face had to be an embarrassment. Then Victoria caught up with him, taking him by the elbow, and he paused, bending down to hear what she was saying. Liberty stayed where she was, eyes wide open and itchy with held-back tears. She saw him give Victoria a little smile and she was stabbed by jealousy. She had told him to go off and spend the rest of his life with Victoria, but did he have to stand there and smile at the woman? She was about to turn round and walk off, when Oscar freed himself from Victoria's grip. He looked up, straight at Liberty, and he too looked as if he was about to start crying. Her face contorting, she clenched her fists so that her nails dug deep into the fleshy part of her palms to stop herself from reaching out and touching his cheek. She had felt as bad once before, when Johnny had been only eight and playing in his first rugby match, he had been tackled hard ending up crying in pain on the ground. She had made to run onto the field to pick him up and hold him, when she had felt the sports master's hand on her arm and his voice saying, 'We don't want Mum on the field embarrassing him in front of his friends, do we now?' So she had stayed back and never

415

stopped hating the master or the game.

With a jingle of bells she turned on her heels and hurried away to the edge of the recreation ground to join the crowd that had gathered to see the trailers and lorries and brightly coloured buses drive on to the field, drawing to a halt, one after the other, at its centre.

'That will be those New Age Travellers,' an old man next to Liberty said. Pleased at the expressions of horror on everybody's face he continued, 'Saw about them on the telly only the other night. They'll wreck the place all right. You just can't shift them. No, we're in for a right old time now.'

'Well there you are, Dad,' a woman spoke triumphantly, 'aren't you glad you're in that nice home, now, instead of here with all this going on? They'll be doing their business in our garden and playing their music all night long. No, you be glad you're away from it all in Fairfield, Dad.'

Liberty turned to see Dad give his daughter an evil look.

'We must call the police immediately.' Nancy had elbowed her way to the front of the crowd, one hand placed protectively on her stomach. 'That field is privately owned. It belongs to Campbell's Farm. It's in use.'

'It certainly is now,' the old man chuckled, 'but Campbell has left it fallow this year and last. There's no crop on it now.'

'The police can't do anything,' someone

416

said.

'We must reason with them, like the good neighbours we are,' Neville appeared with Gladys at his side, his large face bright red under the feathered cap.

Now I'll do it, Liberty thought. I'll run up to Oscar and I'll grab him, and we'll take off across the field and get into one of those old buses and drive away, ram raid out from the ring of rusty—

'Well I'm certainly glad we're leaving. Your life will be a misery, you know, with that lot camped here.' Liberty turned to find Victoria coming up behind her with Oscar, a manicured hand on his arm. Liberty concentrated on the fingernails. A French manicure, Victoria definitely had a French manicure.

'Hello Victoria, hello Oscar. Yes very lucky.' Liberty smiled, her eyes still fixed on Victoria's hand. Lucky, lucky lucky, she thought. You've got Oscar, and a baby, a French manicure and no New Age Travellers. No, forget the French manicure; she never had liked the way the white bits on the tips of the nails were filled in by the white varnish. She herself preferred as little white on her nails as possible. Looking down at her own hands, where the marks from Cissy's teeth were still showing white against the faint tan, she wondered if she was going mad. 'Poor woman,' they would say. 'She became Good and only hours later they took her away. They say it'll be years before they let her out again.'

'I feel a bit of a spoilsport, but I don't really go in for fancy dress, never have.' Victoria leant against Oscar's arm, cool and fashionable in a long navy blue-and-white spotted dress, worn as a waistcoat over a blue linen T-shirt and draw-string blue-and-white striped trousers. It was a look Liberty had admired on the pages of several fashion magazines for months, but as usual failed to follow up. Instead, she had chosen to turn up looking like something that had fallen off the back of a carnival float.

'You look very nice,' she kept smiling.

'I told Oscar that if he dressed up as Robin Hood, I'd divorce him.' Victoria gave Oscar's arm a playful tug. She looked a little surprised as Liberty burst out laughing, a shrill laugh it seemed, even to Liberty's ears.

'I'm sorry,' she said, 'but you didn't really mean that, did you? I mean if I wrestled poor old Neville Pyke to the ground and stripped off his costume for Oscar, would you really divorce him?' She had tried not to look at Oscar but now she saw a small smile twitch at the corners of his mouth. Then he looked away. 'Only kidding,' she pulled a face. 'It must be the heat.' She shifted from one foot to another, jingling her bells.

'Well it's nice that you have the guts to make a fool of yourself,' Victoria said. 'I never would.'

'How sweet of you to say so,' Liberty turned to Oscar. 'It was a nice presentation.'

'Thank you. I like your costume.'

Victoria raised an eyebrow. 'I told him the whole thing was too serious,' she said. 'I mean, it's all a bit of a joke anyway.'

Liberty wanted to ask her to be more precise. What was it that was a bit of a joke? The Award, life in general, people who handed you back your husband although they did not have to?

'I'd better find Mike and get over there.' Oscar nodded to the field.

'Oh come on, it's Saturday.' Victoria tugged at his arm. 'I want to get back home. We've got all that packing to do. Get someone else to do the story.'

'Don't be ridiculous,' Oscar snapped, a look on his face Liberty had not seen before. She had to fight back an impulse to put her hand up and smooth out the frown on his forehead; it was not her job any more. All she could do was stand around in her awful costume, jingling her bells and turning pink from heat and emotion.

Oscar called to the photographer and then he turned away without looking at her, leaping over the stile and striding off across the field towards a camper van painted with huge, triffid-like sunflowers.

Liberty could not take her eyes off him. She did not care if Victoria wondered why she was staring. She would remember him like that,

419

dressed in the crumpled cream linen jacket and blue shirt that was just a shade paler than the blue of his eyes. He looked so good that day, that had she not known better she would have thought he was vain.

'Ask them what the hell they think they are doing,' a man called from the back.

The crowd lining the edge of the recreation ground was getting angry, everyone yelling and shoving to get a better view.

'Get away with you, filthy trash. We don't want your sort here!' a woman shrieked. Liberty had to agree with the sentiments, she just did not like the tone of voice. It was like those court scenes on television when a particularly nasty criminal was bustled inside, cowering under a blanket. Just as she felt herself wishing for the return of capital punishment or planning a spot of lynching with castration thrown in, someone in the watching crowd would start the jeering, face contorted, teeth bared, and all at once you were a liberal.

'Where do you think they keep the blankets?' Liberty asked Victoria. 'You know, the ones they use to cover suspects with. I can't somehow imagine them freshly laundered and stacked in a cupboard at the police station, ready for the next villain.' She paused. 'Then again, why not?'

'I can't say I have ever given it much thought,' Victoria said.

420

'Well nor have I, until now,' Liberty answered meekly.

She scanned the field for Oscar, but he was gone from the sunflower camper, and was nowhere to be seen amongst the jumble of children and dogs and wild-haired adults. 'My goodness what a to-do,' she said, hoping to deflect Victoria's contempt with a thoroughly sensible remark. 'Really,' she added for good measure. When Victoria did not answer she said, 'It's funny, don't you think, how all the men have long hair and most of the women have theirs really short?'

'Well that's the way they are, isn't it?' Victoria said.

Oscar appeared from the throng round the psychedelic fire engine. He was talking to Mike the photographer, pointing in the direction of a small girl, or at least Liberty thought it was a girl with tangled fair hair and dressed in a grubby white shift, standing on her own a little distance away, her fingers in her mouth. Then he was surrounded again as a group of women and children joined hands and began dancing. Liberty craned her neck as, now and then between the prancing figures, she glimpsed him, a head taller than the others, scrubbed and clean shaven, his pale jacket spotless, his expression calm. They could all be part of some Victorian tableau entitled 'The Arrival of Enlightenment', or 'The Natives Welcome Their Ruler After a Long Absence', she thought, amused.

'We must stop them before they start digging the latrines,' Nancy said to a general murmur of approval. Over by the fire engine a couple of men from the village were arguing with a small group of travellers. 'And those dogs,' she added. 'They foul everywhere, they'll run in here too, and then it won't be safe for our children to play. You know what dog dirt does to children.'

'Has anyone called the police yet?' someone asked.

'They can't do anything,' a man standing next to Liberty sneered. 'You must have seen in the papers, it takes weeks, or months even, to get rid of them. They've got rights, would you believe it.'

'Nonsense.' Nancy had elbowed her way forward, her arm protectively in front of her belly still. 'That field is private property, not common land. It belongs to Campbell's Farm.'

'There's no crop on it,' the man said. 'That's what counts.'

Ted Brain had been muttering soothing words of tolerance and alternative life styles. 'I'll talk to them,' he said, taking a step up on the stile. The crotch of his trousers got tangled on the barbed wire below and he grew pinker by the second as he pulled at the pale blue material of the trousers. 'I'll reason with them. I'm sure we can come to some...' with a final yank he was free, '... mutually acceptable

422

arrangement.'

'They've got a cow and all,' a young boy called from his vantage point half-way up an elm tree.

'That's it. I'm going over there.' The man who had been standing next to Liberty removed his black-and-purple shell suit top and folded it carefully before hanging it on a sticking-out branch in the hedgerow. One milky-white trainer and then another climbed onto the stile and he was across before Liberty had a chance to ask him why it was that the cow in particular upset him so.

'We'll have the television down Neville, I'm telling you.' Gladys Pyke craned her neck and tugged at her husband's arm.

'Kate Adie do you think?' Liberty could not help asking.

'She's in Bosnia,' Gladys said matter-of-factly.

So that joke fell flat, thought Liberty, trying to spot Oscar, who had broken loose from the circle of dancers and disappeared. Victoria bent down and picked up her basket of produce from the ground.

'Liberty, would you tell Oscar I've gone home to have a nap. Oh and,' she turned round, 'do tell him not to be long, I've got a list as long as my arm of things for him to do.' She wandered off through the crowd.

After a while people began drifting back towards the stalls and the refreshment tents, and by the time the police arrived, driving their Range Rover up the field to a barrage of cat-calls and the odd unenthusiastic missile from the travellers, only Gladys Pyke and the old man from the home in Fairfield were still standing, staring, on the other side of the hedge.

'They don't want any trouble, so they say.' Oscar had found Liberty back at her stall, sitting on the stool, painting. He shook his head slowly, smiling down at her. 'I'll always remember you in that suit.'

Liberty sighed. 'I was afraid of that.' She put her brush down. 'By the way, Victoria has gone home to have a nap. She asked me to tell you not to be long.'

It was Oscar's turn to sigh. 'Right,' he said, turning away. Still not looking at her, he said, 'I love you, you know that. I think I always will.'

'And I'll never stop loving you. What is it they say? "Until the mountains crumble and the seas dry". In fact, I wouldn't be in the least surprised if I mumbled your name on my death-bed.' Unable to stop herself, she got down from the stool and went right up to stand next to him so that her shoulder touched his arm. Looking around her quickly to see that no-one was watching, she put her hand in his. They stood like that for a few moments with all the shouting and fussing going on around them, then the microphone screeched and Ted

Brain's voice boomed towards them, and they moved apart.

'Ladies and Gentlemen, if I can have your attention for a moment. We have one last item on our agenda. The judging of the Fancy Dress competition. So, could we have all the contenders up here with me, ready for Lady Wilson, our judge.' Lady Wilson, a tall woman with careful hairstyle and an even more careful smile, stepped out from the crowd and strode up to the line of adults and children forming in front of the podium.

Liberty moved behind Oscar, grateful that he had the sense not to suggest she entered. Instead, he whispered, 'Lady Wilson, who is she?' His voice was thick and a little unsteady. Liberty put out her hand and touched the back of his neck with her index finger, just for a second, and his hand flew up and grabbed hers, but he was still looking straight ahead towards Ted Brain and the parade of competitors.

'Awfully grand, that's who she is. She lives in that thirties monstrosity, all red brick and dark tiles, half-way between here and Greenway. Her sons went to Tollymead Manor. She always said she felt more Greenway than Tollymead. I guess she's changed her mind.' With her free hand she fished out a handkerchief from the waistband of her striped leggings and blew her nose. 'Her husband was in garden centres,' she sobbed, 'you know, the kind where they sell furniture and Christmas

425

decorations and china, and where you can even find the odd over-priced plant, if you're lucky.' She sniffed. 'There's one on the Fairfield road, Gardeners' Lodge, open seven days a week. Evelyn hated it.' Suddenly her voice rose. 'She hated it,' and she buried her head between his shoulder blades crying, 'hated it.'

Oscar swung round and grabbed her by the arms, forcing her to look him in the eyes. 'This is ridiculous,' he said. 'I'm going back home to tell Victoria that I love you and—'

'To hell with everything else, including your baby?' Liberty rubbed at a tear and then another one. 'I won't let you and I'm sorry, I should have stayed away from here today.'

The microphone gave a warning whistle, making them both turn. 'The winner of the Best Fancy Dress, and the prize of a twenty-five pound gift token to spend at any Gardeners' Lodge,' Lady Wilson announced, 'goes to Rebecca Flood's Maid Marian.'

A small girl in pink, with a little bow and arrow strung from her shoulders like a dislocated fairy's wing, stepped up onto the podium and Liberty clapped, tears streaming down her face. A stout woman close by turned to her, nodding and grinning, 'Your little girl, is it? I can see you're ever so proud.'

'No,' Liberty said.

The woman looked at her as if she had just kicked a fluffy white kitten, and the old habit of not wishing to cause offence took over. 'I mean no, she's not my little girl.' Liberty dabbed at her eyes with a tissue she had fished out from her sleeve. 'But had she been I would of course have been proud, very proud indeed.'

The woman gave her another look and turned her back.

Liberty stayed looking straight in front of her, tears still running down her face. Oscar's hands gripped her shoulders, and she looked up.

'I can't leave you,' he said. 'Do you hear me? I love you.'

Tollymead: *The award ceremony to present Tollymead with the coveted trophy for Most Caring Village was not without incident. Moments before the vicar of Tollymead, the Reverend Ted Brain, received the award from the Tribune's editor Mr Oscar Brooke, the first of a caravan of New Age Travellers rumbled onto the adjoining field belonging to local farmer Derek Campbell. By the time the fête drew to a close, the visitors were already settled in and washing was drying on the lines.*

There were heated arguments amongst the Tollymead residents as to how to treat the visitors, but Mrs Nancy Sanderson's suggestion to set a nearby herd of heifers on them was comprehensively rejected as uncaring and not in keeping with the spirit of the village. The police were called, however, but explained that there was nothing they could do until Mr Campbell sued for an eviction order.

The barn dance went ahead as planned, held in the Fresh Produce marquee, empty now of prize vegetables, chocolate sponges and home-made raspberry jam. Everyone had a marvellous time, and the few travellers who appeared, lured by the lights and the laughter carried across the moonlit field, soon left again; whether due to the somewhat frosty welcome or the music, Abba, was anybody's guess.

Then, with the music stilled and only a few of us remaining, gathered round the last of the flickering candles, chatting about this and that and life and death, the way one does at 2 a.m., I asked Anne Havesham, who had been taking notes most of the evening, if she never tired of working. Her answer was to recite to us the much loved poem by Longfellow:

Art is long, and Time is fleeting,
And our hearts, though stout and brave,
Still, like muffled drums, are beating
Funeral marches to the grave.

Trust no Future, howe'er pleasant!
Let the dead Past bury its dead!
Act, act in the living Present!
Heart within, and God o'erhead!

Lives of great men all remind us
We can make our lives sublime,
And, departing, leave behind us
Footprints in the sands of time;—

We all agreed that sums it up pretty well; this peculiarly human desire to transcend mere existence.

CHAPTER THIRTY-EIGHT

There was a rumour going round that the travellers, still ensconced in Campbell's field two weeks after the fête, had descended on Tollymead because of the Diary. Pat Smedley told Nancy Sanderson who complained to Ted Brain who told Liberty all about it on the Monday when he came over to talk about dates for Karen's stay. Apparently Pat had a friend in Everton whose accountant son was a New Age Traveller in his spare moments.

'Yes?' Liberty said to Ted over a mug of coffee.

'Well, his mother is an avid reader of the Diary and apparently she had been telling her son all about the new age dawning at Tollymead and her son then went off and told his mates amongst the travelling fraternity that Tollymead was just the place to congregate after the summer solstice. I couldn't trouble you for another cup?' Ted held the butterfly mug out for a refill. It was one of two mugs that Liberty had pinched from Glebe House. She and Evelyn always had their morning coffee together from those mugs.

Taking it across to the Aga, and measuring out the instant coffee she said, 'Maybe the travellers won't cause as much trouble as everyone is expecting.' She could hear herself, how anxious her voice sounded. 'Don't you think people are over-reacting just a little bit? I mean these are not Beelzebub and all his little helpers camped at Campbell's Farm, but just some people with lots of pets and rather unfortunate ideas about personal hygiene.'

Ted accepted the mug, stretching his legs out in front of him, the way Oscar always did, although Ted's legs only reached half the way. 'I don't know,' he grinned at her. 'I have to tell you there's a nasty mood of mutiny in Tollymead that ill befits the Most Caring Village. I wouldn't want to be in the shoes of the author of those entries if it all comes out.'

'Really?' Liberty said brightly. 'You don't think, then, that people will see this as a marvellous opportunity to practise all that Caring?'

'Hardly,' Ted laughed. 'Things have changed, but not that much. I asked Oscar Brooke about it, by the way, but he said they had no idea at *The Tribune* who it was writing in. He did the award ceremony rather well, I thought.'

Of course he did, Liberty wanted to say. He makes love like a dream too, and he's kind and clever and beautiful and sensitive and I love him, but because I've listened far too much to the likes of you I will most probably never feel his arms round me again.

She said, 'Yes he did, didn't he? Actually, there's an ad in this week-end's paper asking

431

the writer of the Tollymead entries to call in at the *Tribune* offices, with a view to extending her contribution.'

Ted stood up. 'Well if I was she, or he for that matter, I would keep my head down for a while. So anyway, you're happy with Karen arriving on the sixteenth and you can meet her at the station?'

Liberty nodded agreement; she had a lot on her mind.

*　　*　　*

Oscar got up from his desk when his secretary announced there was a lady to see him about the Diary. Liberty stuck her head around the door and then, a little awkwardly, the rest of her followed. 'Hello Oscar,' she said, her voice unsteady.

He just looked at her for a moment, saying nothing, then he shook his head, smiling. 'I have wondered for some time whether it was you.' Seeing the look on her face he added quickly, 'The ad was genuine, you know, we really want to talk to you.'

'You sure?'

'Promise,' he said, slamming his fist across his heart. 'Please, sit down.' He indicated the visitor's chair opposite his own and sat down himself. 'So,' he picked up a ruler and turned it round between his fingers, inspecting each side as if he expected to find something interesting.

432

Of course he didn't, so he put the ruler back, looking up at her.

If my love had a colour, Liberty thought, every breath I exhale would colour the atmosphere red.

'So, all that talk about you having given up writing...'

Liberty shrugged her shoulders. 'Well I had, really. The Diary was a bit of fun, or a straggly little life-line, whatever.'

'Oh hell Liberty,' Oscar had picked up the ruler again and he crashed it down on the desk. 'This is ridiculous.' He reached across and grabbed her hand. 'I love you.'

'Human beings are ridiculous,' Liberty said softly. 'But don't you see, all we can do is to be ridiculous with as much grace as possible.' She brought his hand up to her lips and across her cheek, holding it there for a moment before letting go. 'You do understand, don't you Oscar?'

He leant back in his chair, looking at her for a long moment, then with a sigh he said, 'No Liberty, I can't say that I do. But I'll leave you alone if that's what you want.' He crossed one long leg over the other. 'So, the Diary.'

Liberty smiled uncertainly. 'The Diary, yes.'

'How would you like to expand the entries and your cast,' he paused and smiled up at her. 'You made up most of them anyway, didn't you? I mean Anne Havesham, we've had people looking out for her for months.'

433

Liberty shrugged her shoulders, an apology written on her face.

'And the goody-two-shoes Phyllida Medley and Hester Scott OBE? Agnes Coulson and the couple that married, all your own creations too?'

'Yes,' Liberty whispered.

'What about poor Tigger the gun dog and his owners?'

'Well,' Liberty looked down at her hands, 'yes.'

'That's all right,' Oscar was business-like. 'In fact, it's better for what we have in mind. We're not after a Tollymead version of 'Jennifer's Diary', more like a soap, *Neighbours* on the printed page, or *The Archers*, if that sounds better to you.'

'No, *Neighbours* is fine, I'm not proud.'

'There will have to be a trial run, but the plan is to move you away from the Village Diary section altogether, give you about two thirds of a column on page two. Reflect what goes on in the villages around here, but this time it should be all fiction, so you'll be much less constrained. If you could have about four weeks' worth to show Alistair Partridge, that's my successor, when he comes back from holiday next week.'

'I suppose a touch of Armistead Maupin, *Tales of the City*, is a little ambitious?' Liberty had leaned forward, her hands on the edge of the desk.

'A little maybe.' But he was smiling. 'Then again, make it as good as you can.'

'Should I have a strong narrator keeping it together, like in the *Provincial Lady*, do you think, or have an unobtrusive narrative voice?' As she spoke she felt a faint tickle of excitement, feather-light but there, and gingerly she tested its worth. 'You are quite sure you haven't planned this all along to try to make me happy?'

He put his hand out and touched the puckered skin on her cheek. 'Perish the thought.' He grew serious again. 'This might be a small-town newspaper and I might be leaving, but I have more respect for my profession, this paper, and most of all for you, to try that sort of thing. You can be quite sure that this offer, and remember it is only a trial run, is genuine and would have been made to anyone coming through this door this morning saying they had written those entries. Anyway, it was Alistair's idea, not mine.'

For a moment she was quite content. OK, so unless someone came along one day and suggested she collected it all in a book, her work would be of the disposable kind, but was the baker any less valuable because his bread only lasted the day? She took Oscar's hand and lifted it to her cheek, resting against it, thinking how easily she could have it all. She blinked to stop the tears, absent-mindedly rubbing her eyes with the back of his hand. Letting go, she stood up.

'Thank you Oscar. It will be an excellent column.'

Oscar, too, stood up. 'I expect it to be.' He gave her a small smile. 'So you'll be happy now?'

'Happy?' She tried to smile back, but managed only a grimace. 'Straight-backed, broken-hearted. That's not happiness, but you can live.' She studied every feature of his face, she looked at his hands and his arms, at his chest beneath the striped shirt and linen jacket, at his waist and hips.

He put out his hand as if to touch her, then let it drop to his side. 'I'll never stop loving you, Liberty,' he said.

She took a step towards him and this time he pulled her close, and they kissed.

You can't kiss for ever, so finally she freed herself and walked to the door. Maybe when the baby is grown up, she thought, maybe then? Thinking like that was the only way she could leave.

We hope you have enjoyed this Large Print book. Other Chivers Press or G. K. Hall Large Print books are available at your library or directly from the publishers. For more information about current and forthcoming titles, please call or write, without obligation, to:

Chivers Press Limited
Windsor Bridge Road
Bath BA2 3AX
England
Tel. (01225) 335336

OR

G. K. Hall
P.O. Box 159
Thorndike, Maine 04986
USA
Tel. (800) 223–6121 (U.S. & Canada)
In Maine call collect: (207) 948–2962

All our Large Print titles are designed for easy reading, and all our books are made to last.